I0599367

Queen of Illusions

BY THE SAME AUTHOR

Around the World on Five Sous (with H. Chabrillat) – translated by Brian Stableford
Doctor Mystery – translated by Nina Cooper
Miss Musketeer – translated by Stuart Gelzer

Queen of Illusions

by
Paul d'Ivoi

Translated from the French by
Stuart Gelzer

Original illustrations by
Henri Thiriet

A Black Coat Press Book

English adaptation Copyright © 2023 by Stuart Gelzer.
Introduction Copyright © 2023 by Jean-Marc Lofficier.
Cover illustration Copyright © 2023 by Roberto Castro.

ISBN 978-1-64932-214-2. First Printing: August 2023. Published by Black Coat Press, an imprint of Hollywood Comics.com, LLC, P.O. Box 17270, Encino, CA 91416. All rights reserved. Except for review purposes, no part of this book may be reproduced or transmitted in any form or by any means, electronic or mechanical, including photocopying, recording, or by any information storage and retrieval system, without permission in writing from the publisher. The stories and characters depicted in this novel are entirely fictional. Printed in the United States of America.

TABLE OF CONTENTS

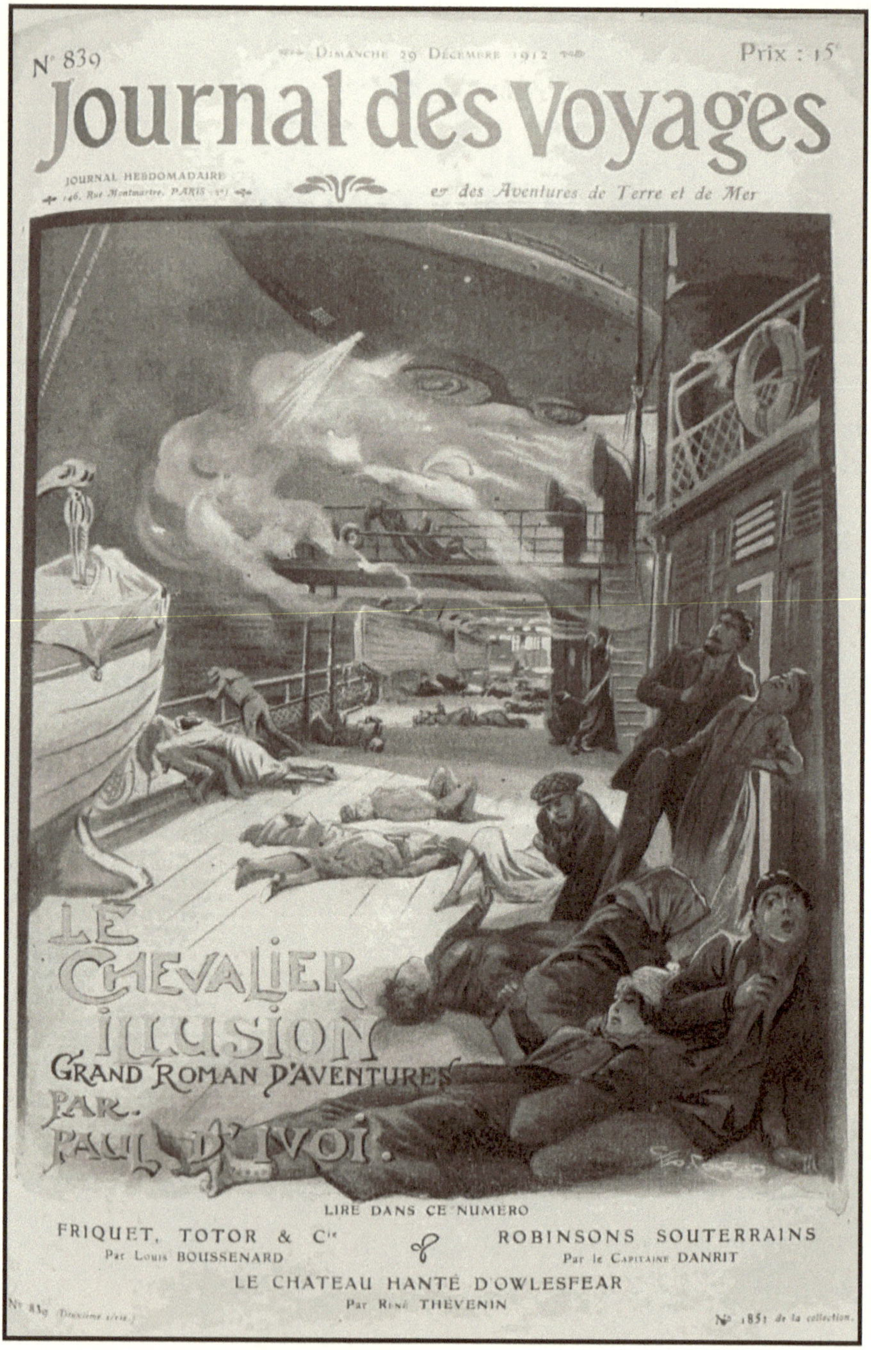

Nº 839
Dimanche 29 Décembre 1912
Prix : 15c
Journal des Voyages
JOURNAL HEBDOMADAIRE
146, Rue Montmartre, PARIS (2e)
& des Aventures de Terre et de Mer
LE CHEVALIER ILLUSION
GRAND ROMAN D'AVENTURES
PAR.
PAUL D'IVOI.
LIRE DANS CE NUMERO
FRIQUET, TOTOR & Cie
Par Louis BOUSSENARD
ROBINSONS SOUTERRAINS
Par le Capitaine DANRIT
LE CHATEAU HANTÉ D'OWLESFEAR
Par René THEVENIN
Nº 839 (Deuxième série.)
Nº 1851 de la collection.

Introduction

Queen of Illusions was first serialized in the popular *Journal des Voyages* from 15 December 1912 to 8 June 1913, under the title *Le Chevalier Illusion* [Knight of Illusions] (which is rather odd considering the gender of its main protagonist) before being republished in book form by Boivin et Cie. that same year under the poetic but somewhat misleading title *Les Dompteurs de l'Or* [The Gold Tamers]. It was the twentieth, and penultimate, novel in Paul d'Ivoi's *magnum opus* series, "*Les Voyages Excentriques*" [The Eccentric Voyages], clearly inspired by Jules Verne's classic *Les Voyages Extraordinaires*.

We presented Paul Deleutre (1856-1915), the writer who signed all his published works with the nom-de-plume of Paul d'Ivoi, in our introductions to *Around the World on Five Sous* (Black Coat Press, ISBN 978-1-61227-369-3) and *Miss Musketeer* (Black Coat Press, ISBN 978-1-64932-108-4). Therefore, those wishing to learn more about him should refer to either of those two volumes.

While taking place in the same fictional universe, *Queen of Illusions* does not feature any of Paul d'Ivoi's familiar cast of recurring characters: Armand Lavarède and his family, Doctor Mystery, Cigale, Miss Musketeer, etc. Instead, it is a stand-alone novel.

Like his more famous predecessor, Jules Verne, D'Ivoi combined geographical adventures and scientific inventions. He took his heroes all around the world, even though he himself had never left France, relying on travel guides and atlases for his documentation. *Le Corsaire Triplex*, with its mysterious hero bent on revenge, commanding a powerful electric submarine, was clearly inspired by Verne's *Twenty Thousand Leagues Under the Seas*. *Les Cinq sous de Lavarède* [*Around the World on Five Sous*], is equally reminiscent of Verne's *Around the World in Eighty Days*, with its hero, Armand Lavarède, following in the footsteps of Phileas Fogg.

However, Paul d'Ivoi cannot simply be dismissed as nothing more than a Vernian imitator. His novels are organized around very different plots. In *Around the World on Five Sous*, for example, the themes of time and money are reversed. Lavarède accomplishes his journey with only five cents in his pocket in a period that greatly exceeds Fogg's 80 days (365 days). Also, the two authors diverge on the question of science. In Verne's works, science is all-conquering, it confronts nature and triumphs over it. Not so with D'Ivoi whose works show a certain disillusionment over the capacity of science to work for the ultimate good of man. Verne made his scientists into superhuman figures whose ultimate goals were scientific recognition and the desire to contribute to the progress of

Mankind. D'Ivoi, on the contrary, depicted them in a far less flattering light, often as power-hungry monsters like Tom Slane in *Queen of Illusions*.

If Paul d'Ivoi was not a predictive visionary like Jules Verne, it was because he wrote at a time when new scientific and technological discoveries followed one another to the point of no longer arousing as much astonishment as they did in the past. Unlike Verne, he extrapolated rather than invented. In *La Course au Radium*, he was inspired by Madame Curie's discovery of radium in 1898 and imagined a radium laser pistol. In *Le Corsaire Triplex*, he played with the research of Claude Goubet (1837-1903), who had developed a small submersible launched in 1887.

If Paul d'Ivoi, like most authors of the times, was an ardent defender of French colonization, which he saw as "civilizing"—while British colonization was considered purely mercantile and hegemonic—he nevertheless portrayed indigenous characters struggling with their Western oppressors. In *Le Corsaire Triplex*, Robert Lavarède must help free the Egyptians from the British yoke if he wants to marry his beloved, Lotia Hador.

Also, unlike Jules Verne, Paul d'Ivoi sought to reach both young boys and girls with his books. In each novel, there is usually at least one female protagonist embodying the feminine ideals of the times, intended to make young boys fantasize, but also to make young girls dream. These heroines are equals in intelligence and courage to their male companions. In *Le Corsaire Triplex*, young Maudlin Green ends up commanding one of the submarines designed by her mentor, James Pack. In *Message du Mikado*, Lydia Honeymoon is a competent spy and plane pilot. And in *Queen of Illusions*, Miss May is an exceptional inventor. Yes, these women are invariably stereotyped as soft and pretty, with marriage as their only possible fate, but they're still a significant cut above the damsels in distress usually found in the literature of the times.

Even more surprisingly, D'Ivoi appeared to challenge the notion of gender. In *Message du Mikado*, a young couple is formed where the hero dresses up as a woman and the heroine as a man in a chapter entitled "Idyll between two transvestites."

Now, read on!

Jean-Marc Lofficier

QUEEN OF ILLUSIONS

PART ONE: PYGMIES AGAINST A GIANT

CHAPTER I
Stepan and Sefra

"Take that, Sefra the Turk!"

"Here's a punch on the nose, Stepan the Bulgarian! A cowardly boy who beats up a woman!"

"A woman? A girl! You're a woman the way an egg is a chicken!"

And the pugilists went back at it even harder.

They were two children of thirteen or fourteen. Stepan, the boy, was well-built, with an energetic wiriness; his very black eyes punctuated a face already tanned by a life outdoors. Sefra, the girl, was sturdy and a little slow-moving, but sweet and graceful even so. Everything in her round face smiled—her lips, her eyes, and her fine nose with its sensitive nostrils. Her lithe, sinuous manner had that mysterious charm that can't be pinned down in some exact description, but whose influence is undeniable.

Right now, both of them were boxing madly. The battle was an unexpected result of the war then going on in Europe, between Turkey on the one hand and the Balkan states—Bulgaria, Serbia, Montenegro, and Greece—on the other.[1] Sefra believed she was Turkish; Stepan considered himself Bulgarian. *Inde irae.*[2]

We've said "believed" and "considered," because the two combatants had no definite knowledge about their own origins. They'd met in the camp of some sort of nomadic group that had emigrated to the United States. They'd earned their living as part of that roving band, sometimes as carnival acrobats, sometimes as fortunetellers, as temporary farm workers, as cowherds or shepherds, as messengers, etc., etc.

For the past month, they'd been on their own. The band to which they'd belonged had suddenly vanished. No doubt some dirty trick carried out by a few of them had obliged them to put a safe distance between themselves and the police of the nearest city: Oakland, a suburb of San Francisco.

The children, who'd been hired on at a farm, had no regrets over the departure of their old companions. Nomads are not people who form close ties. In fact, the children now felt freer and happier. But then a newspaper, the something *Daily*, falling into their hands by chance, had informed them of the fierce struggle whose bloody arena was the Balkan Peninsula.

Impossible to explain why these foundlings, knowing nothing of their origins, their elusive families, their enigmatic homelands, had declared themselves to be: he a Bulgarian, she a Turk. After all, the *friend* you've chosen becomes closer *family* than any other. It's therefore possible that someone devoid of nationality could feel as much loyalty as anyone to the nation he's chosen for himself.

In any case, Stepan and Sefra brought down on each other a hailstorm of blows, every punch delivered with enthusiasm. They looked beet-red, their hair was tangled together, their whole beings tensed with the heat of battle.

"Take that, stupid Bulgarian!"

"Take that, Turkish barbarian! And see how you like this, you ridiculous idolater of the crescent moon and the green banner!"

"Here's your change, you cross worshiper!"

---

[1] The First Balkan War, 1912-13.
[2] "Therefore, anger" (Latin).

"Muslim dog!"

"Christian jackal!"

With those last insults, they suddenly stopped hitting each other. The same idea had occurred to them both. The words "Bulgaria" and "Turkey" meant something to them: they were expanses of land, of forests, mountains, rivers. But the vocables "Christian" and "Muslim" seemed to them to have no definite sense.

Admitting her own ignorance, Sefra murmured, "You're fighting because you're a Christian; do you even know what that means?"

"Sure! It means putting a red cross on your sleeve." Stepan had seen a photo illustration of a group of army medics. "And you," he went on, "what does it mean to be a Muslim?"

She shrugged her shoulders regally. "You put a crescent on your sleeve, and there you are."

"But why a crescent?"

"And you, why a cross?"

They stared at each other, scratching their heads, with doubt in their eyes and their gestures. They smiled awkwardly. Finally, at the same time, they said, "My word, I don't know!"

They lowered their heads, a little ashamed now of having fought without understanding better the cause of their quarrel. Then Sefra burst out laughing, and Stepan joined her in a hilarity as inexplicable as their earlier anger.

"Shall we make peace? It's silly to fight without knowing why."

"You're right."

They shook hands and hugged warmly.

Then she murmured slyly, "You see, Stepan, to earn our living, it'd be better if Turkey and Bulgaria were allies."

That idea brought cheer to their young faces once again.

This conversation was taking place in the main courtyard of the Leslow farm, six miles outside Oakland, a large square bounded on one side by a wall topped with a railing and pierced by a gate opening onto the road. Aligned with that wall, to left and right of the gate, stood the stables, barns, sheep pens, dairies, etc., all of them separated by narrow alleys leading to secondary courtyards, and to haylofts, woodsheds, storage sheds, and tack rooms.

Opposite the gate, on the fourth side of the square, stood the farmhouse, with the comfortable and welcoming simplicity of its long ground floor beneath an attic roofed in glazed tiles of green and blue arranged like a checkerboard.

At the door appeared a woman, no doubt the farm wife, because the children called out, "Mrs. Slane!" She seemed the embodiment of sadness. Tall, hollow-cheeked rather than slim, her head bowed as if by the weight of heavy thoughts, Mrs. Slane had a gentle, resigned face framed by hair that surely had gone prematurely white. Her eyes, which were widened by the habitual tension of her eyelids, expressed worry—the same anxiety that afflicts the eyes of a doe when the baying of the hounds echoes through the forest.

What could she be afraid of, on this farm so close to California's great metropolis? What could she have to fear?—she who'd wronged no one, and who, when she first met Stepan and Sefra after their companions had abandoned them, had said with the simplest charity, "Come in, children. I'll keep you busy, and I'll find a way for you to earn your keep and your daily bread, and even a little weekly pocket money."

With her hand she shaded her eyes, which tears had ringed with dark circles. Seeing that the children were now reconciled, she motioned for them to come to her. A shiver made her voice tremble. "I warned you that you might have to hide."

"Yes, Mrs. Slane. You said the boss doesn't like new faces. Is he coming to the farm?"

"He's on his way."

"Ah!"

"So climb up into the attic, and take along some bread and bacon and cheese and cider. He might stay the night here. Anyway, a few hours of patience will be enough. Once he's gone, we can relax for weeks, maybe even months."

As she spoke, a fog of tears filled her eyes and she sounded embarrassed. Everything about her hinted at an unspoken and unspeakable sadness. Impulsively, the two little foundlings seized her thin, pale hands and brought them to their lips. She understood what was going through their young minds. Kissing them both tenderly on the forehead, she said, "Come. Let's hurry. I tremble at the thought of him catching you here."

"Is he really so awful?" muttered Stepan.

The farm wife's only answer was to lift her arms to the sky and nod her head in despair.

Then she gently led Sefra into the house, with Stepan following. Each of them received a loaf of bread, a rasher of bacon, one of those goat cheeses that in that region are called—who knows why—"oak cheese," and a jug of amber-colored cider. All that was done feverishly. At every moment Mrs. Slane started, listened for sounds from outside, and once she was reassured she hurried on with the task. "Come, come!" she said again.

Carrying their provisions, the two little guests at the farm went to a storeroom for firewood located behind the kitchen, with its vast hearth. A ladder led up through a trapdoor in the smoke-blackened ceiling. Stepan and Sefra climbed the rungs and hopped into the attic.

"Shut the trapdoor," called Mrs. Slane, "and make sure no sound gives away your presence."

She took away the ladder and carried it outdoors. The trapdoor closed silently. In semi-darkness, because daylight reached the attic only through narrow vents spaced far apart, the two young companions in misery found themselves alone amid sacks of preserves, dried vegetables, and smoked meat and fish, all hanging from the roof beams or piled on the floor. Farm provisions filled the attic, though it was more than thirty meters long by a dozen wide.

As if they were stunned by this adventure, Stepan and Sefra stood still a moment, gazing in amazement at the sacks of green beans, lentils, and dried peas, the fruit drying on straw-covered shelves, the brown smoked hams.

Finally, Stepan muttered under his breath, "So this Mr. Slane is an ogre?"

Sefra started. "An ogre! I've heard that ogres eat children! You think...?"

"Of course not. I was just trying to say he must be mean."

"On that count, good Mrs. Slane's terror leaves no doubt... And then, you must've noticed how pale she is, how sad... Earlier, just at the thought of him catching us, she was shaking like a leaf."

"It's true."

There was a silence. Sefra sat on the floor, with her legs folded like a Turk. Stepan propped himself against an enormous sack of potatoes. He seemed to be thinking, weighing the pros and cons of an idea. That interior debate resulted in him exclaiming, "Even so, I'd like to meet the fellow! Wouldn't you?"

She shook her head desperately. "No, no... He'd beat us, maybe throw us out..."

But he stuck to his idea. "So you wouldn't care to show your gratitude to worthy Mrs. Slane, who took us in and gave us a home?"

"How would we show that by meeting the man?"

"I don't know yet. But if we knew what kind of man he is and why he makes her tremble, we might be able to think of a way to rid her of this tyrant... Because only a tyrant could terrorize such a sweet, good woman."

Stepan's suggestion seemed to galvanize Sefra. The fear she'd exhibited just a moment before suddenly disappeared. She stood up and came to him, her eyes shining and her round cheeks blushing.

"Tell me what to do. I'll do it."

The two vagabonds showed their loyal nature.

"Tell me what to do," she repeated.

He shrugged. "You're in too much of a hurry, Sefra." With comical solemnity, his sententious tone echoed some voice he might well have heard long before. "Girls are impulsive—they want to arrive before they've left." She was getting ready to object, but he cut her off. "Come on, let's not quarrel. To take action, we need to know in what direction."

"Of course," she agreed, mollified.

"So the first step would be to find out the reason for Mrs. Slane's terror."

"Well, we already know that!" Sefra exclaimed impetuously. "She's terrified of Mr. Slane."

"Yes, but why?"

She lowered her head, baffled by the question, whose sharp logic required an answer more precise than she felt able to give.

Stepan didn't push his victory too far. "Well, my dear friend, we're in the attic, separated from the ground floor by nothing more than pine boards laid across the ceiling beams."

"Thanks for the news," said Sefra jokingly.

"Mrs. Slane told us to make no noise. And you don't have to make noise to look and listen."

"Look at, listen to... what?"

"Mr. Slane. The man's got to talk, make threats. Well-adjusted ears can therefore figure out his thoughts."

"Okay, and then?"

"When we're in his... confidence, then we can decide."

She clasped his hands warmly. "You know, you're a good Bulgarian."

"And you're a sweet little Turk."

"So we're agreed—we're going to spy on Slane?"

"Absolutely."

"But how...?"

Stepan gestured triumphantly. Pulling Sefra by the hand—which he was still holding—he led her to one of the small vents. Through the narrow opening they could see the farmyard, the rustic gate, and beyond it the road to Oakland.

"This is how we'll see him," he said slowly. Sefra nodded her approval. Then Stepan stretched out flat on the floor and pressed his ear to the boards. "To hear him," he explained.

She clapped her hands in delight—but stopped that noisy display as soon as he said, "Shh! No noise allowed."

She apologized, "I'm sorry. I won't do it again."

Her eagerness to help him made her as pliable as a glove. This little vaga-bond girl, who half an hour earlier had been exchanging fisticuffs with her com-panion, now submitted to his authority. He'd become a master in her eyes, now that he'd found a way—no matter how chancy—to give concrete form to the in-finite gratitude they felt for the goodness radiating from Mrs. Slane, who was so frightened by the still-unknown Slane.

"Horses!"

"A carriage!"

The two exclamations burst from their childish lips. They quickly took off their heavy hobnailed shoes. Then, barefoot, slipping across the attic floor like shadows, they went to the opening they'd chosen as their observation post.

Just then the courtyard gate opened. A light carriage drawn by a pair of horses pulled in.

"There are trunks in the carriage."

"Three people on the front seat. Two men; one of them must be our enemy, Mr. Slane."

"Oh!" murmured Sefra. "You call him our enemy?"

"Sure, since we can already blame him for bringing Mrs. Slane to tears."

14

"That's true," she conceded.

They both fell silent as they intently watched the fast-moving scene taking place in the courtyard.

With fearful haste, Mrs. Slane approached the carriage now stopped in the middle of the open yard. Geese, chickens, turkeys, ducks, guinea hens, surprised by the sudden appearance of the carriage, fled in all directions with harsh cries.

The travelers got down. As the children had observed, there were three of them, a woman and two men. One of the men drew all of their attention, since it was obvious at a glance that the other one couldn't be the boss: he wore clean but unfashionable clothes and had a thick, unruly beard. His wife might be pretty, but she was certainly odd: tall, slim, almost excessively lithe… and then that face—dark-complexioned, with red lips and velvet-black eyes beneath black hair. They must both be employees, subordinates of some kind—that was clear from their behavior. They bustled around their companion: a tall, spare man with a hard, domineering face, and graying hair under a soft felt hat.

If the children had still been in any doubt, Mrs. Slane's behavior would have resolved it. She hastened forward, forcing a smile onto her sad face. She did her best to inject some joy into her broken voice. "Ah, Mr. Slane! I'm delighted by this visit, which I couldn't have hoped would come so soon…"

The man shrugged. "Oh, so you weren't hoping for it, Edith?… Well, I'll take you at your word… and thank you for your welcome."

The poor woman opened her mouth to answer, but he rudely interrupted her. "Let's cut the chitchat, Edith. I haven't got much time, and I need to stick to the point. Have the luggage of my friends Derrick and Freda unloaded. Have them served generous refreshments. As for us, we need to talk."

"Talk?" Mrs. Slane echoed the word in a choked voice. She'd grown paler.

"Yes, talk. But hurry up, please—the clock is ticking."

The words were commonplace, but the emphasis he put on them gave them the weight of an order that couldn't be disobeyed. Mrs. Slane bowed her head, and her whole body seemed to slump. She called for servants and supervised the unloading of the large leather-bound trunks and their delivery to a room at the far end of the house.

Derrick and Freda—since those were the names of Slane's traveling companions—followed a maid who led them to the dining room, where the refreshments ordered for them were served.

With a commanding gesture, Slane grabbed his wife's arm. "Come to the parlor. The doors are padded. That way what we say won't reach any ears but ours."

She considered him with a certain anxiety, but he seemed not to notice. With no apparent effort he pulled Mrs. Slane toward the house.

CHAPTER II
Slane Reveals Himself

Up in the attic, the children had missed nothing Slane had said, and they were afraid of him without even meeting him in person. Their whispered exclamations had punctuated the conversation that took place out in the courtyard.

At Slane's final words, Stepan murmured, "We have to find out what he wants. If he tries to harm Mrs. Slane…"

"What'll you do?" asked Sefra curiously.

"I don't know, but I'll defend the woman who took us in, sheltered us, fed us…"

"Good—me too." She took his hand and shook it vigorously. But then her enthusiasm suddenly flagged. "To defend Mrs. Slane, we'll have to know what threatens her."

"Of course," said Stepan in surprise.

"And the poor woman isn't going to confide her sorrows to a couple of kids like us."

"Of course not."

"Therefore, to learn what they are, we'll have to hear what Mr. Slane says."

"Exactly."

"How? The parlor has padded doors, and no sound can get out." She stopped. He was laughing silently. "What?" she asked.

He put a finger to his lips and whispered, "Come. You'll see. No noise."

As inquisitive as any daughter of Eve, she followed her guide. Together they went about two thirds of the way across the attic that separated the ground-floor rooms from the sloping roof.

Once again, Stepan put his finger to his lips to remind his companion to keep silent. Then slowly, with cautious movements, he knelt on the attic floor. His hands ran across the boards that lay between the beams. Sefra watched the strange action without understanding its point. But then she barely stifled a cry of surprise. Stepan was slowly lifting a disk of plaster cut out of the floorboards themselves.

"What's that?"

"Underneath this is the metal rosette the parlor chandelier hangs from. Through the ornamental cutouts we'll be able to see them and hear them."

She looked admiringly at her friend, who'd uncovered that secret in the house construction. But she needed more explanation. "How'd you find that out?"

"From the workman who hung the chandelier. He cut out this disk so he could see the exact location of the beams—because the screws holding up the chandelier had to be driven into the beams."

"That's true! That's true."

"And now," he went on, "thanks to that earlier work, nothing can keep us from witnessing—with our eyes and our ears—the conversation good Mrs. Slane seems to dread."

Sefra immediately joined Stepan, kneeling by the opening he'd made. She bent closer to see down. He was right: through the copper rosette of the chandelier, which was cut into a decorative lattice, they could look down into the farmhouse parlor.

It was a bright square room, furnished with chairs and armchairs of bent satinwood and a pedestal table of modern design with copper trim. A few color prints and some flowers in vases on the mantelpiece completed the simple but very tidy decor.

"Shh. From now on we can't even breathe." Stepan's warning was self-evident.

The parlor door had just opened, and Slane came in, pushing Mrs. Slane in ahead of him.

The children exchanged a look. Their benefactress looked paler and more frightened than usual. And—as unobservant as young people generally are—Stepan and Sefra had no trouble noticing the shiver that ran up and down Mrs. Slane's body when she spoke her husband's name.

He led off the conversation by pointing to a chair by the table. "Sit down, Edith, and listen to me carefully… and obediently, because what I've decided on is what's going to happen."

The man's cold tone held menace. Again the children exchanged a fleeting glance, then returned their attention to the people they were observing from the height of their lookout spot.

Mrs. Slane sat in the chair indicated by her husband. But fear made her clumsy. She bumped into the table, which caused everything on it—a glass clock, along with a glass platter holding a pitcher, a tumbler, a sugar bowl, and a vase of orange blossoms (a collection of glassware known in the business as a "drinking glass set")—to tremble and throw sparkling light onto the dark surface of the table.

Slane snickered, "You're as clumsy as when I first knew you as a girl."

She didn't react to the insult, and only murmured, "I'm listening, as you asked."

He laughed louder. "It wasn't for the pleasure of criticizing you that I pointed out your awkwardness. You must be aware that your deportment is a matter of indifference to me."

She nodded.

"If, therefore," he went on, "I draw attention to your clumsiness, it's because you're a mother, Edith, a mother! Think about the responsibilities implied by that word. A mother, like a father, is accountable for the well-being of the child she's brought into this world."

She had lifted her head, and her eyes eagerly studied his face. She seemed not to know where this conversation was supposed to lead.

Up in the attic the children admitted to each other in pantomime that they didn't know either.

It must have been part of Slane's plan to explain, because—without giving his wife a chance to ask a question—he went on, "When you were a clumsy girl, only you were harmed. But a clumsy mother would cause harm to our William. And since I don't want to see him harmed, since I want to see him rich, powerful, in short happy, I'll tell you what I've decided."

Up to now the two young vagabonds whom Mrs. Slane had taken in out of charity had observed the fear she displayed toward her husband without understanding it. But they suddenly realized how right she was to be afraid when they heard the man express his wishes. They felt he was capable of anything; that death would follow disobedience. And they clasped each other's trembling hands in a pledge to help each other and defend themselves against the danger that had now become visible.

Unmoving, as if frozen, Mrs. Slane waited.

Slane joked, "You seem upset, my dear. A little orange-blossom water will calm you down enough to discuss our son's future."

He poured out some of the concentrated syrup, added sugar, and cut it with water. When she pushed away the glass he said, "Fine, you're not thirsty now, you'll have this soothing drink later. You're too excitable, my poor dear, too excitable. Here's a glass of something calming, which you'll take in a little while."

18

Then he shrugged and went on, emphasizing every word and articulating each syllable as if to drive them deeper into the mind of his trembling listener. "Outside the little world you claim to live in, Edith, you must've heard mention of Mrs. Hibbett."

He waited a moment for a reaction; getting none, he went on in a tone even more clipped. "No? Well, it's possible. You choose to live so withdrawn. The farm, raising crops, the company of a few farm hands, that's enough for you... Ah, the day I gave you my name, what a terrible mistake I made!"

She murmured dully, "Well then, break the bonds that unite us. You used to think my dowry of fifty thousand dollars was worth the sacrifice of your freedom. Now you think it isn't. Ask for a separation—I won't object."

She stopped, her answer cut short by Slane's guffaw. "Too late, my dear, too late. In any case, spare me your advice and all your interruptions. If I've come to disturb your quiet life for a moment, it isn't to argue with you, but only to inform you of what I've decided, which is what's going to happen."

Since the wretched woman bowed her head—overpowered once again by the voice of this man, whose imperious will she no doubt knew—he went on speaking, now almost good-naturedly. "Since I'll get my way, what's the point of angering me? Open your ears, Edith, and close your mouth. Anything you can say is pointless and futile."

He smiled with satisfaction. "So, I have to explain who the great Mrs. Hibbett is. I say 'the great' because no lesser epithet would do for a billionaire, and she is one. Her first husband left her a widow with the modest sum of four hundred million. That wasn't enough for her. Her second husband was Allan Carter, the oil and gas baron; he was nice enough to die recently, leaving her a fortune greater than any other in America, estimated in round numbers at two billion dollars."

Mrs. Slane didn't move. Her eyes were fastened anxiously on his face. No doubt she was waiting for Slane to make his point clear. And up in the attic, stretched out flat on the floor as they peered with flushed faces down through the openwork rosette of the chandelier, Stepan and Sefra also listened, wondering what the man was getting at.

Slane nodded his approval of his wife's attentiveness, and went on slowly, "By her first husband, Mrs. Hibbett has a son, Lloyd Hibbett, who's now eighteen years old."

"Like our son William," murmured Mrs. Slane.

"Like our son William, indeed. The young men were born a few days apart. But let's put that aside; we'll come back to it later. By her second husband, Mrs. Hibbett—now Carter—has a daughter, a child of three. If I dwell on her children, it's only to explain how, in her capacity as legal guardian of her children, Mrs. Hibbett-Carter inherited the usufruct and direction of those two fortunes."

There was a silence. Mrs. Slane and the invisible listeners overhead felt their hearts pounding: they could tell he was finally coming to the point.

Slane's brow—behind which still lay the thought his listeners feared—creased with deep lines: clearly the man was making an effort to stay calm and to express his intentions coolly. But then his forehead smoothed out, and he spoke again. "Lloyd Hibbett was barely five when his father returned to the bosom of..." Here Slane crossed himself piously. "Now, Mrs. Hibbett is a remarkable mother. She was afraid her son—too rich, surrounded by sycophants—might become one of those worthless wishy-washy creatures who fall prey to adventurers in search of a fortune. She therefore exiled him far away from her. She sent him to England under an assumed name. He completed his studies at Cambridge. He completed them brilliantly, I might say."

"But our William did just the same..."

"Exactly, my dear. Doesn't that resemblance—which has struck you twice in the last five minutes—give you a hint as to the direction of my plans?"

Dimly afraid, she shook her head and stammered, "What's the connection between...?"

He gave a harsh, sinister laugh. "Don't try to figure it out—no point risking brain fever! I came here precisely to explain everything. So..."

He snapped his fingers with brutal carelessness. "But wait—I almost forgot to explain my own situation. You know I founded the Institute of Inventors, by appealing to the vanity of billionaires all over the country. In all my dealings with my benefactors,"—it would be impossible to convey the sarcasm with which he spoke that word—"I dazzled their eyes with the unstoppable power they'd acquire by joining together in a business syndicate whose wealth no one, neither governments nor private individuals, could match. I persuaded them, and I united them. I'm the general secretary of that syndicate... But now they're opposing me..."

He punched the air with a blow intended for his invisible adversaries, panted hoarsely, then went on, "I want control, a monopoly, over all the enterprise in the world, starting with Asia. Hell, not every deal can succeed—no doubt the losses will counterbalance the profits; but for me, or for a president subservient to me, every deal will be excellent, because we—the directors and promoters—will collect not just on the profits but on the capital invested."

He paused in thought for a moment before going on, "Did they understand that? Or were they being sincere when, at our last meeting, they said they liked my plans but they couldn't let me be the one to direct their execution, because I'm not in a position to invest a fortune of my own large enough to persuade those who are hesitating?"

"What does all this have to do with me?" whimpered Mrs. Slane, trying in vain to understand where her husband's explanation was headed.

"I'm getting there, I'm getting there. Oh, I know that you, my dear, are incapable of playing a challenging part in it. That's why I've saved the simplest job for you. You won't have to say anything. All you have to do is keep silent."

"Keep silent?" she said in surprise.

"Keep silent?" echoed the children in their hideout.

"Exactly. But you're not smart enough to get it without having it spelled out, so stop interrupting and do your best to listen. It'll go faster that way."

He went on in the tone of a teacher addressing his students. "Given the current situation, what do I need? To have control over the president the syndicate is going to appoint; or even simpler, to be sure of his cooperation."

Mrs. Slane nodded.

"You understand that much—I'm delighted. Now, do you know to whom they're going to offer that coveted presidency?"

"No, of course not."

"To the candidate they consider to be at the same time the wealthiest and the most capable—because he's been raised far from his kind, like a little bourgeois destined to live out his life in the worst drudgery."

"Lloyd Hibbett!" she cried.

"Bingo! Lloyd Hibbett, who doesn't know his own name, and who won't learn it until he sets foot on American soil again. Lloyd Hibbett, who faces one final test: his mother is going to fetch him in Europe—but first, she's going to follow him without making herself known to him, in order to study him. Ah, that Mrs. Hibbett-Carter is a superior woman, and a principled woman," he added mockingly, "because she'll only give the syndicate a president she considers worthy of the position. What do you think of that, Edith?"

She seemed troubled. Then she spoke up. "You should've made an ally of Mrs. Hibbett."

Slane gestured violently. "And it should've occurred to you that of course that was the first thing I tried."

"And?"

"Mrs. Hibbett turned me down flat."

"For what reason?"

"Because she thinks I'm working mostly in my own interest. The worthy woman is very clear-sighted... clear-sighted, but narrow-minded, because she considers me detrimental to the prosperity of the syndicate."

"I assume she's wrong?" said Mrs. Slane hesitantly.

Slane laughed loudly. "Right or wrong, who knows? Even I don't know. I'm only sure of one thing: that my own personal fortune depends on the success of my plans."

"Your plans are going down the drain," she began, doing her best to seem interested in the problem. But then suddenly she fell silent, frozen by renewed fears.

"Not at all!" Slane rebuked her. "It'd be idiotic to let some woman's ill will scuttle such a colossal venture. I was expecting her to refuse. I gave her a chance to cooperate with me. She rejected it—too bad for her. I still have the option of force."

His voice had acquired a steely tone, ringing like a vibrating blade. It evoked the image of a dagger raised to strike anyone who resisted the speaker.

Choking over her words, Mrs. Slane barely managed to articulate a question. "Force?... What can you mean by that?"

"Lloyd Hibbett," said Slane, his eyes blazing, "raised in England, is completely unknown here, in terms of his appearance. Only his mother could point him out as her son. It's to be expected that, coached by his mother, he'll thwart my plans and maybe even force me to resign."

"That will certainly..."

"That *would*, my dear—if that young man weren't destined to die young, dragging along with him in death his imprudent mother as well as that little girl, his half-sister by the marriage with Allan Carter."

Mrs. Slane stood up, very pale. "What? How?"

He forced her to sit back down. "How? That doesn't matter to you. I'm showing you the future—never mind the details."

He held out a glass to her, the one in which he'd stirred together sugar and orange-blossom water. "Drink this, Edith. I don't mean you any harm, and it bothers me to see you shaking like a leaf in the wind."

She obeyed automatically, with the vague feeling that she had to deflect from herself the rage she sensed was seething in her terrifying husband's heart.

In the attic, the children whispered together:

"Did you see that, Stepan?"

"Yes—he threw some white powder into the glass."

"What was it?"

"That's the question. Maybe a sedative, like some thieves give to people they plan to rob."

"Heaven grant it's only that!"

"Oh! You think it might be poison?"

"Damn... That man's awfully wicked..."

"Well, yeah... All you have to do is look at him... But hush—he's speaking again."

Indeed, down in the parlor Slane's voice rang out once more, with a sound that was hard to define: sarcasm, triumph, menace, all could be heard in his tone. "Edith, don't you want to ask me in what way the death of all the Hibbett-Carters will affect my position relative to the syndicate?"

She gestured vaguely, but when he frowned she hastened to say, "I beg your pardon! I'm asking now."

"About time!" joked Slane. "You just need a little push to be cooperative. So, let me answer your question. Lloyd Hibbett, raised in England, is unknown by appearance in America. His true identity is unknown in England, where they know him only by his assumed name. To put it more clearly, the English see his face under a name that isn't his, and the Americans use his real name without knowing the face it belongs to. Do you understand?"

Mrs. Slane nodded. Oddly, that simple gesture seemed to require an effort. Her face had suddenly grown pale.

The children noticed it and exchanged a meaningful glance.

Sefra whispered, "She looks like she's ill."

Stepan put a finger to his lips.

Maybe the rustle of her whisper had reached the ears of the man they were watching, because Slane looked around in mild surprise. But he must have decided his senses were deceiving him. Turning back to his wife—who'd grown even paler, and whose eyes were now inexplicably clouding over—he announced bluntly, "Our son William is also unknown, since he grew up in England, just like Hibbett. And with the latter dead, there's nothing to stop William from taking his place, from becoming—by my arrangement—Lloyd Hibbett... a Lloyd Hibbett with the same interests as mine; a Lloyd Hibbett under no influence contrary to mine."

Mrs. Slane moved feebly. For a moment she managed to rise from her seat, but then she fell back into it, protesting weakly, "William, an accomplice to such a crime!... Never, never, will I accept that!"

A burst of laughter made her start painfully. Slane observed her, smiling with some kind of delight she couldn't understand. Suddenly he leaned close to the poor woman and said with cynical mockery, "I knew how you'd react, my dear. Thirty years of marriage have taught me the stupidity of your conscience."

She didn't answer. Her eyes, widened by some new horror, were fixed on him. With difficulty she lifted her hands as high as her heart and pressed them to her chest with a grimace of pain.

Slane laughed even louder. "That's good: you've just figured out that I've now disposed of the only influence on William I had to worry about. But I haven't been cruel, my dear—it's just digitalis. In five minutes, your heart will stop beating. *Our* son will become *my* son, and at my convenience I'll train him for the brilliant career I've prepared for him."

She tried to speak, but her lips moved without making a sound. Only her eyes still expressed her final torment. But then they gradually grew veiled, rolled suddenly, and were still: forever immobile.

Without showing the least emotion, Slane bent over his victim and brought a small mirror up to her still-parted lips. No mist clouded the mirror. Then with a gesture of triumph he muttered, "Derrick must've eaten his fill by now. He can help me give this damned Edith a resting place where no one will come bother her."

With that, turning away from the corpse of the woman he'd coldly poisoned, Tom Slane left the parlor and carefully locked the door behind him.

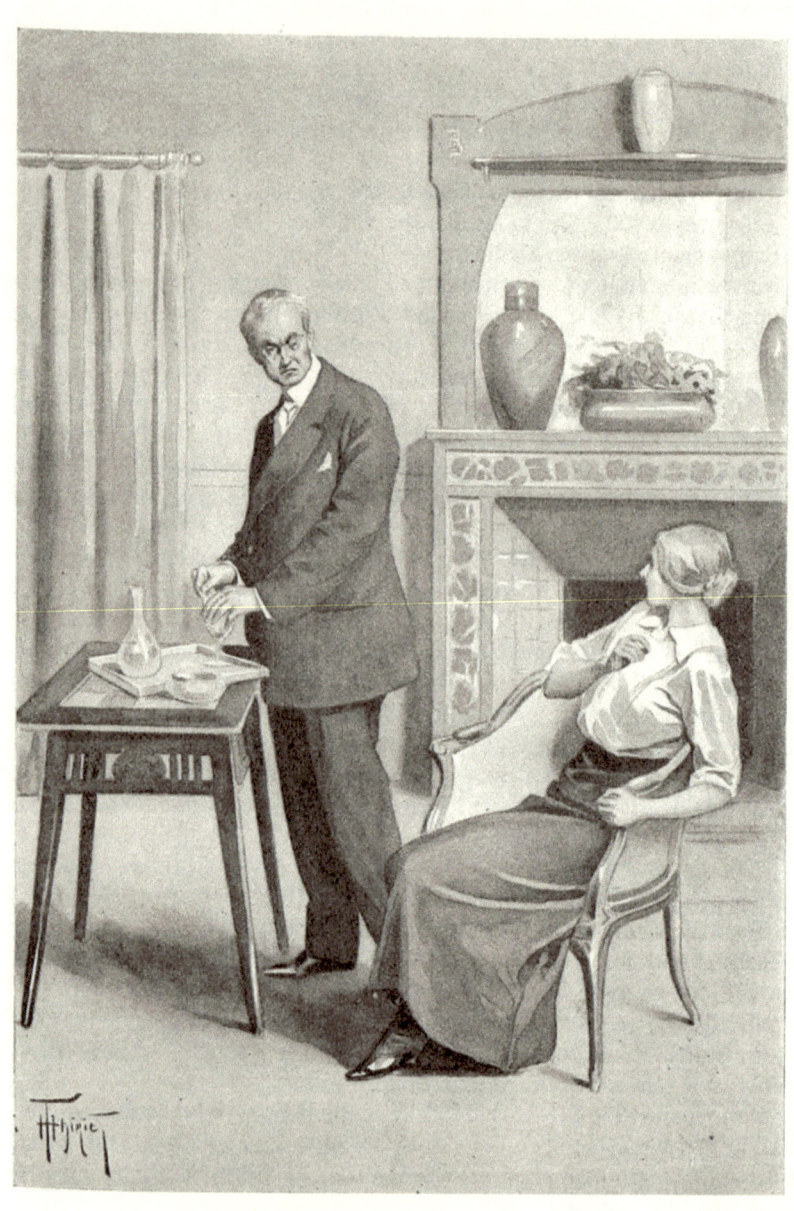

Overhead, above the metal rosette of the chandelier, the two children stared at each other in horror. They couldn't find a single thing to say. Of course, they'd lived a wandering life, among folks whose concept of social morality didn't preclude petty larceny: stealing chickens, fruit, vegetables, sometimes more. But that terrible crime, that sinister act, that takes away life and hurls it into the dreaded unknown that is death, had never met their eyes, never crossed their minds. And suddenly these adolescents, these blossoms barely open to life, were confronted by death's destruction in its most terrifying form—murder. Instinctively they embraced, hugging each other tightly, and dissolved in tears.

How long did it last, that eruption of despair, expressing the heartbreak of two innocent souls struck by a criminal's brutal fist? They couldn't have said. The sound of the parlor door opening brought them back to reality. Automatically, they returned to their observation post.

Slane had come back into the room, but he wasn't alone face to face with the corpse of the poor woman who'd taken in the abandoned children. Derrick and Freda, last seen by Slane's car, stood near him, apparently waiting for his orders.

"Up to this point everything's gone smoothly," said Slane.

"We've followed your instructions," said Derrick in a hoarse voice.

"I know it, my good man, and I'll prove my satisfaction to you—and to the lovely Freda, for helping you."

As they were about to reply he cut them off. "Enough of that. The past is past. We have to bury it so well the future can't ever dig it up." He gave a hideous laugh. "Because the future, my friends, is a notorious tomb excavator." He shrugged scornfully. "For instance, the future can't find what no longer exists... Smoke escapes the curious eye of the law... So we'll leave behind us nothing but smoke."

Derrick and Freda listened in silence, without moving.

Slane went on as calmly as if he were making small talk. "Your trunks are in the woodshed?"

"Yes, boss, they were stored there."

"Tonight we'll load them back onto the car that brought us here. I'll drive you to the Oakland station. I've reserved seats for you on the transcontinental express, which will get you to New York just in time to catch the boat to Europe, where you know what you have to do."

"Yes, boss—but with us on the train and you back at the Institute of Inventors in San Francisco, there'll be nothing to keep some passerby from finding your wife's body, as well as those of the men and women on the farm, that—following your orders—we took care of the same way while we were eating."

"You're mistaken, Derrick."

"No doubt, since you say so, but I don't see how."

"Didn't I say we'd leave nothing behind us but smoke?"

"Yes, you did. But to burn down the farm would be tough."

"That's why we won't burn it down. It'll burn, that's all."

"That's the same thing, boss."

Slane rubbed his hands mockingly. "Not at all—the fire will be considered an accident. It'll rid us of all the compromising evidence, and it'll bring me a profit."

At that last claim, his two listeners couldn't help looking doubtful.

He didn't take offense. "Friends, do you know why I bought this farm six years ago? No, you don't. Well, it was quite simply an excellent investment. My late wife, to whom I gave it as her home, which she gladly accepted—since my company didn't seem to please her, who knows why—my wife never suspected she was spending her days on land that concealed a fortune."

"A fortune?"

"Yes. The ground under these meadows and woods and fields holds oil."

"Oil?"

"Yes, friends. And right here, under this floor, there's a well I installed, that seeps petroleum. You get it? With a simple setup, a flammable fuse, the naphtha gas will catch fire two or three hours after we leave. By tomorrow morning there'll be nothing left here of the buildings or the people but ashes." Slane concluded happily, "And then what do you know—oil will be discovered and my land will skyrocket in value!"

In a different tone he ordered, "Let's get to work. We have to uncap the well and get out of here within two hours." He broke off. "What's that you say?"

The surprised faces of his listeners answered for them. Clearly, they hadn't said a word, and Slane realized it. "My ears are playing tricks on me today. Let's go to the toolshed and get what we need for the job."

Of course, his ears hadn't deceived him. The whispering he'd noticed momentarily had indeed been produced by human mouths—but those mouths belonged to the two children hidden in the attic.

With the corpse of their benefactress before their eyes, gratitude had stirred their hearts, and almost simultaneously, both of them giving voice at the same time to their sense of loyalty, they'd said, "We must go to New York and follow Slane's accomplices and warn this Mrs. Hibbett they mean to harm her."

Sefra murmured, "But people will think we're making up this story to get a reward. Who'd believe two poor vagabonds like us, accusing a rich man?"

"You're right, Sefra. So we won't accuse him. But we'll watch over that lady and her little girl and protect them."

Then Sefra had a new thought that threw both brave children into despair. "To get to New York, and beyond, you need money."

They had no money. And sailing across the Atlantic is expensive, taking the train from San Francisco to New York is expensive. What to do? What to decide? They sat silent, baffled by the obstacle that rose before them.

Then Stepan glanced down through the openwork rosette. The parlor was empty. The criminals had gone to the toolshed. "Come on," he whispered cautiously.

"Where?" she replied.

"You'll see." Triumphantly, with a certain self-importance, he added, "I've found a way to travel without money."

"Without money?"

"Yes, sweetheart. Oh, we won't be as comfortable as in a third-class compartment, but what'll make up for it is..." He paused.

"Is...?" she prompted.

"That we'll be traveling at the expense of the villains who killed our dear Mrs. Slane!"

CHAPTER III
A Series of Surprises

"Whip, I promise you that last night, when we went to bed, there was about half a leg of lamb on Buffet 3, and that bowl was full of a delicious marinated potato and cucumber salad."

"So you say, Hog, so you say."

"Because it's true!"

"Don't get angry. I'm sure you're right—but I can't understand how the salad and the leg of lamb, and even the bone, could've disappeared!"

Two waiters, wearing white jackets over black vests and black trousers, were talking in the dining car of the express making the run from San Francisco to New York.

"Well, I can't explain it either!" cried Hog angrily. "I observe it, and I'm sorry to observe it!"

"A fellow waiter must've served some passenger who was starving in the middle of the night."

"No, no, Whip, you know that can't be it. In place of the missing food we'd have found the receipt. Miss Palanker was on the night shift, and she never forgets. Besides, I asked her: no one ordered a meal last night. The whole train was asleep. The bartender on duty here in the dining car admitted to me that he'd slept soundly. So then?..."

Whip had been infected by Hog's distress, which had also spread to the kitchen, the waiters, the cooks, and the dishwashers. No one doubted the disappearance of objects that were usually quite material: a leg of lamb, potato salad. Vague unspoken suspicions brought frowns of defiance to their faces. But the staff truly panicked when the wine steward swore under oath that two bottles of Veekick Water (the transatlantic version of Evian) had also disappeared. But panicking didn't solve the problem, as was clear, since no one thought of a solution.

A half-hour station stop to change engines, which required some track maneuvers, added to the general distress. While the passengers took advantage of the chance to stretch their legs, a few of the waiters got out on the platform to take a refreshing stroll.

There they ran into a train conductor, who was eyeing the dual-use baggage car No. 5, which stood just in front of the dining car. It was called "dual-use" because a partition, with a door in it, divided it in two: the front half held passengers' luggage, the rear half was used as a pantry and wine cellar for the dining car, to which it was connected by the kind of gangway that made it possible to walk from one end of the train to the other.

Now the conductor, Noller by name, explained that at daybreak he'd gone to the dining car for the milky tea, smoked ham, and toast that constituted his regular "first breakfast"—courtesy of the railroad. On his way back to his post, he'd noticed that the baggage car was filled with the smell of a kind of fragrant blond tobacco called "birds-foot"; he recognized the brand, because that's what his brother smoked. But his brother was back in San Francisco. And he himself had a weak stomach, which kept him from smoking tobacco. So where was the smell coming from? Curious, he'd pushed aside packages and hunted around in every corner—without finding any trace of a smoker. That seemed to him quite extraordinary, and everyone around him agreed... which still didn't solve the mystery.

A few skeptics, like Whip, muttered under their breath that Noller had imagined it, that it was some kind of olfactory mirage. But most of the train crew supported the word of a conductor who was well known for his sobriety and cool head.

Besides, their confidence in him was reinforced by the boy whose job it was to sell cigarettes and cigars in the dining car. Struck by Noller's account, the young man, whose name was Wenham, had rushed straight to the cabinet—which was never locked—where he kept "articles for smokers." There he'd noticed the absence of one of those small painted rectangular tins, each of which held twenty-five birds-foot cigarettes. Some invisible hand had stolen the tobacco, so that it could be smoked in the next car.

On the spot everyone decided it was time to notify the head conductor. He, unable to offer a definite opinion, promised to launch an inquiry. That promise eased their troubled minds a little, though nobody expected much from it, since inquiries rarely produce any light.

The station stop ended. They all went back to work and, absorbed in their jobs, stopped—for the moment—looking for an explanation for those inexplicable events. Of course, undoubtedly someone was responsible. But who? And how had that individual gone about it?

Question marks not followed by answers are torture for humanity. That indisputable fact explains the great charitable motive that inspires so many people when they lie rather than leave one of those punctuation marks dangling.

The train went peacefully on its way. Nothing new happened that day. The early-morning excitement abated. A timid whisper had begun to make the rounds, that Hog, Noller, and Wenham had been mistaken... when a new occurrence reopened the question.

Atkins, who oversaw the sleeping compartments on the Pullman car, was sure—and the manifest agreed—that two of the seats that converted to beds, located in the car behind the dining car, were not assigned to passengers. As we know, those seats, which can be reclined into beds at night, are surrounded by curtains, giving the passenger real privacy, so that decency—every American's right—is preserved. Those curtains must be open and tied back during the day.

Now Atkins was surprised to find the curtains drawn around two unoccupied seats, as if there were passengers sitting there. In his own words, he "tidied up," which is to say he opened and tied back the curtains. And then he discovered to his astonishment that both seats had been converted into beds, and that they *had certainly been occupied*, because there were breadcrumbs on the floor, and an empty bottle bearing the Veekick Farms Water label lay next to one of the seats. So someone had eaten and drunk there!

Atkins was so upset he had kept his discovery to himself, for fear of being mocked—till after the station stop described above; then he told his fellow crew members.

Therefore some person—and it had to be granted it was a person, short of believing in a display by Old Nick (the Devil) himself—had smoked in the dual-use baggage car, taken food and drink from the dining car, and slept in the Pullman car. And that person couldn't be found.

The next few days passed without any new evidence of the stranger. The crew had begun to count on reaching New York in three days without any further alarm... when suddenly the mysterious activity started again.

Noller the conductor had fortified himself against the cold of the night with a small flask that the bartender on duty had generously filled with whisky. He'd left it under the wooden bench he sat on in the dual-use car, to go get supper in the dining car. That was after the last of the passengers had eaten and left, toward ten-thirty at night. Once he'd eaten, he went back to his post. His whisky flask was still there. He sat, rising from time to time to observe the train's progress when they passed through stations, as was his duty. At eleven-thirty—he swore it on the Bible—he had a swig of whisky. At twelve-thirty he had another. The flask itself, still more than half full, proved later that what he said was true.

Well, after his second swig he fell fast asleep. While he slept, a roast veal, two loaves of bread, some fruit, and several bottles of water were stolen from the pantry located in the rear half of the dual-use car. And careful examination revealed that his whisky contained a sedative. That seemed to explain matters: someone had put Noller to sleep so as to rob the pantry undisturbed. Oh, it was easy enough to figure out what "someone" had done—but as for identifying the "someone," that was another matter.

This time, though, the entire train crew flew into a state. The conductors' agitation, and a few overheard words, made the passengers aware of the events—one might say "the regrettable events"—that had occurred on board. From then on there was not a soul on that express train who didn't share in the general excitement.

The person who was the cause of it all didn't reveal himself any further. Though they posted watchmen with regular shifts throughout the night, that fantastical person—who seemed to enjoy fooling everyone—declined to give any sign of himself again.

The passengers' trust couldn't hold up against the stranger's inaction. It's fun to believe in mysterious doings: it gives you a delicious little shiver, an absorbing preoccupation to help pass the time on a long journey... But mysteries that don't occur again the moment you want them to soon grow unbearable. It's tempting, in fact, to dismiss them as the "humbug" of some prankster who's making fun of you. That was the opinion that prevailed. The passengers accused the crew of playing a practical joke on them, and that had an effect on the size of their tips when the train reached New York.

Derrick and Freda, who'd boarded in Oakland on Tom Slane's orders, had paid no attention to the whole story, which they considered to be "nothing to worry about." They left the train followed by a porter who brought their suitcases and their two trunks of yellow leather reinforced with copper corners and ribs, which he'd piled on a luggage cart.

Wanting a walk after six days of confinement on the express, they gave the porter instructions to go to the pier belonging to the White Star Line, an English company whose steamships made the run between Great Britain and the United States, and to load their luggage on the *Tottenham*, bound for Europe.

Derrick and Freda ambled away happily. Looking at them, you'd have taken them for a happy middle-class couple with no serious worries. The most suspicious detective couldn't have imagined that these people had taken part in the arson of the farm outside Oakland, nor that they were now heading to Europe with equally sinister plans in mind. Perhaps even Derrick and Freda themselves had forgotten what they were involved in. If criminals didn't have long stretches

31

when their memories slept, their fear of being arrested and their obsession with the avenging law would soon make them turn themselves in—for anything would be better than being endlessly face to face with their own thoughts.

Certainly at this moment the strolling couple was enjoying a period of forgetfulness.

"The boss promised me," murmured Derrick, "this would be our last 'campaign.'" Seeing Freda shake her head doubtfully, he insisted, "Yes, yes. He explained it to me. Once we're sure we've succeeded, the battle's over. We can focus our lives on more peaceful pursuits."

"I hope you're right," she muttered.

"What? You seem awfully down today."

She gestured wearily. "Not more so than other days. But I'd give a lot for your prediction to come true. I have a constant fear... If we were caught... Oh, prison would be nothing. But the awful thing is that it would be in the newspapers. There'd be plenty to say, wouldn't there, about us, about the boss, about other people."

"Bah! Newspapers! That's the least of my worries..."

She cut him off. "Because it hasn't occurred to you that *she* might see those newspapers."

He started. "Damn!"

"Now you get it," she said triumphantly. "Just the idea has shaken you. You've gone frightfully pale."

Indeed, Derrick's ruddy face had been covered by an ashen veil.

But they were approaching the pier, at the end of which stood the shipping company's tent. The steamship *Tottenham* stretched its enormous bulk along the rock wall. Since the ship's sides rose several meters higher than the quay, a steep gangway enabled porters, sailors, and so forth to reach the deck with the luggage and parcels in their care.

For a moment, Derrick and Freda stopped to take in the lively scene unfolding before them. Then they recognized the porter to whom they'd given their luggage. His job done, he was come slowly back down to the quay. He noticed them too. To their great surprise, he approached them and said mysteriously, "I put the trunks and the suitcases in the gentleman's and the lady's connecting cabins."

"Very good. You've already been paid. But here's a little extra change."

"Thanks," said the porter as he pocketed the tip. "But that's not why I spoke to the gentleman."

"Bah!—then why?"

"To ask him a question. Is the gentleman aware that his trunks talk?"

"Talk?"

Derrick and Freda looked at each other, dumbfounded. Then the same thought came to them both: the man must have hit the bottle. It was in the humoring tone you use when you invite a drunk to go lie down that Derrick replied, "Of course I'm aware... Trunks can talk, just like everybody. There's no problem in letting them chatter a little."

The porter's eyes widened enormously. The cleverness of the remark no doubt escaped him. It seemed to take him an effort to reply, "Ah! And here I thought I was bringing you news. So you already knew trunks complain when you bump then too hard."

"Yes, yes, they complain—and so do I," agreed Derrick to keep the joke going.

"So maybe you already know what they say?"

"When they're bumped?"

"Yes."

"Heck, a trunk must say what any ordinary person says: Ow! Ouch! Ow! Ouch! This brute is hurting me!"

"Exactly," said the porter very seriously. "It surprised me. I thought I ought to inform the gentleman. Now that's done, I'll be on my way."

And with his hands in his pockets and his shoulders hunched, the man went away with heavy steps.

"Well," chuckled Derrick. "Talking trunks! Nothing like whisky to give you notions like that."

Freda just smiled pityingly.

Together they climbed the gangway leading on deck. A ship's officer pointed the way, and they went to their quarters. The suite occupied by Tom Slane's accomplices consisted of two adjoining cabins, each opening onto the corridor—or "passageway," as they're called on ocean liners—and with a communicating door between them. For anyone who knows the price of a transatlantic steamship ticket, it must be clear that Slane was doing things handsomely. Cabins of that kind are roomier. Even with the two trunks present, there was plenty of space by the bunks and in front of the wash stands.

Derrick snickered, "Well, good old trunk, you who talks to porters, you should at least—just out of politeness—say hello to your owner." He burst out laughing, his harsh voice ringing in the cabin. "No, really, when you're sober you could never think up the crazy ideas you get from liquor!"

Hearing no answer from the adjoining cabin, he went to the door between them to find out why Freda was silent. Kneeling by her own trunk, she was hunting through a key ring, loaded with many keys of all sizes, for the one that fit the locks of her luggage. Hearing Derrick come in, she turned. "We're sailing tonight, at the turn of the tide. I'm taking advantage of the time till then to sort my things a little."

"Oh, leave all that. We'll have plenty of long days of sailing. Better would be to go back on deck and go have dinner somewhere near the pier. Remember, we'll be stuck on board till we reach England."

She got up promptly. "Whatever you say, Derrick."

"Thanks, Freda."

Moments later they were back on the quay. A ship's officer had told them departure wouldn't take place before nine o'clock at night—or at twenty-one hours, to follow the modern style. They therefore had three hours to spare.

Once they were gone, their cabins were silent for a while. Then there was a slight snapping noise, like the grinding of a badly-oiled hinge. Where did it come from? The source of the noise was soon clear: the lid of Derrick's trunk rose very slowly. The movement stopped, then started again, as if someone crouching inside was making sure there were no spies around. That inspection must have produced a favorable result, because the lid opened all the way; the upper tray was stuffed with clothes tightly secured by straps. How could those clothes have caused the lid to open? Usually, clothes packed in a trunk are completely powerless to open it.

A minute went by. Then there came a cautious whistle. Was there an echo? Because an identical whistle answering the first seemed to come from Freda's cabin. And then—that porter earlier had been exactly right—the trunk spoke, uttering the onomatopoeia, "Hup!"

The monosyllable still rang in the air when a visible change took place: in both cabins the upper trays of both trunks rose, revealing beneath them, and supporting them with outstretched arms like caryatids or telamons,[3] Stepan and Sefra, the children we last left watching and listening from the attic of the farm where Mrs. Slane had been killed.

The idea of avenging their benefactress, along with that of protecting Mrs. Hibbett and her children from some danger—an unspecified one, except that its intention was quite simply to eliminate them—had aroused in the two children the desire to follow the perpetrators of the planned crime. Derrick and Freda would lead them to Mrs. Hibbett, and once they'd warned her she'd be on the lookout.

Yes… but following someone isn't as easy as it seems. The railroads consider passengers without money "undesirables." And yet they absolutely had to stick to Slane's accomplices, who—as they'd overheard in their hiding place—would be sailing for Europe six days later, as soon as the express train reached New York.

Necessity is the mother of invention. While Slane and his accomplices were busy with the complicated process of setting fire to the farm and erasing all clues to their crime, Stepan and Sefra left their observation post and went to the storage shed where the trunks had been left.

Along the way, they found the male and female farm workers fast asleep in the kitchen, where the remains of a substantial log fire smoldered in the vast hearth. They ought to wake them! But the hope kindled by that idea was soon

---

[3] Caryatids and telamons: respectively, female and male figures used in architecture as ornamental supports, seeming to "hold up" a column or archway.

snuffed out: all their efforts were in vain. The sedative they'd heard about had been served out liberally.

Stepan realized it was pointless. Surveying the sleepers with pity, he said, "There's nothing we can do here. Let's focus on the others, the ones who can still be saved."

The boy's cold decision reflected the years of hardship he'd already lived. With a sigh, Sefra followed him. She too understood the priorities of the moment. Having both lived among vagabonds, always in conflict with local residents or the authorities, they had a very different sense of society from that of children lucky enough to grow up in their own families.

In the toolshed they found everything they needed: hooks to manipulate the locks of the trunks, and screwdrivers to control those locks from the inside. They hid the second and third trays of both trunks in a barn and slipped into the space they'd occupied. The lids closed. With a sound of screwdrivers turning, the locks were relocked. When the owners of the trunks came to get them and depart for the Oakland station with their boss Tom Slane, they had no inkling the contents of their trunks had undergone a significant change. The presence of the children in the trunks, and their ability to get out whenever they wanted, explained all the mysterious events that had livened up the six-day train journey.

And now, standing together by the reclosed trunks in Derrick's and Freda's cabins, Stepan and Sefra talked in low voices.

"We're aboard the ship about to sail for Europe. Now what?"

"Go look for the cabins belonging to Mrs. Hibbett and her staff."

"If we go look, we'll be seen..."

"But not noticed. At departure time we have nothing to worry about."

Not convinced, Sefra shook her head.

Stepan insisted. "I'm telling you, believe me. Anyway, do you have a better idea?"

With an impatient gesture, she admitted defeat, then said, "All right! We find Mrs. Hibbett. Then what?"

"Then we tell her what we know."

"And if she doesn't believe us? After all, if we hadn't seen and heard what we witnessed in Oakland, we wouldn't believe such things could possibly be planned."

He shrugged philosophically. "It's a chance we have to take."

"But then..."

"She'll either believe us or she won't. In the first case we'll follow her guidance. In the second case we'll get back on the quay and we'll find a way to earn a living. There's work in New York, just like in San Francisco." And with a smile he concluded, "And if we don't like the town, we'll leave. Now we know how to travel without spending a cent."

That idea amused her, and she replied thoughtfully, "All right, let's do it... Especially since I think you're right: there's nothing else we can do."

Together they slipped into the passageway. A steward going by helpfully answered their questions: Mrs. Hibbett, her daughter, and a nursemaid had the suite on the aft quarterdeck.

"I should've known," said Stepan when the steward was gone. "As rich as she is—according to Slane—of course she has the finest cabins on the ship."

"True."

"But let's not waste any time: we have to decide what we're doing before the ship sails."

Without hiding, feeling sure no one would pay any attention to them so near departure time, the children went aft and found the luxury cabins whose doors opened directly onto the quarterdeck. They reached the Hibbett suite; there could be no doubt—a card fixed to the door announced the name of the woman they were looking for.

Together they knocked. The door opened immediately, and the nursemaid, a big blonde girl with a mild, sleepy air, appeared in the doorway and asked, "What's the purpose of your call?"

"Is Mrs. Hibbett there?"

"Of course she is, but she can't receive everyone who calls. So tell me what you want, and I'll ask her."

Those words ended in a cry of surprise. Taking advantage of her being off guard, with a quick shove Stepan thrust the nursemaid to one side and, with the way now clear, leaped into the cabin, followed faithfully by Sefra. Before the servant could recover from her astonishment, the two children had crossed the first cabin and stopped respectfully at the door to the second cabin, which belonged to Mrs. Hibbett and her little daughter. The mother and child were there.

Mrs. Hibbett was about forty, slight and fragile, with fine features expressive of both decisiveness and melancholy. Blonde hair shot through with gray framed her wide forehead. The billionairess herself was brushing the hair of a child of about three, adorable but unruly, whom she had trouble holding onto as she sat on a berth.

The sight of the two children seemed to amaze her. "Who let you in here?" she asked curtly.

Sefra was inspired to answer immediately, "Providence, that must want you to be saved, along with this lovely little thing."

That clear, disturbing reply froze the words on Mrs. Hibbett's lips. Taking advantage of that, Sefra quickly continued. She spoke of their stay at the farm outside Oakland, and of their affection for the woman they'd assumed was the farmer's wife, Mrs. Slane.

"Slane," interrupted her listener.

"Yes, Slane. That name is known to you, isn't it, ma'am?"

"Indeed so, but he's not a family man. I was thinking of someone who's the Director of the Institute of Inventors. He obviously has no connection to the person you're talking about."

"Wrong: he's her husband."

"Husband!" Mrs. Hibbett seemed struck. Between clenched teeth she muttered unconsciously, "He claimed not to know where his wife had gone." Her young visitors now interested her enormously. "Go on, children, go on. I'm listening."

No doubt she was prepared for some sensational disclosure—but her expectations were about to be horrifically surpassed. In broken sentences, Sefra and Stepan took turns explaining their presence in the attic and the openwork rosette that enabled them to witness the conversation between Slane and his victim. They laid out the vile plot Slane had devised to substitute his son William for Lloyd Hibbett, whom she was now on her way to Europe to bring home. Then they described the poisoning of Mrs. Slane, the intention to burn the farm, their own decision—inspired by their gratitude to the dead woman—to find Mrs. Hibbett, to warn her, and if she wished, to put themselves under her orders to watch Slane's accomplices, who'd boarded the ship and were staying in cabins 5 and 7. If necessary Mrs. Hibbett could have Derrick and Freda arrested, and finish her journey without being followed by her enemies.

But she shook her head. What pretext was there to arrest them? How could she accuse Slane? No one would believe accusations based entirely on the word of two poor little vagabonds.

"Then keep us with you, ma'am," murmured Sefra.

"Keep you?"

"Yes! Your children and you yourself are threatened. We'll be shields standing between your enemies and you."

The heroic simplicity of the offer deeply moved the woman it was intended for. The children seemed unaware of the magnificence of their gesture—they were merely acting out of instinctive devotion.

Not wanting to expose these poor children to danger, Mrs. Hibbett was about to decline, when Sefra went on, "Your little girl will be bored without playmates… We'll play with her… Plus which, seeing you with companions always around you, maybe Slane's accomplices will abandon whatever it is they're planning that we don't know."

She sounded so candid, so honest, that Mrs. Hibbett was moved to say—without realizing she was speaking her thoughts aloud—"But if I understand them right, these children are offering me their lives!"

"Oh, it isn't much," replied the girl, "but it's all we've got."

Certainly Sefra and Stepan—who nodded to show his support—were quite unconscious of the heroism implied by their words. And it occurred to the rich American woman that she could make the fortunes of these poor children. She could guarantee the prosperity of these young people who had put their future at her disposal… as long as she herself eluded the traps they'd warned her of. With the inherent optimism granted by her millions—an optimism that resulted from leveling out her path with hammer-blows of gold—she thought the danger might

38

not be so great. Wealth blindfolds its possessor. A person who can spend money without counting it acquires from the blissful admiration of the needy masses the sense of being some kind of divinity, a sacrosanct creature fate cannot touch.

Placing her delicate hands on the young heads bowed before her, she agreed. "From now on you'll be the companions of my darling little one."

She called, "Lunny!" When the nursemaid appeared immediately, she told her, "I'd reserved the neighboring cabins, to be spared any contact with other passengers. Inform the captain that I'll be occupying them from here on. After that, you can help these young people settle in."

The nursemaid hurried off with an energy that showed she meant to prove her zeal.

Mrs. Hibbett studied her new servants. "We'll have to dress you properly, children. It won't be easy on board. Oh well—we'll manage, and you can begin working."

Then she turned to the toddler, who'd been watching the whole scene with her big innocent eyes. "You see, dear Jane, they'll play with you."

"All the time?" she lisped.

"Yes, all day."

Jane clapped her hands with glee. But suddenly her face darkened. "And at nighttime?" she asked anxiously.

"At night, darling, they'll sleep in the next cabin."

"And if Jane wakes up, they'll play with her?"

Mrs. Hibbett tried to resist the dear tyrant's whim. "Nighttime's not for playing..."

The toddler frowned, trying to make her doll-like face look menacing. "But if Jane wants to play?..."

"Oh, you stubborn little thing, I certainly can't have them sleep in your cabin... Them and you and Lunny—that'd surely be too many."

A mother who reasons with her child is beaten.

"I don't need Lunny," insisted the sweet little blonde child with all the authority she was capable of. "She just needs to dress me in the morning and undress me at night."

"But, listen here..."

"A good little mother tries to please her daughter."

That argument seemed unanswerable. What mother could resist her child in those circumstances? "All right, then, you'll share their cabin."

Jane threw her little arms around her mother's neck and pressed loud fast kisses onto her cheeks, saying in a sweet singsong, "What a good little mother, what a good little mother!"

Her mother forgot how improper the arrangement she'd just agreed to would be considered in the world's eyes.

An hour later, after long blasts from the ship's siren, the ocean liner set off down New York harbor, passing close to the light housed inside Bartholdi's

Statue of Liberty. Neither Stepan nor Sefra witnessed the grand spectacle of the docks of the great city surrounded by the Hudson and East Rivers. Thanks to the diligence of Lunny—who was motivated by Mrs. Hibbett's orders but also perhaps by the pleasing thought that if darling little Jane had new playmates her own job would become a sinecure—Stepan and Sefra, under the nursemaid's eye, tried on clothes she'd gathered from just about everywhere.

When Stepan had been dressed like a cabin boy, and Sefra was proud of how good she looked in a black dress with a wide collar and white cuffs—the whole outfit borrowed from the closet of a young chambermaid on board—when therefore the two children were free to go up on deck with Jane, who was delighted with her new "living toys," the American coast was no more than a grayish line on the horizon.

That evening the customary peace and quiet on board were shaken by an event quite out of the ordinary. Derrick, opening his trunk to get warm clothing needed against the sea fog, was stunned to find that at least half his luggage had disappeared. That made Freda, though she needed nothing, open her own trunk, where she discovered the same thing. No one hates being robbed more than a thief. Even worse was the exasperation of two thieves who'd both been victims of the same robbery. Their cries rang through the ship. The captain, the second in command, ship's officers of all ranks, doctors, pursers, sailors, servants, all threw themselves furiously into an investigation doomed to be fruitless.

"There's been a robbery," they all said, "therefore the missing articles will be found on board."

They couldn't have known that the said articles, having been left behind at the farm outside Oakland, had been consumed in the fire set, at Slane's orders, by the robbery victims themselves. Without that first link in the logical chain, Sherlock Holmes himself, in spite of his astonishing powers of deduction, couldn't have shed light on the mystery.

After forty-eight hours it was discovered that... not the slightest clue had been discovered. Scintillating debates livened up the evenings in the lounges. All the great thieves, past and present, had the honor to be named in interesting extempore argument. Fra Diavolo,[4] Cartouche,[5] Mandrin,[6] the Chevalier du Pou-

---

[4] Fra Diavolo ("Brother Devil") was the nickname of Michele Pozzo, a real-life bandit and guerrilla leader around Naples during the Napoleonic occupation of Italy (1796-1814), famous as the subject of an 1830 opera (and a 1933 silent film post-dating this novel) as well as being the inspiration for Paul Féval's sinister Colonel Bozzo, the leader of the Black Coats.

[5] Nickname of Louis Bourguignon, a highwayman around Paris during the French Regency (1715-23), who allegedly stole from the rich and gave to the poor, and was celebrated in ballads and prints.

[6] Louis Mandrin (1725-55), another French highwayman and smuggler with a Robin Hood reputation that still endures in the Dauphiné and Savoie regions.

lailler,[7] the robbers' bands of the Black Forest, of the Forest of Bondy, of Corsica, of Calabria, paraded by, ending with modern burglars, real or fictional (even Arsène Lupin was mentioned). Naturally those debates didn't lead to the discovery of so much as a pin, but they did at least vastly amuse the only two passengers who knew anything about the mystery: Stepan and Sefra.

But perhaps the children would have been less pleased if they'd been aware of one consequence of the fruitless investigation: Derrick and Freda, convinced they'd been the victims of a "colleague" of disconcerting skill, became suspicious of everyone on board. And as a result, they naturally noticed the children. Their appearance, which would have placed them among the lowest-ranked of the passengers rather than among the aristocratic tourists on the quarterdeck, prompted inquiries by their enemies.

Lunny, happy to talk to "swanky" passengers—since Derrick and Freda were in first-class cabins, the nursemaid had no doubt about their swankiness—Lunny needed little prompting to tell them all about the two "young things" who'd been hired as playmates for Miss Jane at the moment of departure.

That led Derrick, once he and Freda were alone, to murmur the vague threat, "We'll have to see. These urchins who show up suddenly, who get themselves put in charge of minding little Jane and thereby make it harder for us to carry out the boss's orders... Seems suspicious to me."

"Bah! Just a couple of vagabonds who've found a way to travel to Europe for free."

"Maybe so. But what if they stay in Mrs. Hibbett's employ?"

Turning pale, Freda answered in an odd voice, "Then, too bad for them. They'll suffer the same fate as the others."

"That's right."

"Two more or two less, what do we care?"

They stared at each other in anguish. Finally Freda blinked. Tears clouded her bright eyes, and with a shake in her voice she murmured, "*She* was a little thing like that once... Oh, may she never learn whom she has to thank for becoming what she is now."

An infinite sadness seemed to weigh on them both. They stayed there, without moving, without a word, their tense faces the evidence of their devastating inner thoughts.

A few feet away from them, Jane filled the air with cries of delight as she played enthusiastically with her new friends, whom she didn't want to part with even for a moment.

But, when the child paused for breath, Sefra whispered in Stepan's ear so quietly that he barely heard her, "They're watching us, Stepan."

---

[7] The Chevalier du Poulailler ("the Knight of the Henhouse"): Jean Chevalier, another famous Parisian "gentleman" brigand, who was caught and executed in the 1780s.

"They have a right to. They made us welcome in their trunks."

"Involuntarily."

"Sure, but we have no reason to deny them the pleasure of watching us."

"I'm scared of them."

"Me too. But I think the danger won't come till we're in Europe, when we've met up with Lloyd Hibbett. So we can relax till then."

At that moment Jane threw herself on them. "You've gone to sleep... You've stopped playing!"

And so the game picked up again, even livelier than before.

PART TWO: THE TRANSPACIFIC LINER CYCLOPIC

CHAPTER I
Miss May and Mr. August

All the newspapers had published articles like the one in *The Times*, of which here is a carefully clipped-out extract:

DEFINITIVE VICTORY FOR SUFFRAGETTES

Without a doubt, the rise of the fair sex to all positions heretofore reserved for men is now a fait accompli. Under pressure from public opinion, the universities have opened the doors of their schools of engineering to young ladies, and yesterday the first "engineeress" graduated at the head of her class.

Her name: Miss May. Her age: sixteen. You read that correctly—sixteen years old, while the youngest of her rivals were at least twenty. According to her professors, frail, graceful, pretty Miss May is a mathematical phenomenon.

Nothing could stop her, nothing in her technical studies seemed hard for her. To sum up concisely the judgment of the teaching faculty, we quote here a representative statement by the Regent of Cambridge University: "Looking at Miss May," said that eminent man, "you would think that if mathematics didn't exist, this strange young woman would invent it—naturally, effortlessly, the way a bush grows flowers..."

As we known, the English, though mistakenly reputed to be phlegmatic, are susceptible to enthusiasm. From Lords to Cockneys, Great Britain was excited. Reporters took to the field. In a few hours they'd learned that the heroine of the story lived in London, on Ladbroke Grove Road, at the boarding house of the respectable Miss Tolham. Soon Ladbroke Road, one of the largest thoroughfares in London, was filled with gawkers. But no matter how suffocatingly they crowded around, no one caught sight of so much as Miss May's shadow.

Miss Tolham reported that the young lady, diploma in hand, had suddenly vanished... suddenly, but voluntarily, according to the letter she'd left in her room. And the papers had to settle for publishing that brief message, along with photos of Tolham House, and the dining room, and even the kitchen.

The letter ran as follows:

To Miss Tolham, from her student and dear friend Miss May,

My very dear and respected teacher, I'm infinitely grateful for your goodness. So that you don't take it as a sign of my forgetting what I owe you, I want to tell you why I'm leaving without—for the first time—seeking your wise affectionate advice.

My dear respected teacher, life is mathematical. Every person is an integral... or the differential function of an integral. And just as trigonometric sines and cosines are fated to form angles, so do different obligations fail to run parallel. The consequence is the painful duty to leave one line and follow another.

I'm convinced that those who have paid my expenses up to now, whom I've seen too infrequently, are poor. They paid for my education with their blood, their very existence. I don't want them to suffer any longer on my account. So I'm off to apply what I've learned, to gain a fortune that I'll share with them.

When that man and that woman, those sublimely good people, come to you, show them this letter. They'll see my feelings for them and for you, and my intention to work for the benefit of all.

My fondest thoughts remain with you, my teacher, and I hope your good wishes will follow your devoted young former student,

—May.

The reporters filed long articles of commentary on that letter. They explained to their readers that every year two people had covered the expenses of Miss May's education. Every year those strangers had spent a day with their protégée. But who were they? Where did they come from? Where did they go after those visits? No one could find out. According to the few people who'd seen them, they were a man who looked like a working man in his Sunday best, with a beard and hair of dark brown, a dark complexion as if from exposure to the sun, and a sturdy build suggesting physical strength; and a dark-haired, olive-complexioned woman with large black eyes. That was all. In any case, public curiosity soon found other nourishment.

That great British shipping company, the Blue Star Line, had just launched its giant ocean liner, the *Cyclopic*,[8] with a length of three hundred meters and a beam of thirty-five, driven by engines with a capacity of a hundred thousand horsepower, with room for five thousand passengers and crew, with a swimming pool, a theater, a "children's palace" of attractions for the young, and so on.

That maritime leviathan, that gargantuan luxurious floating city, captured the public attention. Five hundred thousand rubberneckers flocked by rail, automobile, yacht, dirigible, and even airplane to Liverpool, home port of the *Cyclopic*. The cheers greeting its launch rose to the skies. The crowd spoke the ship's name together with that of Mr. August, the young engineer—whom no one had the pleasure of spotting—who, according to scientific journals, had brought about a genuine revolution in the application of machinery. The addition of a simple bent tube to the steamship's boilers had increased the power of its engines by thirty percent, so that now the *Cyclopic*, instead of sailing at the top speed of twenty-five knots predicted by its builders, could achieve thirty-two nautical miles an hour—as fast as an express train.[9]

According to well-informed people, the engineer was on board. He'd given his invention to the Blue Star Line at no charge, in exchange for the company taking care of the patent filings and for guaranteeing the inventor a substantial share of the resulting profits. But August remained invisible. *Punch*, the great English satirical magazine, joked about the gawking crowds in a piece that proved very popular:

Your Cockneys were all in the springtime month of May. They've suddenly moved to the stifling summer month of August—at the risk of upsetting the smooth order of the Gregorian calendar. Luckily the seasons have resisted their influence. We're happy to notify our readers that they will still be able to enjoy the months of June and July.

People always assume that men who tower over them by their learning, their valor, their talents, must also tower over them by their physical height. To no one did it occur that a young man with a rosy face and soft blue eyes and blond hair escaping from under a sailing cap with ear flaps—a man of average height, as slim as a girl, looking quite elegant in yachting clothes of navy blue

---

[8] The name *Cyclopic* is presumably d'Ivoi's ironic reference (as was Souvestre & Allain's *Gigantic* in the last *Fantômas* novel) to the *Titanic*, which sank in 1912, two years before this novel was published.

[9] The speed of a ship is measured using a "log," a rope with a knot in it every fifteen meters. You count the number of knots that pass in half a minute, or thirty seconds. That number corresponds to the number of nautical miles (a nautical mile equals 1852 meters) covered in an hour. [*Note from the Author*]

with gold buttons—was in fact the very person whose name was on everyone's lips.

And yet that gentleman, who looked like a child barely past adolescence, was leaning on the rail of the spar deck smirking down at the gawkers crowding the quays, the jetties, and the breakwaters to see off the *Cyclopic* and wish it a safe voyage. The enormous ocean liner was bound on a journey around the world, on a cruise for millionaire tourists, via the North Atlantic, Gibraltar, the Mediterranean, the Red Sea, the Pacific, and Cape Horn before returning to Liverpool.

A stateroom on deck cost £8000 sterling (two hundred thousand francs) a person; a private cabin, £4000; a shared cabin, £3000 a berth. It was said the ship, valued at the tidy sum of forty-three million pounds, was carrying over a hundred million pounds in cash and bills, and almost that much in jewelry. Those vast sums rang in the ears of the public and produced looks of astonishment and greed, along with a vague hint of haunted unease, while the ship, steered by a port pilot, drew away, followed by a launch, which next to the enormous ocean liner seemed shrunk to the size of an insect.

The *Cyclopic* dwindled to a dot on the sea. Philosophical onlookers observed that distance reduced the great monster built by men to something tiny compared to the vastness of Nature.

Mr. August was still leaning on the rail of the spar deck. A few feet away from him one of the chambermaids assigned to the lady passengers went by. She was a woman of thirty or thirty-five, with unusual looks: she was tall and rangy, and lithe and sinuous in her ship's uniform—a light blue dress and an apron with a bib decorated with lace; a blood-red orchid was tucked into her very black hair, which framed an olive face marked by dark eyes.

The chambermaid's eyes fell on the engineer. She started in surprise; some indecipherable emotion made her tremble all over. She stood there a few seconds, her hands clenched unconsciously. Then she seemed to come to a decision; she moved away without attracting the daydreaming August's attention and disappeared down one of the hatchways leading below decks.

Her descent from level to level—in such haste she was practically falling—brought her to the engine room. There, like the legendary devils of Hell, the stokers labored before the flaming mouths of the boilers. The roar of the fires, the whistling of the air rushing through the vents, the ringing of the heavy iron pokers that stirred the glowing coals on the furnace grates, all rose in a deafening cacophony well worthy of the scene that met the chambermaid's eyes.

But she didn't seem at all struck by the spectacle, nor did she react to the terrible heat that prevailed in the engine room. Her black eyes darted about; she was clearly looking for someone. No one paid her any attention. The chief engineers stood by the boilers, a little concerned about possible damage to the brand-new engines, which for the first time were facing a real-life test.

Without anyone stopping her, the woman approached a sturdy bare-chested stoker in tight canvas trousers who was busy stirring the fire assigned to his team. "Derrick," she said.

The deafening noise in the engine room drowned out her voice, and he didn't hear her. She had to shout to get his attention. "Derrick!"

He turned with a sudden gesture of suspicion, as if he feared being surprised by some enemy. But his face—black with coal, and tense from inner anguish—relaxed at the sight of his visitor. Still, he sounded surprised. "Freda?... What do you want? Have you forgotten we're supposed to be strangers till... then?"

She interrupted him. "I've forgotten nothing... But something unexpected has happened, and I'm frightened."

How had Tom Slane's accomplices, last seen crossing the Atlantic as first-class passengers, been reduced to menial workers aboard the great ocean liner *Cyclopic*? Their transformation resulted entirely from Stepan and Sefra having gone to work for Mrs. Hibbett. When the *Tottenham* reached Liverpool, a few days before the launch of the *Cyclopic*, Slane's people had realized those "damned kids" were watching them. If either Derrick or Freda appeared, the children quickly arranged to get between them and the child. It became clear that if they were known to be aboard the great ocean liner *Cyclopic*, bound on a sensational pleasure cruise around the world, their presence would surely arouse the children's suspicion, and perhaps by extension that of Mrs. Hibbett. They sent Slane a telegram, using a prearranged code. Once he was brought up to date, he modified his previous instructions. And Stepan and Sefra rejoiced at being rid of the enemies of the family whose protection they'd undertaken.

For now, the children were focused on loving the spoiled toddler with all their hearts. Never till now having experienced the sweetness of affection, they'd discovered, through knowing the mother and her child, that there exist fortunate beings who have only to be born to be guaranteed the ultimate joy called love.

As a result, their own mutual friendship had grown. It had once seemed merely instinctive; now it became rational. What had been a vague, poorly defined tie had become the relationship of a devoted brother and sister. Delighted with loving each other, delighted at the thought of having left their enemies far behind, they stood together on deck, watching the port, the shipyards, and the docks glide by. Or they pointed out to each other the ship's officers, and famous or wealthy passengers—and especially the blond young man who was still leaning on the rail.

"Mr. August." They spoke the words with unconscious respect. They admired the engineer, whose scientific expertise of course lay far beyond their comprehension. Their tranquil mood would have been shattered if they'd suspected that the adversaries they assumed were far away were in fact at that very moment in conversation in the engine room.

And yet at that same moment Derrick and Freda were thinking neither about the children nor about Mrs. Hibbett.

"Something unexpected has happened that's frightening me," the supposed chambermaid had just declared. Her features betrayed confusion and terror.

"What?" said Derrick, eyeing her with concern.

Freda took a deep breath, as if her lungs were starved for air, then went on in a low voice, "*She*'s on board!"

He growled and dropped the poker he was holding, so that it rolled across the tiled floor with a sinister ring. "*Her*? You're mad!"

"No, Derrick. I saw her as clearly as I see you."

"Are you sure?"

"Could we mistake someone else for *her*?" Her voice trembled with some inexpressible despairing tenderness.

Derrick seemed to have no reply to her emotion. Forcing himself to stay calm, he said, "Well... what protects us will protect her too. Find out where her cabin is, and..."

"But if she ever suspects!..."

They both bowed their heads, as if overcome by the idea.

"She'd be horrified by us," went on Freda, her voice shaking.

Derrick clenched his fists and said vehemently, "We don't matter. Let's save her, and then... then... My poor Freda... We have to accept things as they are... It was always going to end badly for us, wasn't it?"

The two of them, standing in the red glow of the furnaces, speaking of things that seemed tragic, were the very picture of despair.

Finally the stoker went on, "We'll think about ourselves later. For now, we have to save her. And if we're going to succeed we have to make sure she doesn't recognize us."

"Once I know where her cabin is, I swear I'll never cross her path."

"As for me, I'm well hidden down here. It'll all work out. Come on, Freda, run along, and buck up."

Slane's accomplices shook hands. Then, without a word, the chambermaid left the stoker. Moving fast—but as cautiously as an Indian on the warpath—Freda climbed the ladders and went along the passageways past the cabins, till she reached the purser's office. With the pretext of learning the names of the passengers in the cabins assigned to her, she leafed through the ship's manifest.

"Good," she said to herself after a few moments. "The Blue Star Line has managed things well. Mr. August has been given cabin number 2, on the quarterdeck. I'm assigned to regular first class. It'll be easy to avoid him..."

But then she broke off with a muffled exclamation. "Well, well, well!" She chuckled as she went on, "Number 4 is occupied by James Lipson... So they're neighbors—one of whom is doomed while the other must be saved! How very odd!"

That was all. Freda shrugged, and left the office. Why did she go back on deck? The peculiar woman couldn't have said. She was obeying some presumably unconscious inner impulse. Hiding behind a corner of the lounge, she looked eagerly at the place where earlier she'd spotted the man, the sight of whom had agitated her so much.

August, the blond young engineer, was still there. But he was no longer alone. Now a tall young man—presumably a passenger—looking sturdy and distinguished in a dark brown travel suit, was deep in animated conversation with him. Their gestures and their expressions indicated their mutual engagement in the discussion.

"Lipson!" stammered the chambermaid, turning pale. "Lipson!"

But her distress lasted only a moment. Once again she shrugged her shoulders, in a characteristic gesture that suggested a change in her thoughts. "Cabins 2 and 4," she said to herself. "I should've expected that. Bah! It doesn't change anything. But I'll have to be on my guard. The child shouldn't get too close to this Lipson. That would only mean suffering later, and I don't want her to suffer."

It would be impossible to express the savage intensity contained in those words. Freda was frowning. Her features—oddly beautiful in repose—were rigid with anger mingled with tenderness. A wild animal might look at her young with that expression, in which menace and affection were mixed. But then the peculiar woman's face relaxed. "What's written is written," she muttered. "The time for action is still far away. Let's let things take their course. For now we just have to keep her from knowing we're on board."

A few minutes later she'd vanished below decks on the enormous ocean liner—just when the harbor pilot, having steered the *Cyclopic* out to the open ocean, rejoined his launch to return to port.

"I beg your pardon, sir. It'll be a long cruise for us, since both you as engineer and I as a passenger are bound for San Francisco. People our age are scarce on board. You're traveling alone, I believe, as am I. So I think introducing ourselves will help us both stave off the monotony of the crossing."

That was how Lipson had approached August, who was still leaning on the rail, watching the land vanish over the horizon. The engineer had sized up the newcomer with one sharp glance. The verdict must have been favorable, because he replied, "The thought is as clear as an axiom: one and one make two."

"Thanks for the equation, which is encouraging if somewhat mathematical. Since you permit me, sir, I'll therefore introduce myself." Pointing to himself, he went on, "I'm James Lipson, graduate of Cambridge. But I must warn you that my name—though it's the only one I know of for myself—is probably not the one I'm entitled to. I've deduced that from a few things my solicitor let slip when he was serving as my man of business and providing for my upkeep while I was studying in England. Plus which, the cost of my allowance, of my education, and of my passage on this luxury liner for a cruise reputed to be perfection itself, all lead me to believe I must come from a wealthy family. And finally, the news that once I reach the United States my legal and financial status and so forth will be regularized prompts me to believe that I'm an American citizen. And now you, if I may ask?"

August had smiled as he listened, and now he replied with a warm smile, "I'm Mr. August, an engineer. But I should tell you that my last name is not just probably but quite certainly an assumed name."

"No problem! I'll use it because it suits you."

"No, no," cried the young engineer, "it doesn't suit me at all. But I use it for several reasons, the first of which is that it's the only name I know of for myself."

They both burst out laughing.

"Good!" cried Lipson, "in fact very funny. Each of us presents a self that is unknown to him."

"As you say. But we can still consider the introduction valid."

"Naturally!"

"And I'll prove it by observing that in sailing on the *Cyclopic*, by way of the Mediterranean and the Indian Ocean and the Pacific, you've chosen the longest possible way back to America."

"Sir, I pointed that out to my man of business."

"Ah?... And what did he say?—if it's not indiscreet of me to ask."

"Oh, not at all. We're going to spend many long days together on this ship, so the way I see it, we'll have to confide in each other. As for my man of business, he didn't object at all to the fact that a transatlantic ocean liner would get me to New York in six days, and in six more the transcontinental train would get me to the San Francisco rail terminus—my official destination."

"Whereas on the *Cyclopic*, counting ocean crossings and stops in port, it'll take several months..."

"It seems my unknown family wants it that way. Till now I've acquired only book learning, and the steamship journey will allow me to form a general impression of the globe and its inhabitants. In short, pleased at being free and curious about the voyage, I didn't object. I submitted to the wishes of my family, which could've been a great deal more unpleasant."

That conversation was the start of a true friendship between the two young men. From that moment, in fact, they were hardly ever apart. The proximity of their cabins, as well as certain tastes they shared, helped bring them closer. Together they visited the cities the ship stopped at along the way—Port Said, Aden, Bombay, Colombo, Singapore, Batavia[10]—talking, debating, sharing their

---

[10] The Dutch colonial name for modern-day Jakarta.

observations. In the evenings, rather than linger in the lounge, where an expert orchestra gave much-applauded concerts, the two met in either cabin 2 or cabin 4, where, while sipping flavored tea, they compiled the diary of their tourist impressions. That literary collaboration sealed the connection between them. They were no longer apart, except late at night, to go to sleep, and again for a few minutes in the morning.

Every day at that time, August the engineer went down to the engine room to calculate the distance traveled by the *Cyclopic* versus the amount of fuel used, and each day he returned delighted. His engine was performing even better than he'd expected. The ship's engineers, along with the captain, said so to anyone who'd listen—to the point that, if he'd wanted to, the young inventor could have let himself become an idol admired by all the passengers. But whether out of pride, or modesty, or disdain for worldly success, August had evaded all applause and discouraged all overtures.

Only three people, besides Lipson, had managed to get close to him. One was a little girl named Jane, a sweet blonde child of about three, whose ailing mother hardly ever left her cabin; the job of supervising the child had fallen to a nursemaid, Lunny, and to two devoted teenagers, Stepan and Sefra.

Neither August nor Lipson suspected that their acquaintance with the three children had been entirely Sefra's work. Here was how it happened:

Mrs. Hibbett rarely left her cabin, which soon prompted Sefra to say in surprise, "Hey, Stepan!"

"What do you want?"

"Information. When we were listening to the wicked Slane, at that farm outside Oakland, didn't we hear him say the villains planned to substitute Slane's son William for Mrs. Hibbett's son?"

"Yes, exactly. And that the latter was named Lloyd Hibbett."

"All right. Then that Lloyd Hibbett must be aboard the *Cyclopic*."

"So it would seem..."

"Sure—but he's not on the passenger manifest."

"Then he must not be aboard."

"I'm not so sure. He might be here under another name."

"Why another name?"

She laughed. "Well, um, to disguise himself."

Stepan scratched the tip of his nose with a puzzled look.

Sefra went on, "Come on—it's possible. I'd even say it's definite, because I've noticed Mrs. Hibbett is pretending to be ill..."

"Oh!"

"She's a little sick, but not as badly as she pretends, not to the point of having to stay shut up in her cabin."

Confused, Stepan raised his arms high. "What are you trying to prove with all this? I don't get it."

"This: thanks to us, Mrs. Hibbett has been forewarned of the criminals' plans."

"Fine. Then?"

"She's an educated woman, who knows a lot of things we can't even imagine."

"Fine again. Keep going."

"Her son, Lloyd Hibbett, grew up in England without knowing his true origins."

"That's what Slane said."

Sefra cut him off with a curt gesture. "Well, maybe he still doesn't know, and he's on board the *Cyclopic* under another name."

With genuine admiration Stepan murmured, "You're so clever! How'd you think of that?"

"It was the way Mrs. Hibbett stayed in her cabin..."

"That gave you the idea?"

"Of course. Her enemies know her well. So if they're lying in wait for her, she's no safer in her cabin than outside."

"True!"

"Ah, you're getting it. Now let's assume Lloyd Hibbett is a passenger, going by Peter or Jack or some other name."

"I'm assuming it."

"When she saw him—she who is his mother, separated from him for so long—wouldn't she give herself away? Wouldn't she betray him to the criminals by a gesture, an action, a word? To avoid that, she stays in her cabin." Sefra leaned over to whisper in Stepan's ear, "Luckily for us, she doesn't always stay there."

"Now what are you saying?"

"This: she sometimes walks on deck."

"And?"

"And I've noticed that, if she thinks no one's looking, she obsessively watches Mr. August the engineer and his friend James Lipson."

"So one of those two is her son?"

Sefra burst out laughing. "Her son would be Mr. Lipson, since Mr. August is an engineer with the Blue Star Line, and is known to the company, and is here under his own name."

Stepan's mouth hung open. Her deductions floored him. But his surprise grew to astonishment when she went on, "If I'm not mistaken, we have to look out for him, the way we do for little Jane."

"Yes, but how?"

"By befriending him and being around him as much as possible."

He gave a grimace of worry. "It won't be easy."

"Sure it will. Very easy, in fact."

"Easy?"

"By persuading little Jane that she likes those gentlemen a lot."

"Jane! You want to trust that kid?"

This time Sefra laughed so hard she allowed herself to slap Stepan's shoulder. "Not trust her, guide her. Poor Stepan! It's so true, what they say: boys are a lot more naive than girls."

With that piece of wisdom handed down through the ages, she let her friend recover his good humor while she went off to be with Jane, who'd been driving her nursemaid Lunny crazy.

It was after that conversation that Jane was "steered" toward August and Lipson by her playmate Sefra. That clever vagabond girl had no trouble persuading the child that those young men would tell her wonderful stories and play with her. Since the two friends, feeling a little isolated on board, had been entertained by the little darling's advances, and by her whimsical bodyguards, Stepan and Sefra, they'd made the trio welcome. And, with the typical tyranny of small children, Jane now wanted nothing but to be with them.

Lunny, the nursemaid, had protested at first, but she'd quickly realized that the company of those two grown men, on top of that of Stepan and Sefra, would make her own presence redundant. The prospect of freedom beckoned to her, and Lunny was soon as eager as Jane for the child to be with the young men. As can be imagined, as soon as Jane had gone to her new friends, Lunny gave Stepan and Sefra a few instructions and then melted away, to enjoy the pleasures of endless chatter with the ship's staff, the other passengers' servants, the crew, and in short anyone able to stand her continual prattle.

She even came gradually to think of the young men, along with the teenagers, as "adjunct nursemaids," and to rely entirely on them. Eventually she began to forget to go fetch Jane from August or Lipson's cabin, where the child had spent the whole evening; and more than once the little darling slept there overnight under the care of those strangers—one of whom, as Sefra had deduced, was the child's unwitting brother. At first Lunny had apologized for forgetting, but soon she saw no reason to: after all, she was making the gentlemen very happy by confiding to their care such a sweet companion as Miss Jane. They owed her their thanks, and would no doubt have been surprised if she'd apologized. So now she limited herself to collecting the little darling in the morning. She took her back to Mrs. Hibbett's cabin to be washed and dressed, after which she faithfully restored her to her "supplementary nursemaids."

For the first two months of the cruise, broken by long stops in port, August never crossed paths with the couple who'd been so interested in him: Freda the chambermaid and Derrick the stoker. Clearly those two had taken precautions.

But a single drop of water overflows the glass, a single word unleashes a great war, and a single smile determines a man's destiny. All their precautions came to naught for one tiny reason: Stepan, goaded by Sefra's triumph in figuring out Lipson's possible parentage, was looking for his own chance to shine. Not finding an opportunity right nearby on deck, he sought it elsewhere in the ship. And that was why, on the morning of the sixty-first day of the voyage—the *Cyclopic* having sailed from the port of Batavia in the middle of the night and now coasting along that enchanting island named Java—Stepan surreptitiously followed August on his way down to the engine room, as was his daily habit.

The stop in Batavia had been stretched to six days at the request of wealthy passengers who wanted to take excursions in Java—a land that has rightly been called "nature's pearl." The engine fires had been put out, to be relit only a few hours before sailing. August wanted to check that the interruption hadn't reduced the performance of his invention.

He was engaged in a technical discussion with the chief engineers when he was interrupted by a strangled cry from Stepan, who'd followed him. The boy was pale, and his eyes popped in a wild stare aimed at the open bay of one of the boiler chambers. A figure the boy knew too well had just appeared there, leaving him dumbfounded.

The electric lights were aimed at the engines, not at the passageways between them. And yet August, following the direction of Stepan's eyes, in turn gave a strangled cry. There could be no doubt: he too recognized that figure—as one of the two people who'd cared for him in childhood. How could Mama Freda, as he called her, be here? How, and why? August didn't ask. Impulsively he ran to the woman he'd spotted so unexpectedly.

She made as if to flee; but, no doubt realizing she didn't have time, she changed her mind and turned to face him. "Well, yes, it's me! You've got to make a living somehow, don't you?" Pointing behind her to a stoker hunched over the furnace he tended, she added, "Derrick!"

August had seized her hands. With great feeling he said, "Mother!"

She pushed him away almost roughly. "Don't call me that. A chambermaid shouldn't be the mother of an engineer."

"But you are—because of the care with which you raised me. You're the mother of a foundling who owes you everything: his life, his education, even the position he's going to reach in life."

"All right. It was our pleasure to devote ourselves to you. Isn't that so, Derrick?"

The stoker had straightened up and was trembling as he listened. He answered his wife with a nod.

"Anyway," Freda went on, "you don't understand. We were drifters. We lived by night. One evening we found you by the road, crying with hunger. Where did you come from? Who were you? You didn't know. We gave you food. Watching you eat eagerly, we loved you..."

"Deeply," agreed August with affection. "The work I find you doing now proves how much it cost you to educate me. Whether you like it or not, in my heart I'll always call you Mom and Dad."

"You can't. It would cause you difficulties in the world."

"I'd be despicable if I thought about it that way."

55

"No—you have to do it, for us."

"For you?"

"It would be too cruel if, out of misguided affection, you made all our work pointless. We wanted you to have dignity, honor, high rank... Your success is our reward..."

August bowed his head. His rational mind was persuaded by Freda's argument. He knew the peculiar woman was right. The Blue Star Line would obviously not have welcomed him if he'd introduced himself as the son of a stoker and a chambermaid.

"All right," he said finally. "I'll say nothing during the cruise. But when it's over you'll quit your jobs, and it'll be my turn to support you and ensure your happiness."

Freda seemed to stagger, but then she straightened up and managed to murmur brokenly, "Oh, you dear beloved darling!"

Without knowing its cause, August had noticed her distress. He embraced her. "I understand everything—your silence, your mysterious behavior. But now that I've found you, I can't agree to pretend you're not on board."

She tried to speak, but he put his fingers gently on her lips. "Be quiet and listen. By day I won't see you. Notice that I'm doing what you want. But in the evening, when your shift is over, when my father Derrick has been relieved by the night crew, you'll come to my cabin so I can hug you and we can plan our future life."

Freda still stubbornly shook her head. August went on more insistently, "Yes, that's how it'll be. That's what I want, and I won't allow it to be otherwise. Think: I'd be a coward, unworthy of your love, if I gave way... So it's settled. To start with, this very evening I'm inviting you to come have tea."

"This evening?" Derrick and Freda both repeated the words, like some dismal echo.

"Of course, this evening. But what's wrong, Mother?"

A look of inexpressible distress had passed across Freda's face, as quick as thought. In a voice ringing with infinite despair she said, "That's what you want?"

"Yes, Mother, that's what I want."

"Then it's agreed. Now go away. The engineers are watching us. They're surprised at how long we've been talking. Go away, and think about how, for us, the greatest misfortune would be if, having worked to clear all obstacles from your path, we ourselves became obstacles."

Her voice was so urgent that August didn't try to object. "I'll obey, Mother, I'll obey. This evening I'll see you both—I have your promise."

And he went back to the engines.

Stepan—stunned, astonished—had witnessed the whole scene from a distance. The fragments he whispered to himself expressed his dismay. "So! The engineer knows the criminals! He's their friend! Look at him shaking the villains by the hand! Is he part of the gang too?" But then he shook his head firmly. "No, that can't be. Mr. August is good, and honorable... But then he must not know what they are. Yes, that's it, he doesn't know. He thinks they're trustworthy working people." A thoughtful look crossed his face. "The criminals might be planning to dispose of Mr. August too... And besides, this doesn't make our guard work any harder." He laughed. "Where there's enough guarding for two, there's enough for three."

Stepan had unconsciously drawn closer to the group he was focused on. Suddenly he stopped still, as if his feet were welded to the floor. He'd just heard the engineer say, "So it's settled, tonight I'll offer you tea in my cabin."

But the boy soon recovered. "Tea!... Well, Sefra and I will be there too! I've got to go tell her the whole story!... Ha, ha! I think I've got news of some importance!"

No one was paying him any attention. He was able to slip away from the engine room without anyone noticing.

Meanwhile Freda remained with Derrick. They eyed each other in confusion, drops of sweat beading their brows.

Finally he grumbled, "Tonight... tonight, just when *that man* is to meet us."

She sighed sadly. "Yes." Then, her breast heaving with a sob, she added, "We'll save our child. Let all the others die on this accursed ship, so long as *she* lives."

"By God, I agree!" he replied. "But I believe we're approaching the moment we've always feared."

"I think so too, my poor Derrick."

"We can't save her without telling her..."

"No, we can't."

He clenched his fists. Fat tears rolled down his cheeks. "And our child will despise us!"

"Damn it! She's respectable!"

There was a silence. Then in an anguished whisper Derrick spoke again. "Yes, it's true: retribution always comes."

"Always."

"You love a little creature, you wish for her to grow up happy, decent, honorable... in short, everything we aren't! But the thing is, that takes money. And then you wind up in the clutches of *that man*. And you have to obey him, since that's the only way to get the money you need. And when the child is small, you think she'll never grow up, she'll never demand an explanation."

"That's exactly what you think!" moaned Freda.

"And then the time comes. The education you've given her, the intelligence you've nurtured so proudly, leads her straight onto the *Cyclopic*, this enormous, idiotic, doomed ship."

"Alas!"

"We got ourselves hired on, following the boss's orders. But we were going to save our dear child as well. For two months we managed to avoid her."

"Another twenty-four hours and she'd never have suspected anything."

"As you say… But now the whole plan is in ruins."

"She'll know."

"She'll despise us."

"She'll never want to see us again."

They clasped each other's hands and stood there for a moment, breathless, trembling from some internal turmoil.

Then Derrick muttered, "Too bad! First we'll save her. After that, we'll see."

Freda shrugged. "Oh, after that, it all follows, my poor Derrick. We gave that sweet beloved creature our whole hearts. Afterwards we'll have lost a child—and we'll have lost our hearts."

"And then?"

"And then, all we'll have left to give her is our lives."

"What are you trying to say, Freda?"

She smiled sadly. "You don't understand. You must be slow."

"Could be."

"Come on—could you live without her love?"

He gave a roar. "No, of course not!"

"Me neither. So then…"

"You're right. We'll slip away into death. That's easier than suffering for years… In fact, that's the only solution."

A voice rang out. "You're letting the fire die!"

Derrick jumped at that warning from the foreman, and hurried to shovel coal into the furnace he was responsible for.

CHAPTER II
A Tragic Tea

"Yes, James, I'm sure you're a kind-hearted man, and I believe you're a friend."

"You can be just as sure of that."

"That's what I meant to say! And my confiding in you is proof of my esteem. When I told you about the humble people who raised me, I shared a secret with you that no one else knows."

"I'm all the more obliged to you."

"I expect them at any moment. It might displease you to meet them. I won't be offended if you feel you prefer to leave."

Lipson and August were speaking in the latter's suite. The young engineer had thought it was his duty to warn his friend—which is what he now considered Lipson—of the low rank of the guests he'd invited for tea. Lipson had responded to that sign of his confidence in the most cordial way.

But he was barely finished when they heard the delightful babbling of a child. "How about me?" said a gentle voice. "Am I allowed to stay too?"

It was little Jane, settled as usual in her grown-up friend's cabin, and covering sheets of paper with shapeless drawings with the help of Stefan and Sefra. Lunny, the nursemaid, was now completely used to this routine. At the beginning she'd sometimes come to fetch the child around ten, scolding loudly about

59

the unhealthiness of staying up late. Now she regularly forgot, and the little girl—over whom the teenagers had no authority—often slept all night on a fold-out couch that was part of the furniture in both Lipson's and August's cabins. In that case the inseparable Sefra and Stepan stretched out on the carpet next to the child's bed.

August replied without hesitation, "Your good reputation, little darling, is not at risk!"

That made Jane laugh, and they all shared in the hilarity.

A steward brought in tea, cookies, and liqueurs. A moment after he left there was a quiet knock at the cabin door.

"Come in!"

The words were still ringing in the air when the door opened slowly, and Derrick and Freda appeared—red-faced, awkward, emotional. Seeing Lipson, Jane, and the two teenagers, they made as if to retreat; but August ran to them and drew them into the cabin, saying, "James, here are the kind, affectionate people I was just telling you about."

Lipson graciously extended his hands to the newcomers. "I'm honored— yes, absolutely, honored is the right word—to meet you."

His words and his tone of voice ought to have dissipated the visitors' embarrassment. On the contrary: they seemed more self-conscious than ever. Perhaps they were feeling what Stepan had thought earlier—that they were criminals. They stammered unintelligible words, leaving August surprised at their unaccustomed shyness.

Derrick pointed out Lipson, Jane, and the teenagers. "Will they be having tea with us?"

"Of course."

"Is that appropriate for them?"

It was Lipson who replied emphatically, "I find it perfectly appropriate for passengers like us have tea with honest, devoted people like you."

A fleeting look of joy crossed the faces of the stoker and the chambermaid, but their expressions soon darkened again. They exchanged a meaningful glance. Finally, with a shrug, Derrick sat on a couch. "Well, after all, if someone extends you an honor, you can't exactly refuse it. Still, I'll say many thanks."

Turning to Freda, who stood immobile by the table that held the teapot, the hot water, and the cookies, he said, "Take care of serving, Freda. These gentlemen will surely allow you to do that job. It's not work tonight, it's pleasure."

Without waiting for their assent, she began to make the tea—that fragrant beverage whose preparation has such importance in the eyes of the English.

Stepan and Sefra had gone back to playing with little Jane; but anyone observing them would have noticed that out of the corner of their sharp eyes they were watching Derrick and Freda. Without any thought for their own danger, the teenagers were keeping up their self-assigned task as bodyguards.

As for August, he considered his adoptive parents with anxious surprise. They seemed to be not themselves right now. What could have changed them like this? Lipson's welcome had been such as to leave no room for misinterpretation. So what was it? Could it be the presence of the children that was displeasing to them? Unconsciously, August's reflections led him to fix his keen, insightful attention on Freda. His whole being—driven by his wish to understand the unhappiness he sensed in these two people he loved so much—gained unaccustomed powers of observation. That led him to notice the chambermaid making some odd gestures. What was she doing? Why was her hand moving that way over the steaming teapot? Why was she furtively raising it to her mouth?

Here was an odd coincidence: at that very moment, the stoker gestured in a way that drew August's attention. Derrick too had raised his hand to his lips—exactly like someone eating a candy, a sugared almond, or a piece of chocolate. Both of them, at the same time, seemed to be concealing gluttonous behavior.

Perhaps in another context those details wouldn't have struck the young engineer as significant. But at this moment some vague instinct asserted itself deep within him. And that instinct led him to intuit that something abnormal was going on, something he had to understand, expose, and fight! But once again, what exactly was there to fight? Here his rational thinking ran aground. He could pin down nothing definite. He had no clear idea—not so much as the embryo of an idea.

Meanwhile Freda went on with her voluntary work. She held out the sugar bowl to Lipson, to August, to Derrick, to the teenagers, and to little Jane, for whom she'd made a cup of weaker tea with extra milk. Finally she served herself. Suddenly she began to talk, quickly and volubly—as if to keep her listeners from interrupting her. She spoke of her maternal love for August, of the happiness and pride she felt in his being willing to acknowledge such humble adoptive parents, and in the fact that his friend Mr. Lipson—won over by August's praise, no doubt exaggerated by his affection—was willing to do them the honor of sitting with them at the same table. Smiling, assiduous, she urged the young people to drink up their steaming tea: tea was worthless once it got cold, right?

Lipson had drunk two cups. Little Jane, following her grown-up friend's example, had drunk the same amount of tea with milk. And then suddenly the child fell gently backward in her seat and closed her eyes. She was asleep. Stepan too was losing consciousness. Lipson was staring absently at the ceiling.

August was astonished at this sudden onset of sleep. He was about to drink. He set his cup back on its saucer and turned to Lipson to express his surprise—only to be astonished once again: Lipson looked benumbed. His eyelids fluttered, suggesting how hard the young man was fighting to stay awake. Well! What could be the meaning of this soporific epidemic?

Derrick and Freda weren't asleep. But it seemed to August that his adoptive father was casting a sarcastic eye on Lipson, on Jane, and on the teenagers.

The stoker and the chambermaid had drunk their tea, but it hadn't made them sleepy.

Then August vividly recalled the gestures he'd noticed earlier: a hand passing over the teapot, hands putting something surreptitiously into their mouths. An explanation occurred to him: did the first gesture mean a sedative had been added to the tea? And did the later gestures mean the two had given themselves an antidote? What a mad hypothesis! What reason would Derrick and Freda have for putting their companions to sleep? And yet August couldn't shake off the idea. So, taking advantage of a moment when his adoptive parents were both checking their watches—with a degree of attention that suggested how important the time was to them—he emptied the contents of his teacup onto the thick carpet covering the cabin floor, then set his cup down on its saucer.

At the gentle sound of porcelain, Freda turned, and saw that his cup was empty. August would have sworn she looked delighted. So—she must want him to fall asleep, just like the others! Oh, he had to find out the reason behind these incomprehensible events. He pretended to close his eyes, so as to make them think he too had succumbed to the sleep that had already overpowered the others. And now he witnessed inexplicable actions, and overheard conversation he couldn't fathom.

Neither Derrick nor Freda moved for several minutes. They looked from one sleeper to the next, with a mix of sarcasm, concern, and satisfaction in their eyes. Then the chambermaid got slowly to her feet. Her peculiar face, with its big black eyes, shone more than usual. Her nostrils quivered. She looked once again like some gypsy fortune teller, a caster of lots, the eternal drifter of humanity.

With steps so quiet that August couldn't hear them, she went to little Jane, shook her, took her into her arms, and set her down on the couch. Then she shook Sefra and Stepan the same way. She smiled broadly, revealing small sharp white teeth. She looked pleased that sleep had made the three children unconscious. Then she approached Lipson and shook him roughly. The young man moaned indistinctly—just an automatic protest arising from the depths of his sedation.

Derrick and Freda exchanged a look of triumph. Then he pointed at August. She nodded, approached the young engineer, put her hand on his shoulder, and gave him another rough shake. Of course the pretend sleeper was careful not to move. Freda turned to Derrick, who'd stayed where he was. Unconsciously she lowered her voice to murmur, "They're asleep! The opium has done its job!"

Derrick nodded his agreement and muttered, "They don't know the antidote, like we do. Slane's sugared almonds are the best!"

"Shush! Don't speak the boss's name!" she interrupted with obvious fear.

"All right, all right! We won't say it. But we'll have to talk about him, if we're going to tear our darling from his clutches—our girl who was unlucky enough to be aboard this damned ship."

"We'll save her."

"Fine! But the others—James Lipson, little Jane, these kids who work for Mrs. Hibbett—what about them?"

"We'll worry about that later. For now, don't you feel how cold it's getting?"

Cold! What could Freda be talking about? Cold... fifty or sixty miles off the north coast of Java, practically on the equator, in one of the hottest regions of the globe?

August almost forgot his pretense of sleeping to question them about it, but he caught himself. Still, those surprising words had given him the irresistible wish to unravel the mystery behind his adoptive parents' inexplicable actions.

"Quick, get the electric heater! Otherwise we'll turn into blocks of ice within the hour!"

Derrick didn't act the least surprised at those strange words. And—incredibly—the temperature did indeed seem to be dropping.

The stoker hurried outside and was gone for a few minutes, then returned carrying a copper device that August—peeping through his lowered eyelashes—had no trouble recognizing as an electric radiator of a particular kind: electromagnets and a small box shaped like a battery pack led the young engineer to conclude that the device itself produced the heat it then radiated. In short, it was a self-contained radiator.

"Turn on the machine!" ordered Freda.

Derrick must have obeyed, because there was a slight click. Almost immediately a barely audible hum filled the room. The radiator's copper filaments reddened, and a gentle warmth spread through the cabin.

"Damn!" said the stoker. "A little heat sure feels good. Outside it's as frigid as Siberia."

"It'll be worse later. Gosh—along with those black rays, the boss's artificial clouds help produce the temperature of deep space, which is to say more than two hundred degrees below zero Centigrade."

Derrick sat close to the radiator, muttering, "Say, Freda, do you even understand what you're talking about?"

She shrugged. "I sort of understand. Anyway, one thing's clear: those damned clouds make it freeze, and the devil of winter himself can't match that."

"Oh, sure, no doubt about that."

"Well, that's all we need to know. The rest of it doesn't matter to us." She broke off. "The cold's coming in through the keyhole—I'll put the key back in the lock."

Oddly, to do that, she held the key with her apron, as if she were afraid to let her skin come in contact with the metal. Then she sat down by Derrick.

"Will it be much longer?" he murmured.

She replied in a low voice, "A half hour, the boss said."

"And it'll all be over?"

"Everything!"

"The passengers, the crew?..."

"The *Cyclopic* will be like the ghost ship of legend, you know: there'll be nothing but corpses aboard."

Suddenly she stopped speaking, and gave a hoarse cry, while on her face was a look of some indecipherable horror. Two trembling hands had been set on her shoulders. She turned. Leaning over her, his face tense and dead white, she saw August—awake and shaking with superhuman fear.

The young engineer said, "What are you talking about? Mortal danger threatens everyone on this ship?! I have to get out, I have to warn them..."

Derrick leapt up and put his back against the cabin door, barring the way. "Don't plan on getting out now."

"So you're accomplices in this incredible crime?—one my rational mind still can't credit!"

The heavy silence that followed those words seemed to hang dolefully in the room. Derrick had lowered his head. But then he straightened it, and with wild resolve on his face he cried out hoarsely, "You'll hate us, you'll despise us—so be it! But at least you'll be saved. We sacrificed our lives to build yours. We knew very well this present moment would come; we went on even so. Too bad for us!"

And in a harrowing voice Freda echoed his words: "Too bad for us!"

CHAPTER III
Polar Cold at the Equator

"Dick?"

"Mr. Locke?"

"You hear that?"

"I sure do!"

"And what do you think?"

"That if it wasn't nuts out in the middle of the ocean, I'd say it sounds like the engine of an airplane."

"Exactly! In fact, that very same thought came to me."

Up in the maintop sat two sailors responsible for the wireless service that had been installed on the *Cyclopic*, as on all transoceanic steamships. With their noses in the air they were scrutinizing the cloudless celestial vault whose indigo was punctuated by twinkling stars.

"A real airplane," went on Locke with all the authority of a sailor wearing the wool braid of rank.

"You can say that again," Dick agreed courteously.

"But an airplane doesn't go wandering around all by itself this far from land."

"That's what I keep saying, Mr. Locke."

"So then?..."

"That's what I'm asking you."

There was another silence.

Then suddenly Dick pointed to the sky. "Mr. Locke, look over there, to port!"

"A rock?"

"No, no, it's not on the surface of the sea—it's above, in the sky!"

"What do you mean, in the sky?"

"A plane heading straight toward us!"

"My word! By the devil's forked tail—it's true!"

Indeed, its black shape standing out against the deep blue of the sky, something was moving at high speed. Nothing about it resembled the traditional form of an airplane, and yet it was obviously a flying machine. Where did it come from? Where was it going? The two sailors were in no position to settle those points. But with lively curiosity they followed the course of "the object in question," as they referred to it—having no other name to give it.

Dick was right: the "object" was headed straight for the giant ocean liner. "They might be planning to land on deck," he suggested to his superior.

"It wouldn't surprise me," agreed Locke. "They'd have no trouble—the *Cyclopic* is big enough to handle the extra weight!"

"Without any inconvenience, Mr. Locke!"

They both burst out laughing, finding their observation remarkably witty. But they soon had to admit they were wrong in their conjectures. When the "object" reached the *Cyclopic* it was still three hundred meters overhead and gave no sign of any intention to descend.

"Ten thousand devils!" muttered Locke. "What kind of acrobatics are they up to up there?"

Dick shook his head. "All those aviators have to be at least partly crazy in the head, right? Otherwise, instead of climbing aboard a kite, they'd choose to have the solid deck of a good sound ship like this one under their feet."

"That's right, Dick, my boy."

"Look—they've stopped right above us."

"They're matching their speed to ours."

"It's like they're escorting us."

With his fist, Locke gave his own skull a blow that would have knocked out an ordinary man. "Dick! We can find out who the aviators are!"

"All right. So you say, and I believe you. But I sure don't see how."

"By broadcasting the question on the wireless!"

Dick roared his agreement. "Perfect! Someone will answer…"

"And we'll know who the jokers are who think they can taunt us incognito!"

Together they climbed into the small shelter that held the wireless transmitter. Dick got straight to work. "Northeast of Java, about a hundred and fifty miles offshore. Unknown aircraft circling above steamship *Cyclopic*. What machine, and what pilot?"

The two wireless operators rubbed their hands. In a few minutes the nearby airport from which the mysterious craft must have taken off would reply with all the information they needed.

Just then the duty officer telephoned them from the bridge, asking the radio operators the very same questions they'd just broadcast into the ether. They told him they were waiting for an answer at any moment. But they didn't get the one they expected.

Suddenly Locke cried out in surprise, "I'll be! The aircraft itself wants to answer—it's coming down!" After a moment's thought he added, "A surprising machine! It's descending perpendicularly! What kind of aircraft is that?"

No doubt they'd soon find out. The plane now floated at the height of the *Cyclopic*'s topmost mast. They could see it clearly: it had the shape of a very elongated fish, the shape commonly seen at one time in "dirigibles." But no means of propulsion was visible: no propeller blades could be seen anywhere on the exterior. And yet the rumbling of the engine proved that some apparatus of that kind must be involved.

"Look, now it's making clouds!"

Dick's remark was prompted by a strange phenomenon: a sharp whistle had pierced the air, like some gas under high pressure escaping from a tank through a narrow opening. And then an opaque milky fog had suddenly enveloped the aircraft, hiding it from view.

"This beats playing shuffleboard!" muttered Locke.

"Or playing cards with a Chinese deck!" agreed Dick.[11]

"The fog seems to be forming up above before dropping toward the surface of the sea."

"Well, it'll reach the sea, Mr. Locke."

"I'm not so sure, Dick."

"Yes, yes! Look. It's dropping, it's dropping."

---

[11] An expression suggesting very great difficulty. Chinese playing cards do in fact exist, but there is no settled value for each card; the values change depending on the players, and vary from one town or village to the next. [*Note from the Author*].

It was true: the mysterious fog, clearly much heavier than air, was now falling around the masts. In a few seconds it had reached the transmitter shelter on the maintop.

"We won't be able to see a thing!" cried Locke. "Light the lantern!"

"Aye, aye, sir."

The fog blanketed the maintop. The wireless operators cried out in pain, "It's cold as hell!" Then they collapsed on the narrow platform, unmoving, as if dead.

Still the fog dropped, blanketing the bridge, the top deck, the promenade deck, its billows curling into the lounges, into the dining room, falling through the hatchways and down the ladders, filling the passageways lined with cabins, and the holds, the kitchens, the engine room.

And everywhere the terrible cloud produced the same effect as an extreme cold snap. Men dropped in place, as if felled by a sudden stroke. Water froze instantly, shattering the vessels of glass or porcelain that held it. The boilers in the engine room went out, and the stokers and machinists and engineers froze hard where they stood.

What horrifying disaster was befalling the *Cyclopic*? What unprecedented cloud was wiping out the crew of this vast floating city—which, based on its size, its tonnage, its power, should by rights have been untouchable by the elements? Instead, in calm weather, in the middle of a peaceful night under a star-studded sky, a fog had arisen, and this leviathan had been transformed into an enormous necropolis.

Not a sound now rose from within the ship. Icicles hung in the corridors, on the varnished cabin doors, on the gilt moldings in the lounges. An intolerable hyperborean cold prevailed on the ship—so recently the fastest vessel afloat—which now, with its fires out, its boilers cold, its engines immobilized, drifted like a buoy at the whim of the waves.

But now the fog was thinning out, growing moment by moment more transparent. Soon it was all gone: the clouds had completely dissipated. The airship could no longer be seen in the sky. And the warm air of an equatorial night gradually drove away the freezing wave that had blanketed the *Cyclopic*. There was a genuine thaw. Icicles melted and ran in rivulets across the decks and the carpets in the passageways. Things returned to normal again... only the people remained inert, overcome.

In August's cabin, Derrick still stood blocking the door with his fists at the ready, as if to repulse a possible attack. "No one leaves here till Freda says so!" he growled roughly.

Facing him, August also had his fists clenched. Frustrated by his powerlessness, he roared, "You despicable people!"

The stoker went pale. "Yes, despicable! You can say that again! But later, when you've calmed down, remember that Freda and I have been despicable for your sake."

"For my sake! I forbid you to say so. I reject any connection…" The young engineer's entire body was stiff with disgust.

Derrick shrugged. "Go ahead and reject us, that's fine with me. Sure, we're scum, I know that. Sure, people can despise us, fair enough. But in the end you alone, August—you alone, Miss May—you shouldn't condemn us without hearing us out."

There was a kind of poignant agony in Derrick's voice. Freda went to him, squeezed his hand, and turned sadly toward the engineer. "Miss May, we're not asking for your forgiveness. Drive us out of your presence, out of your heart: we're prepared for that. But at least don't condemn us out of ignorance."

May—who'd disappeared so suddenly in London and whom no one had suspected in her new persona—gestured vaguely in assent.

Freda went on, "Listen, Miss May. We would never have spoken of all this, if what's happening hadn't happened."

The young woman nodded in agreement. Unwittingly, despite her anger, she had to acknowledge the devotion of those who'd raised her.

"But now," Freda continued, "we really have to talk things over. You know…" She paused, then went on quickly, "You know, Miss May, we found you at low tide, fastened to a small raft the waves had pushed onto the rocks. Why did we untie you? Why did we give you milk from a bottle we were carrying in our caravan? You can never know the answer to that kind of thing, any more than you can explain why, watching you drink, we admired you as if we'd never seen someone drink before."

She paused, her breath laboring.

Derrick took advantage of the pause to murmur, "The fact is, it's a funny thing to be grateful to a baby for being willing to drink when it's thirsty!"

Freda silenced him with a gesture and went on, "Anyway—what's the use of trying to understand what's written in the book of Fate? No doubt we had to love you, had to submit to the job of keeping you alive… That's what we did."

"Oh!" whimpered May, hiding her face in her hands.

The chambermaid wiped a tear away from her black eyes, and said more harshly, "You do what you can." Louder still, she clarified, "What you *can*, never what you *want*." Then in a kind of haste she added, "We were part of Slane's gang. We only knew how to steal. Up to then we'd done it for a living. Now we'd do it to raise the little darling chance had given us as our daughter."

"Not chance, Providence!" cried the young woman. "Providence gave you a duty, made you able to understand it and accept it—so as to redeem you, to inspire you to leave the path of crime!…"

But there she broke off, stunned by her listeners' reaction: they were laughing bleakly. Her nerves sadly shaken by their mirth, she asked, "What's the matter with you?"

Still in the grip of his awful laughter, Derrick said, "Leave the path of crime! You say that like a naive child! Can a fish escape from a net? Well, it was the same thing!"

The young woman's eyes suddenly filled with pity. The stoker's words had made her see the truth that a man becomes the prisoner of his crimes, as he does of his virtues.

It was Freda who continued, "All right, we have to explain everything. We never thought of changing our life. First of all, we knew no other work. We'd grown up among vagrants without any fixed address, we were used to thinking of sedentary people as our enemies, we didn't even think we were doing anything wrong by taking what they had plenty of. That's fair in war."

"Alas!"

"It was later, much later, when you, Miss May, were growing up... and you were getting an education... and you spoke from a heart as pure as a lily... that's when we understood that next to you—our little white angel—we must look like the blackest of devils."

"Freda!"

"No, don't interrupt. I have to get to the end. That day we felt proud of your purity—and at the same time we shuddered with horror at our own unworthiness." She shook her head sadly. "Hell—we're no dumber than anyone else! We said, the day our dear little lamb sees us as we really are, she'll be horrified! Sacrificing yourself isn't enough—children also expect you to sacrifice yourself correctly! You can't hold it against them: it's not their fault they're so rigid. They don't know anything about life." She gave a single sob.

Unable to resist the impulse, May hurried to the poor woman and hugged her tight, stammering, "Don't cry! I forgive your past, all of it! But now that's over. You don't need to grovel in disgrace anymore. I'll make enough money to support all three of us..."

She stopped right in the middle of her fine speech. Derrick and Freda were shaking their heads vehemently. Stunned, shivering with inexplicable fear prompted by their refusal—a refusal whose motivation escaped her—she said, "Why not?"

"The boss wouldn't allow it."

"But why?"

"Because you can't let those who know your secrets go free."

"Well! We'll do without his permission!"

Again, the young woman's adoptive parents shook their heads firmly. Annoyed by their resistance to her wishes, May growled, "You're afraid!"

"Afraid for you," said Freda gently. "You, whom he'll strike to get back at us."

"Oh! We could fight him..."

"No, no... you can't fight him."

May clenched her fists. Her soft blue eyes shot daggers. "No matter how strong and powerful a man is, you can find a chink in his armor."

They said nothing, but their faces expressed their skepticism. May gestured wildly, and her voice rang like metal. "Anyway, who is this person you seem to think is invulnerable?"

Together Derrick and Freda said in muted voices, "Tom Slane."

This time it was May who was left speechless. Tom Slane! Was that the name she'd just heard? Tom Slane, Director of the Institute of Inventors—that remarkable establishment which concealed beneath its modest name a university full of engineers dedicated to research on scientific discoveries... which were then developed and distributed around the world by a powerful investment company. What were the chances that such a person could be the leader of a gang of criminals?

"Tom Slane," echoed the young woman aloud, as if to make sure her ears hadn't deceived her.

"Yes, Tom Slane," they reiterated.

"The scientist?"

"Yes."

"Him? Impossible!"

"But true."

The vehemence of their harsh reply made her tremble.

Derrick explained, "Only a scientist could have refrigerated everyone aboard the *Cyclopic*."

May's teeth chattered at that reminder of the drama that had unfolded around her. "Why that monstrous crime?"

"To get his hands on the fifty or sixty million dollars worth of cash and jewelry all the millionaires were foolish enough to bring with them on the cruise."

"But then the ocean liner will be found, drifting with its crew of corpses?"

"Nothing will be found," said Freda bleakly. "The *Cyclopic* is going to vanish with all hands." She stifled May's cry of horror by putting her quick, delicate hand to the girl's lips, and went on hurriedly, "We were aboard to pass along information. At every stop we met with the boss's agents to give them..."

"Be quiet! Be quiet!" cried May in agony.

But with a tragic gesture Freda stretched out both her arms—which gave her a heartrending resemblance to someone crucified. In a voice made hoarse by emotion, she went on, "I have to tell you everything. You have to know everything." She gave a single sob. "Imagine our distress when we saw you among the passengers. To be working to bring about your death—you, our heart, our soul, our redemption!... No, it was impossible! It couldn't be!"

"Poor Freda," sighed the young scientist.

"Yes, you can say that again. We'd been given a special electric radiator. We were instructed that at the moment of the crime we had to hide ourselves in a cabin, switch on the radiator, and wait half an hour. Well, we decided to hide you with us. And then... then..."

She gave a deep sigh and clenched her fists desperately. "Tom Slane is cruising in the Malay Archipelago on his yacht *Follower*. The airship that dropped mortal cold on the *Cyclopic* has by now gone to join him. How soon will the *Follower* intercept the Blue Star Line's great ocean liner, now become a floating tomb? I have no idea. But we'll have enough time to lower a boat to the water. You'll get into it, with provisions, a compass, everything you need. You'll make for Batavia..."

"Where I'll accuse..."

"No one!" cried Freda, "no one! Because that would be condemning to death not just us—no great loss—but yourself at the same time: you, who are to live your life happy, respected, enjoying everything we were denied."

"To live in silence is to be complicit..."

"It's to withdraw from a battle you can't win... Think about who Tom Slane is—a man idolized by the newspapers in two hemispheres! Who'd believe *you*, you poor dear little thing? You'd be broken in the attempt..."

"You'll testify..."

"Us?!" Freda burst out in demented laughter, which Derrick joined. "Us, a couple of gangsters! One word from Slane would send us to the scaffold. We'd be accused of outrageous extortion, and our unsavory reputation would drag you down with us in dishonor."

Her argument seemed unanswerable. May felt it. She bowed her head. A thousand thoughts raced through her mind. What to do? What to decide on?

She started when Derrick's voice broke into her train of thought. "The half hour has passed. It's time to think about saving our little May."

"He's right," agreed Freda. "Come."

But the young woman pointed out Lipson, little Jane, Stepan, and Sefra, all still asleep. "And them?"

Freda's cheeks grew pale. "Them?... They're doomed, like the others—even more than the others."

"In that case I'm staying."

The older woman's eyes flashed with an angry fire. "Oh, we'll force you to go."

"To get into a boat, maybe. But how will you stop me from slipping into the water later and finding my own death?"

The two criminals shuddered. They begged her, "May, May, try to understand! But it's true—you don't know! Tom Slane has a son, whom no one in America knows, because he was raised secretly in Europe. Well, Slane's ambition is that his son will gain a position of such power that the greatest monarchs will envy him."

"What's that got to do with what I want?" growled May scornfully.

"You'll find out, since you hope to die. Slane wants his son to be the head of a syndicate of American billionaires. You must surely be aware that those men, who control the world's wealth, have formed a syndicate to fight the forces of democracy in the United States…"

"I know that, but again, what can that possibly have to do with me?"

"That sought-after position will go to the heir to a great fortune."

"Good for him."

"It's Lloyd Hibbett."

"The son of the late coal and railroad tycoon?"

"The same! Now, that son, raised in England, educated at Cambridge, is unknown in America. He himself knows nothing of his birth. His mother, who became a widow when he was barely three, wanted it that way. She thought if he was unaware of his own wealth, he'd work harder and become more deserving of his high destiny. He doesn't know his own name. He doesn't know that his wise mother, remarried and widowed a second time, is aboard the *Cyclopic*."

"You mean Lloyd Hibbett is aboard as well?"

"Under the name of James Lipson."

"Him?"

"As we speak, the mother is dead. The young man's little sister by the second marriage will soon be dead: that's little Jane. And he himself is due to vanish, to make way for William Slane, who as of tomorrow will be known to all as Lloyd Hibbett."

Distraught, May stared at Freda without speaking or moving. What she'd heard had literally petrified her.

"Well," cried a cheerful voice suddenly, "I don't see any reason why the boat—intended only to save Miss May—couldn't just as easily take along Mr. James, darling Jane, and Stepan and me!"

Freda and May started. Who'd spoken? It was mischievous Sefra, delighted to have escaped—by her presence of mind—the sedative that immobilized her companions.

Freda stammered, "She wasn't asleep!"

The girl replied cheerfully, "Luckily! That way I was able to overhear that you're not as devoted to Tom Slane as I thought."

"You knew about…?"

"Everything—since the farm outside Oakland. But let's leave that aside. Miss May is an honorable person. So we should respect her wish, which is to save everyone here."

At the sound of Derrick's heavy footsteps, Sefra broke off. The stoker went to the door and slowly and cautiously opened it… which suggested that he still considered the girl's intervention irrelevant. "We can go now. Quick, if we want to save our May."

His words seemed to pull the young scientist out of her shock. "I'm willing—but with them," she said, in support of Sefra's plan.

"But…" objected Derrick and Freda.

She cut them off abruptly. "I understand. James, Jane, and Stepan know nothing—and they'll go on knowing nothing of what you've confided to me."

"Then why not abandon them here?"

May leapt to embrace Freda. "Listen," she said affectionately, "do you want me to love you the way I used to? Do you want me to forget what I know of the disgrace and the crimes you confessed?"

"Oh, if only that were possible!"

"Anything is possible for someone who atones."

"What do you mean?"

"I mean that I'll keep silence… but that from now on Slane will have an enemy, one resolved to use all her scientific knowledge—all the knowledge she owes to you, who were just weak accomplices of an evil genius—to fight against that human scourge. And that you'll help me."

"Us? How?"

"You're his assistants. He trusts you."

"Sure."

"It goes without saying. He's told you about all his plans, so… you're going to betray him to me."

"You? Urging betrayal?"

"Betraying a criminal to make restitution to his victims! My father, my mother by adoption… I'm enlisting you in the guerrilla war for good. I'm in no position to condemn you—I who owe you everything. Make it possible for me to love you unambiguously."

"You're talking about a clay pot trying to fight an iron pot."

"Bah! Engineers have files and hammers—tools that can break an iron pot." Then, with a smile that revealed the indomitable courage blossoming within the charming young woman in these terrible circumstances, May went on in a persuasive, enticing, authoritative voice, "Are we agreed? Do we still love each other? Do I have a father and a mother? Or are you leaving me an orphan?"

With some awkwardness, Freda pointed at Sefra. "But what about her? She knows…"

"She'll keep quiet for as long as Miss May orders her to say nothing," cried the girl firmly. "It's not hard to understand that, with a gentleman like your friend Tom Slane, you don't want to give away secrets that would displease him!"

"I'll answer for her," said May slowly.

Derrick and Freda gave up their resistance. They didn't accept the hug May offered them, but they seized their beloved child—the bright blue flower in their bloodstained lives—by her slender hands and kissed them with fervent devotion. "We'll obey you, dear. To do what you want, we'd even die in the attempt… unless by chance we succeed." And in discouraged voices they added, "Which we don't count on."

Without answering those pessimistic words, May led them to the door. As we know, the supposed Mr. August occupied a luxury cabin that opened directly on deck.

The vast *Cyclopic* had stopped, its boilers had gone out, its engines were still. It lay unmoving beneath the starry dome of the sky, splashed by the lapping waves like some drifting reef. Solemn silence reigned. No more conversations, no more songs, no more tinkling pianos. No more orders, no more sailors' shouts. It was the silence of a graveyard. The great leviathan, built by the powerful Blue Star Line at a cost of millions, carried within its hull nothing but an army of the dead.

CHAPTER IV
The Night-vision Binoculars

A large boat was lowered to the sea. When its sail was hoisted, it left the great ship behind.

May was alone at the tiller. Stretched out in the bottom of the boat lay Lipson, Stepan, and little Jane. They were still asleep. Sefra, unmoving, sat curled up in the bow. May looked at them all. She felt deep pity for the two Hibbetts, the brother and sister who knew nothing of their parentage and who were doomed perhaps never to know it, who had no idea they were orphans from now on, and that back there, in her luxury cabin on the *Cyclopic*, their mother lay in the eternal sleep of death.

Before leaving the ship, the young scientist had gone to find the dead woman. She'd kissed her white brow and quietly vowed to her to dedicate her young life to avenging her and to giving her children back the name they'd been robbed of.

But money is the sinews of war, and without hesitation May gathered up the jewelry and the bundles of cash that belonged to Mrs. Hibbett. For the cruise around the world, the billionairess had brought along five or six million dollars—a pittance for someone who possessed fifteen hundred million, but a fortune for the castaways who were preparing to fight against Tom Slane. The mother's spirit would join them in battle; the deceased mother would support her children by the help of her gold.

Oddly, the young woman felt no sadness. So much had happened that night! She'd learned that her adoptive parents had lived as criminals, that every scrap of her own education—in science, in moral principles—had been paid for by crime, or at the very least malfeasance!

And then that slow walk she'd made through the *Cyclopic* now devoid of life! What could be more horrible than those lounges, where the passengers had been overtaken by death in the midst of laughter, of a half-finished gesture, of a chord banged out on the piano? May had brushed by them on her way to Mrs. Hibbett's cabin, and then again to help Derrick and Freda lower the boat to the sea. She'd shivered at the sight of those creatures—so recently as alive as she was, and now looking like statues of stone. But she was unable to feel sadness. A single idea dominated her thoughts and lifted her above the circumstances of this hour: she'd committed herself to war—to victory—for the sake of those who now slept in the bottom of the boat as it slowly drew away from the enormous ocean liner.

And the magnitude of the task didn't frighten her. She intended to crush Tom Slane, the director of the great Institute where a thousand scientists and inventors labored unceasingly to supply new innovations to the colossal scientific and commercial enterprise conceived and brought into being by the very same criminal who tomorrow, thanks to mass murder—the Homeric slaughter of the thousands of passengers, sailors, servants, stokers, and so forth aboard the *Cyclopic*—would become the de facto leader of a syndicate of billionaires and would hold within his hands a power before which men, rulers, nations would have to bow.

And yet she, May, a mere engineer of no account, with the help of her devoted Derrick and Freda and these children now asleep at her feet, would rise up against that criminal with the hope of bringing him down someday. It was a blessing of her mathematical mind that she couldn't see how unequal were the forces arrayed. "One brain against another brain. A scientific bandit against an honorable daughter of science—that's all that matters."

That's what she said to herself calmly. But then she shook her head thoughtfully. "Where he has an advantage is in money—the money that buys support. And he'll have plenty of it." She began to laugh. "That's true. But my advantage is to be unknown to him. I know I'm his enemy, and he doesn't. I've got my eye on him, but to him my puny self wouldn't seem worth a moment's thought." She rubbed her hands together in real satisfaction. "That restores the balance. We're equal in strength. We've each got as much for us as against us."

May turned to look back at the ship, which could now barely be made out in the darkness. Without the bright points of its signal beacons, she wouldn't have known exactly where the vessel was. "Good," she said to herself, "in another few hundred meters I'll lower the sail. This little boat will be completely invisible—which will allow me to see."

With her foot she nudged the crates fastened under the thwarts. "While my dear gangsters were putting provisions on board, I went to the captain's cabin. I gathered some useful instruments—above all his night-vision binoculars, Farnham and Cowe's latest model, whose lenses and prisms are made of a special alloy that transforms black light into light visible to the human eye."

She was right: that unusual property of glass containing a certain proportion of rare earths was just beginning to be exploited by the British Navy, which is always ahead of the world's other navies. As can easily be imagined, the Blue Star Line had drawn on the most up-to-date technology in outfitting its luxury ocean liner *Cyclopic*. The relative ease with which the pseudo Mr. August, and his invention to increase engine power, had been welcomed showed the owners' concern that no one get an advantage over them, and that they stay abreast of every new advance.

For another quarter of an hour the boat sped through calm seas. Then, with unexpected skill, May lowered the sail. When that was done, she picked up those binoculars and aimed them in the direction of the ocean liner. To her eyes the *Cyclopic* stood out against the darkness that veiled it, and the young woman could see the ship as clearly as if it had been lit by the noonday sun. She could even make out two human figures leaning on the top deck rail, and who seemed to be examining the horizon.

"Freda and Derrick," she said softly to herself. "They're trying in vain to spot us in the dark. You poor bandits who love me, I'll free you by punishing the man who made you do wrong."

But then suddenly she broke off. "Another ship!" she stammered. In her viewfinder appeared a second vessel, much smaller than the *Cyclopic*, and drawing closer to it. The ship's horn could be heard calling in the night.

"They're acting out the part of finding the wreck," May muttered to herself. "If by chance some other ship is in the area, there'll be a witness to testify that Slane deserves commendation for hurrying to the assistance of a vessel in distress." She laughed. "But I know the truth—and the villain doesn't know I do. He thinks his plan has unfolded without a flaw." She paused before concluding, almost happily, "I therefore have the first advantage."

But soon she was concentrating on watching what was going on around the *Cyclopic*. The night-vision binoculars enabled her to follow everything her enemy was doing. Slane's yacht, the *Follower*—she could read the name on the bow—lay next to the ocean liner, whose sides rose almost ten meters above the smaller vessel. Immediately a line of sailors ran up the gangway ladder, and there followed a busy back-and-forth of men carrying packages. But all the packages being taken down to the *Follower* looked quite small.

May understood: all the valuables and jewelry brought along on their world cruise by carefree millionaires were being transferred to the criminal's yacht. He was extending the string of crimes his sinister mind had conceived— with robbery at an unprecedented scale. Indeed, the six hundred and twenty different insurance companies who'd underwritten the various policies covering the *Cyclopic* had to pay out—leaving aside compensation to the families of the dead—a total of two hundred million dollars, of which fifty million was just for the vessel itself.

It was easy for May to understand what had happened on the ocean liner: on Slane's orders, the crew of the *Follower* had divided up to search every cabin; each sailor was responsible for a certain number of cabins. The freezing gas disgorged by an airship developed in Slane's own Institute—and that he bragged to the newspapers he would offer to the United States War Department after he'd tested it—had brought down everyone on board the *Cyclopic*. Without a thought for the dead, the evil genius's minions made off with all of the victims' valuables and jewelry.

May watched as, one by one, the crew came back on board the yacht. Among the sailors returning to the *Follower*, she could even recognize Derrick and Freda. Finally the yacht drew away, and sailed off into the night. Soon only the reddish glow of the sparks rising from its smokestacks showed where it was.

The *Cyclopic*, with all of its dead—the *Cyclopic* robbed even of the wealth of those whose lives the criminals had already taken—drifted inanimate, silent, on the choppy swell of the Java Sea.

In some surprise May reasoned, "But whoever finds the abandoned ship will certainly notice it was the scene of a terrible crime!"

Just then a jet of fire shot into the sky, and a wave of smoke rolled out across the ocean. A few seconds later the sound of a violent explosion reached the young woman's ears. When the smoke had cleared, no trace of the *Cyclopic* remained. The giant Blue Star Line vessel, disemboweled in an explosion triggered by Slane, sank into the depths of the ocean, taking with it all evidence of the crime.

The criminal sped away as fast as the *Follower* could sail.

And, standing in a small boat rocked by the swell, with James Lipson and little Jane and Stepan asleep at her feet, and Sefra sitting in the bow as if petrified, May—a young woman, practically still a child in spite of her position as an engineer—dreamt of vengeance that, realistically, seemed impossible.

PART THREE: THE EMPEROR'S DAUGHTER

CHAPTER I
The Typist

"Hello!... Yes, perfectly. Your instructions will be carried out."

The young blonde typist, who'd raced across the office to answer the ring-ing phone, returned to her busily typing coworkers. "Ladies, stop whatever you're doing! We have to make three hundred copies of the press release!"

"Oh! It's as urgent as that?"

"It has to be distributed today to the American newspapers, and wired to China, Persia, Europe, and so forth."

There was a commotion. All the typists pulled the pages they'd been work-ing on out of their machines and replaced them with sheets of blank paper. Then there was silence. All eyes were on the one who'd just passed on the boss's orders—a slim, adorable girl, elegant in her simplicity, and with a pretty face framed by a halo of blonde hair.

She gestured with her hand. "Get ready! I'm starting." Then in a slow clear voice she dictated: "Lloyd Hibbett, president for the past four years of New York's syndicate of five hundred American billionaires, and Tom Slane, general secretary of the same, have rented San Francisco's Buena Vista Park for tomorrow."

"That can't be cheap!" murmured all the women as they typed the words. "What do you think, Miss May?"

She shrugged. "I don't know. But going on…" And she resumed her dictation: "These gentlemen do not intend to deprive the citizens of San Francisco of their favorite place to stroll."

"Oh, really!"

"On the contrary, they invite the public to turn out to attend the celebration of Lloyd Hibbett's betrothal to Princess Liao, favorite daughter of the emperor recently dethroned in the Chinese Revolution, and till just recently an outstanding student at the New Feminist College, where she gained all the acquirements that can adorn the heart and mind of one already admirably endowed by Nature."

"Come on!" joked Lily, the youngest typist. "Daughter of the ex-emperor of China, filthy rich, engaged to Lloyd Hibbett, who has even more money—it's no surprise she's perfect in every way."

"She is, Lily!" insisted May.

"Do you know her?"

"No, but…"

"Well, I do! Yes, in fact I do! Before I came to work for Tom Slane, I worked in the accounts department at the New Feminist College. Well! Princess Liao's not bad, even for a Chinese girl. She's a pretty Chinese girl, I grant you that. But she's a phony, and she wasn't the brightest bulb among her classmates."

"Ah," cried another typist, "listen to Lily running her down! Lily had matrimonial plans that included Lloyd Hibbett, so she's just picking on her rival!"

That provoked a burst of laughter.

"Let's keep going!" they all cried. "If the boss shows up and his communiqué isn't ready, look out!"

"Three hundred copies," repeated May, "that makes thirty each. Let's not waste any time."

For a while the only sound in the room was the clatter of typewriter keys.

But then the incorrigible Lily called out, "Does the daughter of a dethroned monarch still have the right to call herself a princess?"

"Absolutely, you chatterbox. Besides which, by Chinese law she can give her husband the title of prince."

"So Lloyd Hibbett will become Prince Lloyd?"

"Yes."

"Prince Lloyd—that sounds like it comes right out of a fairy tale!"

"Thirty copies, don't forget!"

Once again all heads had gone up to enjoy Lily's jokes—she being the "kid sister" of the typing pool—and once again they were lowered, and the clatter of typing resumed and was no longer interrupted.

Soon May gathered up the three hundred copies required. "I'll take them down for dissemination," she said. "Back in a while."

She left the room and went down a long corridor flanked on one side by doors marked *Offices 1 to 10... 11 to 20... 21 to 30...* And so on, up to 100.

A hundred offices in that building on Kearny Street, just to process accounts receivable or payable: that simple fact suggested the volume of the business at Hibbett's and Slane's Institute of Inventors, rumored even in America to be the number one corporation in the world. The other side of the corridor was lined with windows looking out on Kearny Street, a loud, busy thoroughfare crisscrossed by trolleys and teeming with automobiles and vehicles of all kinds. The sounds of a multitude at work came through the windows, while the clink of gold and the rustle of paper money could be heard through the office doors.

No doubt May was used to all that, because she went on her way without seeming to pay it any attention. At the far end of the corridor a narrow staircase led down to the lower floors.

"An old building—no elevator," she laughed. "Though it's true there are only four floors, instead of the fifteen or twenty in a proper American office building!"

In any case, she went down only a few steps before stopping at a door cut into the thick wall. Opening it, she found herself on the grand main staircase, with an ornately carved banister and steps covered in soft carpet. Here an elevator—or a "lift," as the British say—filled the center of the stairwell. May summoned it, and moments later she stepped out on the ground floor of the building.

To her right a large entranceway was marked *Office of the Director of the Institute.* Beneath that title ran a very American warning: *Do Not Disturb Without Serious Cause.* It was known throughout the country that it was a good idea to pay attention to that sign. Several important people—so it was said—believing themselves entitled to enter, had been thrown out with a harshness they wouldn't soon forget.

The typist didn't seem daunted by the warning. She went through the entranceway and greeted in passing a sturdy doorman sprawled in an armchair. She was about to reach the door to the director's office when a page intercepted her.

"Good morning to you, Miss May."

She looked him over. He was a well-built teenager, and under his green and gold uniform he seemed both strong and agile.

"And good morning back to you, Stepan. Are you stopping me like this because you need some help or advice?"

"Thanks, but no: I just wanted to show you that I'm carrying out conscientiously the job you got for me."

"Oh, don't mention it. I just had to ask Mr. Alexius here…"

"And it was granted on the spot," came the deep voice of the doorman, half rising from his armchair. "I have to say, Miss May is by far the hardest-working girl in the typing pool. And I should add that my trust in her recommendation has been amply rewarded. Her young protégé here has proved well worth her glowing praise."

She thanked him with a bow and rested a friendly hand on her protégé's shoulder. "You hear that, Stepan? I'm proud of you. Continue keeping Mr. Alexius happy."

The doorman puffed himself up with pride—his vanity so perfectly tickled that he didn't notice the quick gesture that allowed the page's and the typist's hands to touch briefly and pass a rolled-up slip of paper from Stepan's fingers to May's. It happened in a flash.

The typist waved goodbye, then entered the director's office without knocking.

"Who is it?" cried a commanding voice—which softened immediately. "Ah, it's you, miss."

"I've brought you the three hundred copies…"

"All right!" The speaker pressed a button, and boys in uniform appeared instantly.

"For full distribution," said Tom Slane briefly—for it was he. "Fifty copies to the local press. The rest as telegrams and cablegrams, according to the list drawn up by the publicity department. Go! In an hour I want to hear it's all done."

The message boys vanished with a speed that hinted at the habitual obedience of the staff. Indeed, Slane never tolerated slowness—to say nothing of lack of zeal.

Tall, spare, with a forceful clean-shaven face and salt-and-pepper hair, he exuded strength and authority. "Well, miss," he said to the typist, "any comments upstairs?"

"Just one. The betrothal party is going to cost a lot of money."

Her answer seemed to please him. With a warm smile he said, "Your friends are right. As proof, they're all going to get a dollar bonus today for doing that little job."

She bowed her thanks.

"And what about you, Miss May? What did you think?"

"I thought the betrothal would bring Mr. Hibbett a title of nobility, and he probably cares more about that than about spending money he doesn't need."

Slane burst out laughing. "Well reasoned, Miss May, very well reasoned! I've always known you had excellent judgement." He hesitated a moment, then seemed to come to a decision. "You're a very responsible worker, Miss May. You're never late, you never make mistakes. How much do you earn?"

"Thirty dollars a week."

"Would you like double that?"

"Oh, who wouldn't want that?"

"You'd have to be Princess Liao's personal assistant."

May started. Her blue eyes looked questioningly at her boss.

"All right, "he said, "you're too smart not to understand I'm offering you a position of trust."

"One that'll be hard to carry out?"

"Yes," he agreed without hesitation.

"Then I'd need more pay."

Slane smiled triumphantly. "I never bargain, as you know. So listen to what I expect from you."

May bowed. No doubt that seemed to him to be agreement enough, because he began, "You know the circumstances. Lloyd Hibbett, president of the syndicate of American billionaires, is about to marry Princess Liao, daughter of the exiled emperor of China."

She nodded.

"The dethroned monarch has made a political calculation. The enormous sums Lloyd Hibbett can set in motion could finance a successful attempt to restore him to the Celestial throne." He paused with a mocking smile. "Well thought out, right? Unfortunately Princess Liao doesn't have the slightest dynastic ambition."

"Really!"

"That surprises you, as it does me. But the fact is, when it was proposed that they honeymoon in China, she objected, saying it was her firm wish never to leave the United States again, and to live here in the peaceful enjoyment of her wealth."

"How very philosophical!"

"Maybe so. And maybe she doesn't really care that much for Lloyd Hibbett. Whereas I? I love that young man like... like a son." With some kind of hidden sarcasm Slane went on, "A son—that's the very word. He owes me his life. Am I not the one who, when the *Cyclopic* went down after running onto some unknown reef in the Java Sea, picked him up, along with a couple of servants from the unfortunate liner, all of them half dead from hunger? Three survivors, whom I vowed to take care of, precisely because of the favor I'd done them."

"It was you who had Mr. Hibbett—who was on his way back from an English university—officially identified; you who made sure he came into possession of his family's fortune; you who propelled him to the presidency of the syndicate of five hundred American billionaires."

"Making sure, by doing so, of unparalleled support for the Institute, where I've brought together inventors and researchers of all kinds. From that point of view I've been fully repaid—and more—for rescuing him. Anyway, I'm only thinking now of my affection for him. I want Lloyd to be happy. For him to be happy, his honeymoon journey must take him and Princess Liao to China."

"Why?" murmured the typist as if despite herself.

Slane frowned. "The reason will be made clear later. There is one, that's what matters. Well then! I want the young lady to have with her a female companion who's under my orders, and who can sweep away the princess's stay-at-home hesitations and persuade her to act in a way that's consistent with my dear Lloyd's happiness."

May's eyes flashed with a spark that was quickly suppressed. "And so you chose me?" she asked calmly.

"Would you accept?"

"I'd be hesitant…"

"I haven't yet mentioned the perks of the job."

She shook her head. "It's not about that. I have the dedication and the desire to succeed—but do I have the skills needed?"

"I believe so."

"You?"

"For the six months since you entered the typing service, I've been observing you. You have a first-class intelligence. You grasp everything effortlessly. It's natural—and no surprise to your fellow workers—that you've risen to be the de facto leader of the typing pool. A leader without a title, but whose authority is all the more legitimate because it's accepted by co-workers who think of themselves as your equals."

A blush spread quickly on the young woman's cheeks. Clearly, her boss's praise gave her real pleasure. "If that's your judgment, Mr. Slane," she said quietly, "I'll do my best to justify it with respect to Princess Liao."

He rubbed his hands together vigorously enough to take off skin. "Now you're talking! So, hand over your duties to Diana Holt, and—armed with the letter of introduction I'll give you in a minute—go see Princess Liao at her mansion on Fulton Street, by Golden Gate Park."

"Does she know about it?"

"Yes. She's tired of her Chinese companions. She says she'd prefer the company of an American girl."

May bowed, took the letter of introduction he handed her, and asked, "Any special instructions for tomorrow's betrothal party at Buena Vista Park?"

"You'll accompany the princess, and do your best to persuade her to be nice to Lloyd."

In the elevator on the way back up to the floor where the typing pool worked, May unrolled the piece of paper Stepan had slipped into her hand earlier. She read, *Jane unbearable. Never stops asking for you.*

"Poor darling," she said to herself. Then she put the message in her mouth and swallowed it to destroy all trace of the mysterious correspondence.

A few minutes later May left the Institute. On her way down the sidewalk on Kearny Street she had to dodge the busy passersby who hurried along with the well-known American indifference for other people's ribs. She glanced back at the Institute with a worried look that suggested some vacillation. Perhaps unaware that she was putting her thoughts into words, she murmured, "He's so powerful! Millions of dollars, sixty factories, two hundred laboratories where the scientists he recruited work nonstop doing research into every field of human endeavor—submarines, railways, aviation, electricity, telegraphy whether wired or wireless, etcetera, etcetera!"

But then she sliced the air with a wave of her hand, and shook her head. "Bah! What am I risking? Dying in the attempt. And I know very well that Derrick, Freda, James—all of them would be cut down by the same blow."

Firmly she willed herself to drive away that gloomy thought. "I'm not going to waver now. For four years we've been preparing for this struggle. Thanks to the considerable sum I was able to take from the late Mrs. Hibbett's cabin on the *Cyclopic*, I've been able to pursue my research." She laughed, because Tom Slane wasn't aware there'd been a female inventor at his Institute. "Now we're ready. Slane has every weapon at his disposal. We have only one—but it's unknown, an innovation. Therefore victory isn't out of reach…"

She stopped cold. Coming toward her she recognized Freda and Derrick. She held out her hand. "Good morning! A quick word. I'm to be the personal companion to Princess Liao." She cut off their expressions of surprise. "There's no time. Where's our little Jane now? I need to see her. Apparently she's misbehaving."

"Oh! She's at the house on Fulton Street, next to the Chinese girl's mansion."

"And James?"

"Still working as a servant for Princess Liao."

"So he's the one who persuaded her that she'd rather have an American companion?"

Her adoptive parents shrugged to show they didn't know.

But May smiled gently. "I know you dear people don't understand my plans. I love you all the more for being loyal to me without asking for explanations. So I wasn't questioning you, I was simply observing that our scheme is working."

They both smiled. "Are you happy, May? Then we are too."

With deep affection, Freda added, "We could never have hoped things would work out so well: to see you all the time, to work alongside you… Sure, without understanding what's going on, as you say—but what does that matter, as long as we're helping you?"

"While risking your lives, you poor dears."

"Who cares! We've always risked our lives, but this is the first time we've enjoyed it."

May smiled in acknowledgment of Freda's devotion, then said quietly, "Time to split up. Go! Let's make sure no one suspects that our little Jane is at the Fulton Street house." Then, thoughtfully, with a look of concern, she added, "It's for that little darling that I'm most afraid. Only seven years old! She's defenseless."

"Oh, she won't give herself away. She knows nothing."

"Are you positive?" They looked at her in surprise, and she went on, "I feel like, for a while now, she's been more affectionate to me than before."

"Oh, she loves you! That's natural, since you take care of her and brighten her days. Everybody, big or little, loves you!"

May shook her head. "That's not it! I see something in the little darling's eyes, some thought I can't pin down. The child's mind escapes me."

Neither Derrick nor Freda, those simple souls, understood the meaning of the young scientist's words. They watched her in puzzled silence, no doubt waiting for instructions.

She gestured in resignation. "Oh well, maybe I'm wrong. But let's be extra careful, that's all."

They clasped hands hurriedly, and all went on their way.

But May had gone no more than a hundred meters before she stopped again with an anxious exclamation. She'd just bumped into a dark-complexioned girl of thirteen or fourteen, who was fairly pretty in spite of her mismatched multicolored clothing and the evident distress in her face and her gestures. The girl had come to a stop in front of May, and she opened and closed her mouth without making a sound.

"Sefra!" murmured May finally. "What are you doing here? Why have you left your post?"

"I was running to the Institute to alert Miss Freda…"

"Alert her of what?"

"Of the abnormal thing that's just happened."

"Something abnormal has happened?"

"Yes, of course! At least I think so. I'm watching over little Jane, right, and I'm supposed to report on anything unexpected."

"Well, come on, explain! You're making me dread something awful! Is it awful?"

"I don't know, miss." Then in a rush, as if her tongue had loosened and she urgently wanted to be rid of burdensome news, she went on, "You told me, 'Sefra, you're a good child, you're loyal to your friends, you used to be devoted to Mrs. Hibbett, and now you're anxious to devote yourself to her child. Would you be willing to watch over the little girl, whose life will have to be more precious than your own, more precious than those of the people you love most?'"

"Believe me, I remember."

"And anyway, haven't Stepan and I been devoted to Miss Jane ever since the *Cyclopic*? I'd pass through the eye of a needle for the dear little thing if I had to."

"I'm sure—but what's upset you?"

"It's this. You put Jane and me in that house on Fulton Street, right next to the Chinese princess's house."

"Yes, yes, cut to the chase!" muttered May with open impatience.

"I can't, as you'll see! For several days now, Jane has been taking an interest in what's going on at the princess's mansion."

May started, and echoed in a troubled voice, "Taking an interest?"

"Exactly. She's been watching the comings and goings and asking me for the names of the visitors: Lloyd Hibbett, Tom Slane, and lots of others. Plus which, she recognized Mr. James even in his servant's uniform."

"She recognized him—that's bad! We'll have to move somewhere else!"

Sefra shook her head anxiously. "Too late, miss!"

"Why too late?"

"Because a little while ago, as I was getting dressed, Jane went out."

"Out... onto the street?"

Sefra nodded vehemently. "Oh, she didn't go far. She knocked at the door of Princess Liao's mansion..."

"What?"

"It's true, miss!"

"Go on," panted May.

"I only found out later, from Mr. James. He ran over with a message from Princess Liao—that's the kind of work servants do, you know—to tell me the princess wished to serve lunch to the little girl who'd 'come to pay her a neighborly call.' Apparently that's how the little tyrant introduced herself."

Listening to that account, May had gone terribly pale, and a look of great distress filled her face and her haunted eyes. Through trembling lips she managed to stammer, "All is lost! Jane—a child too young to understand—will say something that the fiancée of William Slane, who's now passing as Lloyd Hibbett, ought not to hear."

And yet young Sefra was eyeing her questioningly. May knew she was waiting for instructions. She had to hide her distress. She willed herself to be firm. She managed to put on a neutral expression. Het voice didn't give away the terrible anxiety she felt at the thought that her darling protégée was with her pitiless enemy's fiancée. "Go warn Miss Freda, and tell her that you've reported to me."

"Yes, miss."

"Then go back to our house on Fulton Street, and wait till they bring Jane home..."

"And I swear on my life I won't let her escape again!"

"I'll give you instructions about that later. Go!"

For a moment May watched as the girl dashed off. When she knew Sefra could no longer see her, she began to hurry—almost running—in her haste to get to Princess Liao's mansion.

She soon reached Fulton Street: on one side stood the elegant mansions of the wealthy; on the other side ran the fence bounding Golden Gate Park, the locals' favorite place to stroll. She slowed down. The closer she came to her destination, the more hesitant she grew. She had to present herself to Princess Liao, since that was Slane's order. To fail—or even just to be slow—to carry out the instructions of the Director of the Institute of Inventors would be enough to raise the suspicions of her all-powerful adversary—a man against whom her only chance of success lay in surprise.

Of course, that meant Jane would see her. But how could she possibly obey her orders without the child seeing her? The poor little thing wouldn't hide her pleasure at seeing May, whom in her baby talk she called "big sister." She'd jump into her arms as usual. And then... then... how would she explain?

Suddenly an idea crossed her mind with the speed of a sharpened arrow. "But she must already have recognized James Lipson! Of course she's already announced that he's her friend. So the jig is already up..."

She gestured with resolve. "Oh well—I'll soon see. We'll have to disappear, lie low for a few months. After all, I don't know where Slane's plans are leading, and I feel like I have to find that out before I can locate the chink in his armor. Time to go into exile! It doesn't matter... It's just a delay that'll push back the hour of the ultimate battle."

A moment later she stopped before the great door that stood in the middle of the monumental façade of Princess Liao's mansion.

CHAPTER II
The Mind of a Little Girl

Erected by an industrialist who—by means of the kind of bold speculation that's normal in America—had become a billionaire in a matter of months, the mansion was graced by a large garden, something uncommon in San Francisco. The mansion itself was built in the typical style of architectural bluster that prevails throughout the United States. The whole place gave an impression of ponderous wealth. The walls, the tiled floors, the marble balconies proclaimed the vast sums spent on them—without quite achieving elegance.

Having sprouted like a mushroom, the industrialist who'd built the mansion had collapsed just as fast. He'd disappeared—though he might well surface again with some new scheme. The mansion had been put up for sale by his creditors, and was bought by Tom Slane, who was pleased to offer it to Princess Liao as her residence. Of course the new owner had seen fit to connect the mansion on Fulton Street to his Institute on Kearny Street by telephone, telegraph, and telephote.

A little door for pedestrians was set into the great double doors. At the sound of May's knock, it opened. She entered the tiled vestibule. In front of her she saw an inner courtyard, bounded on three sides by the wings of the mansion, and on the fourth by the garden, with its artfully arranged trees and flowerbeds.

A gatekeeper burst out of the lodge to the right of the entrance. "What's this concerning?" he demanded with a mix of obsequiousness and insolence. Servants give off impressions their masters don't always notice.

May noticed, but didn't react. She looked the guard up and down, and said calmly, "Sent by Mr. Slane. Message for Princess Liao."

She hadn't even finished before the man bent double. "I believe the Princess to be in the dining room, with some little devil who managed to get in in spite of me." He stopped talking long enough to pull a cord attached to the wall. "I will nevertheless notify her of your arrival. A messenger come from Mr. Slane isn't just anybody!" By now perfectly friendly, he added, "Take the stairs ahead of you. The staff on the second floor will meet you."

May didn't wait to be told twice. She headed quickly up the grand staircase, the wooden banister of which had once railed off the choir stalls of a Gothic church in France. The brave young woman was now in a hurry to confront the danger that earlier had made her shiver.

Upstairs she suddenly found herself face to face with a tall servant, who had a distinguished look in spite of his uniform. May started.

The man leaned closer. "Don't worry, miss. It's me—James."

"And Jane?" she murmured.

"The child's as quick as a little fly. Not a move, not a word gave away that she recognized me."

"How's that possible?" The young woman clasped her hands. It was something she hadn't dared hope for: some instinctive, intuitive caution had sealed the little girl's lips. She was almost calm as she went on, "And our experiments?"

"Going wonderfully, miss! Wearing the electric bodysuit, which amplifies my will at least ten-thousandfold, I believe I could control the minds of five hundred people simultaneously... and when I say five hundred, I might as well say five thousand. There's no limit to the collective hallucination that arises."

"Ah, James, you've restored my courage."

"I'm simply returning it," he said in an emotional voice. "Don't I owe all the courage I have to you—the tamer of the kings of gold?"

Blushing, she interrupted him. "Oh, that tag again!"

The pseudo-servant said very quietly, "I won't use it anymore if it displeases you, miss. But I'll go on thinking that it fits a young woman scientist who's succeeded effortlessly, by ingenious electro-mechanical means, in producing mind control."

May's blush deepened, and she had to control her voice to say, "Princess Liao is still at lunch, isn't she?"

"No, no. She went to the cinema-telephote parlor to entertain the kid, who's positively enslaved her. They must be enjoying themselves, because when the butler came to announce lunch was ready, the princess sent him away with orders to put it off for half an hour."

"In that case you could announce me right away."

"All the more so because you're expected. Slane phoned to say you were on your way."

"Ah! What did she say to that?"

"She said, 'Finally!' Oh, the suggestion I planted in her mind was as extreme as you asked for."

"Thank you. But please announce me, James. Later I'll be able to thank you as you deserve."

The pseudo-servant gave her a tender look, then turned on his heel and vanished into the next room. He was gone only a few seconds. When he returned he'd assumed the tone, the look, the manner of a well-trained servant. "If miss would be so kind as to follow me…"

She couldn't help a slight smile, but she soon regained her serious expression. In this house that Tom Slane had equipped, danger lay all around her. She had to put aside pleasant thoughts.

Lipson set off, and she followed him. They passed through a series of rooms furnished in a remarkably odd style: next to somewhat over-gilded American or European pieces stood bookcases, chairs, and incense burners fashioned into mythical animals and grotesque dragons, in the fantastical taste of craftsmen from the Celestial Kingdom. Apparently the young woman who lived in the house, having grown up in the Imperial City of Beijing, had brought with her into exile a love of the rococo designs of her ancestors. She must have ransacked San Francisco's Chinatown to collect the countless examples of Chinese art now displayed in her house.

Lipson stopped and pointed out a closed door. "Here it is." He knocked three times discreetly, then opened the door and stood aside to let the visitor pass, while in a loud voice he announced, "Miss May, the person sent by Mr. Slane."

In spite of her courage, May had to pause on the threshold. She felt as if her feet were nailed to the floor. In the spacious room into which she looked, Princess Liao—a dark, saffron-complexioned young woman with tiny mannered gestures, wearing three Chinese tunics, her hair in a bun fastened with gold pins—sat facing a large telephote screen, on which appeared a succession of images transmitted over long distances by wireless: a device every sufficiently wealthy American is able to have at home. As we know, the telephote transmits images the way the telephone transmits sounds.

Next to the young Chinese woman, a little girl with a lovely face—skin of peaches and cream, large eyes of a blue so deep they look violet—under a dazzling crown of golden hair, was in the middle of applauding. And indeed at that moment the screen presented a marvelous spectacle: May could see that the princess was showing her little visitor the various workshops at the Institute founded and led by Tom Slane.

Unknown machines, belted wheels, turbines, pistons moving at dizzying speed, machine tools, smelters, kilns... it was enough to astonish even professionals, engineers. The Institute was like a summation of global industry—not the industry of today, but of that which would belong to the world in fifty years.

The little girl seemed to be vastly entertained by these things, which she must have found incomprehensible. Her pleasure led her to exhibit an almost religious worship for the master of all these marvels. Presumably the princess had mentioned his name, because over and over the child repeated, "Always Tom Slane! Always Tom Slane!"

May's entrance interrupted the scene. Princess Liao examined the new arrival, then—in excellent English, with only a singsong intonation betraying her foreign origins—she said, "You're Miss May. My friend Tom Slane has spoken very highly of you."

"I will strive to earn an equally good opinion on the part of Your Highness."

The young Chinese woman deigned to smile at that respectful reply. "How nice. Have you been told what I expect of you?"

"I presume I'll accompany you on walks, read to you..."

"Exactly." With somewhat haughty condescension the princess went on, "This morning you'll have lunch with me. That way I can get to know your mind. Your outer self is pleasing to look at, but your inner self should please me too, shouldn't it?"

"I'm entirely at Your Highness's orders."

"Ah. And then this afternoon we'll go out. A few purchases for tomorrow, the great day of my betrothal."

May bowed in acquiescence.

Suddenly Princess Liao cried, "How you do stare at that child!"

It was true: May had unconsciously been watching little Jane, with a deep fear that at any moment she would throw herself into her arms—and thereby give away her connection to the supposed typist. Would the princess's remark itself trigger the affectionate impulse May dreaded?

Trembling all over, May nodded; she felt unable to utter a word. Her heart pounded in her chest. What would little Jane do? The child had turned when she heard the princess refer to her. She seemed to be waiting for the reply. Her eyes were fixed on May—who was surprised to read in the little girl's expression some kind of veiled sarcasm. But that was all: nothing suggested the little girl had ever met the new "personal companion" before this moment. She greeted her like a stranger when Princess Liao presented her as "Miss May."

But as they were going to the dining room, the child, maneuvering to make the princess take the lead, stood quickly on tiptoes and whispered so softly that May could barely hear her, "You know I recognized you, right?" Then she put a finger to her lips. "Now you'll be able to come see me openly, since we've been introduced at the Chinese lady's."

May was dazed. So the girl understood—at least the overall situation! But she had no time to question her: little Jane bounded away to follow the princess downstairs.

Moments later the three of them were taking their seats in the dining room on the first floor, whose large bow windows of high-quality glass looked out on the interior garden of the mansion.

The new "personal companion" hardly noticed what she ate. She had to answer Princess Liao's questions, while concealing her own growing astonishment.

Jane seemed as calm as if she had nothing to hide. She spoke to May as if to a stranger, with a child's familiarity. "What's your name, blonde lady?"

"Miss May."

"Oh, what a pretty name!... And you're pretty too, you know." Then she added slyly, "My name is Jane... Do you like it?"

The child truly seemed to be enjoying the life-threatening intrigue unfolding around her. She maneuvered through it easily, with no apparent effort. Children have a remarkable intuitive gift for subterfuge, and they listen to and assess those around them with powerfully accurate judgment. Yet those who've moved on to the age of reason can claim, with more naivety than insight, "Oh, children don't notice anything!"

Jane was triumphant proof to the contrary of that common misperception. "The lady's very nice," she went on, now addressing Princess Liao. "I like her. When you're not around, I'll play with her."

"Why not when I'm around too?" asked the princess, who was clearly amused by the child's chatter.

With a shrewdness that continued to astonish May, the little girl replied, "Oh, then I'd rather play with you!"

That earned her a kiss from the young Chinese woman. Once again a little flatterer lived at the expense of whoever would listen to her, and the fable by the great La Fontaine found resounding confirmation.[12] And once again a child outwitted a supposedly sensible grownup. Those were May's reflections, while in the grip of considerable emotion.

Lipson entered, bringing the portable telephone, whose wire uncoiled behind him. "Princess," he announced loudly, "Mr. Hibbett and Mr. Slane ask to speak with you. Given Your Highness's upcoming betrothal, I thought it best to bring the receiver in here."

"You were quite right."

---

[12] Jean de La Fontaine (1621-95), poet and author of the famous *Fables*. The fable referred to here, with a paraphrase of its moral, is *Le Corbeau et le renard*, a verse retelling of Aesop's "The Fox and the Crow."

When the phone had been set down next to her on the table, she spoke into the receiver in a soft, musical voice. "Hello! Hello!... You say you can see me... I understand—you're at the Institute, looking at the telephote screen. Mine's in the Red Parlor and I'm in the dining room now, so I'll have to settle for listening to you... Yes, Miss May, the girl you sent over to be my personal companion, is here with me now... The little girl? Oh, you're curious about the little girl? You want to know who she is?"

As May deduced, by the princess's replies, the questions coming through phone, she felt faint. Slane and the false Lloyd Hibbett were interested in Jane— Jane whom they'd made an orphan, whom they'd doomed to live without a name, under May's frail protection, while May herself was engaged in an unequal struggle! All of her blood rushed to her heart, and for a moment she couldn't breathe.

But, oblivious to the anxiety being felt so near to her, Princess Liao went on, "A little neighbor, on a child's whim, decided to pay me a neighborly call... Exactly. She's as darling as can be—even more than you can imagine. I've had her stay for lunch, and now the little thing is busy trying to make a conquest of Miss May. Isn't that right, miss? Oh, you can answer. My friends can see us and hear us just as clearly as if they were sitting right here."

"In that case," murmured May with an effort, "I'll admit, I'm under the spell of this darling little creature."

"Well said!" added Jane solemnly.

That made Princess Liao laugh, and presumably did the same to the listeners at the other end of the line, because the princess went on, "You see how entertaining she is!" Then her face brightened. "You're coming over... with some nice jewelry. You'll be very welcome, and the jewelry too... That's right. See you soon."

The princess hung up the receiver. Lipson reentered the room just then, and she called out gaily, "Put away the phone, and have coffee served in the Red Parlor. We'll have it while we're waiting for our visitors."

She turned to May—who was immobilized by worry over Slane's arrival, which would place him in the presence of Jane, the darling victim who'd escaped from the hecatomb of the *Cyclopic.* "You'll go in before me, please. I have to check my hair. As you can imagine, when you're meeting your fiancé, your 'sweetheart' as you say in America, it's a good idea to primp your curls!"

Laughing, the princess went out of the room, leaving May alone with Lipson and Jane. The scientist and the pseudo-servant exchanged a long look, as if they were questioning each other.

Finally the young woman said, "We can't act till we're sure of ourselves."

"I'm absolutely sure."

"Then the screening parlor would be ideal... Let's strike the first blow, since you've made up your mind."

Lipson nodded his approval. Then, remembering his role as a servant, he picked up the phone and carried it out, while May, taking little Jane by the hand, led her toward the Red Parlor.

In the vestibule Lipson bumped into Freda, who'd come rushing in. "You, Freda? And running? What's your hurry?"

"Lloyd Hibbett and Tom Slane are on their way here. I overheard them talking, and I raced over—not to mention, Sefra warned me..."

"Indeed, they telephoned."

"So do we need to hide Jane?"

"No! They already saw her on their telephote screen."

They were speaking in cautious voices on the threshold of the open main door, through which came the sound of traffic on Fulton Street.

"But what if they question the little girl?"

"They won't."

"How can you be sure?"

"Because the visitors won't even think of it, considering the little distraction we're preparing for them."

Surprised, Freda paused a moment before going on in a whisper, "Is this our May's invention?..."

"Yes."

"And you, Mr. James, a scientist, you're confident that...?"

"So confident, Mrs. Freda, that it's I myself who'll carry out the test."

Her mouth widened to an O—as we know, the universal expression of astonishment. "So you understand?"

"And so do you, I believe..."

"Than you believe mistakenly. No offense, but the fact is, I might understand if it was really explained to me—but someone would have to explain it."

"All right, I'll try. You believe, don't you, that some people—hypnotists, mesmerists, and so forth—can transfer their own will to another person's mind."

"Oh, everybody knows that."

"They can give their subjects genuine hallucinations, leading them to think, speak, act, however the controller wishes. However, here's the catch: that transfer of will is extremely tiring for the 'operator.' It can only be done by someone with especially strong nerves."

"So far I'm following you, Mr. James."

"Our Miss May, as you call her so affectionately, therefore asked herself whether it might be possible to amplify the operator's will—ten times, a hundred, a thousand, ten thousand times—so that with minimal or almost no effort he could control the thoughts, the actions, the vision, not just of one subject but of everyone gathered nearby, without exception. You can then see the advantage such a weapon would give people ready to sacrifice their lives for a just cause."

Freda clasped her hands in a gesture more eloquent than any words of admiration.

"She's worked on the problem for four years."

"With your help?"

"Like any humble lab assistant helping an inventor of genius. And she solved it."

"This is where everything becomes murky to me."

"Of course the details are beyond you, Mrs. Freda, since you haven't studied physics, chemistry, physiology, and so on. But at least the basic principle should be clear to you."

"Clear, clear—if you say so... But just between us, it's not a blinding clarity."

"All right, moving on. Against your skin you wear a kind of chain mail, designed by Miss May, consisting of the components of electrical batteries, whose current is channeled in such a way that it amplifies the psychic effluvia— or, if you'd rather, the current of animal magnetism projected by the will."

"Oh, my head!" moaned Freda, pressing her fists against her temples.

"I'll stop."

"No, no... But for me, all your talk about currents is just a Latin mass for the papists. Just tell me, does this chain mail suit give you a lot of power?"

"You can decide for yourself. May's latest refinements are such that, if we assign my own will a value of one unit, when I'm wearing the bodysuit it's raised to at least a hundred thousand."

"A hundred thousand, you say?"

"And I'm certainly underestimating. But even if we stick to that figure, I say that if a thousand people were gathered in one spot I could impose on all of them the same hallucination at the same time, with an effort barely a tenth of what would be needed by an operator who wasn't wearing the amplifying apparatus."

Freda was transfixed. But still she seemed not to grasp the full scientific meaning of what he was saying.

Lipson could see that, and with a smile he went on, "Just remember one thing, Mrs. Freda: I can control a thousand minds at one time. You're going to witness a much reduced test..."

"When?"

"In a few minutes. I can see Slane's car at the far end of Fulton Street now. Run to the Blue Parlor, which is only separated from the Red Parlor by a door. From there you'll see and hear everything. That demonstration will be worth more than any explanation."

She was about to speak again, to ask more questions, but he interrupted her. "The car will be here in ten seconds. If your 'boss' sees you, you can be sure you won't be observing any tests."

Putting it that way made it very clear to her. Freda dashed off and soon vanished into one of the parlors opening onto the vestibule.

Just in time: the car pulled up in front of the mansion. Two men got out: Slane and a tall young man dressed a little affectedly, and sporting a monocle. In spite of all his undeniable contrivances of stylishness, beneath the gentlemanly elegance of his appearance the fellow couldn't hide something vaguely common—imperceptible to most people but very clearly visible to the elite accustomed to noticing fine distinctions.

"Ah!" cried Slane heartily as they entered, "the worthy James was waiting for us."

"Sir has been so generous," replied the pseudo-servant with feigned obsequiousness, "that I feel in conscience bound to open the door for him myself. When one expects a visit from a gentleman such as Sir, one should meet him with all doors thrown wide open."

The Director of the Institute of Inventors, obviously flattered, puffed up with pride. Smiling, almost cordial, he said, "And is that also Her Highness Princess Liao's opinion?"

Lipson shrugged with the discretion of a well-bred servant, in whom familiarity and respect are not at odds. "Oh, Her Highness is a girl, as Sir is aware. The visitor she anticipates most is the gentleman accompanying Sir."

His eye fell on Lloyd Hibbett, who'd been standing by calmly watching the exchange. All three men laughed—Slane and Hibbett loudly, the pseudo-servant with a little more discretion.

Then Slane asked, "Where will we find our charming princess?"

"In the Red Parlor, Sir, where Her Highness has had coffee served."

"Ah! If I remember right, that's the room with the telephote screen that connects to the Institute."

"Indeed, Sir. No doubt Her Highness thought that, if necessary, Sir would have no difficulty getting in touch with the Institute. It's well known that Sir is the busiest man in the United States."

Clearly very susceptible to flattery, Slane once more nodded his approval. "Yes, yes," he said with false modesty, "I'm fairly busy. Not too much work—no, no, there's never too much—but enough... In truth, if you could pack forty-eight hours into the day I wouldn't complain."

Lipson led Slane and Hibbett to the Red Parlor, a long rectangle whose walls were draped in red and gold, except on one of the short sides, which was entirely filled by a mirror of uncommon size. We should explain right away that the mirror—whose presence neither good taste nor necessity could justify—was part of a technical apparatus. It replaced the usual projection screen of a telephote, which would have looked much too ugly in a parlor for receiving company.

Princess Liao, May, and Jane were seated around a small pedestal table finely inlaid with mother-of-pearl, ivory, and gold, on which stood a beautiful coffee service in greenish porcelain from the Eleventh Dynasty.[13] They all rose as the visitors entered, and the princess deigned to take a few steps forward. She stretched out her long, slim, delicately amber-shaded hand to welcome the newcomers. She shook Slane by the right hand in the American manner, let her tapered fingers linger for a moment in Hibbett's grasp, then indicated where they should sit.

"Will you join us for coffee?" she asked with a sweet simper.

"I'd join you in death!" cried her fiancé, seizing an opportunity to serenade her—with all the grace of a bear digging up a root. "How could I turn down a cup of the mocha whose aroma perfumes the whole room?"

Princess Liao didn't react to the absurdity of his words. Perhaps—with the typical naivety of girls, who take for pure gold the gilt paper flowers of their admirers' cheap rhetoric—she just didn't notice. Whatever the case, she turned to her new personal companion and said, "Miss May, would you serve the gentlemen?"

May did so immediately, without seeming at all daunted by a task for which her training as a typist wouldn't normally have prepared her. But if the others present had bothered to pay attention to a person of so little account, they might have noticed that she kept looking insistently at the drapes behind them, on the wall opposite the telephote mirror. Those drapes covered the partition separating the Red Parlor from the Blue Parlor.

As if her very eyes were making them move, or as if some inexplicable draft were lifting them, the drapes billowed three times. But May might not have seen it, because at that moment she picked up the gilt silver sugar bowl and said respectfully, "If the gentlemen will be so kind as to serve themselves the sugar."

Slane was reaching for the sugar tongs when he stopped in mid-motion at the ringing of a bell.

"Telephone!" they all cried as one.

"Would you get that, Miss May?" said the princess nonchalantly.

The former typist, having hurried to the receiver, came back almost immediately. "It's a message from Mr. Slane's Institute, asking us to switch on the amplifying plate of the telephone, so that we can all hear without using earpieces, and also to switch on the telephote."

"The telephote too? Damn, it must be an important call," muttered Slane. "We'll do as asked and find out."

With just a couple of metallic clicks, May carried out the instructions. The telephote mirror grew cloudy, then turned a dull gray, as if it were reflecting a fog—though there was no trace of fog in the Red Parlor.

In their astonishment they all cried out, "What in the world is that?!"

---

[13] The Yuan Dynasty (1279-1368), famous for its Mongol founder, Emperor Kublai Khan.

As if in answer, the fog condensed into well-defined shapes. On the mirror-screen could now be seen a small bright square room, furnished with chairs and armchairs of bent satinwood and a pedestal table of modern design with copper trim. A few color prints and some flowers in vases on the mantelpiece completed the simple but very tidy decor of this room unknown to May, to Princess Liao, and to Jane, who all murmured, "What's the screen showing?"

Slane, however, had jumped. He knew that room, where four years earlier he'd begun the series of crimes that had allowed him to rise to the summits at which his greedy ambitions aimed. It was the parlor of the farmhouse outside Oakland! How could that room, destroyed by fire—a room that no longer existed outside the memory of the general secretary of the syndicate of American billionaires—appear on this screen now?

The question was choked off in his throat. There was motion on the screen: two people, a man and a woman, came into the parlor and sat by the table.

"Mr. Slane!" cried Princess Liao. "And who's the woman who's there with you?"

With an effort that almost broke him, Slane gave a shrug of ignorance. And yet he knew it well—the ghostly image of his wife, that fine woman Slane had murdered. She was tall and very thin, almost gaunt. Her drawn features suggested that suffering had cost her the beauty whose traces could still be seen. Her hair, parted in the middle, had once been black but was now streaked with white.

"Who is that woman?" repeated the princess. May and Jane said nothing, but were full of curiosity.

Slane and Hibbett remained silent. They'd both gone terribly pale. Their lips quivered. A subtle enough lip reader could have made out in that quivering the words, "My wife!" and "My mother!"

Suddenly Jane pointed out on the screen the openwork rosette on the ceiling, from which the chandelier over the table hung. "Look at the rosette! Through the holes you can see someone's eyes looking!"

It was true. Whose eyes? It was impossible to tell.

Slane shuddered. He remembered that, before starting the fire at the farm, he'd found signs that someone had been up in the attic, by the rosette. He'd never figured out who'd been there, and it didn't seem to matter, so he'd forgotten about it. Why was the screen reminding him of it now? Why was it replaying that hour of horror?

He tried to rise. His intention was obvious: he meant to go to the screen and switch off the device... but in vain. Some unseen force held him as if he were nailed to his chair. He looked over to Lloyd Hibbett, but the young man was motionless, in some kind of stupor.

Meanwhile the man and the woman up on the screen continued to move, and the amplifying plate of the telephone projected their voices around the Red Parlor. Slane's image was speaking, in a calm, harsh, commanding tone. "My dear Edith, you're the stumbling block in my path. I'm not going to allow you to jeopardize my son William's future."

"Me—jeopardize his future!" she cried in astonishment.

"If you weren't my wife," he went on cynically, "when Mrs. Hibbett was widowed I could've gotten around her and gained the upper hand over her son Lloyd—and had no trouble replacing him with our son William."

"Oh!" cried Princess Liao in astonishment. But, like all the others present, she felt as if she were fastened to her seat by invisible bonds. She looked around desperately at her new personal companion, and little Jane, and her guests: all of them sat unmoving, as if turned to stone. Their eyes, wide with intense curiosity, were fixed on the telephote screen, the source of these shocking surprises.

CHAPTER III
Slane's Thoughts Up On Screen

Through a narrow gap in the drapes that separated the Blue Parlor from the Red, Freda had been observing these events. "What room is that on the screen?" she whispered.

Lipson stood next to her, with his arms stretched out and his fingers aimed at the spectators who sat facing the telephote screen. "It's the parlor of the farm-house outside Oakland, near San Francisco, where Mrs. Slane lived five years ago. I've made it so that the criminal recalls all the circumstances of his crime, and that his memories take the form of a hallucination, not just for him but for all those around him."

"Terrifying," said Freda, her voice trembling. She shivered, knowing she herself, along with Derrick, had been with Slane at that farm of dreadful memory outside Oakland. Yet her interest in the present scientific phenomenon predominated. She whispered, "But how can you make the telephone and the telephote obey you?"

Smiling, Lipson shook his head. "It's simple: they don't. In fact the tele-phone is silent, the screen is actually blank. Only the spectators—including you,

Mrs. Freda—under the power of a shared hallucination, a genuine waking nightmare, imagine they can see and hear Slane's memories." His voice softened with deep joy. "What do you think of the powers invented by your own May? No, don't answer. Watch and listen; you'll have plenty of time to voice your admiration later."

Lipson's fingers pointed even more rigidly at the people gathered in the Red Parlor. It seemed to Freda that some kind of emanation—almost invisible yet still perceptible—flowed from his fingertips and wrapped itself around the heads of the spectators. Was she imagining it? Was it real? She had no time to puzzle out the mystery.

The strange scene leading up to the crime from the past was still unfolding on the telephote screen—which Freda now knew was actually blank. Mrs. Slane had stood up. "Give my son William to that woman? I refuse!"

Slane's image gave a disagreeable laugh. "Dear Edith, you don't understand the situation. I'm the general secretary of the syndicate of American billionaires, but they're shrugging off my criticisms. I want a monopoly on all business undertakings in Asia, and they don't agree, because they don't think I have the financial wherewithal to commit myself far enough to inspire their confidence." He passed a hand across his brow and went on sarcastically, "I therefore have to put at the head of that syndicate the richest member of all that capitalist army—someone who, by committing his wealth even more than the rest, can break down all resistance."

"Why don't you make a deal with the great Mrs. Hibbett?" Mrs. Slane asked sharply.

Slane's image shrugged. "It must be obvious to you that that's the first thing I tried."

"And?"

"Mrs. Hibbett turned me down flat."

"Why?"

"Because she thinks I'm working mostly for my own advantage, and that as a result my plans must be detrimental to the prosperity of the syndicate." Slane's image gave a tragic laugh. "I was expecting her to refuse. For a long time now I've been aware that she distrusts me. But I'll get what I want. She's left me no way to get it except by criminal means. So here's to crime!"

Mrs. Slane tried to rise, but he pushed her back into her seat. "Her son Lloyd is studying at an English university. No one knows him here. His education is almost finished. He'll soon be brought back to America. He's already heard, from sources other than me, that he'll be appointed president of the syndicate of American billionaires. It's easy to predict that, coached by his mother, he'll thwart what she thinks are my plans... thinks correctly, in fact."

"That's certainly what will happen."

"It would happen, you mean to say, you naive woman, if that young man weren't doomed to die young."

"Why should he die?"

"Along with his mother and his little sister, the child by her second marriage."

"But why?"

"So that our William can inherit his name, and his entire fortune, and the presidency of the syndicate of billionaires, so that he can lead that organization—the most powerful in the world—in a way that suits my plans. His wealth, and mine, will reach magical heights: wealth that can bring down governments, that can ruin whole nations!"

Mrs. Slane cried out in protest, refusing to go along with his bold, sinister plot. But Slane, up on screen, forced her to drink a little orange-blossom water, to which he'd added poison. Soon the poor woman died. A brutal expression crossed his face, and he laughed harshly.

Slane called in Derrick and Freda, and told them about the oil well hidden under the floor. The car drove off, carrying Slane and his accomplices and their trunks—inside which, though the murderer didn't know it, Stepan and Sefra, those witnesses to the crime, were already hiding. The farm outside Oakland went up in flames, erasing all evidence of his vile deeds.

Suddenly the scene changed. The telephote screen transported the spectators to England. On the dock at Dover, far from eavesdroppers, Slane explained the details of his plans to his son William, who listened carefully.

"From now on you can think of yourself as Lloyd Hibbett, because that young man will be leaving England in two weeks, aboard the *Cyclopic*."

"All right—but people are going to notice the switch..."

"I already explained this: I raised you in isolation. Your face is unknown to anyone who might get in our way. So in a few weeks I'll set sail in my yacht *Follower*, while you, under an assumed name, will go to Batavia."

"In Java?"

"There you'll test the airship invented by my picked engineers. When it's time to act, I'll let you know. You'll announce that you're going to take the plane for a cruise over the Java Sea. That way you can fly over the *Cyclopic*. The point is—and nothing could be easier for you—to use the liquid carbon dioxide spray to wipe out all life aboard the ocean liner. When that's done you'll ditch the airship, whose wreckage will be found later. That'll establish the death of the pilot, X... whatever name you'll have been going under in Batavia. In fact, meanwhile, you'll make your way to Lloyd's cabin—Lloyd, whom my trusted men will already have sent to a discreet watery grave. And in his cabin is where we'll find you later. So even my accomplices will believe you're the real Lloyd Hibbett."

"Do we need to be so cautious? Our men can be trusted, we've got a hold over them..."

"The day after the big deed, son, they'd have a hold over us. By God, I wouldn't care if they tried to blackmail me. We'll be so rich we can let ourselves

106

be robbed with a smile. But one indiscreet word could topple everything we've built. So we can't let them speak that word. Therefore they'll never know what happened on the *Cyclopic*, and they'll believe absolutely that you're the real Lloyd Hibbett."

There was a long, heavy silence. Neither Princess Liao nor May nor Jane nor even Freda moved a muscle. Their faces were frozen in horror. Their eyes were fixed on the screen that had delivered such awful news. Tom Slane and the false Lloyd Hibbett, meanwhile, squirmed in their seats, struggling in vain against the mysterious force that paralyzed their will.

Trembling all over, Freda whispered into Lipson's ear, "After that he got Derrick and me hired on board the *Cyclopic*."

"Where, in saving your May, you also saved me, and my darling little Jane."

She nodded.

His voice growing sad, Lipson went on, "But who am I? We know Jane is Mrs. Hibbett's daughter. But whose son am I? Whose? I'd been told the name I used before wasn't my real name. Then what is my real name? Who's my family?"

Freda's lips trembled, and she looked at Lipson with pleading eyes. Perhaps at that moment—in spite of May's reiterated instructions—she was on the verge of telling him everything those devoted children Stepan and Sefra had found out about his origins.

But a gesture of Lipson's stopped the words in her throat. By sheer willpower the young man forced his attention back on the present. He stretched out his arms toward the Red Parlor and murmured, "On to the crime! Thoughts of the criminal, make yourselves manifest to all! Show us the crime!"

And then Freda, along with all the spectators gathered in the other room, witnessed a series of scenes, one after the other, like the scenes projected by a cinematograph—but more vivid, more affecting, more terrible. It was no longer a representation of life, it was life itself.

They saw the deck of the *Cyclopic*, and the officers on the bridge, under a blue-black sky spattered with stars. Strange! A woman, a passenger, was strolling by. Seeing her, May, Freda, and Lipson all felt the same shock: in that passing image they'd recognized Mrs. Hibbett.

By what amazing confluence of unknown wills, arising from the mystery of the hallucination induced by Lipson, had his own mother, and Jane's mother, been conjured up at that moment? Perhaps it was Slane's own mind that had retained the ineradicable image of the woman on whose account he'd condemned to death those hundreds of strangers aboard the *Cyclopic*.

They were all so shocked that none of them noticed Jane's reaction. The little girl had gone pale, as all her blood flowed to her heart. She clasped her hands and sighed, so quietly than no one heard her, "Mama!" The child's heart had retained the memory of the vanished woman.

But now the events on screen rushed along. A strange kind of aircraft appeared above the ocean liner. It dropped lower. An opalescent cloud shot out from the underside of the airship. It sank—such a heavy cloud!—it enveloped the maintops, and the sailors on lookout—and they collapsed, frozen into stiff attitudes. Still the fatal fog descended. It struck down the officers on the bridge, the man at the helm... and it put a fatal end to Mrs. Hibbett's stroll on deck. It blanketed the decks, and through every open hatchway it flowed down the stairs to the cabins. And still the airship sprayed out more fog, to follow endlessly what it had already spread. The machine in the sky poured death down onto the vessel in the sea. It was liquid carbon dioxide, turned into a gas by a special apparatus, that performed the role of messenger of death. To all aboard the ocean liner it brought not only a wave of cold—two hundred degrees below zero—but asphyxiation to finish anyone who might have survived freezing.

Then all the clouds dissipated, and the airship came down and alighted on deck, as gently as a bird. A man got out. Horrors! It was William Slane—that criminal who, till just recently, they'd all been calling Lloyd Hibbett.

He activated certain controls on his airship. It rose into the air, flew off into the distance, and disappeared. A few kilometers away from the *Cyclopic*, under its own power, it fell to the sea, where it floated: it would become the wreckage Slane had planned.

Meanwhile William strolled along the deck, indifferent, clearly without remorse for the slaughter he'd just caused. He vanished into a cabin, presumably the one assigned to the real Lloyd Hibbett.

Clearly Slane was fighting against the waking nightmare whose mysterious manifestation in the room terrified him, because now the scenes began to rush by as if he were trying to drive them from his thoughts.

The yacht *Follower* appeared and came alongside the *Cyclopic*. The spectators in the Red Parlor witnessed the looting of the Blue Star ocean liner—that enormous methodical robbery after the monstrous killing. They watched as the crew of the *Follower* ransacked the floating tomb and made off with the wealthy passengers' cash and jewelry.

And then the thieves left the ocean liner, and the *Follower* drew away. The yacht was not yet over the horizon when a blast of fire and smoke shattered the deck of the *Cyclopic* and punctured its hull, leaving gaping holes through which water poured into the ship. The great vessel sank to the bottom. The ocean surface was indented for a moment by the suction; then the waters closed over the spot and once more were calm.

No trace of the crime remained: that thought occurred with shocking clarity to everyone in the room. But then, in the minds of May and her friends, it was succeeded by a contradictory thought: one trace did remain, an intangible trace... the murderer's memory. And at that very moment the memory had been awakened. Why? How? Only May, Lipson, and Freda knew that the reconstruction of a past that seemed forgotten forever was a work of science—the accomplishment of one young woman. What had it taken to achieve that extraordinary result? Not much: only that an abandoned child grow up to become an engineer, thanks to the sacrifices of two rascals who, fed up with the bitter taste of crime, hungered for the sweetness of giving their love and devotion.

Behind the drapes, Lipson let his arms drop to his sides. Immediately the mind control that affected all of them dissipated and vanished. No more horror, no more images, nothing. In the Red Parlor, if it weren't for the pallor and terror lingering on their faces, no one could have guessed at the ghastly tragedy that had just played itself out in their minds.

Tragedy was the right word—a moral tragedy of astonishing brutality. Princess Liao had just learned she was betrothed to William Slane, a murderer hiding under the name of Lloyd Hibbett. Slane and Hibbett knew they'd been exposed, and they trembled—but they still didn't suspect that little Jane, seated near them, now knew who had murdered her mother.

The distress of every one of them would be impossible to describe. Each of them was in a state close to madness. The perpetrators and the victims floundered equally in their dismay. At first no one thought either to make accusations or to defend against them. They all had to recover some equanimity after that incomprehensible experience. It was as if they'd all forgotten they themselves were personally involved in the terrible story they'd suddenly witnessed. Their curiosity about how it had happened outweighed the horror it had caused, and that tone dominated their first exchanges.

"Did you see that?" whispered the princess to May.

The latter paused for a moment, then assumed an expression of surprise before answering calmly, "See? What should I have seen, Your Highness?"

"Why—the explanation for the disappearance of that English ocean liner, the *Cyclopic*, lost with all hands for reasons unknown!"

May was ready for the question. With astonishing coolness, she caused her delicate features to express even greater surprise. "I beg your pardon, Your Highness, but I don't understand."

"What?! You didn't see the terrifying images projected onto that telephote screen?"

"The screen was blank, Your Highness. I could swear it."

The princess gestured impatiently, but then she smiled, and took hold of Jane's hands. "Little Jane, did you see it?"

May started. For the same reasons she herself was denying the story, she hoped the little girl would deny it too. She worried that the formidable enemies against whom she'd just struck the first blow would have their suspicions, and she felt it would be best to let them face only Princess Liao as they struggled to explain away the bleak hallucination.

But alas—the child was going to tell the truth! Yet this time May was taken utterly by surprise. Jane looked straight at her with an inscrutable expression in her eyes, then in her sweet voice she answered, "I'm like your blonde friend.

You were staring at the screen, so I looked at it too, because you seemed to be seeing something. But I didn't see anything."

Slane was listening with an expression of dismay. What May and Jane said reassured him a little and let him recover some of his composure. He didn't think to doubt Jane: a child of her age was surely incapable of the logical sequence of thought that might have motivated May's response. He didn't realize that, apart from the complicated motives he could attribute to his own employee—for that was how he still thought of May—namely a wish to support him and to prove her zeal, there was another motive, one that on the surface might appear too straightforward, but that produced the same result.

"I love May," the little girl had said to herself. "I don't understand why she's claiming to have seen nothing. But I'll say the same thing, and that'll make her happy, which is what I want most of all."

So now Slane was reassured and comforted, almost smiling, as he drew encouragement from the little girl's words. By God, he himself had certainly suffered a hallucination, no doubt about that. But Princess Liao couldn't have experienced the same one, that stood to reason... It would be a good idea to question her.

Calmly and quietly, Slane asked, "My dear princess, what was it you saw up on the screen?"

The Chinese girl shuddered all over. She stared with genuine anxiety at each of them in turn. Then suddenly, veiling her dark pupils behind eyelids shining with mother-of-pearl and bordered by the dark line of her long lashes, not daring to speak but afraid to say nothing, she stammered, "Nothing, or almost nothing. I have a bit of a migraine. I was disoriented. If you don't mind, I'm going to retire."

Without waiting for their consent, the princess moved to the door, left the Red Parlor, and hurried to her room, where she wept desperately.

Slane and William exchanged a look. There was no doubt in their minds: the princess had fled to avoid answering Slane's questions. If her own hallucination hadn't been at the very least unflattering to him, she wouldn't have sought refuge in saying nothing. Her silence therefore loomed threateningly. Those threats didn't worry the two men personally: who could be powerful enough to harm them in their unassailable position of strength? But from the fact that they themselves were untouchable, it didn't follow that their plans were secure. And the linchpin of their schemes was the marriage of Princess Liao to the false Lloyd Hibbett.

In any case, clearing up the matter seemed impossible for now. The father and son withdrew—but not before Slane had warmly shaken May's hand and said, "I'm concerned about out lovely princess's health. Please bring me word at the Institute."

"I could phone you."

"No, no, don't use the telephone. My staff can be nosy and talkative. On the eve of the official betrothal, there's no need for us to hand material to the gossips in the crowd."

"I understand. I'll come as soon as Her Highness has let me see her."

The young woman accompanied the Slanes out to the street, leaving them—in spite of all their troubles—flattered by the obvious deference of their "employee."

But once the heavy front door had closed behind them, and the rumble of the engine made clear that their car was pulling away, May hurried back to the Red Parlor, where Jane, and now Lipson and Freda, were waiting for her. She cut short their praise for her skill as an inventor of hallucinations, and gave them instructions in a kind of nervous haste. "My dear Freda, you'll take Jane back to the house... And you, little Jane, promise me you won't sneak out again the way you did today."

The little girl shook her blonde curls rebelliously. "I'm bored all alone with Sefra. Oh, she's nice, and very obedient. She does everything I ask... But it's important to spent time around a variety of people!"

She spoke those last words with such comical gravity that the others couldn't help smiling.

"Of course, you've got to have variety, little angel," May agreed affectionately. "However, at the same time it's also important to consider the consequences of your actions."

"What consequences do you mean, my dear big sister?"

"I'll explain, little one. You love me dearly, don't you?"

"With all my heart, and even more," said the child loyally.

"You'd be sad if you didn't see me anymore?"

"Not see you anymore? That couldn't happen."

"Well, darling, your little escapade today, coming over to this house, could've separated us forever—by putting between us a barrier that can't be crossed."

"What barrier is that?"

After a pause, May said gently, "You're too young to talk about such things." The barrier she meant was death... and the young woman didn't want to utter the funereal word, which she imagined would rend the child's ears.

To her great surprise, little Jane burst out laughing—one of those crystalline laughs whose notes rise and fall over a rapid succession of thoughts and that express the joy of all children. Displeased by the unexpected effect of her words, May just listened. But she was shocked when little Jane recovered from laughing and went on, "Oh, you won't say what the barrier is."

"Why won't I?"

"Because I'm too young. You're worried about scaring me by telling me that my being here in Princess Liao's house could've led to your death, and that of all our friends, and mine too."

Freda cried out in dismay, "She knows what death is?"

"No, no…" began Lipson.

"Of course I do," interrupted Jane, still smiling. "It's when you're deceased, and you can't move, and you can't speak, and you can't breathe, and they put you in a room underground, that you never get out of again."

Their jaws dropped as they all listened.

She went on triumphantly, "Just like the people we saw up on the screen earlier—the lady at the farmhouse, the passengers on the *Cyclopic*…"

Her voice shook slightly on those last words. Suddenly she threw herself into May's arms. Burying her face in May's breast, she cried softly and sadly, "My mama! I recognized her walking on deck." She wept gently.

They all stood silent, shaken by this sudden glimpse into the mysterious depths of a child's heart. Though to them she'd still seemed to be no more than a darling little plaything, Jane had concealed within herself an acute understanding of the tragic struggle they were engaged in, and had taken on the burden of the grief they'd thought she was too young for.

Already the little girl had gained control over her passing emotions. She wrapped her arms affectionately around May's neck and pressed her rosy cheek to May's cheek, so that her blonde hair was intermingled adorably with that of the young scientist. Then she said slowly, "You see, I already knew everything you could say… You can see now that I already knew it. So I said to myself, it's a nuisance that I can only hug my May in secret. And just then you phoned to tell Sefra to be even more careful, because you were about to become the personal companion of our neighbor, Princess Liao…"

"You knew all about that too?"

"Of course, since it was about you."

That sweet reply earned the little girl a kiss. Encouraged, she went on, "Right away that gave me an idea—to have the princess introduce us. That way everyone would know we knew each other, and I'd be free to see you."

Lipson and Freda considered the girl, who showed so clearly the faculty of logic and the ability to reason that superficial observers deny children are capable of.

Unconsciously, May pressed the little darling closer to her heart. Her protégée's diplomatic subtlety astonished her and filled her with relief. She needed to understand more completely, so with a kiss she asked, "You didn't know the princess?"

"Of course not."

"In that case, how could you know she'd agree to introduce us?"

That prompted the child to burst out laughing once again. "Aren't children allowed to do whatever they want?" she said with a knowing air. None of them was able to keep a straight face. Though she'd grown serious again, Jane gave them time to laugh, then said calmly, "Follow my logic, sister May, and you'll see I had to succeed."

112

"I'm following, darling," said the young woman, curious for this insight into her little protégée's mind.

"The princess is a woman of the world, isn't she? The world of important people…"

"Important Chinese people," said Lipson playfully.

Jane paid no attention, and went on addressing May. "Therefore she'd take notice of a polite gesture. Oh, I know a grownup couldn't have dropped in for a neighborly visit—but a little thing like me could."

"I grant that. But once you'd paid your call, you could just go home again…"

"You're right, but that's what I didn't want to do."

"Well, you little schemer! You weren't counting on the princess keeping you…"

"On the contrary, that's exactly what I was counting on!" Seeing the look on May's face, Jane went on, "That surprises you… Ah, I'm pleased to be able to surprise a clever person like you. I'll explain everything. You remember the story you made me learn the other day, the fable by a French poet from far away across the Atlantic… There's a crow sitting in a tree with a chunk of cheese in his beak. At the foot of the tree there's a fox. Foxes can't climb, but this one sure wants that cheese. And he gets it, you remember, because 'flatterers live at the expense of those who listen to them.'"

"What are you talking about?"

"That fable. You must've forgotten it, but I remembered. I was inspired by the fox. I flattered the princess, and princesses appreciate that as much as other women, and so she couldn't do without me. There."

That unexpected application of La Fontaine's sublime fable, *The Fox and the Crow*, stunned the little girl's friends. She'd shown herself to be skillful, clever, even—why not say the word—a diplomat.

As if she could read her companions' thoughts, she hugged May tighter and said, "You know, I'll play the fox only with other people. With you, with James and our friends, I'll never be the fox—never, never."

From May's arms, Jane moved on to hug Lipson and Freda. Then, at May's urgent request, she obediently took Freda's hand and let herself be taken back to the house next door, where Sefra was still waiting anxiously to learn the result of the little girl's invasion of Princess Liao's mansion.

May and Lipson remained alone together in the Red Parlor. The pseudo-servant's eyes were fixed on the young woman with a look of such tenderness that she started. A shadow passed across her face, and her eyes were troubled for a moment. With her clenched hand she made an unconscious gesture of resolve.

"What's wrong, miss?"

Words alone are nothing—only the tone in which they're spoken gives them meaning. And the way Lipson had just asked that question turned it into the most loving of expressions. Everything about him hinted at the attachment he felt for the unknown young woman he'd met long ago on the *Cyclopic*, and whose ally he'd been for the past four years in the quest for vengeance and justice.

He'd agreed to follow her orders. He knew he was fighting on behalf of a certain Lloyd Hibbett, about whom he knew nothing—what he looked like, where he lived, nothing. What did it matter to him? By taking him off the doomed *Cyclopic* May had saved his life; naturally he'd dedicated that life to her. He'd loved her almost without knowing it. Every day he'd found another reason to love that young blonde agent of his own salvation. He'd discovered her charm, her grace, her courage, her moral and intellectual superiority, like an excited explorer in some marvelous new land.

May had long since understood that. Did she feel attracted by his affection, following the old saying—as true and as false as all old sayings—"Love elicits love"? If so, she hadn't admitted it even to herself. May's mathematical mind protested at the idea of a union between the Hibbett heir and the foundling child who'd been raised by a couple of wretches and who'd become an engineer thanks to the money her adoptive parents had set aside for her education from the profits of their crimes.

Today, when she launched her attack on the Slanes' peace of mind, she'd also promised herself to reveal to Lipson his true identity. He needed to know he was fighting on his own behalf, to avenge his mother, murdered far away on the fatal deck of that Blue Star ocean liner. And then, once he knew he was so wealthy, so far above other people in America, he'd be cured—so thought May—of an attraction she ought not to encourage.

The time had come to dress that moral wound: that was how the engineer described it to herself. But why, as she opened her mouth to begin the planned explanation, did she feel an ache in her heart? Why was her voice shaking? She didn't want to know, and she forced herself to do what she considered the logical and dutiful thing. "James," she began in a dull voice that gradually gained confidence, "back then, when we were all looking at the telephote screen, did you notice that woman passenger who was strolling on deck just before the attack?"

"Of course!"

"No doubt you recognized her?"

"On the *Cyclopic* I thought too much about Mrs. Hibbett to have forgotten her. You'll recall that I tried in vain to find her son, that son who was so carefully disguised."

"And did you find him?"

"Alas, no."

"Now that we're locked in battle against the vile Slane, I want you to know. Before now, it would've been too much for you—the news would've seemed too heavy to bear. Waiting anxiously for me to perfect my invention was hard enough."

Lipson watched her with growing surprise. "How strange you sound!"

"Rightly so, my friend, because poor Mrs. Hibbett's son, darling Jane's older brother, is..." She paused for a moment. Suddenly she felt out of breath. Her lips refused to finish speaking the words.

Not noticing her struggle, and impelled by curiosity, he prompted, "Is?..."

"Is you, Lloyd Hibbett," she said finally, her voice cracking.

He cried out, "Me! Me!" Then he came to her, his hands outstretched, his face shining. "Ah! If it wasn't for avenging my dear mother, and restoring Jane's fortune, how little I'd care about this news!..." But then his tone changed abruptly. "No, that's not true. A man needs wealth to adorn the altar of his divinity... And my divinity—now it's my turn to reveal something to you, May—my divinity is..."

Everything about him expressed the thought, "is you!" But he didn't get to utter the words that would have committed him for life. Instead she interrupted him fiercely. "Are you so superficial, James, that you're prepared to spend your time on matters of no account?"

"Of no account!" he echoed, stunned.

"Absolutely. To avenge your mother, to restore Jane to her rights, those are the only duties that should guide you..."

"Sure, but after that..."

"After that you'll still have to render one final satisfaction to the spirit of the dear departed woman, which must be wandering sadly and anxiously around us. She wanted you to take the leadership of the syndicate of American billionaires, so that you could foil Slane's plans and replace them with beneficial initiatives."

"Am I saying I won't?"

"No. But you can't imagine the work that'll be necessary to bring that about. To achieve what Mrs. Hibbett wanted, you'll have to drive all other concerns from your mind and your heart. From now on your time, your blood, your heart, your mind, must all be devoted to that task and to nothing else! The slightest distraction would be a betrayal—and the worst kind of all: the betrayal of the dead!"

Cowed by the young woman's tone, and with the despairing feeling that a barrier had risen suddenly between them, obscuring the joyful romantic dream that had sprouted in his heart, Lipson was left speechless, motionless, his face frozen bleakly with the look of those who've just felt the slap of the black wing of Fate.

May gave him a look of infinite sweetness—then abruptly seemed to recover her resolve. "Do you understand, Mr. Hibbett?"

"Oh!" he protested, "don't address me as Mister and break the equality between us!" He meant that, in English usage, only an inferior addressing his superior uses the title Mister in front of his name.

She still had her bright eyes fixed on him with the self-sacrifice of martyrs in the arena impassively facing down the lions and the crowd eager to enjoy their suffering. Only a slight roll of her shoulders suggested the great desperation of her sacrifice. In an artificial tone she said, "It would be more proper, given our respective positions. But it's not important, and I won't insist. Whether I call you Mister or not, it won't change the fact that you'll still be the heir to the greatest fortune in the world, and I'll still be a humble engineer raised on the charity of a couple of criminals whom I love and whom I forgive for branding my forehead with that mark of shame."

He held out his hands pleadingly to her, everything about him expressing his love.

She replied with a gesture that seemed to sever all bonds between them, and in a harsh, almost curt voice she said, "You understand, James—I'll have to call you that for the time being. From now on you must think of no one but your mother, who has passed on to the other side, and your little sister Jane, whose fate is tied to yours."

With stiff steps—like a statue walking, to use a common expression that's simultaneously naive and picturesque—she left the Red Parlor.

But when the door had closed behind her, her strength deserted her. A sob shook her whole body, and she had to lean against the wall to keep from falling. But the valiant young woman allowed that weakness to last only a moment. By sheer willpower she regained her self-control, forced her heartbeat to return to normal, dried her tear-filled eyes with an impatient hand, and lifted her head.

"Come on now, May, drive away those foolish notions. A mathematical mind shouldn't give way to the ridiculous dreams of those amiable crackpots known as poets. Think about nothing but the duty you've taken on." She raised her big blue eyes to heaven. "Mrs. Hibbett is watching you," she added. "And when the job is done, and you go to join her, she'll say, 'Thank you, my child!'"

CHAPTER IV
A Cage for a Mechanical Bird

Half an hour later, May emerged from the bedroom on the ground floor of Princess Liao's mansion, where the princess had locked herself to hide her emotions after seeing those upsetting visions on the telephote. The two young women stood in the doorway with their hands clasped together, seeming to have some difficulty letting go. The princess's slightly almond-shaped black eyes, her delicately amber-colored face, her posture, all betrayed fear and alarm. Lowering her voice, she whispered, "I can't understand it. It's all witchcraft. It's beyond the power of human beings."

"But I've told you," said the scientist a trifle impatiently, "it was just a simple scientific demonstration."

Like a guilty schoolgirl caught in the act, the princess went on, "Don't be angry. Perhaps my Chinese education keeps me from taking these things in all at once. In the Forbidden City, neither the servants who took care of me as a child nor the scholars who educated me ever spoke to me of such marvels of science. I'll do my best to adapt to this new knowledge." She went pleadingly, "What does it matter to you, anyway? I trust you—you who dropped so suddenly into my life to warn me of the pit I was about to fall into. I'll obey you."

Slane would certainly have been surprised at the princess's striking submissiveness to the former typist. He'd have been worried by the authority the new personal companion had assumed over the descendant of the Manchu conquerors[14]—a princess till now so vain about her high birth and so haughty that Tom and William Slane themselves had been forced into unaccustomed deference so as not to offend the proud daughter of the emperor who'd been driven from the Imperial City by a revolution of the Han Chinese.

But now May went on, "So you'll keep little Jane and her servant Sefra with you?"

"As I've promised."

"And tomorrow they'll go with you to Buena Vista Park."

"Yes, yes, as I said. Have I not set your will over mine?"

May pressed the princess's slender fingers affectionately. "I beg you, Princess, don't speak of will. Say only that you've entrusted your heart to mine."

That way of putting it brought a smile to the princess's lips. "That's what I'll say," she promised. "I'll say it all the more willingly because I believe it expresses the truth." She went on admiringly, "You're so brave! A little while ago I was in despair, ready to escape into the death that leads to the feet of the Ten Thousand Benevolent Buddhas. Then you came, and I've regained hope. Those villains who lied to me no longer seem invincible…"

"And they aren't—as long as…"

"As long as they don't suspect what we're really thinking. Oh, that's clear to me, very clear. Don't worry. Our Chinese courtesy—so much greater than that of white men—has trained us in the art of constant dissembling… I'll behave to our enemies with imperial courtesy."

They smiled at each other, bonded forever by the danger they were going to confront together.

May grew serious again, and unclasped her hands from the princess's. "I'm going—there's still so much to do. Believe me, Princess, either you'll be rescued or I'll die trying."

"I believe you."

For one moment longer, the black eyes and the blue eyes exchanged a promise of absolute trust. Then, at a sign from May, Princess Liao returned to her room, while her personal companion hurried down the stairs and out onto Fulton Street.

She didn't go far. Barely fifty meters from the Liao mansion she stopped before a small house of modest appearance, whose narrow front seemed to have

---

[14] The last Chinese imperial dynasty, the Qing (1644-1911), was established by invasion and conquest from Manchuria. The 1911 Revolution that overthrew the Manchus was led by native (ethnically Han) Chinese.

slipped humbly into position between the grand façades of the luxurious mansions lining Fulton Street. There was a copper knocker on the door, but she didn't use it. After glancing around to make sure no one was watching her, she put a key into the lock, turned it with a light click, and opened the door. She went inside and closed the door quickly, keeping curious passersby from seeing in.

But she hadn't taken three steps across the tiled vestibule before a living projectile threw itself upon her, while a childish voice cried joyfully, "It's sister May! It's sister May!" and little Jane wrapped her arms around the young woman's neck.

Sefra appeared behind her, scolding, "All right, Miss Jane, enough!"

The scientist interrupted her. "Don't scold her, my dear. The instructions I just sent you must've made clear that our battle plans have changed." Before Sefra could express her surprise, May went on, "This evening you'll take Jane back to Princess Liao's."

"To the princess?..."

"Hurrah!" cried the little girl, clapping her hands.

"Yes," continued May. "You'll both have dinner there: Jane with Princess Liao, you with Mr. James."

"Very good, miss."

"The princess will want the child to spend the night. You won't say no, but your condition for agreeing will be that you too can stay over at Her Highness's house."

Sefra's eyes widened. Clearly these unexpected instructions gave her pause.

It was Jane who answered May. "So, are you satisfied with your little sister, May?"

The young woman smiled. "A little sister who began by making me very afraid."

"Yes, yes," said Jane with a knowing air, "you were worried I'd tell people things that were none of their business." And with a sarcasm unusual in a child of her age she went on, "There was no risk of that. There are matters I don't understand very well, but I knew... Oh, I knew perfectly well people would try to kill you, and kill James, if they found out all three of us love each other." She danced on one foot. "Now you and I can love each other, since we've been introduced at the princess's."

May's only answer was to press the child to her heart. Then she set her down again. "The minutes are flying by," she said to herself. Aloud she said, "Jane, you don't need to worry about the princess anymore. She's one of our friends now."

"All the better!"

"Why do you say that?"

"Because she's nice. I didn't like thinking of her as one of the bad people."

"Ah, perfect. Well, she's no longer one of them. But it's possible we'll be dragged into a journey, maybe even a long journey, with the men you saw at Her Highness's."

"Mr. Slane?"

"And the one who calls himself Lloyd Hibbett."

"And who's actually just Slane's son, William... We learned about that from the screen."

May nodded in approval. Her remaining fears were evaporating before this new proof of the seven-year-old girl's lively intelligence. "All right, listen to me now, just as carefully as you paid attention to the screen..."

"Oh, sister May, I'm always happy to listen to you. You've got such a lovely voice... You see... I don't know quite how to put it... But anyway, there's nothing I like quite so much."

While she spoke, the affectionate little thing was putting out her lips for a kiss, which May didn't refuse her. "Darling, if the journey I predict takes place, we'll have be on our guard constantly against the Slanes."

The little girl solemnly held out her hand. "Oh, those nasty men are stupid. You saw how they didn't suspect we had an understanding. We'll keep it up. You can't imagine how happy it makes me to work for my beloved big sister's victory."

There followed another flood of kisses. May had trouble disentangling the child's arms from around her neck. Then she moved toward the front door—but Sefra came quickly to her, and in a shaking voice she stammered, "And what about Stepan, miss?"

May stroked the girl's hair. "Don't worry, poor Sefra. You'll see your friend Stepan tomorrow at Buena Vista Park."

"Oh, thank you, miss! That's all I need."

"I'll let Freda know too. It's important that she go with you tomorrow."

Then the front door closed, and May was gone. She hurried away down Fulton Street, her heels ringing rapidly on the sidewalk. She was retracing in reverse the route that a few hours earlier had led her to the mansion of the daughter of the emperor who'd been overthrown by the Chinese people.

She soon reached Kearny Street, and followed the line of great buildings of the Institute of Inventors: the business offices, the labs, the workshops where practical products were created from the theoretical discoveries of the researchers employed by the vast enterprise Tom Slane had managed to bring into being. Her pace had slowed, as if she was hesitating about which direction to go. Indeed someone who could read her mind would have heard her thinking, "I have to warn Derrick. Could I do it later? Better to take a chance on bad luck than show up in the workshops before the appointed time. Besides, Stepan is a reliable go-between."

She nodded firmly. Her hesitation came to an end, and soon she passed through the entrance leading to the administrative offices of the Institute of Inventors. She crossed the antechamber of the director's office without slowing down, greeting in passing the imposing doorman still ensconced in his armchair. Stepan wasn't there; presumably he was out on some errand. She didn't seem to register his absence and went straight to the door to Slane's office. This time she didn't go in without knocking first. On the contrary, she rapped twice on the door, quietly yet very distinctly. She waited ten seconds, then finally made up her mind to enter that room—where the hopes of all the unrecognized inventors in the United States came to rest, to flourish, or to die.

But certainly at that moment the man in the room—the room where he'd forced the brain of the New World to pulsate—had nothing of his normal dictatorial look. Slumped at his grand desk, his face buried in his hands, Slane seemed lost in some dark daydream that shook his sturdy body. Across from him, William nervously smoked a cigarette. The young man's pale face and haunted eyes suggested that at present his thoughts too had nothing rose-tinted about them.

At the sound of the door opening quietly, Slane looked up. His eyes shone as he recognized May. He rose partway to point her to a chair—an honor he reserved for very few people—and then said hoarsely, "Well?"

"I've just come from Fulton Street, sir."

"Were you able to talk to Liao?" His troubles made Slane forget to call the princess by her title.

May seemed not to notice the unconscious omission. "I was indeed, but without achieving much."

"What do you mean?"

"That I didn't get a definite answer. The princess suffered a hallucination, that's for sure. Anyway, she's not trying to hide it. But even when I showed a friendly interest, and questioned her about it..."

"Well, she must've said something!"

"Of course."

"Give us her exact words. They might help put us on the right track."

"'Dear Princess,' I said, 'tell your personal companion—who already feels as devoted to you as an old friend—what frightened you. The memory of it will weigh less on you.' She took my hands and pressed them to her heart, which was pounding wildly in her chest. But the only words I could get from her were, 'Horrible! Horrible!'"

Slane and William shuddered. May's report added to the unease they'd felt since they left Fulton Street. They'd returned to their office in a state of unspeakable anxiety. They were shaken by the strangeness of what had happened, and by their inability to explain it plausibly. May's arrival had given them reassurance... a reassurance that her explanation was now undermining.

"In short, she refused to tell you...?"

"Refused? No, she didn't refuse. She seemed distracted, unable to hold a conversation, lost in her thoughts. The proof that she didn't refuse is, when I grew quiet—discouraged by my lack of success—she began to talk. Oh, just to herself! She'd obviously forgotten I was there."

"What did she say?" The father and son had straightened up, their whole bodies eager for answers.

May appeared to be somewhat embarrassed. "I beg your pardon for what I'm about to repeat—but it's my job to repeat everything, isn't it?"

"Of course, speak without the slightest fear."

"All right. Princess Liao cried, 'I can't go through with the betrothal! I mustn't go to Buena Vista Park tomorrow!'"

"By the devil," growled Slane angrily as he slammed his fist onto the desk, "if she stays away it'll be the ruin of all my hopes!"

May smiled—a smile whose subtle sarcasm escaped her listeners. "Don't worry, sir. Knowing that a man like you doesn't do anything without a reason, I persuaded the princess not to provoke a scandal."

"You did?"

"Very easily. 'Your Highness,' I said, 'the betrothal is nothing but empty show—only the wedding counts. Now, the invitations for tomorrow have all been sent, and accepted. To cancel the event now would bring down severe discredit not only on Mr. Slane and Mr. Hibbett but on you...'"

"Very well argued."

"It was easy," said the young woman again modestly. "In short, she'll be there. However..." Once more she seemed to hesitate. "She plans to cancel the wedding itself—and in spite of all my efforts I couldn't change her mind about that."

Slane clenched his fist as if he were about to slam it on the desk again. William ground his teeth.

May calmed them by going on in her gentle voice, as mildly as if nothing unusual were being discussed, "The important thing, it seems to me, is to get her to Buena Vista Park tomorrow."

"How?"

"Well, my idea might be good or it might be bad—you be the judge. What if you throw a lunch on board the new airship built at the Institute? Combining the betrothal with a little free publicity, if you get me?"

"And then?"

"What's to keep you from flying away—with Princess Liao and a few of your loyal staff: me, your mechanic Derrick, your trusty Freda, your errand boy Stepan..."

"Kidnap her? And take her where?"

"Anywhere you want, sir—wherever you feel like holding the wedding. Didn't you already announce that the wedding wouldn't take place in San Francisco? Obviously your preference was to hold it somewhere else."

"You figured that out?"

"You have to admit it wasn't hard: all the signs point to it."

"No, no. Other people didn't understand it was my *preference*. They thought of everything, except that it was a preference guided by my interests. You're very intelligent, and you'll have proof of my satisfaction with your services."

The two men's faces had brightened. The young woman's words seemed to them the epitome of wisdom.

Slane shook her hand enthusiastically. "That's fine, Miss May! I'll certainly remember you. By Old Nick's forked tail, I'll do exactly as you suggest. So, till tomorrow. Go back to that impressionable Liao, and make sure she doesn't create any new difficulties for us." But then he changed his mind. "No, first, come see the airship with us. I have complete trust in you. I want you there when I plan the flight." He added almost warmly, "You know, if you have any criticisms, don't hesitate to share them. You're smart enough for it to be worthwhile to let you say whatever you want."

She bowed as if flattered by the compliment. But she was actually thinking to herself, "This way he'll lead us where he wants to go—he'll show us his real goal. And that's exactly what I need to know to defeat him, and to give James and my darling Jane back what they've been robbed of!"

Though Slane, clearly content with her apparent loyalty, motioned for her to precede him out of the room, she stepped aside to let him pass, murmuring, "I wouldn't presume, sir. I'm not worthy."

And that only added to the satisfaction of the Director of the Institute of Inventors.

But thanks to that gesture May was able to hang back a few steps as they crossed the antechamber, so that she could whisper into Stepan's ear, "See Derrick this evening and get his instructions for tomorrow."

The boy nodded slightly and seemed to be absorbed more than ever in the illustrated newspaper in his hands.

Meanwhile May hurried to catch up, and joined the father and son in the elevator, whose sturdy gate Slane had opened with a tiny key. A locked elevator was strange enough; even stranger was that the machine didn't rise to the upper floors, it dropped into the cellar—a "lift" that sank!

Through lowered lashes, the young woman gave a sharp, inquisitive look around. She realized she was about to enter the subterranean plant—entry to which was strictly forbidden to the staff in the offices and workshops aboveground.

Indeed the Institute had workshops on two levels: On the surface were those dedicated to making steel plates for battleships, steel canons, and metal armatures; to assembling electrical devices of all kinds for heating, lighting, telecommunications, etc.; in a word, to meeting the demands of all the normal industries of the world. The uninitiated public admired those workshops, without suspecting that the visible facilities were the less interesting half of the Institute of Inventors.

What would be the point of setting up hundreds of labs, in which—like monks of science—inventors, engineers, chemists, doctors, bacteriologists, etc. etc., lived and worked... if their research were confined to the limits of conventional industry? Among those researchers were a few whose work had resulted in unprecedented discoveries. The underground laboratories were set aside for them. Restricted access—tightly patrolled around the clock by well-armed guards—gave them the security they needed to work in secret on inventions whose later dissemination stunned the world.

Vague rumors had spread of the existence of workshops hidden underground. May had often heard about them in more detail from her adoptive father, Derrick, who—along with others whom Slane trusted completely—had free access to them. She'd trembled as she imagined the incredible power of the weapons produced in those mysterious labs and available to the enemies she'd sworn to defeat. More than once she'd expressed her mathematical regret that she couldn't assess with her own eyes the output of the "forbidden workshops."

And now she was about to have her anxious curiosity satisfied. She would see and even touch the machines—and all with her enemy's permission! Wasn't it like some kind of warning from the Infinite that presides over human affairs? The complacency of the Slanes was their first flaw. Didn't it hint that other flaws would follow? That the triumph of crime had lasted long enough? That the murderers, unwittingly driven along by destiny, were moving from the dazzling heights of the Capitol toward the abyss at the foot of the cliff crowned by the Tarpeian Rock?[15]

The sinking "lift" stopped without a bump. May estimated they'd descended forty or fifty meters—between twelve and fifteen floors—perpendicularly. Once again Slane used his key to open the elevator cage, and William and May followed him out into the underground space.

They were standing in a circular hall whose vaulted ceiling, made of mortared blocks of the kind of limestone used for millstones, was broken only by the dark opening of the elevator shaft rising toward the light of day. Facing them was the entrance to a corridor, three or four meters wide, that was lit by electric lamps fastened to the walls. Motioning to the others to follow him, Slane started down the corridor.

After thirty paces they were stopped by a heavy oak door reinforced with iron. But all the Director of the Institute of Inventors had to do was press a button hidden in the ornamental ironwork; the lock turned, and the door swung slowly on its hinges.

---

[15] In Ancient Rome, traitors and other high criminals were executed by being thrown off the Tarpeian Rock, a cliff near the Capitol (the seat of power). The expression "the Tarpeian Rock is close to the Capitol" means that the fall from high to low can happen quickly.

May couldn't stifle a cry of admiration. Before her she saw an immense hall filled with the hum of countless turbines spinning with dizzying speed. She could tell at a glance both that this was the generator room, producing the power needed to run all the machine tools in the underground workshops, and that electricity alone was the generating force.

A guard seated in a glass booth next to the door with a revolver in his hand rose menacingly. But when he recognized the director he saluted in military fashion and sat back down.

Slane had heard May's stifled cry, and he turned to her. "Do you find it beautiful?"

"I couldn't have dared dream of anything like it," she answered quite sincerely.

Her words pleased him, and he went on, "Good. When I trust someone enough to reveal this to them, I'd like them to be aware of what it says about the abilities of the boss they're working for."

She bowed.

"That's why I invited you to come along," he said. "An intelligent and logical young woman like you will find a stroll through this workshop quite enlightening."

This time she felt obliged to thank him. "I'm most grateful to you... But I wonder if I might be allowed to ask for an explanation."

"Of course. Ask away."

"These turbines here... What power drives them?"

"A waterfall."

Stunned, she echoed, "A waterfall—here?"

Her reaction seemed to amuse Slane. A silent laugh creased his face. "We're near the sea, you curious typist. A channel cut through bedrock brings water from three miles offshore."

The stupefaction on her face made him laugh even more. In fact Slane's answer had petrified May. In a flash her mind had calculated the vast sums needed to carry out a job like that. And that fresh realization of the enormous means at the disposal of her terrible enemy made her heart ache.

But Slane had put his arm through his son's and set off again. May wandered along after them, looking around her with wide eyes. They crossed the turbine hall and entered a workshop where giant flamethrowers hurled fire that melted metal blocks almost instantly. Showers of sparks rose everywhere— green, blue, red, yellow, violet, depending on the metal being treated. The effect was magical, enchanting.

"The foundry," explained Slane with some arrogance. "We no longer have furnaces and ovens, which cost so much to install. Instead cylinders to store liquid hydrogen, and these flamethrowers, are all we need to exceed any temperature reachable by conventional industry. As you see, we can instantly liquify copper, iron, platinum, granite, basalt..."

May nodded to show she was grateful for the explanation. But she didn't say a word. The young woman, overwhelmed by the power on display, was incapable of making a sound. The use of liquid hydrogen, on a scale unknown to industry, crushed her spirits by reemphasizing in her thoughts the power of the man she meant to defeat. And through her mind ran the troubling question confronted by all the philosophers who've come face to face with evil geniuses: How had he turned to crime? Why had this man of supreme intelligence sunk to villainy, when the road to virtuous success was open to him?

They saw one workshop after another. One of them, into which they didn't go, looked to May like a giant lantern, whose facets shone with blinding light.

Slane explained, "The sides appear to be glass, don't they?"

"Indeed they do!"

"They're steel plates!"

"Steel!" she stammered. "But what kind of light can pass through them like that?"

"Radiation from the rare earths, that's all it is."

Of all the rare earths, the best known is radium! May shivered. What kind of gargantuan experiments were going on in those underground workshops to produce that flood of radiation? Every step brought her new proof of the almost limitless power gathered by the man now guiding her.

His explanation finished, Slane had walked on. Now the corridor led past the doors of workshops from which escaped a deafening din. Shouting, singing, snatches of orchestral music, all blended together in the most appalling cacophony.

"Cinema images and phonograph sounds," called out Slane. "We're very close to the commercial launch of the first genuine and perfected Talking Pictures—the exact representation of life, toward which all the other industrialists are still just groping clumsily." He went on sarcastically, "It should sell very well. Ha, ha! The science involved is insignificant, but you can't pooh-pooh the commercial side of it, as you can imagine, Miss May!"

His laugh had something metallic about it, something that left an unpleasant impression. May's heart ached, and her lips trembled.

Luckily Slane didn't think to observe her. He was going straight ahead, made giddy in a sense by the enormous organism his own willpower had created. The hum of machinery, the clicking of switches opening and closing electrical circuits, the whistling of gas jets breaking up larger masses into smaller, the purring of transformers—all of it was like a concert in his honor. The hundreds of sounds all sang of the power of his mind, and of his organization. He'd outdone all the rulers, all the tyrants whose memory is preserved in human history. They'd reduced men to slaves; he had tamed science, which is to say the power of the mind.

With a strange rustling, a tall plate of steel that blocked the corridor slid aside on rolling rails, revealing an arched opening—and May couldn't hold back a cry of admiration. "Oh!"

Slane smiled. He'd been expecting that reaction, and in fact had provoked it, by calling ahead on the internal phone line with an order to close the entrance to the airship hangar.

The young woman now followed him into that hangar. It was a vast rotunda, thirty meters high, whose steel ribs curved down from the ceiling to the floor like lines of longitude on a terrestrial globe. The surface between those metal joists was covered with ceramic tiles in an array of bright colors.

But the *container* held May's attention for barely a moment; her eyes were fastened helplessly on the thing *contained*—the precious machine for which this monumental hangar had been built. It stood in the center of the hall, enormous, its hull vaguely resembling that of a ship, its sides dotted with round shapes that the engineer had no trouble identifying as the mouths of turbines, no doubt used for propulsion.

"The Slane airship," said the Director of the Institute of Inventors with emphasis. He said no more; those few words seemed sufficient.

And indeed they appeared to have overwhelmed the young woman. She stood there motionless, suddenly recalling in her mind's eye the fatal vision of the *Cyclopic* under attack in the middle of the Java Sea. The machine that had rained down freezing cold and asphyxiation and death on the ocean liner had also been an airship, the ancestor of the one before her now. She stared at it desperately, as if gripped by the mad notion that she could spot the stigmata of the crime—as if inanimate objects could remember.

Then she started: Slane had begun to speak again. He was addressing a group of men who'd come toward them without May noticing. They weren't workmen, since they were dressed a little like sailors in uniform.

"Captain Bubany, Lieutenant Black, men… We'll be taking off from Buena Vista Park tomorrow with a few passengers on board. The time for the payment you've been promised is coming soon."

"Hurrah!" cried the men, galvanized by his words.

"Hurrah, if you say so," agreed Slane in a sarcastic tone they missed. "In any case, I'm counting on you. Tonight you'll take our *Vulture*"—he pointed to the airship—"out of the hangar. Tomorrow, promptly at my signal, you need to be ready to land at the central roundabout in Buena Vista Park. That way everything will be in position for the betrothal of Mr. Hibbett and Her Highness Princess Liao."

As she stood there quietly and listened, it struck May that for her those orders spelled the irrevocable start of the all-out battle. Just then she felt a hand touch her arm gently. Next to her stood Derrick, dressed in a mechanic's blue overalls. Without betraying the least surprise, May murmured in a voice as quiet as a whisper, "He means to kidnap Princess Liao."

"We'll be on board," he answered in the same way. "Should I warn the others?"

"Only Stepan. He'll join you when he gets off work."

"But what about Freda and Mr. James?..."

"I've taken care of that."

Slane turned to her with a smile. "I'll take you on a quick tour of the *Vulture*. In order to make the princess comfortable on board, you'll need to be familiar with its features."

May nodded, and hurried to follow Slane, who was already climbing a light retractable staircase that provided access to the inside of the airship.

For half an hour the villain led her around the interior of the airship, over which she repeatedly exclaimed in admiration. She was certainly sincere: she was awed by this tremendous machine that gave its owner the mastery of the skies. But at the same time she blessed the benevolence of the mysterious fates that had come to the aid of the good people fighting against the criminals—a benevolence thanks to which Slane himself was making it possible for her to reconnoiter the ground on which she and her friends would have to do battle.

When she finally left the Institute she returned to her house on Fulton Street, where she found Lipson waiting for her. They held a short conference in low voices, a conference that ended with these words: "We're risking our lives, James. One last time I have to warn you of that."

"Fine! You know, May, you're risking your life entirely out of friendship for us. It'd be shameful if I hesitated to risk mine." He thought for a moment. "Unless you agreed to withdraw from the whole business."

She broke in, "Never!"

"Then let's go ahead. Anyway, I have to tell you, May, I wouldn't find dying with you at all unpleasant!"

The following day seemed like some kind of national holiday. Buena Vista Park was lavishly festooned. Temporary pavilions set up for the occasion provided plenty of buffet tables where the guests, in spite of their great numbers, could eat and drink without waiting or being crowded. Attendants at the park gates let in only those with invitations, and were deaf to the appeals of the gawkers crowded outside, who stared curiously at the multitude of financial, commercial, political, and scientific eminences who'd come running at Slane's and Hibbett's invitation, and who were delighted and enchanted to be there.

Unobservant people said, "Oh, this marriage will join together hundreds of millions of dollars—but it'll also be the union of two lovestruck hearts!"

But anyone looking more closely could have noticed a number of signs suggesting that the parties involved were deeply worried. From time to time Slane and Hibbett were unable to suppress a surreptitious gesture, an anxious glance, triggered by some unexpected noise—or perhaps just by some hidden thought.

Princess Liao's submissiveness now—after her reaction to the hallucination scene—struck them as troubling. Though they had complete confidence in May, they were filled with a nameless dread: they were still convinced the Chinese princess had experienced the same hallucination they had. If so, then how—why—had she been willing, after that, to carry on with the plans for the marriage?

Presumably to some extent she'd been influenced by that loyal little May's reasoning and persuasion. And yet the princess's complete obedience now struck them as unbelievable. Had she just fooled her new personal companion by pretending to agree with her? For all they knew, Princess Liao might have some thunderbolt planned, some twist that would expose the Director of the Institute and the Hibbett heir to accusations, and perhaps even lead to an unprecedented scandal that would put their positions at risk. As a result, Slane and Hibbett remained in unspeakable anguish.

And yet the time went on and nothing untoward happened.

Soon a rumor, news heard up to now by only a few privileged people, began to travel from group to group. Tom Slane was going to show off to his guests a brand-new marvel created in the Institute's laboratories on Kearny Street: an airship that had been undergoing trials for several years, and that gradual improvements had brought to perfection, and that would be donated to the United States government after one final demonstration.

Though Americans weren't as obsessed with aviation as Europeans, the news caused a genuine sensation. Bets were taken on the shape and the novel features of the airship, on the power of its engines, on the diameter of its propellers, on the size of the crew needed to steer it, etc. The people of the most wager-crazy country in the world gave themselves free rein, this time apparently with good reason: they claimed this new machine would be completely different from every airship already in operation anywhere.

What was more, it was a first-rate warplane, able to launch, not bombs like most warplanes—bombs that were now known to be relatively ineffective—but freezing clouds, or something like that, clouds that were heavier than air and that dropped automatically to the ground, where they wiped out all life. How was it done? What gases made up the fatal clouds? No one knew. The inventor and maker had jealously guarded his secrets. No matter! The plans for the airship, the chemical composition of the gas, the engines—everything about it was American, conceived and brought into being by citizens of the United States.

The result was inexpressible excitement. The "hip, hip, hurrahs!"—those cries of joy in the land of the dollar—mingled with the Spanish "vivas!," the German "achs!," and many others, since all the languages of Europe are spoken in the United States.

Suddenly the crowd froze. The drinkers set down their glasses without emptying them. The diners dropped their knives, their forks, their spoons. Everyone, nose in the air, was mesmerized by a moving dot that had appeared high in the sky.

"The airship! The airship!" The word went around, the volume rising as the news traveled out through the gates of the park and was repeated by the gawkers who hadn't been let in. They were delighted to be able to witness the one part of the ceremony that wouldn't be hidden from them by the trees in Buena Vista Park.

Meanwhile the airship was descending, following a long spiral. Its shape became clearer. It truly resembled some kind of submarine that, by magic, had been given the power to fly through the air. It came closer still. Now they could make out the rapidly spinning turbines placed along the underside, which accounted for the way it hovered and moved. They could even see the undercarriage that would allow it to land. A newer, longer, louder roar of acclaim shook the air inside and outside the park. For once the millionaire class and the working class were in agreement: the airship was a marvel. Still it descended.

Then gently, without a bump, the airship—thirty-five meters long, ten meters wide—set down in the middle of the central roundabout of Buena Vista Park. A tight pack of policemen burst from the shrubbery and spread out in a circle around the airship to keep anyone from approaching it. Inside the protected ring stood Slane and the man everyone knew as Lloyd Hibbett. They were anxious and impatient, as if waiting for something they'd given up hoping for. They craned their necks and stared down one of the avenues that ended at the roundabout. What were they looking for?

Princess Liao appeared, accompanied by May. Skipping along happily between the two young women, and holding them both by the hand, was little Jane. Some distance behind them came Lipson, walking with the calm dignity befitting a well-trained servant, and occasionally exchanging a few words with that other servant, young Sefra, who walked beside him.

Unconsciously, the Slanes shook hands. Hurrah! That little typist had persuaded the princess to come! If only the Chinese girl didn't change her mind now! If only she agreed to get on board the *Vulture*! Once she was on the airship, she could rebel all she liked—it wouldn't matter anymore. Hearts pounding, the Slanes kept their eyes on her. No... so far nothing was upsetting their plans. The princess started up the retractable staircase leading to the airship. Her companions followed her. Slane and William hurried after them, and began to run: now victory was theirs!

The top side of the airship fuselage resembled the bridge of a ship. Several people stood there, leaning on the steel balustrade and watching the new arrivals climb toward them. Stepan waved to welcome Sefra. Next to him, Derrick and Freda seemed paler than usual, and in low voices they spoke to each other poignantly.

"Right now all of us might be bidding farewell to life, Derrick."

He shrugged. "Oh, for you and me that farewell doesn't mean much!"

"Well, it's not for our sakes that I'm worried, that I'm trembling all over."

"I know that. You're worried about her, about our May... And what about me—you think I'm tickled to see her here? But she's the one who wanted it, she's the one who ordered it. We can't go against her wishes."

They both shook their heads sadly.

After a pause, Derrick went on, "She said, 'The airship itself will provide the first proof of the Slanes' guilt.'"

"That's what she said."

"Do you have any idea how this damned machine is going provide that proof?"

"No more than you do. But shush! They're coming up, they're almost here."

She was right: the little group of passengers coming aboard were now halfway up the retractable staircase that connected the roof deck of the airship with the ground. Not long after that, they were all aboard and lined up along the steel balustrade. Down below, still held back by the ring of policemen, the guests in the park greeted their appearance with loud cheers.

Slane seemed to have recovered his customary nerve. "Champagne!" he ordered happily. Servants came forward with silver trays bearing exquisite glasses of crystal ornamented with silver and precious stones. Slane leaned over the balustrade, put a megaphone to his lips, and roared, "We raise our glasses to the grand old United States! I would ask you all to please do the same!"

Cheers rolled across the sky like the rumble of thunder. The buffet pavilions were besieged. Within five minutes all the happy guests at this most original betrothal party were brandishing glasses, and self-appointed servers fanned out to pour rivers of foaming champagne.

Those libations didn't take people's attention off the stars of the celebration. The crowd could see Tom Slane, Lloyd Hibbett, and that Chinese girl, Princess Liao, holding up their glasses to toast. Down on the ground they all did the same, and proclaimed their patriotism in a loud hurrah in honor of the great Republic. No one could remain indifferent. The sight of the airship had fired up their imaginations to red hot. Notions of conquest, of global hegemony, bubbled to the surface in the presence of that airship—which they all realized could be an incalculably significant factor in any conflict between nations.

And no one noticed Slane pulling the princess inside the airship. The young woman had suddenly staggered, and her eyes blinked desperately.

With feigned concern the false Lloyd Hibbett cried, "She's fainting!"

Slane replied with a chuckle, "Yes, it must be the champagne."

Putting his arm around the princess, he held her up and practically carried her inside to the lounge. So far only William had followed him. When they'd stretched the princess out on a couch, the young man muttered, "You know, the sedative seems unnecessary. Even with her eyes open, what could she do to stop the airship taking off?"

133

Slane shrugged. "The park is full of photographers. You want someone to take a photo of her resisting?"

"I take your point. Now, when are we taking off?"

Slane began to laugh. He pressed a button to ring a bell. Then with a hint of triumph in his voice he said smoothly, "We've taken off."

From now on Princess Liao would have to give up hope of anyone rescuing her. She was in his power. She would have to bend to his will. Nothing stood in the way of the success of the terrible villain's plans.

And yet, at that very moment, out on the airship's roof deck, May gathered Lipson, Jane, Freda, Derrick, Stepan, and Sefra around her and said mysteriously, "Do you have the first message for the world?"

"Yes, yes," they all whispered.

"In that case, let it all go!"

No sooner had she finished speaking than a torrent of leaflets—typed and then mimeographed—rained down toward the ground. They tossed batch after batch overboard, while the airship, powered by its engines, rose into the deep blue sky. Of course the crowd ran to pick up those leaflets—a greeting from the great mechanical bird created by science—the moment the airship had lifted off. The police cordon was broken. Some of the leaflets, carried by the wind, came down outside the park and provoked open fighting among the gawkers, so eager were they all to get a copy. Insults and blows were exchanged, both inside and outside the park.

In the end, the leaflets wound up in the hands of the strongest or the cleverest, and they generously agreed to read aloud to their immediate neighbors the "ethereal communication"—as they insisted on calling it. The listeners were struck dumb when they heard what was written on those leaflets, which was as follows:

Princess Liao has been abducted by force, because she intended to refuse to bind herself in marriage to her fiancé. Why would she refuse? She believes she has evidence of a crime. She claims that, some years ago, Tom Slane and his son William caused the sinking of the ocean liner Cyclopic, *after the mass murder—by means of freezing gas, which their prototype airship was already able to spread—of the thousands of passengers, sailors, crewmen, etc., who were aboard the doomed vessel.*

The real Lloyd Hibbett, who is not the impostor presented under that name by Tom Slane, miraculously escaped from that hecatomb. He has sworn to avenge his mother, who was among the victims. He hopes soon to be able to unmask those murdering thieves, against whom he will file official charges with the legal authorities.

The press, and the syndicate of five hundred American billionaires, are urged to sever all ties with any entity connected to the perpetrators.

The world was left stunned. The newspapers and the telegraph lines carried endless commentary on the terrible accusations, some denying them, some leaning toward supporting them. The very fact of the debate undermined the position—heretofore unassailed and considered unassailable—of the Director of the Institute of Inventors and of his protégé, "Lloyd Hibbett in his own mind," as the more humorous papers called him.

May had struck the first blow of the ax against the criminal's power. But she was his prisoner aboard an airship that, flying at an altitude of two miles above the sea, was carrying her west at incalculable speed.

PART FOUR: TRIAL BY ILLUSION

CHAPTER I
Tom Slane's Plans

The interior of the airship—heavier than air in every sense, since its hull was made of interlocked aluminum plates—was laid out in an unusual way. A corridor ran around the entire circumference of the hull, encircling the various cabins, a lounge, and a dining room. Only at the rear was there a single spacious cabin that occupied the full width of the airship, with windows in the hull that brought in daylight.

A narrow staircase led down to the lower level, which housed the crew's quarters, the fully electric-powered engines, and the control room, whose principal equipment was an instrument panel filled with buttons labeled with symbols; those buttons directly operated the various functions of the airship. There was an exact duplicate of that instrument panel in the large rear cabin, which Slane and

William had taken as their own quarters. That way, if they wished, the two men could steer the airship themselves. All they had to do was to notify the pilot, via acoustical tube, that they were assuming control. The pilot switched off his instrument panel, and that was that.

That evening Slane and William had retired early, leaving May and Princess Liao in the lounge. Gathered around them like attentive servants were Lipson, Derrick and Freda, and young Stepan and Sefra. Darling little Jane seemed to be dozing in a rocking chair.

The criminals had withdrawn to escape from the princess. When she awoke from the artificial sleep produced by the sedative she'd drunk when the *Vulture* was still on the ground at Buena Vista Park, she had overwhelmed her kidnapers with endless awkward questions. Locking themselves in the rear cabin saved the villains from the annoyance of answering. They stood together, looking out through a window.

"We're over the Pacific," murmured William.

"And already fairly far from the coast," his father replied cheerfully. "We left San Francisco at four in the afternoon—'sixteen hundred hours' as the advocates of clock reform say. It's now eight—or twenty, if you prefer. We're traveling at about a hundred and fifty miles an hour. So that would put us about eleven hundred kilometers from land."

"And where are we going?... If the question isn't indiscreet."

"Not at all. We're heading straight for China, toward Mongolia,[16] where the dethroned emperor is waiting for us..."

"He's really waiting for us?"

"Eagerly, my dear 'Mr. Hibbett.' Because he assumes your marriage to the lovely Princess Liao will produce a flood of dollars—a flood that he intends to use to thwart the plans of the young Republic of China." Slane was chuckling as he spoke.

"Is he mistaken?" muttered William. "Please explain, because I'm never sure about anything with you."

That admission seemed to amuse Slane. He went on cheerfully, "Of course he's mistaken. What would be the goal of a syndicate of practical men like the one we control?"

"To make money, by God!"

"Exactly. In this case, to secure mining, railroad, and shipping concessions from the Chinese government."

"Concessions in everything, in a word."

"The very word. So our interests require smoothly functioning public services, civil order, and peace and quiet."

---

[16] D'Ivoi writes "Mongolia" here, thought later he places the ex-emperor firmly in Tibet.

William nodded. "Therefore what the ex-emperor wants is the opposite of what we want."

"Diametrically."

"So why make me marry that Liao, who inspires in me none of the feelings a wife is supposed to, at least according to the Holy Scriptures?"

Slake looked both amused and surprised. "That sounds like you're asking for an explanation."

In spite of his father's sarcastic tone, William didn't hesitate. "Certainly. I feel like a person works more effectively and more happily when he understands the point of what he's doing."

Slane had already recovered his gravity and self-control. In a benevolent tone he picked up where he'd left off. "Anyway, you'd have to find out before we reach China. One day sooner or later makes no difference. So listen carefully."

He led William to a seat, sat down himself, and cautiously lowered his voice as he went on. "Would you assume that a person who held the secret of the ex-emperor's hiding place, and who also held a precious hostage in the form of little Liao, might get anything he asked for from the government of the Republic of China?"

"Undeniably!" cried William, delighted to have been given a glimpse of Slane's plans. Nothing in William's mind balked at the betrayal implied in what he'd heard: the son was worthy of the father.

"Here's the situation," continued the latter, "a simple diagram of the politics involved. The existing status quo has everything to fear from the partisans of the previous status quo. Our 'living trump cards' make us in a sense the guarantors of the new regime. We can keep the peace or we can unleash civil war, just as we wish... Haha! It takes a great doctor to have the power, with a wave of his hand, to grant either sickness or health. Yes... and someone like that gets well paid, my boy—don't you think?"

"Very well paid," chuckled William.

"Even better paid than you think. While in China we'll be arbiters of peace and civic order, at the same time in Persia we'll be defending the prerogatives of the Shah against Russian and British encroachment."

William leapt to his feet and exclaimed in surprise, "Persia now? You've never spoken to me about Persia!"

"I wanted to keep it as a pleasant surprise, son," said Slane evasively.

"But why and how will Persia be mixed up in this?"

"I'm sorry to see you haven't studied contemporary history, my poor boy."

"Oh, never mind the platitudes about history, please. I'm only interested in the story you're telling me."

"I'm flattered. But you're wrong to disparage history, because it alone can shed light on your question."

"History?"

The look of alarm on his son's face made Slane laugh loudly. Then he raised his hand to get William's attention. "Princess Liao's mother was sister to the Shah of Persia. Therefore, you ignorant boy, by marrying the Chinese girl you become that monarch's nephew. I hope you can see the consequences. Thanks to your nepotistic intervention, the American billionaires' syndicate can get the Persian railroad concession, the river and maritime shipping concession, the mining concession—controlling the mines that once provided the wealth of the Persian dynasties and the power of the great cities of Babylon, Nineveh, and so on. A nephew inspires more trust than some English or Muscovite stranger."

"And he deserves that trust." William winked cynically.

"He deserves it," echoed Slane firmly. "Because it would be worth nothing to him to betray that fine sovereign…"

"But then…"

"Whereas of course his own interest dictates that he remain loyal."

"And how! I feel a burgeoning sense of loyalty…"

"That way you can smooth out whatever difficulties the Americans can't overcome."

"I'm not much of a diplomat."

Slane slapped him affectionately on the shoulder. "It's very straightforward diplomacy. The difficulties in question are all a matter of formalities."

"What do you mean?"

"That the Shah requires of his concessionaires a certain degree of outward show of respect toward his august person and toward his ministers: genuflection, granting precedence, you get the idea?"

"Perfectly. A nephew doesn't see these things the way foreign plenipoten-tiaries do. He can put up with anything to make his excellent uncle happy."

"Exactly."

"I see, I see. I secure all the profitable concessions…"

"No, no—the bad ones as well as the good ones."

William pressed his hands to his head. "Ugh! Now I don't understand again."

"But it's childishly simple. The good ones will become American compa-nies…"

The young man cried joyfully, "I get it! Whereas the bad ones will be passed on to the British, the Russians, the Germans—who'll take them, first of all to get a foothold in business in Persia…"

"And then," went on Slane solemnly, "to keep their competitors from gain-ing the same advantage."

"And those who take the concessions," added William, "will have to meet all the protocol demands my uncle the Shah requires—since we'll already have agreed to them when we first got the concessions!"

The two men fell back in their seats and gave way to helpless laughter. They'd just shown their true—greedy, savage—natures openly. They were *busi-*

nessmen: ready to sacrifice nations, partners, friends, for the sake of deals that would bring incalculable profits to them personally.

Suddenly they frowned: someone was knocking quietly at the door to their cabin. They exchanged a questioning, almost worried look. Every unexpected event seems menacing to a criminal. Who could have come to disturb them? The crew and the officers on board, long since trained, knew very well the Slanes tolerated no interruptions in their private cabin. What could be the meaning of this violation of the standing rules on the *Vulture*?

To that unspoken question Slane answered quietly, "To find out, let's see who this unwelcome visitor is. If his business doesn't justify this intrusion ten times over, we'll cure him of his untimely zeal."

William nodded and called out harshly, "Come in!"

The door opened slowly to reveal a ruddy man with graying hair, wide shoulders, and a stocky build. The gold braid on the cuffs of his jacket and the uniform cap he held in his hand indicated his rank: captain and crew chief of the airship.

"What?! You, Bubany?" cried Slane. "What could possible be going on for a man as scrupulous as you to break the rules?"

The captain bowed, without seeming at all bothered by his employer's tirade. "Incredible things are going on, gentlemen. So incredible that they seemed to me to warrant breaking the rules, as you say."

Taken aback, his listeners stood there with their mouths hanging open.

To explain, Bubany added, "If I believed in the horned Devil—and what man of common sense would dare deny his existence?—I'd say the Lord of the Fires of Hell himself is at work aboard the *Vulture*."

"The Devil now! Why the Devil? Explain yourself, Bubany. Otherwise you'll lead me to doubt your sobriety!"

"My sobriety is well known," the captain answered gravely. "In drinking contests I've put away forty-eight whisky cocktails without any more effect than a baby with a glass of milk. So Your Honor can rest easy. My mind isn't wandering because of liquor, but because of inexplicable goings-on."

The captain spoke with such conviction that his listeners were struck.

"If you want to convince us," said Slane, "please tell us about it."

"I came for no other reason, gentlemen. I'm glad you're allowing me to carry out my duty."

The Slanes had always found the captain a little talkative and rambling, but right now he'd become absolutely unbearable—to the point that William couldn't help growling, "Speak, but in the fewest possible words!"

Bubany wasn't at all offended. "I'll do as young Mr. Hibbett asks. But I'll need enough words to make myself clear, just the way you need enough cloth to make a jacket. Any tailor can tell you, if you're even five centimeters short on fabric, the garment goes all to hell. If it's even one word too short, a report will be unintelligible."

141

As can be seen, William's comment had done nothing besides force the Slanes to listen to an interminable digression. They bit their lips to keep from swearing at the incorrigible talker. But they realized the best way to speed up a tale told by someone suffering from compulsive verbosity was to let him go on without interruption.

The captain went on calmly, "All that said—not to dispute your excellent suggestion, but to prove I'm worthy of your confidence, since I understand the proper value of words—I'll tell you what upset me."

"Finally!" they sighed.

"As you know," went on Bubany unperturbed, "our *Vulture*—since that's the name you thought right to choose for the airship we're on—carries a crew of sixteen men, divided into two watches that are on and off duty every six hours."

"Oh, yes, we know," nodded Slane with resignation.

"So, counting Lieutenant Black and myself, that makes eighteen men. I'll refer only to them, because there've been no modifications among the passengers, so there's no call for including them in the count."

"What are you babbling about with your *modifications*?" growled William as he ground his teeth.

"No, no, young sir," the captain hastened to say. "Don't try to make me think I'm babbling. I know that can't be—because I've got no more voice than a sardine in oil. I'm just reporting. As for the word *modifications*, which seems to have drawn your attention, it's warranted anytime there's been a change in the personnel on an airship."

"I'm aware of that. But why have you made this modification?"

"Alas, gentlemen, I haven't made it! I've been forced to put up with it, that's all, because I've been able to figure out neither why nor how it came about." Observing their impatience, he went on, "But I'm making my report of the fact. A noteworthy fact, truly! Of the eighteen men who make up the crew, I can only find ten. The other eight have vanished, evaporated."

At that bizarre news the father and son exchanged a sarcastic look. All the evidence suggested the worthy Captain Bubany had made a sacrifice at the altar of the divine bottle—and a very potent sacrifice, given that, as he'd claimed earlier, not even an army of drinks could cloud his judgment. This time, however, his mind was heavily clouded. Eight men evaporated! What a ridiculous joke! It was too bad the alcohol the captain had obviously put away hadn't evaporated just as fast.

Looking to have some fun at the expense of the man he considered a drunkard, Slane asked mockingly, "Did you order Lieutenant Black to find the cause?"

"Yes, sir!"

That firm reply made the Slanes jump. Well, now… might there be some germ of truth in this apparently fantastical tale? They suddenly felt interested—

though not yet worried, oh, no. Together they asked, "Well, can you give us the details?"

"I repeat, gentlemen, I came here exactly with that intention." Standing straight, with his arms hanging naturally and his little fingers along the crease of his trousers, Bubany said, "You'll recall, gentlemen, you had dinner this evening in the dining room with your passengers."

"Yes, of course, but cut to the chase, I implore you," growled Slane, at the limits of his patience.

"I beg your pardon, I can't cut to the chase, because this is where it begins."

The Slanes clenched their fists. The captain's obsession with minutia was wearing down their last nerve. And yet to learn anything they had to let him talk... so they held their tongues.

Taking advantage of that, Bubany went on, "As is my practice, I was on duty in the control room to make sure the airship was running smoothly, so the gentlemen and their guests could enjoy their dinner without incident."

The chatterbox's listeners ground their teeth. "After that? After that?"

But without speeding up his delivery the captain said imperturbably, "To get to *after* you have to start with *before*, right? So I was at my post right up till the moment when, having finished your meal, you yourselves came to relieve me at the instrument panel."

Slane roared, "By Satan himself, we know all that!"

With the greatest politeness, Bubany nodded. "No doubt, gentlemen. But the reminder was necessary, to prove to you that I couldn't supervise the crew at the same time. As a matter of fact, neither could Black. He was in the engine room with the crew on duty. As for the off-duty crew, who'd been relieved at six o'clock in the evening, they were—at least I assume so—in the crew's mess having their own dinner."

"Ah! Get a move on!" begged father and son. "We arrived to take over from you. You left..."

"The very word. I left the control room. I said to myself, 'Duff...' Duffert is my first name, you see, just as Bubany is my last name."

A violent gesture by Slane put an end to the new digression the captain was on the point of launching.

"So I said to myself, 'Duff, you're hungry. Everyone else on board has fed. I think it's your turn now, old boy.' Famished, I headed straight... to my cabin, where before we left Frisco—the usual nickname for San Francisco, you know—I'd stored a pâté and various other equally delectable goodies I got from one of those buffet tables at Buena Vista Park. I took nourishment, which in the weakness of my nature I needed badly. Then the call of duty pulled me to my feet. I realized I ought to pay a visit to the engine room. Lieutenant Black is a reliable man, without a doubt, but it's a good idea for a captain to keep an eye on reliable men too. On the way, I passed the control room, as you're already aware."

"And then?"

"Usually we don't require silence on board, and since the crew's mess is on the lower level a little noise wouldn't bother the distinguished passengers upstairs. So usually, as I say, the men talk and sing and make a racket that, just between us, sounds more like the growling of bears than the twittering of hummingbirds. But now there was absolute silence from the crew's mess."

"Absolute?" echoed his listeners, suddenly seized by a vague anxiety. The logical, sequential unfolding of events in the captain's account troubled them and led them to doubt their earlier assessment of his condition. They let go of the thought that he'd drunk more than he should have. Now they felt he was telling the truth. They were both eager and afraid to hear the rest of his report.

Meanwhile Bubany kept on going at his usual pace. "I stopped. I listened. The silence continued. I was surprised, and I opened the door. The crew's mess was empty."

"Empty!" cried the Slanes, jumping to their feet.

"Completely, gentlemen. Now, during the night shift—from six in the evening till six in the morning—the men who aren't in the engine room are confined to the mess."

"Naturally."

"That's to avoid disorder on board."

"Why tell us what we know as well as you do?" grumbled Slane. "What did you do when found out?..."

"That my men were missing? I looked for them, of course."

"Where?"

"Everywhere. In the engine room, in the hold... I even asked your passengers, who were chatting peacefully in the lounge. Naturally they didn't understand what I *meant*."

"They hadn't seen the missing men?"

"No sir, they had not. And I can't blame them, because I couldn't find them any more than they could."

For a few seconds his listeners stared at each other with a stunned look on their faces.

Bubany was the first to break the silence. "In conclusion, gentlemen, I instructed Mr. Black to conduct a general search."

"And?..."

"He's just reported back to me. He found no trace of the fugitives anywhere." The captain shook his fist in the direction of some imaginary enemy, and went on angrily, "I say *fugitives* to convey that they're no longer with us. But to be a real fugitive, you have to flee. And may Old Nick impale me with his pitchfork if anyone can show me how it's possible to flee from an airship flying at high speed and at an altitude of two thousand meters above the ground!" There was a muffled croak. The captain had turned crimson. "The ground!... Again, not the right word, because we're over the Pacific Ocean, and the nearest coast lies a thousand or twelve hundred kilometers away!"

Flushed and breathless, Bubany stood facing his listeners with anxious eyes. He seemed to hope these "gentlemen" could offer some explanation for the inexplicable. The Slanes, who'd created this airship and solved the difficult problem of transporting a number of people across great distances, should easily have solved the mystery that was making their subordinate's mind spin. And to see them standing there, speechless, frozen, their faces tense from the vain search for a plausible solution, left Bubany even more demoralized than he'd been by the event itself.

Father and son realized they must take action—or at least pretend to take action. Right away, in a voice that he managed by force to appear confident, Slane said, "Lead the way, Bubany. We're going to repeat the search you made. So you believe, as we do, that it's impossible to leave the *Vulture* when it's flying at this kind of altitude?"

"Unless you're a bird, gentlemen, I say the thing is impossible."

"All right. Your men weren't birds. Therefore, they must be hiding somewhere or other. Six eyes will see better than two. We're bound to spot some clue that'll put us on their trail."

To say the captain was convinced would be an exaggeration. He knew he'd searched with his own two eyes as well as any ten, or any hundred, could. But the "boss" had spoken, and there was no sense contradicting him.

When the three of them had explored every corner of the airship, and had questioned Lieutenant Black and the engine-room crew, without finding a hint, no matter how slight, that shed any light on the fantastical disappearance of eight missing men, they returned to the upper level reserved for the owners and their guests. A vague hope had brought them back here: perhaps the men had hidden in one of the passenger cabins—no matter how unlikely such behavior seemed on an airship where the Slanes imposed iron discipline. Why would the crewmen have done something like that, which could only end in harsh punishment? They didn't ask: as long as it carried with it some feeble hope, even an absurd hypothesis was welcomed uncritically by the three men who confronted the inexplicable.

Of course, when they threw open the doors the cabins were empty. It could hardly have been otherwise.

In the lounge Princess Liao was playing bridge with May; she'd honored her valet, Lipson, and that mechanic, Derrick, by inviting them to be the third and fourth players at the table. Stepan and Sefra sat nearby on the carpet, looking through a picture book. Curled up in an armchair, little Jane seemed to be asleep, with an enigmatic smile on her rosy lips. Freda sat near her, doing embroidery.

When the Slanes appeared, followed by Bubany, May stood right up and said quietly, "Do you need me to do anything?"

Slane shook his head almost rudely. The young woman's words had closed off another theory: obviously, none of the passengers had any inkling of the strange incident that had thrown the owners, the officers, and by now the remaining crew of the *Vulture* into confusion. The passengers were oblivious to the unexplained and inexplicable disappearance of eight men who'd been present at six o'clock and had vanished by nine—from an airship in mid-flight. The mystery grew ever more confounding. It was impossible to make sense of it.

You could escape from a prison on land. A crashing wave could wash a sailor off the deck of a ship. The absence of a prisoner, the loss of a sailor, could be accounted for. But at an altitude of two kilometers, no wave could take away a man, no cell door could be opened to freedom. Above, below, to the left, to the right, everywhere, there was nothing but thin air. Of course, you could fall, or jump. But that would be either an accident or a suicide. And neither an accident nor a wish to die would strike eight men at the same moment—men untouched by scruples or remorse, eight criminals confident they were on the verge of earning a substantial reward, a payout that would make their fortunes!

Tom Slane employed only the most hardened souls. That criminal mastermind trusted only wretches who'd proved their wickedness. And he insisted on proofs of such a high standard that, if it could be put this way, his companions formed a world-class criminal elite. What's more, those proofs of their troubled pasts gave him a hold over them. How could eight men like that—picked for an expedition they knew very well would make the dollars rain down into their pockets—possibly think of suicide, of the terrifying drop into the two-thousand-meter abyss that yawned beneath the hull of the airship?

Those questions were rattling around in the Slanes' and Bubany's minds. Lost in their thoughts, they didn't notice how odd they themselves looked. They'd stopped at the door to the lounge, unmoving, their eyes unfocused, as if they were daydreaming, quite forgetting that the passengers were watching them in some surprise.

Princess Liao's voice made them jump. "What's wrong with you?" she mocked. "Are you so sorry you sedated me and abducted me from San Francisco? Or are you hoping I'll forgive you for that action unworthy of real gentlemen?"

William was too much on edge to be teased. His anger burst out brutally, causing his usual mask of cautious courtesy to drop. "I care no more for your forgiveness than a hen does for a ball gown! You're in my power now, far from the protection of the foolish law, whose nets just hamper the movements of men of action! Therefore, you'll obey!"

But Slane clapped his hand harshly over his son's mouth. "Shut up, I tell you!" Then, recovering his composure, and aware of the need to keep up the lie by which he'd substituted his son for the real Lloyd Hibbett, he went on, "Be quiet, Mr. Hibbett, be quiet. This child can't possible understand the vast plans that guide our actions. The arcana of high policy aren't within the grasp of the lovely beings known as young ladies."

He softened his voice, working with devilish duplicity to correct the impression William's clumsy outburst had created. "Her father, the unfortunate dethroned ruler of the Middle Kingdom, will explain these things in a way that will lead her to trust us. And then, my dear Lloyd, Princess Liao will regret the injury her childish notions have caused you, and she'll admire in you the great citizen that your modesty too often conceals."

Without waiting for an answer, Slane bowed and withdrew, pulling his companions along with him and heading back to the control room. He sat at the instrument panel and studied the pressure gauges, the chronometers, and the route drawn automatically by a device, a secret invention of his, that was connected to the engines and that showed on a map, up to the minute, the exact location of the *Vulture*. Finally, in a low voice, as if he were talking to himself, he said, "At eight or nine in the morning we'll be passing over the Hawaiian Islands. I want to stop there."

"Why show ourselves foolishly and give away where we're going?" cried William impulsively. He stopped short. His father was looking at him with undisguised scorn.

Shrugging angrily, and with a mocking smile adding an edge to his words, Slane said, "We'll set down out of sight of anyone, on one of the unclimbable peaks that rise over the islands." He added bitterly, "I want to carry out a thorough investigation, a search of the entire airship, with the help of the men who are now tied up operating it. I want to get to the truth about the desertion of those eight rascals, in whom I had... in whom I still have complete confidence, because they know they couldn't possibly gain anything by hatching a plot against me!"

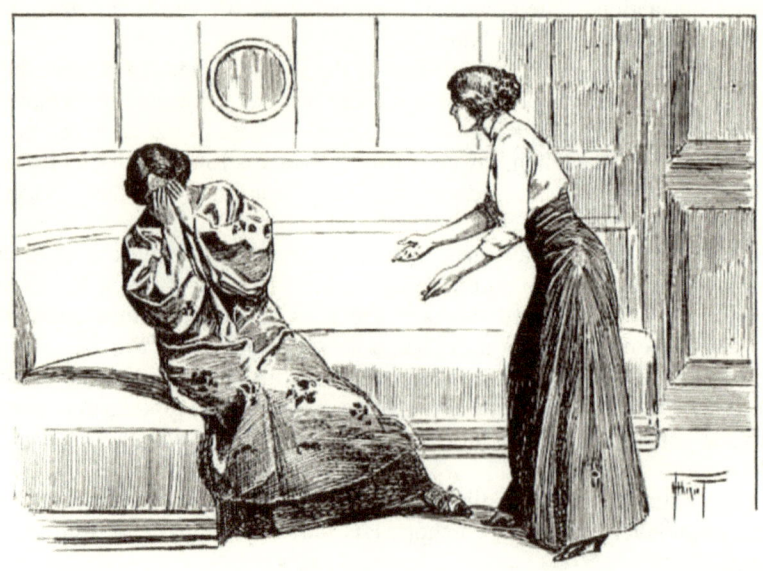

CHAPTER II
The Green Fairy

In the interests of his *investigation*—to use the same term he'd used—Slane would have been well advised to listen the conversation that took place, after he left the lounge, among the passengers who earlier had been so absorbed in the divine delights of bridge, as the afficionados of that game call them somewhat hyperbolically.

No sooner had Slane gone, dragging William and Bubany along in his wake, than Princess Liao rose suddenly. The rest did the same, the bridge players putting down their cards, Jane dropping her nonchalant pose, Stepan and Sefra abandoning their picture book, Freda setting aside her embroidery.

Silently, on tiptoe, the princess went to the door. She glanced sharply outside, to make sure the Slanes had really gone away. At a signal from May, Freda joined the princess and said in a low voice, "I'll stay here, Your Highness… If anyone comes, I'll warn you. You can talk without fear."

The princess whispered her thanks and returned to her place at the table, around which all the others had now gathered. "Well, Miss May?" she asked. "My hallucination—since that's what you call what I thought I saw the other day on the screen in the Red Parlor in my house on Fulton Street—my hallucination seems more and more to match the truth."

"Didn't I promise you that's what would happen?" May replied gently.

"Yes, yes, don't take what I say the wrong way. I don't mean I've lost faith in you. I believe in you, and in Mr. James. I trust your devoted companions. I just wanted to say that my... enemies themselves are nice enough to make clear their real thoughts." She shivered. Her whole body seemed to sway in fear, the way a palm tree sways in the wind. She went on, "You heard the way Lloyd Hibbett"— she caught herself quickly—"Sorry, you told me he has no right to that name... Anyway, you heard how that.... individual spoke to me just now."

"Like a bandit who's dropping his mask—yes, Your Highness, I heard. For a moment I thought he was going to give himself away completely, which would leave you in no possible doubt about the absolute truth..."

"Of the tragedy you caused me to see up on the screen? Oh, my dear Miss May, I have no doubts about that, believe me. His father, that sinister man, did his best to interrupt him and find some cunning way to distract me... but I'm sure it was the Benevolent Buddhas of the Celestial Empire who allowed me to see the past revealed. Oh, don't try to make me think it was a hallucination: I don't have a gift for science, I don't understand it. I'd rather believe the gods manifested themselves to me, because they wanted me to know they were watching over me. That way I... I can find more courage."

May bowed without replying. What difference did it make whether the princess put her trust in gods or in science? The only thing that mattered was that she placed herself in the hands of those who wanted to save her.

"Can I ask you something more?" went on Princess Liao shyly after a short silence.

"As many questions as you'd like, you know that."

"Thank you, I'm not especially brave. I'd much prefer a life where I wasn't forced to exhibit courage. So I'm surprised that, given the danger that surrounds us—and such danger, O Buddha!—you didn't expose the Slanes for their crimes while we were still living in San Francisco. Being on American soil would've guaranteed us the protection of the law..."

The scientist's tinkling laugh cut her off.

"You're laughing?" asked the princess in some disappointment.

"Certainly, Your Highness. Not at you—but at the naivety implied by your suggestion. What? You think accusations coming from me, a typist, or from James, a domestic servant, would be listened to—when they were aimed at men who, by their scientific achievements, by their status, by their wealth, were protected by invulnerable triple ramparts? Alas, you haven't learned the bitterness of the struggle for life. No court would accept our account—though perfectly true—of the loss of the *Cyclopic*... an account supported, I'll say it again, only by the testimony of people whose social position is so humble compared to that of the accused. To file complaints, to press charges! The only result of doing that would be to find ourselves accused of slander and thrown in some jail or other... leaving you alone and defenseless, in the clutches of adversaries who will never hesitate before any crime that serves their interests."

May had grown animated as she spoke. The princess bowed her head. Her delicate amber face expressed her sorrow. "In that case," she stammered, "if we're not allowed to expose them, I'm lost!" There was an unspeakable horror in her voice, the kind of instinctive, unreasoning terror that leads to panic.

May smiled at her gently, and with the grace of a young mother comforting a child frightened by some tale about a bogeyman, she took the hands of the overthrown emperor's daughter. They made a charming pair: the dark Chinese princess the picture of weakness, and the blonde English engineer the picture of strength and valor. May said, "No, no, you dear timid princess! I don't think you're lost at all! There's no effective way for us to expose the Slanes, that's true. But they can expose themselves, they can confess their crimes, they can make restitution to their victims for the fortune they stole from them."

"Oh, they'll never agree to that!"

"Sure they will! I haven't given up hope of making it happen!" Then to persuade her May continued, "We have only one weapon to set against their gold, their machines, their many unscrupulous followers... But our weapon is a good one: illusion! Ah, Princess, I would've thought that after what happened to those eight rascals you'd be a little more persuaded!"

"Horrible!" moaned the princess, hiding her face in her hands, while her frail body shook convulsively.

What had provoked that reaction? Simply that Princess Liao knew the answer to the mystery of the *Vulture*'s missing crewmen—the mystery Slane and William and Bubany were trying in vain to solve...

After dinner, when the two Slanes had withdrawn to escape from a conversation they didn't enjoy listening to, May had tiptoed to the door of the dining room, and in one quick glance had examined the neighboring lounge. Coming back to her friends, she'd murmured, "Captain Bubany left to go have his own dinner. The coast is clear."

Her words appeared straightforward, yet all of her listeners started, and May herself seemed to be in the grip of some strong emotion. Her usually rosy cheeks were pale, and there were dark circles under her eyes. But by sheer will-power she forced her graceful body to stand up straight, and with her face clear and calm she said firmly, "The time has come to act. From now on, any of us might suddenly find ourselves unexpectedly in danger. Each of us must therefore be ready to overcome that danger. I'm going to give you a weapon that is also a shield."

They all remained still, watching her in silence.

"Wait here for me." With those words, May left them and ran to her cabin, where she opened a suitcase and took out a fairly large flat box, which she carried back to the lounge.

No one had moved. Derrick and Freda still sat at the table. Princess Liao stood with her head bowed. Little Jane had taken Lipson's hand and stood by his side, making use of every inch of her small stature. The calmest of all were certainly Stepan and Sefra. The scene made no special impression on them, since they'd witnessed such terrible things long ago, when they were penniless wanderers at the mercy of whoever they met on their way. Past experience had left them a little jaded.

May set the box on the table and took off the lid, revealing a pile of objects made of navy blue cloth. What were they? She spread one out. Well! It was like one of those knit undershirts worn next to the skin to protect against the cold of winter. Oddly, it had no sleeves. Was it an athletic vest, the kind worn to go rowing? But it wasn't clear what need there might be for rowing on an airship racing across the sky, two kilometers above the surface of the sea.

Their confusion was brief, because now May said, "Each of you will take one of these tunics and go put it on right now."

"Why?" murmured Princess Liao.

"To acquire the power to control the minds, the wills, the actions, the senses of your opponents."

"So this is your invention?"

"Yes."

"This is what provides such power over minds that…"

"That at your house on Fulton Street, all Mr. James had to do was say to himself, 'I want the Slanes to recall the sinking of the *Cyclopic*. I want those details—in the form of a hallucination—to be visible to all, up on the screen, like a telephotic projection.'"

"And that was enough to cause all of us to see those events from the past," stammered the princess with a shiver.

"Ah!" cried Lipson, gazing admiringly at May, "the weakest person, if he's wearing this electric tunic, can overpower the strongest and manipulate his senses in the strangest ways! For example, the subject will see you—or not see you—just as you wish. He'll see what's real or what's imaginary."

With a pleading gesture, May cut off his panegyric. "Time's a-wasting! All of you, take one of these tunics and go put it on. Hurry!"

Derrick, Freda, Lipson, Stepan, and Sefra each took one of the strange undershirts, and one by one they left the lounge.

"What about me, big sister? Is there one for me too?"

The scientist smiled at little Jane's question. "For you, darling? Oh, this isn't a toy for children."

"I know that, I was paying attention!"

"All right," interrupted May, not wanting to argue about it now, "take one and stop pestering me!"

The little girl didn't wait to hear her say it again. She grabbed one of the navy blue tunics and ran off with her prize.

Only Princess Liao hadn't moved.

"Well, Princess," said May gently, "don't you want to be protected from attack, like the rest of our friends?"

The Chinese girl responded with a gesture of horror. "Yes... yes... But not that way. No, not that way."

"Let me explain..."

"Don't say anything, May—there's no point. I don't understand your science. To me, your corselet is the diabolical work of evil genies, and I couldn't possibly imprison my body inside it. Please don't ask me to, I beg you."

All the superstition of China trembled in the princess's admission. May didn't insist. She closed the box and took it quickly back to her cabin.

When she returned, she found all of her companions gathered once again in the lounge. She studied them for a moment, then with an effort she said, "James, are you wearing the electric tunic?"

"You ordered us to, May, so the question is unnecessary."

The young Englishwoman smiled sadly. "I apologize for giving such orders, but the circumstances..."

"... Give me the pleasure of obeying you," Lipson impulsively finished her sentence. After a pause he added, "Anyway, even if you didn't order it, I'd still do what we agreed on. The victims must be avenged."

"By becoming a murderer," moaned Princess Liao.

But Lipson shrugged, and—showing to what degree revenge seemed right and normal and necessary to him—answered mockingly, "Would you rather marry the murderer?"

The princess hid her face in her hands with a low moan.

"All right," said Lipson, "that's settled. I'm going to introduce those rascals to the *Green Fairy*."

"What's that?" stammered his astonished listeners.

"Just something I thought up. It hardly matters what the hallucination is, right?"

"Right..."

"So, whether I lead them along by one vision or by another isn't something we have to debate." Then, slowly in an ambivalent tone in which mockery and dread were mixed together, he went on, "If you feel strong enough for it, ladies, I'd ask you two to go out onto the roof deck of this accursed airship. Seeing you there—yesterday's victim and tomorrow's victim—will give me courage."

"I'll go," promised May.

Deep emotion shook Lipson's voice as he stammered, "Thank you, Miss May, thank you. You saw firsthand the people who went down with the *Cyclopic*; may your eyes now witness the first act of the punishment."

As if to stop him, Princess Liao—her frail body rigid with horror—held out her arms. Too late: Lipson had hurried out of the lounge.

Before the princess could say a word, May seized her wrists and begun to pull her toward the door.

"What do you want?" sighed the Chinese girl.

"To take you to the bridge."

Princess Liao struggled desperately. "But I don't want to go! I don't want to watch!"

Almost rudely, May replied, "You have to!"

"No, no! Don't force me!"

"Would an emperor's daughter refuse to grant the encouragement of her presence to one who was devoted to her?" With increasing roughness May went on, "Do you think James enjoys this aerial combat? No! No, if you have even a trace of that idea in mind, banish it as a lie. He was born for goodness, for the tender emotions, to spread happiness around him. If he now acts in a way that allows you so cruelly to display your horror, that's because we're young women—who might lack the needed strength when the moment came to strike the blow." She lifted her eyes to heaven as she added, "We ought to be eternally grateful to him. And it must be our greatest duty to show that gratitude. What would he think if we refused to do the little he asks of us, when his own heart breaks at the awfulness of what he has to do?"

The princess had bowed her head. She no longer struggled as May pulled her along. Not that she was persuaded: but she'd been raised in the imperial palaces of the Forbidden City and kept in a state of passivity, without the capacity for independent will or argument, that was once typical of feminine upbringing in the Celestial Empire, and she was now unable to resist. Her few objections had exhausted all the energy she could summon.

As if in a dream, the princess mechanically followed May along the corridor that encircled the lounges, the cabins, and so forth. Freda and Derrick followed in their footsteps, and they in turn were followed by Stepan and Sefra—who were extremely curious about the mysterious Green Fairy Lipson had mentioned earlier. Collectively they resembled a parade of statues along the corridor: their stiff movements, their tense features, their staring eyes all contributed to the likeness. What could be going through their minds that was awful enough to disturb even Derrick and Freda?

At the center of the airship, a spiral staircase made of steel led up to the bridge—which was what the crew called the open roof deck on top of the hull; indeed the flooring, made of dovetailed planks, along with the metal railing surrounding it—which was collapsible and could lie flat on the flooring—lent a certain vague resemblance to the bridge of a naval vessel.

They climbed the stairs. Pulled along by May, the princess went up, step by step, with growing horror. She felt a kind of holy terror, like a desire to be dissolved in the infinite represented by the priests in the Chinese faith, as if she were inhabited by the Ten Thousand Benevolent Buddhas and by their servants, the priests, as well as by those mortals who had achieved death while following

153

the philosophical path of Confucius or Lao-Tse or the Buddha himself. She was no longer conscious of living, of acting. A foreign will had in some sense drawn her out of her own self.

The princess now found herself on the bridge, leaning on the steel rail—that delicate barrier separating those who stood on the curving convex roof deck from the dizzying abyss over which the *Vulture* was flying. The rumbling of the turbines that powered the airship, and the hard wind that whipped her face, showed her how fast they were flying.

A pain in her wrist caused her to look down. It was May's hand, still holding on tight: the engineer had not let go of her during the entire tragic walk. Her clenched fingers sank into Princess Liao's delicate skin like a living vise and left bruises. Yet the princess didn't protest—she would have lacked both the courage and the strength. Still, her fear grew: in the young Englishwoman's convulsive grip she sensed a horror even greater than her own. For May—so strong-willed, so energetic, so superior to the average woman—to lose awareness of her own actions, a storm must be raging within her, she must be experiencing an emotion at the limits of her capacity to feel. And that realization of May's paroxysm devastated the princess.

The two of them, tottering, supporting each other, stood there in the howling wind, with the feeling that they were living through a nightmare, were being dragged headlong by some unstoppable flight of Fate.

Perhaps Derrick, Freda, Stepan, and Sefra, who stood unmoving a few feet away from the two young women, felt the same way. They discreetly held each other, and kept their eyes fixed on Princess Liao and on May—the beloved adopted daughter of two of them, the chosen sovereign of the other two—who had pulled them along in her orbit.

"I say this Colorado ham is prime, fellas—though having your mouth full isn't ideal for conversation."

"All right, Cox knows his mouth is full, but he feels like talking anyway. Eat your ham, man, and talk afterwards. Your voice and our ears will be better off for it."

An epic volley of laughter greeted that sally by Joker, the acknowledged clown of the watch that had just gone off duty in the *Vulture*. Those eight men were gathered in the crew's mess, eating voraciously. Certainly after a six-hour shift in the engine room a man was entitled to feel like recovering with a solid meal—and an even better way to recover was with jokes: laughter is the best digestive.

At least that must have been what Joker thought as he made fun of Cox, his usual victim. But Cox seemed to be in a bad mood, because he answered with a growl before achieving real speech: "Joker, I'm warning you, from now on leave me alone."

"Hah!" cried the other, "Cox thinks being left alone is something you can buy at the store, like a plug of tobacco."

"I reckon you annoy me, and I've had enough. So…"

"So… what?" Joker turned to face Cox and glared at him menacingly to express his anger that his habitual butt had dared to rebel.

Accustomed to yielding, Cox hung his head.

"Ah!" said Joker, calmed by that gesture of submission. "For a moment I thought you were about to challenge me to a knife fight."

The other men snickered. But they all fell silent when Cox replied, without raising his voice, "That's exactly right—a knife fight."

Shocked this time, Joker took a step back. "I must be dreaming! Cox wants to play at Bowie knives!"

"That's right, Joker."

"How did that stupid idea take root in your thick skull?"

"It's your fault."

"What's that you say?"

"I say you've annoyed me enough to wear down my patience. So I said to myself, this has gotta stop."

"Really?"

"And it's gonna stop," said Cox, who, now that he was fired up, was not at all intimidated by his adversary's mocking tone.

"Hah! And how exactly do you think you're gonna keep me from having fun?"

"With my knife."

"Idiot! I'll carve you up like a side of beef—which has about as much brains as you do!"

No one laughed. The other men just listened, guessing this argument would end in bloodshed. They were certainly interested; but the anticipation of a fight made Joker's witticisms seem stale by comparison. Usually the slightest thing he said made them laugh.

The sudden impassiveness of the spectators hurt his pride as an artist, if it can be put that way. Joker realized his eloquence was losing its edge. With rising anger, through clenched teeth, he said again, "I'll carve you up…"

To his great surprise, Cox calmly interrupted him with, "Could be, but it could just as easily be that my knife will cut your hide to ribbons."

"Never! You're done for."

"Anyway," said Cox, "it doesn't matter in the least as far as this is concerned."

"Wrong! I'd just as soon it be your skin in ribbons than mine."

Imperturbably, Cox shrugged with complete indifference. "Poor Joker, you don't get it."

The other man started. "Now I don't get it, he says! Cox thinks he's passed his stupidity on to me!"

"No, not at all."

"Then explain yourself! Because, by all the devils in Arizona, you'd drive even St. Peter at the Pearly Gates nuts!"

"In that case I'll explain," said Cox, as calm and serious as ever. "What is it I want? To stop being the butt of your jokes, because I'm tired of it. If I kill you, that'll be the end of your jokes. If you kill me, I won't be around to hear 'em. Either way, I'll get what I want. So now you can see why I don't care whether your jokes end one way or the other."

For once, Joker found nothing to say. The other man's logic had stunned him, even disturbed him. Unfortunately, the spectators greeted Cox's answer with discreet laughter, and once again Joker felt his status as the acknowledged wit on board was under threat. Every smooth talker has the soul of a showoff. His nostrils flared, his eyes darkened. In one quick move he drew from its sheath the knife he kept at his belt, like all of his companions. "All right then, Cox, let's get on with it! I'm eager to satisfy you."

Those two crooks working for Slane were about to come to blows. The blades shone blue under the electric bulbs that lit the mess. The bystanders craned their necks, eager to see blood spilled. Suddenly they all froze. They'd heard the metallic ring of a sharp knock. Before any of them could make a move or say a word, the door swung open.

Lipson came in slowly. With military precision, all of the crewmen automatically stood at attention. Slane recruited criminals, but he enforced strict discipline. To these men, Lipson was nothing more than Princess Liao's valet—but the princess was the fiancée of Lloyd Hibbett, who in turn was the friend and associate of Tom Slane, which meant her valet was someone not to be scorned.

Lipson was very cordial. "Evening, fellows, don't take any trouble on my account. I just came by to ask you about something that quite surprised me, since it's my first voyage on this extraordinary airship."

"Oh," murmured Joker as he sheathed his knife, "I would've thought that, working for a princess, nothing could surprise you anymore."

The visitor smiled. "You're right. There aren't many things that could. And yet, the one I'm talking about has me completely astonished."

"And you hope we can explain it."

"I don't hope—I'm sure you can."

"Damn!" Clearly the crooks were flattered. Still, their suspicion that the princess's valet might be overestimating their powers made them smile and frown at the same time—producing bizarre expressions that in other circumstances Lipson would have found comical.

Right now, he seemed not to notice. "You'll understand right away why I feel so sure. You're part of the *Vulture*'s crew."

"Of course," they all replied, happy to have begun with a point obvious to even the slowest of them.

"Therefore, you're familiar with the way the sky can look when the airship is in mid-flight, or stopped, or indeed at any stage."

The crewmen exchanged amused looks. They didn't know where the valet was going with this, but the odd way he was leading into the subject entertained them and reassured them about the nature of the questions to follow.

As if oblivious to their reactions, Lipson went on more cordially than ever. "Just now I went up onto the bridge to get some air."

"It couldn't do you any harm," said the incorrigible Joker.

"And it wouldn't have done me any, my friend—if..."

He paused long enough for all of them to ask, "If?..."

"If I hadn't unluckily looked around me—that is to say, to put it as accurately as possible, looked around the airship."

His listeners were dumbfounded. What—this valet said he'd "unluckily" seen what was around the airship? Had he gone mad? Or maybe... It wasn't long since dinnertime. Maybe the princess's valet had on the distorting glasses liquor puts over the drinker's eyes, and he was seeing through the bottles he himself had emptied! But that theory had no sooner occurred to them than they discarded it. Lipson's behavior, the perfect poise of his gestures, his relaxed expression, all contradicted that notion.

"And?..." they all prompted.

"And indeed, as I was saying, I looked around outside. I expected to see clouds, and far below—I was told we're flying at an altitude of two thousand meters—the surface of the sea, or at least the mist that sometimes covers it."

"Well?"

"Well, nothing like that at all. The truth is, the view was completely different. It seemed to me the *Vulture* had landed on the top of a grassy hill."

"A hill? The *Vulture* landed?" The chorus of shouts would have reduced any ordinary speaker to silence.

But Lipson wasn't at all disconcerted, and he went on, "My eyes told me the airship had come to a stop. My ears told me it was still traveling at high speed—the turbines were roaring, and I had to hang onto the rail to keep from being carried away by the wind."

This time not one of the crooks had anything to offer. What the visitor was saying, in a voice that gave complete authority to his words, appeared inexplicable to them. They were convinced the valet was in his right mind. They couldn't attribute what he said to drunkenness or stupidity. So in that case... They all stared at each other open-mouthed, flabbergasted, unable to form a logical thought.

"Given those circumstances," Lipson went on, "since my senses were no help to me, since reason insisted that an airship couldn't be in motion and stopped at the same time, and likewise a grassy hill couldn't keep pace with a flying airship, I decided the wisest thing was to come ask you about it, and invite you to take a look for yourselves, so you could apply the benefit of your experience and give me the explanation I'm sure would occur to you."

Well, dammit, that valet was certainly right: they had to go take a look—though his story sounded utterly preposterous. The *Vulture*'s crew had never observed anything remotely like what he was describing. In an uproar, they all followed him out the door and into the corridor and up the stairs to the passenger level. Neither Lipson nor the men behind him noticed the door to one of the cabins open quietly as they went by. They didn't see little Jane slip out into the corridor and follow along at their heels. They didn't hear the darling child muttering to herself, "Why should I be the only one not to see what my big sister May is going to do up there?"

They all climbed up and emerged onto the outside bridge. But no sooner had they set foot on the roof deck than the crewmen cried out in pain and covered their eyes with their hands.

The moment Lipson stepped through the door leading outside, he spun around, raised his arms, and spoke mysterious words: "The Green Fairy! See her there! Follow her wherever I want her to lead you!"

For just a moment his eyes fell on May, who leaned against the fragile rail a few feet behind him, surrounded by Princess Liao, Freda, Derrick, Stepan, and Sefra. Then once again he gave his full attention to Slane's henchmen.

Though the princess was distraught, though May was trembling, though the others were in anguish, what struck them now was not so much the drama of the scene as it was the extraordinary change they saw in Lipson: the strength of his will seemed enormously magnified by the electric tunic May had ordered him and all the rest of them put on.

Leading the group of crewmen, Joker cried out joyfully, "The Green Fairy!"

His companions all echoed him, "The Green Fairy!"

For the second time, the passengers were about to witness an illusion created and inserted into human minds by means of a device that looked like a piece of clothing. The disproportion between cause and effect, and the mystery of the projection of the will, added to their turmoil. The words "Green Fairy" had made them all jump. Isn't that what Lipson had told them in the lounge, the illusion he'd said he would create? What could those words mean? None of them could say.

But events were now accelerating. The criminals didn't seem to notice the presence of the passengers. Their eyes wide, their faces ecstatic, their arms out as if to grab hold of the apparition they'd been made to see, they walked in single file to the rail that surrounded the roof deck.

Princess Liao gave a muffled moan, which was answered by a small frightened cry from the hatchway that stood open in the middle of the roof deck. No one noticed that unexpected echo. If May had looked that way, she would have seen the tense features of Jane, who stood on one of the last steps of the spiral staircase and leaned out to watch the scene planned by her friends.

But the speed with which events were unfolding monopolized the spectators' attention.

"Here I come, good Green Fairy!" cried Joker tenderly. And with one quick hop he hurdled the steel rail and threw himself into the void. His action froze the spectators, but seemed to galvanize the other crewmen. "Wait for us! Wait for us!" they shouted in voices that were barely human. Pushing each other aside in their hurry to chase the vision only they could see, they ran to the rail and climbed over it as Joker had. For just a moment, while the *Vulture* continued on its course, the spectators could see dark shapes falling through the clear night toward the ocean, in whose murky waters eight bandits on Tom Slane's payroll were entombed forever.

Only the passengers remained on the bridge, speechless, unable even to form a thought, crushed by the terrible spectacle that had unfolded with the speed of a dream.

"Good gracious heavens!"

"You can say that again!"

Those two exclamations, so cogent in spite of their brevity, burst from the mouths of Stepan and Sefra. For the duration of that tragic minute the two foundlings had been squeezing each other's hands as if for strength and support.

And at that same moment, Freda, leaning against Derrick's sturdy form, was stammering in fear and exultation, "We're going to win! We're going to win! To think our little May made this happen!"

But Lipson didn't leave his friends time to express their reactions. Returning to the breathless group, he said, "Let's go back to the lounge. That's where we have to be found once the absence of those men is discovered. Because, don't forget, their disappearance will be even more damaging to our enemies' morale if they can't explain it." Then, like an officer checking on his men's equipment, he added, "If any of you have not yet put on the electric tunics Miss May handed out earlier, do so now. The war has begun, and we need to be armed."

"I've put mine on," said Derrick with pride in having done his duty.

"Me too," echoed Freda.

"Us too," cried Stepan and Sefra in poignant unanimity.

May only gestured to show she too had on the apparatus that wildly magnified the wearer's willpower. What need had she to speak? Wasn't it obvious that the young woman who'd invented the marvelous device would be among the first to put it on for defense?

"And you, Princess Liao?"

Shivering at the question, the Chinese girl shook her head desperately.

"What? You refuse to be armed? Think about it: the Slanes will be furious, and their anger will be directed at you more than anyone, since you're the keystone of their whole plan."

"Never," she murmured, her voice breaking. "I'll never agree to make use of that diabolical power!"

"Bah! Even just to defend yourself?…"

"No, no!"

"Think about it. We're gambling our lives. Even the will of a small fragile child wearing the electric tunic would be powerful enough to plant a hallucination in the mind of an athlete! You don't have to attack, if your feelings forbid you, but at least defend yourself!"

Though May added her arguments to those of Lipson—the real Lloyd Hibbett, orphaned and robbed of all he possessed by the evil owners of the *Vulture*—it was in vain: nothing could change the princess's mind.

"Oh," she said, "I know what you're thinking. The descendants of the Manchus are cruel at heart. You're right. Perhaps I wouldn't shrink from a dagger, poison, a revolver; but I'm afraid of a tunic that enables you to drive your opponent mad. I don't understand how it's possible, and that mysterious magic terrifies me." She clasped her hands. "I beg you, don't force me. I'm eternally grateful that you've espoused my cause. My heart blesses you for it. But I cannot do battle with the weapons you offer me." And then, in an atavistic surge of the Manchu spirit of her warrior race, she added, "If the pain is too great, I'll know how to die. Don't force me to use the witchcraft you call science."

They all understood there was no point in insisting: Chinese people rarely think scientifically. They live in a world of dreams, of skillfully tangled stories.

They're happy to account for all natural phenomena as arising from the actions of the Dragon and the Tiger, symbols that have become real to them. Lipson and May could see that nothing would overcome their companion's instinctive—even atavistic—resistance to the influence of factual science. Any attempt to explain would be fruitless. Princess Liao had etched within her confused, stubborn Chinese mind the idea of witchcraft, and nothing in the world could erase it. She could never see the tunic—whose *electric* current magnified the *magnetic* power of the wearer's will—in its true light. Too bad: the princess's obstinacy would add yet another danger and make it even harder to protect her.

With a gesture of resignation, Lipson murmured, "Let's get back to the lounge."

But as he approached the hatchway leading to the narrow spiral staircase he let out a muffled cry. "Someone was spying on us!"

"Who?" cried his companions as they rushed forward, gripped by dread of the coming battle and the fear that yet another tragic execution would be called for.

"I don't know—I heard the stairs ringing, as if from light footsteps."

They heard only part of what he said, because he was already rushing down the spiral stairs. Spurred on by fear, they all hurried after him. A mad rush brought them to the lounge, where they found little Jane looking through a picture book.

"Darling, did you see anyone going by?" asked May.

The child affected a look of surprise, and answered with another question. "Who would I have seen, since you'd all gone out?"

There was no point in pressing the child further.

Jane, seeing their attention was no longer on her, went back to her book. The story it told in pictures must have been very engaging, because her cheeks were rosier than usual, and if her friends had thought to look carefully they would have seen that her chest was heaving at a rate that gave away her breathlessness. That would have led them to wonder how a little girl sitting reading a book could be panting so hard.

But they noticed nothing, because they were absorbed in their concern about the supposed spy. They now discussed the likelihood of a false alarm: the noise Lipson had heard might have had some mechanical origin. The rapidly spinning turbines made the metal frame of the *Vulture* vibrate, and that vibration was passed along to the metal plates of the hull and to the airship's internal bulkheads. It seemed reasonable to assume that was probably all Lipson had heard.

Indeed, Lieutenant Black and the eight remaining crewmen were all busy in the engine room, for the work there couldn't be neglected, no matter what the reason. The very survival of the airship accounted for the tone of the notice posted by the engines—a tone that had made the passengers tremble: *Anyone on duty who abandons his post will be punished by death.*

As for Captain Bubany, he was dining in his cabin, and anyone familiar—
at first hand or not—with the routine on board the *Vulture* knew that worthy officer took his meals very seriously and would suffer no distraction, much less be
found wandering around the airship. Nothing and no one could have interrupted
him while he was eating.

That left Tom and William Slane.

A careful tour along the corridor gave Freda confidence that the Slanes
hadn't left their cabin. As has been said, it was a security feature of the airship's
design that the instruments in the control room were duplicated in the owners'
cabin, so that if the pilot suddenly stopped doing his job, whether by accident or
for any other reason, the *Vulture*'s masters could instantly take control of flying
it.

Reassured, they all took their seats around the card table. And that was the
staging that fooled the Slanes when—alarmed by Bubany's disconcerting report—they came into the lounge while they were searching the airship. The
bridge game kept them from suspecting that their passengers had it in their power to resolve completely the mystery of the disappearance of Joker and his seven
companions.

Furious, with a vague terror eating at them—nothing is as demoralizing as
the inexplicable—the father and son returned to the control room, followed by
Bubany, who was panting like a seal. None of them had the slightest explanation
for what had happened. Curses, angry questions that went unanswered, fists
striking the furniture, heels stamping on the floor, all betrayed the three men's
fear and rage, and their inability to imagine a solution to the enigma.

While they were wasting their energy in vain outbursts, Princess Liao went
back to her cabin, along with little Jane—who that evening, in an unexpected
burst of affection for the Chinese girl, had announced that she wanted to stay in
her cabin. Normally it fell to May to take care of the girl, but the Englishwoman
had agreed without protest that the little darling's whims should be obeyed.

It has to be said that her willingness was the result of Lipson having whispered to her, "Perfect! That way we'll be free to act."

"We won't get much sleep," muttered Derrick in his rough voice, which he
tried in vain to keep low.

"We won't get any sleep at all."

"What are we going to do?"

"Keep on going."

Derrick started, and Freda, Stepan, and Sefra all cried as one, "We're going
to send the rest of them over the rail?"

Lipson shook his head. "No, no. But we're going to drive them mad. We're
going to make them think they're dreaming. We need them to focus their fears
on their criminal masters. The first time the *Vulture* lands, we need them to flee
the Slanes' airship."

"Why?"

163

"So that only we remain on board with our two enemies."

"And then we won't keep them around for long?"

Lipson shrugged sadly. "Who knows?"

"What do you mean, who knows?" cried his listeners.

"Before we punish them, we'll have to pick up another passenger..."

"Who?"

The question was echoed by many voices; Derrick and Freda, Stepan and Sefra, all were eager for an answer. Only May seemed to understand Lipson—the genuine Lloyd Hibbett to whom she'd dedicated herself since the *Cyclopic* disaster.

"Princess Liao's father," the young man finally answered in a low voice. "Princess Liao's father, the target of the Slanes' plot, is in definite danger, whose nature we don't know. And what's the point of protecting her if we allow those villains to have a hold over her—which they will if we abandon the emperor to their clutches?"

He cut short the questions his companions were beginning to ask. "Enough talk for tonight... It's time to act. We have ten men to bring under mind control: Bubany, Black, and eight crewmen. Miss May and I will take care of three each. Derrick, Freda, Stepan, and Sefra, you'll divide up the other four."

"When do we start?"

"Right now."

Their faces lit up with joy. On tiptoe, without a sound, they all left the lounge.

Meanwhile, in the control room, Slane, William, and Bubany had gradually calmed down. Of course, they had no more idea than before what had happened to half the crew; but their furious shouting and carrying on had eventually "worn down their nerves," as the Dutch put it so well. They'd reached a kind of truce, so that without being aware of it they lowered their voices and restrained their gestures. Part of that calm was the result of exhaustion and even discouragement. Nothing is so calming as despair—though it was true that in this case calm was synonymous with defeat. When victory appears unattainable, the fighter stops looking for it. He lies down willingly and closes his eyes, hoping for the sleep from which no one awakes. To some degree the Slanes had reached that state. They'd stopped talking, and Bubany joined them in silence.

The door opened quietly. May stood on the threshold, her hands raised to point at the three men. Presumably by doing so she was confusing their eyesight, because none of them seemed to notice she'd come in. She smiled, and across her sweet lips and in the dimples on her cheeks there passed a quiver of triumph. She thought to herself, I've used science to do the impossible, something that till now was considered to be the fantastical domain of legend. And the comparison

164

was unavoidable: the mythological Ring of Gyges[17] made whoever wore it invisible; the electric tunic May had invented kept the enemy's eyes from seeing whoever wore it. In the end the result was the same: whether you were invisible, or whether those you didn't want to see you were unable to do so, the secret of your presence was equally safe. It was peculiarly like enchantment: all it took was for a young woman to wish it so, and the miracle thought to be impossible took place.

Gently, cautiously, avoiding any noise that might give away her presence, May crossed to the back of the room and slipped behind a table that would prevent any of the men from bumping into her. It was all very well to be invisible; but it was also necessary not to be given away by unexpected contact. The enemy would be surprised to come up against some invisible obstacle, and that would be enough to put him on his guard.

She also had to avoid giving herself away to their ears… and that was exactly what she did unintentionally: though May's footsteps were light, still a floorboard creaked. She froze, holding her breath.

But Slane and his companions had started. They looked curiously around the room.

"Did you hear that?" whispered Slane to his son.

William nodded.

"How about you, Bubany?"

"I'd be lying if I didn't say yes, but…"

"Why are you hesitating?"

"Because you appear to be worried, gentlemen, and I fear I'll make you angry if I say that the creaking we heard seemed completely natural."

Slane frowned. He didn't like his subordinates to be able to detect anxiety in his expression. "By Jove, I assume it's natural too. Wood moves, doesn't it, and when it moves it creaks. That's the explanation you were about to give me."

"Indeed, that's what I meant to say."

"Well, Bubany," said Slane, trying to mask his true feelings under an appearance of heartiness, "it just proves we're always in agreement, old fellow."

But in spite of all the reassuring words, their faces remained tense. Each of them, when he thought no one would notice, searched the room with suspicious eyes.

A sharp knock at the door made them all shiver.

William roared furiously, "Holy devils! Can't we be left alone? If the idiot who's interrupting us now doesn't have a really good reason, I'm going to blow his brains out with my revolver!"

---

[17] In Plato's *Republic*, the myth of Gyges—a shepherd who finds a magic ring and uses its power of invisibility to usurp the kingdom—is cited to question the idea of what motivates just and unjust behavior.

At a sign from Slane, Bubany opened the door. Then he cried, "Black! You here?"

"Lieutenant Black!" echoed the two Slanes in shock.

If Black had left the engine room, when it was his duty to be there to oversee the crew, that was a bad sign. What could have happened to make him do what he knew was punishable by death? In fact, the lieutenant looked stunned, broken. This tall, slim, red-haired, ruddy man, always calm and even-tempered, whom neither men nor things could upset, now looked agitated, hasty, out of tune—to put it in a way that best expressed the change in him.

Before the others had a chance to ask him anything, he cried, "Captain Bubany, take over the controls!"

"Isn't Bols at his post at the instrument panel?"

"No! I had to have Nell replace him. But the poor fellow doesn't really know what he's doing, and I'm afraid he'll make some mistake."

Without waiting for him to finish speaking, Bubany leapt with a cry of fear to the seat at the duplicate instrument panel. The seat broke under his weight. It was as if the substitute pilot, that man Nell whom Black had mentioned, had been waiting for this moment to make the mistake they expected. The floor seemed to drop away beneath their feet.

"We're falling!" shouted Slane and William and Black.

"We're falling!" moaned May, still invisible to the others but forgetting her caution in the grip of an all too justifiable terror.

Luckily Bubany was a man of action. His fists came down on multiple levers. The airship's descent was stopped. The shutters that covered the portholes in the hull rolled up with a snap, enabling them to see out.

And then, as calmly as if nothing out of the ordinary had taken place, Bubany said, "We're out of danger. I won't leave the controls. But I can listen to your report, Black. What happened to Bols, that you had to give his job to Nell?"

CHAPTER III
From Shock to Shock

"Just a moment," growled Slane.

They all turned to look at him.

"No doubt my ears are deceiving me. But I want to clear up one point. Just now, as you all heard, none of us was able—because the emotion was perfectly natural—to keep from crying, 'We're falling!'"

"I did it myself," admitted Bubany candidly.

"So we're all agreed on that. But after that, I think I heard something else."

They all looked at him in surprise. "Say! So did I!"—"Me too!"—"Me too!"

"A woman's voice repeating the same words. I would've thought it was an echo if it had been a man's voice. But a woman's voice? No echo can alter a sound like that!"

"That's right," muttered Bubany. "No echo can change the gender of a voice!"

"Well then?"

Slane's question astonished his listeners. "Well..." they stammered. "Damn! Then it's pretty surprising."

"Look," said William, "it defies common sense. No one here is a woman. Therefore, we took some random sound for an echo of our own words. It happens all the time. There's no woman here, like I said, and I defy you to prove me wrong. Therefore, we were the victims of an illusion."

May had trembled at Slane's observation. But now William's explanation reassured her. By the power of her will—vastly magnified by the electric tunic—her enemies were unable to see her. How would they be able to detect her presence?

Anyway, Slane had come around to his son's point of view. But was he convinced, or did he just think it wiser to bring to a close a debate that could only end in yet another inexplicable phenomenon? She couldn't tell.

The fact was, turning to Lieutenant Black—and suppressing the shaking in his voice with an effort that was visible in the tension written on his face—Slane said, "Lieutenant, tell us what happened in the engine room."

Black shook his head, puffed out his cheeks, and replied hesitantly, "Sir, I believe Bols got a bee in his bonnet about something."

They were all surprised. "What leads you to think that?"

"His behavior. Judge for yourselves. He was seated at the instrument panel. Suddenly he jumped in the air and shouted, 'Damn it to hell!' Then he looked around menacingly..."

"Go on."

"I have to point out that all the others were at their posts, and Teddy, the one closest to him, was at least a dozen feet away."

"Surely that doesn't matter!"

"I must absolutely beg your pardon, sir, because Bols accused his mates of having kicked him in the part of his anatomy that wasn't protected by the rather narrow pilot's seat."

"Kicked him?"

"And you say Teddy, the closest man, was a dozen feet away?"

They were all speaking at once.

Still perfectly solemn, Black replied, "That's what I said, sir, and that's exactly what makes me think poor Bols has lost his mind."

There was a silence. May—still invisible—smiled. None of these criminals was now thinking about the woman's voice they'd heard before. She thought to herself, "That must be the work of Derrick or James or one of the other of our friends doing their part." She had no doubt her companions, having made themselves invisible like her, had begun to terrify the remaining crewmen.

But of course, that explanation wasn't available to Slane. He muttered, "Bols must have rheumatism or gout. He probably mistook a sharp pain for a kick."

Black shook his head firmly.

"You disagree, Black?"

The lieutenant nodded. "I'll say it again: no, sir. Gout might produce the effect you describe—but once, not twice. And it certainly doesn't drive a man responsible for piloting an airship to quit his post suddenly…"

"He quit?…"

"I'd call it quitting, sir. He stretched out on the floor, on his back, and said that way he could keep from getting kicked again in the spot I mentioned before."

Slane and William leapt to their feet with unspeakable astonishment in their eyes. "This is unbelievable!" muttered Slane in exasperation at the series of incomprehensible occurrences. "I'll go see for myself. Bubany, don't leave the controls."

The captain nodded firmly. The two Slanes rushed out of the cabin, followed by Black, who was as dumbfounded as they were. It took them only moments to race along the corridor to the spiral staircase leading down to the engine room, and to tumble one after another down the stairs. They were spurred on by feverish haste—haste mixed with fear.

Yes, these criminals, having risen, thanks to uncommon good luck, to the summits of power and wealth, now found themselves suffering from vertigo. Was the long series of mysterious events—starting with the projection of their past on the big screen in the Red Parlor at the mansion on Fulton Street—a forerunner of a turn in their luck, a herald of their defeat? Accustomed only to victory, Slane and William were thrown into confusion by the counterattack of an enemy they couldn't put their hands on.

They picked up their pace, and Black had trouble keeping up. But as they entered the corridor at the far end of which stood the door to the engine room, a group of men surged around the corner and collided violently with them.

"By all the devils in the Rocky Mountains!" roared Slane. "The first one who doesn't go back to his post is a dead man!"

Indeed, these fugitives were the crew: overcome by panic, they'd fled down the corridor. But Slane's threat brought them to their senses, and one of them even tried to explain. "It's not our fault. The airship is haunted…"

His words ended in a whimper: Lieutenant Black had grabbed the man by the throat, and was shouting, "Nell, you wretch! I made you responsible for piloting—which is to say responsible for the lives of all on board, and you deserted your post!" He was shaking the man the way you'd shake a tree to get the ripe fruit to fall.

But Loeb, a German who'd recently joined the crew of crooks working for Slane, intervened firmly. "He's right! It's not his fault!"

"Not his fault? I'd like to see you prove that." But in spite of the skepticism in his words, Black had stopped shaking Nell.

"I can try, at least," said Loeb. "Nell was at the controls. Suddenly we all heard the sound of a slap—a slap that could knock a horse over!"

"I forbid fighting on board," said Slane in a menacing voice.

"No one was fighting, sir."

"But what about the slap?"

"Nell certainly received one—his cheek went as red as a beet. But none of us delivered it."

"Are you pulling my leg, Loeb?"

"No, no!" cried all the other crewmen. "It's the absolute truth! Nell got a slap that no one gave."

Just like earlier in Slane's cabin, a heavy silence fell; they all stood there gloomily. Once again something inexplicable had happened. And Slane noticed that, with trembling lips, the men kept whispering over and over, "The airship is haunted!"

Haunted! That stupid explanation might be enough for simple minds. But he—a scientist, an engineer, Director of the Institute of Inventors, armed with a skeptical mind and scorning anything that couldn't be tested experimentally—what explanation could he put forth to counter that of the ignoramuses standing before him? Slane was afraid to admit that nothing came to mind—a mind usually overflowing with bold theories. Events unlike anything he was familiar with, and contrary to all the laws of nature, were taking place on board the *Vulture*—events that gave him the feeling, just like his men, that invisible enemies were moving all around him. The idea expressed by that naive word "haunted" had taken terrifying hold in his mind. Ah! With all his strength he pushed it away. Maybe so... but in the workings of the mind, you can only get rid of a theory by replacing it with a different one. And where was that different theory?

The crewmen around him, Lieutenant Black, even his own son William, all stood watching him, stunned and afraid. He knew that at this terrifying moment they were all waiting for words of reassurance from him. Simply to have something to say, he announced, "Let's go have a look."

He led the way. Forcing himself to walk with confidence, he headed toward the engine room. Suddenly they all came to a stop, their legs shaking. Someone had just cried out loudly, and a quick glance around showed them it must be Teddy, whom they now realized they'd left behind alone at the controls.

The cry had brought them to a halt, but the words that followed it froze them with terror. Their companion was roaring and panting as if he was fighting an unequal battle: "Ah, I've got you now! You've blinded me—I can't see you—but I've got you now, and hell if I'll let you go!"

Who could he possibly be holding, since he was alone? Left to themselves, the crew would certainly have fled without waiting for an answer to that question. But Slane was there with them, and Teddy's words had kindled a spark of hope in his mind: the enemy they'd sensed behind all of the night's strange events must have let the crewman take him by surprise, and now they were fighting.

Instinctively, Slane rushed toward the sounds, and that gave his men courage, and they followed at his heels. Elbowing each other, they all crowded into the doorway to the engine room... but there they froze in place.

In the middle of the large square room, Teddy was fighting like mad, bumping into the dynamos, the machines that drove the airship. The witnesses would have sworn he was furiously battling an invisible opponent.

"I see you, captain! I see you all, mates! I'm not blind, and I've got that slapping fellow!"

Where was that slapping fellow? No one could see a thing. They all looked at each other, reluctant to get any closer to Teddy, who went on fighting wildly—and then something unexpected happened: his features straining, his breath whistling through clenched teeth, his voice choked and muffled, Teddy cried, "Ah, rascal! You're strangling me! Help!"

But his cry was cut short. A loud bang shook the air, and Teddy dropped. There was a hole in his head, and a puddle of blood spread out around him.

Someone had fired a revolver—there could be no doubt about that. The sound of the shot was familiar to all these professional criminals. But where was the gun that had gone off? Where was the hand that had pulled the trigger? They could see no gun, and no hand. And yet the cloud of smoke that had suddenly appeared in the middle of the room carried the whiff of gunpowder.

What nightmare were they trapped inside? Because this could be nothing other than a nightmare! How else to explain a revolver whose presence was manifest only by its smoke? And, as the whitish cloud with its scent of gunpowder slowly began to dissipate, there lay Teddy's corpse, with a hole in its temple: it wasn't a dream. A murder had taken place in the presence of Slane and of them all—one of the crew had been gunned down.

Suddenly a thought occurred to Slane, a thought that restored him to his wits for a moment: what if Teddy, in the grip of his fever, had shot himself? That idea gave renewed courage to the terrible leader of all these criminals. He glimpsed a practical solution to this one mystery among so many mysteries.

He ran to the body and turned it over. First disappointment: Teddy's revolver was still deep in his pocket. But hope drove Slane to seize the gun by the grip and pull it out of the pocket. He examined it eagerly. William, Black, and the seven surviving crewmen crowded around him curiously, sensing their leader was on the trail. But they all experienced the second disappointment: Slane stared at the cylinder, stunned. All the bullets were in place; none had been fired.

While he stood there, frowning, his brow furrowed, a volley of curses and oaths made him jump. When they came forward to gather around him, the men had left the doorway clear. And now a hail of blows—truncheon blows, they claimed—were raining down on their heads, their shoulders, their shins. In fact, bloody welts could be seen across several of their faces. Even William had been hit hard, and his clean-shaven face carried a noticeable red mark.

For one long minute they all stood there, as if they'd been overwhelmed by that invisible bastinado. And then the instinct to flee awoke. A wild panic seized them, lashed them on, and extinguished all hope for reason. Like a herd of wild animals startled by the sound of the hunter's gun, they thought of nothing but escaping from the place where their companion had fallen.

They gave way to a mad scramble down the corridor to the spiral staircase. They felt dizzy, and as they ran they bumped into each other, they raised their fists and struck out at each other with instinctive violence, each fleeing man afraid to fall behind the rest. In their minds, driven mad by events that seemed supernatural to them, one thought prevailed: the man bringing up the rear would be the most exposed to attack by their invisible enemies. And those enemies they'd now recognized and identified: they were spirits, ghosts, the kind of beings summoned by mediums. Nothing could now rid the men of the idea the airship was haunted.

When they reached the bridge, the open roof deck swept by the wind of the speeding airship, under the indigo dome of a sky dotted with stars, the crewmen stopped to catch their breath. But though the fresh air calmed them for a moment, it also gave them new energy to announce to their boss that they no longer wished to serve aboard the *Vulture*.

"In a few hours we'll reach the Hawaiian Islands," they said vehemently. "Drop us off near the capital, Honolulu. We'll get back to the States[18] on some good ship where evil spirits don't beat up on the sailors."

In vain Slane and William tried to reason with the frenzied crew. No argument had any effect; they were no longer listening. In vain the Slanes pleaded and threatened. And Lieutenant Black, usually so impassive, was now as distraught as the men: he too would get off at Honolulu. He too was desperate to get back to the States, to set foot on solid American soil, where those evil spirits out of ancient legends wouldn't dare show their faces.

"The *Vulture* is haunted! The *Vulture* is haunted!" Slane's henchmen could give no other answer. That refrain was an obsession, a leitmotif for the fear that shook them all.

The Slanes realized they had no choice but to give in. After all, the *Vulture* could get by without these idiots who were deserting it. A single man was enough to fly the airship. The supply of electricity to power it took place automatically. They could do without the cowards, and so they'd do without them. They'd be let off in Hawaii.

But even as they mocked the men for their cowardice, Slane and William were shaking on the inside. They too were afraid—and the more so because they didn't know what to fear. And yet they had to go back to Bubany, whom they'd

---

[18] The Unites States had annexed Hawaii in 1898, but it was only an American territory, not a state, till 1959.

left alone at the instrument panel in their cabin... always assuming nothing bad had happened to the captain—because really, absolutely anything could occur on this damned *Vulture*. That thought crossed their minds, but they dismissed it by reasoning, "If Bubany had been forced to abandon the controls, the airship would crash. Since it hasn't..."

But in spite of that logic, they hurried back to their cabin. A new surprise awaited them there. When they entered the room, all seemed normal. Bubany was at his post: he stared out the porthole with his right hand on the steering joystick and his left hand hovering over the instrument panel. The captain seemed to be carrying out his duty imperturbably. His calm manner reassured the Slanes. Seeing him so much at ease and focused on his job, they were able to breathe again: what a relief not to be surrounded by crewmen blinded by panic! So they still had one reliable companion. They wouldn't have to count on themselves alone to fly the *Vulture*—aboard which, they couldn't help admitting, some very odd things were going on. One single henchman wasn't much, if you were supposed to be the head of an entire criminal gang; but compared to being all alone, having one loyal man felt like having an army.

But their satisfaction was brief. Without leaving his position as attentive pilot, Bubany murmured, "Ah, it's you, gentlemen. I was waiting for you to return, to request that you let me off at the nearest dry land, because I can't stay on this hellish airship any longer."

The Slanes just stood there a moment, stunned. What? The captain wanted to quit, just like the rest! So, all of them? Not one would stand by them. They'd be left to carry on the struggle alone... But they quickly straightened up and pulled themselves together. Ah, the Slanes were still tough competitors, men of action! What did it matter if everyone else abandoned ship? Weren't they leaders, ambitious and brilliant men who'd designed these innovative machines, and set up a vast criminal organization, and built labs and workshops, and recruited scientists? They could get by without the help of all these losers turning tail at the first skirmish!

Slane asked in a harsh voice, "What made you decide that, friend?"

Without turning around, still carrying out his duty as pilot, Bubany replied, "Because the *Vulture* is haunted."

"Haunted!" Father and son both echoed the word that had been following them everywhere.

Bubany himself repeated it. Like Lieutenant Black, like all the crewmen, he shrank from the idea that word expressed.

They had to find out what could have motivated such sudden weakness in a brave man. Suppressing the anger that shook his voice, Slane asked, "Haunted! I wouldn't have thought a fellow like you, Bubany, would repeat nonsense like that."

"Oh, I wouldn't have believed it myself," agreed the captain. "But things have been happening—and what you once considered absurd suddenly occurs to you as the only possible explanation for what's going on." He reached briefly for a lever to trim their course, then went on, "Anyway, can you, sir, the cleverest of the clever, give me another explanation for what's been happening to me?... I'm not stubborn; I'd be happy to adopt your explanation, with my thanks."

The Slanes relaxed: at least Bubany hadn't gone mad—he was open to discussion. So, talking over each other in their relief, they both cried out cordially, "Speak, Bubany, don't be afraid! We, of course, are scientists, and for us the idea of haunting is inadmissible. Still, we respect your courage, and we'd be happy to rid you of whatever crazy notion has taken root in your mind."

"You'd be doing me a great favor by getting rid of it," muttered the captain. "In any case, here's what happened."

Breathing heavily, he leaned toward the porthole and cast a curious glance outside. Then, with both hands on the instrument panel and his eyes on the way ahead, like one of those Asian deities who seem oblivious to the rites carried out in their honor, he spoke. "So, a while after you left with Black, to go to the engine room..."

"How long after?" interrupted William.

"That I couldn't say for sure. Being alone here, and responsible for flying the *Vulture*, you can understand I wasn't able to keep an eye on the clock."

"Of course. Go on," said Slane quickly to head off a pointless debate.

Anyway Bubany needed no encouragement. He went on, "Suddenly I heard shouts coming from the engine room. Of course, the bulkheads muffled the sound, but even so I couldn't be mistaken: someone was shouting. I was mighty curious, because it's not acceptable to make a lot of noise while serving under your orders. Without noticing I was talking out loud, I said to myself, "Well! What's going on in the engine room?"

"A perfectly reasonable question," said Slane with a vague smile.

Bubany slowly shook his head, then went on quietly, "I hadn't even finished the words when a very soft voice right next to me whispered, 'What's going on? It's very simple. Good spirits are punishing the guilty.'"

The Slanes stared at each other in astonishment.

"Oh, come on, Bubany! You're pulling our legs!" yelped William.

But the captain solemnly protested, "No, no, you're mistaken. I would never dare make fun of you, sir."

"And yet you're telling us a bedtime story!"

"A bedtime story? Oh, sir, I don't know if it strikes you as something that would make you sleepy, but I can assure you what I'm telling you will keep me awake for a long time."

Once again Slane found it necessary to intervene. "Let Bubany explain. And you, captain, keep going. Tell us everything! Again, Mr. Hibbett, please stop interrupting this good fellow's report."

It should be noted that Slane remained coolheaded enough to call his son by his assumed name.

"I have to admit," went on Bubany, "it made me jump. Then I had to laugh at myself. 'Your ears are deceiving you, buster!' I said to myself. 'Now you're hearing voices!'"

"Very well reasoned!"

For a moment the captain eyed William, who'd interjected those words of agreement. "Very badly reasoned, Mr. Hibbett, very badly. Because right away the soft little voice said, 'Stupid man, have you ever known your ears to deceive you with sentences as clear as the ones I'm now drilling into your thick skull?'"

"Not a very friendly voice."

"Indeed not. But I'll admit, it didn't occur to me to take offense. No, it didn't even occur to me. I was too astonished by that voice coming out of an invisible mouth. Anyway, to find out, you have to ask, right? So I asked: 'What do you want with me? Who are you?' The answer came right away: 'Who am I? A spirit of justice! What do I want? To save you!' 'Save me? From what danger?' I asked, trying to joke a little. But that devilish little voice brought me right back to seriousness. 'Everyone on board the *Vulture* is in danger,' it said. 'Have you already forgotten the eight men who went missing?' 'Hell, no!' said I. 'When you're captain, that's not the kind of thing you forget.' Then, on my honor, the room was filled with soft laughter. I swear, it sounded like a girl giving way to gentle amusement. Then it stopped suddenly, and that damned voice went on, 'You can stop looking for those eight men. They're dead, and the ocean has received their bodies.'"

"Dead, and thrown into the Pacific!" cried the Slanes with a shiver.

The captain shrugged with the insouciance of a man used to risking his life. "Bah! You've got to go one way or another, gentlemen. I didn't have time to ask her who'd killed them—because suddenly I heard a bang from the deck below. I couldn't help crying out, 'A pistol shot, now!' 'Another of your men struck off the crew manifest!" said the voice.

Slane and William listened without making a move. Fear gripped them again, fraying their nerves, closing in on their minds. Bubany's composure accentuated the upsetting nature of the astonishing things he was reporting. As he told his story he acted like a spectator, someone outside the action: he had the impassivity of a cinematographer filming a movie villain.

And now, as phlegmatic as ever, he went on imperturbably, "Then I heard the sound of the door opening. I thought it was you coming back. I glanced over. Well, by the Devil, here's the strangest thing of all: the door had opened wide, but there was no one there. I said to myself, 'All right, it's only a gust of wind. When the gentlemen left, they didn't shut it properly.'"

"That's possible," agreed Slane.

"No, no, sir, it wasn't."

"How could you tell?"

"Because of what followed: it must've been the strangest gust of wind ever."

"What are you trying to say, Bubany?"

"That after the door opened, it closed again. Yes, it closed again."

"It closed again?"

"You can be as staunch as you want at your post, you can disbelieve old wives' tales all you want, but there comes a moment when you lose your bearings. That voice, and hearing half the crew was dead, and the pistol shot, and the door opening and closing all by itself—it was too much all at one time. For a moment I forgot about the instrument panel, I forgot about flying the airship, everything. I held my head in my hands, because I could feel my brains boiling, as if some cook were sauteing them in black butter sauce. And then, wham! Another shock."

Slane and William unconsciously took a step forward, as if to get closer to the words that were coming.

Bubany didn't seem to notice. He went on, "A perfectly justified shock too. The controls on the instrument panel began to move all by themselves... and so capably that they were doing exactly what I'd have done myself."

"But that's madness!" cried his listeners.

The captain shrugged. "Madness or wisdom, that's what happened. But listen to what came next. As you can imagine, seeing the controls moving all by themselves astonished me. But it also called me back to my duty. I reached out for the controls. It was obvious the slightest move would lead to something incredible. Truly, gentlemen, I swear, it was enough to make you lose your mind. My fingers struck something I couldn't see. I seemed to have hold of someone's arm. I say I seemed, because I couldn't really tell for sure. Anyway, things were happening so fast I didn't have time to think. So I was gripping that invisible thing that seemed to be an arm. I beg your pardon if I'm expressing myself awkwardly, but I'm trying to convey my impressions as best I can. Just then I heard a shout of fear, or maybe anger, I can't say for sure."

"A shout, now!"

"Yes, gentlemen, a shout. And right away a voice—rougher than the first voice—rapped out these four syllables: 'Too bad for him!' And then a fist punched me right in the face... at least it felt like a fist, and a punch hard enough to stun an ox. Automatically I put my hands over my left eye," he said, "letting go of whatever I was holding without seeing it, and forgetting that the slightest instability could make the *Vulture* crash."

"In fact, I don't understand why it didn't," muttered William.

"Oh, Mr. Hibbett, because the spirits didn't want it to. While I was holding my eye, click, click, click—the control levers began moving once again. That went on for a minute, long enough for me to recover, and then the second voice said, 'Bubany, the spirits wanted to warn you, because you're a good man it would be a shame to launch prematurely into the darkness of oblivion. Take over the controls again. But at the first stop, get away from those who are doomed!' Then it sounded like the voice was getting further away. 'What's more, you won't be the only one doing so. As we speak, the entire crew is demanding to be released near Honolulu, which the *Vulture* will reach this morning. I say this morning, because it's already three a.m.' Well—a spirit telling me the time, like a clock! And then whoosh, the door opened, and closed again. That was it. I tried to keep the conversation going, but the spirit didn't answer anymore. And that, gentlemen," concluded the captain with dignity, "is why I say the *Vulture* is haunted, and it's why I insist on leaving it as soon as possible—because I'm convinced something bad will happen to anyone who tries to fight for control with the spirits who've decided to live here."

Bubany's voice conveyed an unshakable resolve. Like Black, like the entire crew, he was filled with an irresistible, almost pathological desire to escape from the airship, which had become a stage for displays of some incomprehensible power.

Slane realized debate would be pointless, and maybe even dangerous; it was better to give way gracefully. "You can do exactly as you wish, Bubany. I'll set you down on land, along with the rest of the crew."

"So they really asked for that, like the spirit said?"

Slane grimaced at that renewed mention of the spirit, but he contained himself. What was the use of trying to apply reason to a matter he himself didn't understand in the least? "Yes, they did. But I'll require all of you to promise your silence. The *Vulture*'s itinerary must remain a secret."

"It'll remain a secret, sir. Right now we're all frightened out of our wits, but of course not one of us would think of betraying so generous a boss as you've been. And even if we won't serve you in the air, I hope we'll still be allowed to serve you on land."

Slane bowed to express some vague form of consent. "So I won't let you off in the plains right near Honolulu. Since I want to keep the *Vulture*'s movements hidden, neither the native Hawaiians nor the Americans who've occupied the islands can be allowed to see the airship. I'll set you down in the mountains in the middle of the island, where I'm sure to find somewhere to land out of sight of gawkers."

"At your convenience, sir."

"A couple of days' walk will get you to Honolulu. That won't alarm men like you."

"Of course not, boss."

Bubany turned to them for the first time since the conversation began, and the Slanes couldn't help crying out in surprise: the captain's left eye was swollen and surrounded by a purple bruise. The punch he'd received from the spirit had marked him unmistakably. That spirit must have had a fist as strong as a boxer's.

CHAPTER IV
In the Crater of the E'akiro Volcano

As the reader will have deduced, May and Lipson, assisted by the devoted Derrick, Freda, Stepan, and Sefra, were responsible for all the commotion. Their willpower—vastly amplified when their own magnetic emanations were combined with the current generated by their electric tunics—had completely prevented their adversaries from seeing them in action.

It's important to understand that May and her friends had *not made themselves invisible*; they had simply *made their enemies hallucinate* so it was impossible for them to see in the usual way the people and objects before their eyes. To make yourself invisible implies an almost magical transformation of your own physical nature, since a normal eye can no longer see you. Hallucination or mental suggestion, on the contrary, forces the observer to see, not what actually is, but what he has in some sense been directed to dream, or—to put it another way—to see only a fraction of reality. If you suggest to a subject that he's alone in a room, he will no longer see the author of the suggestion come in. Now, everyone under the influence of the electric tunics became a "subject";

what defined being a subject was the difference in power between the respective mental wills of the subject and the "operator."

Of course, the operators had faced some challenges. Because of a wrong move, Derrick had fallen into Teddy's grip, and to get free he'd had to shoot him with his revolver. As for May, she'd been using the instrument panel to keep the *Vulture* from crashing while Bubany was distracted, when she felt the captain's hands seizing her arm. If Lipson hadn't been there to deliver the stout punch that freed her by "mechanical impetus," catastrophe might have followed.

Once Bubany had resumed his job as pilot, Lipson led May out of the Slanes' quarters and back to her own cabin, saying, "I've asked all our friends to go back to their cabins and go to bed. Please do the same. Slane will probably make a tour of inspection. He has to find all the passengers sleeping innocently."

With a stifled laugh, they parted on that light note.

But Slane knew nothing of all that. Sunk in a chair with his hands clutching his head, he sat unmoving as he called in vain on all his powers of reason. Occasionally he glanced around the room at his son, as deep in thought as he was, and at Bubany, steering the airship with practiced gestures amid the regular clicking of the controls.

And then Slane fell back into his own bleak reflections. Bleak indeed! The balance sheet for that one tragic night would have frightened the bravest man: of the eighteen men—counting officers and ordinary airmen—who made up the crew, nine were dead. The rest would be leaving the *Vulture* in a few hours, having been driven mad by the inexplicable actions of some mysterious and invisible adversary.

Slane's thoughts hung on that last adjective. "Invisible! There's no such thing as an invisible enemy!" he muttered to himself. He clenched his fists in anger, and a savage grimace contorted his features. "No one's invisible. That's fairy tales, fantasy, and the like. Anyway, there are no strangers stowed away on board. Ergo, there must be one or more traitors on the *Vulture*."

The villain was getting close to the truth—though his adversaries deserved to be called not traitors but avengers. Lipson had foreseen it, which is why he'd asked his friends to allay suspicion by shutting themselves in their cabins.

"Traitors… Yes, that must be it," went on Slane to himself. "But who? Who?"

His eyes were bloodshot. He stared straight ahead, frowning in his frightful attempt to apply his intellect to solve the terrible puzzle. His gaze moved unconsciously from the walls of the cabin to the ceiling and then the floor. Was he looking for some trace of whoever had struck his henchmen so hard? No—at least he had no exact conscious intention of carrying out such an examination. Rather than being driven by his wish to unmask the perpetrators, he was just giving in to an anxious need for physical action of some kind.

Suddenly he roared loud enough to make his companions jump.

"What now?" stammered William uneasily.

"This." Slane bent down. From the floor under the instrument panel he picked up a red stone, a translucent gem the size of a pea.

"A ruby," murmured William, who was observing his terrible father's actions.

"Yes, a ruby—but not just any ruby: a ruby that might put me on the trail of the truth."

His son shrugged rather irreverently. "Come on!"

"Look at it closely. Do you notice anything special?"

William examined the precious stone with care. Suddenly he too cried out, "By the Devil! It looks like…"

"Go ahead, let's see if we have the same idea."

"Well, it looks like a stone from the Indochinese bracelet I gave Princess Liao."

Smiling happily, Slane rubbed his hands with satisfaction. "My dear Lloyd, that's exactly what I thought. I'm delighted you agree."

"You're too kind," said the young man with a bow. "But I have to admit I don't why you're so delighted."

Slane gave his son a look heavy with sarcasm. "Yes, of course, the young don't excel at cause and effect. Listen—listen so you can learn how to connect the separate elements of an equation." He raised his hand, as if to express the undeniability of his words. "If this ruby was dropped here in this cabin, it must be because the bracelet it was on came in here."

"The French call a truism like that a *lapalissade*," laughed his son.[19]

But Slane didn't seem at all offended. "Call it a *lapalissade* if you like, my boy, but that self-evident truth leads to another one: since the bracelet couldn't get here by itself, it was therefore brought here by its owner."

William dropped his attitude of mocking indifference. "You're trying to say Princess Liao came into this cabin, which is also a control room…"

"And where she had no business being, my boy… and where we were unaware of her intrusion…"

Slane broke off. Once again, his son was laughing. "You're not really going to deduce that that poor little Chinese girl threatened the crew, killed those men, punched the pilots…"

"No, no, I'm not dumb enough to say that."

"Then what?"

"Then, my boy, I think since we left San Francisco Liao has considered herself our prisoner, rightly or wrongly."

"We can speak the truth between ourselves," teased William. "Let's say, rightly."

---

[19] *Lapalissade*: a tautology, named after a 16th-century French nobleman, La Palice (or La Palisse), whose epitaph was (wrongly) said to have read, "Here lies the Lord of La Palice. / If he weren't dead he'd still be alive."

"Fine! As a result, she shares the obsession of all captives..."

"The obsession with escape. All right! But a prison flying two kilometers above the sea is a little harder to get out of than one that's built on the ground."

The young man's good humor was infectious, and Slane went on in a more relaxed manner, "Of course, of course! But I deduce that someone pining for freedom would naturally look for allies among those individuals *who know how to fly the airship*!" Slane gave disturbing emphasis to those last words.

William took his father's hand and shook it vigorously—not without some genuine respect for his display of deductive logic. "You know, old man, you're certainly still the sharpest one around!"

"So you can conceive, as I can, that Liao bought the allegiance of some of the men, and therefore that there are traitors on board, which accounts in a perfectly reasonable way for all the inexplicable things that have happened on the *Vulture*."

They'd both lowered their voices. They exchanged a look, drawing each other's attention to Bubany at the controls, where he was fully absorbed in flying the airship. The captain was thinking of nothing but reaching the Sandwich or Hawaiian Islands, and getting off the haunted *Vulture*, aboard which his unease was intensified by a constant reminder of his bewildering adventure, in the form of his swollen black eye.

But now suspicion had entered the Slanes' minds, and it forced them to mistrust everyone. Almost in a whisper, they went on, "The loyal airmen were killed. So the traitors are among the survivors. Let them get out on land! Liao will stay on board, with her valet Lipson. On our side we'll have our faithful Derrick and Freda and those bold youngsters Stepan and Sefra. In those conditions it won't be hard to make her confess the whole truth."

Father and son exchanged another look—the threatening look of an executioner considering his victim.

William murmured anxiously, "If they plan to alert the authorities to meddle in our business..."

A scornful gesture cut him off. Slane snickered. "You forget, I'm the director of the Institute, and you, Lloyd Hibbett—as everyone knows you—are the president of the syndicate of American billionaires. No, no, don't worry about a frontal attack; it would just break our enemies. Our position makes us invulnerable." A cruel smile exposing his yellow teeth, he went on savagely, "Plus which, I'll take over the steering controls as we approach Hawaii. I'll find a spot to land where the men will have to hike for two days before they get to someplace inhabited. Two days! By that time we, and the *Vulture*, and Liao, will be far away."

Then, as if inspired by a new thought, Slane rose. "Come, William. It occurs to me that we need to make an inspection round."

"Why? We know those frightened rascals of ours are still up on the bridge."

Once again Slane showed his teeth in a scornful laugh. "No point checking on them. I locked the hatch leading back into the airship. Those idiots will only get off that roof deck when they step off onto land."

"Ah, good! Perfect! So then we'll just have to throw out Bubany here."

"You got it."

"In that case, I'll say again, given all that, I don't see why we're taking the trouble to make a pointless inspection round."

No doubt the young man regretted his words once he saw the look of pity his father treated him to.

"Haha! A pointless round," Slane hissed. "Pointless to make sure our *friends*"—he emphasized the word—"May, Derrick, Freda, and company, are sleeping, and nothing bad has happened to them. I'd also like to make sure Princess Liao and her valet Lipson—whom I don't trust at all—are properly in their cabins."

William bowed his head; he understood his father's thinking.

Following the deserted corridors, they went around the *Vulture*, cautiously opening the doors of all the passengers' cabins. They had no trouble doing so, because—unbeknownst to the people they were inspecting—the Slanes had duplicates of all the room keys. The inspection was pointless: everyone the masters of the *Vulture* observed was asleep.

At least, that's what they thought. May herself, following the pseudo-servant Lipson's instructions, had slipped into her cot, where—helped by the strong emotions of that night—she was now fast asleep. Luckily for her, her regular breathing had convinced Slane to give her no more than a cursory inspection. If he'd come closer to his former typist, he would certainly have noticed her left arm, which lay outside the covers. Around her wrist a gold bracelet, carved in the form of fighting dragons in authentic Indochinese style, formed a shining circle. Slane would have noticed that one of the rubies decorating that valuable piece of jewelry had come out of its mount, leaving a gap.

If he'd noticed that, the inquiry it prompted would certainly have informed him that Princess Liao, having lost the bridge game that evening, had given the young Englishwoman her bracelet as security till she could pay her card debts the next day. May tried to refuse, but the princess—with the great seriousness the Chinese bring to everything related to gambling—had stubbornly insisted, to the point that the scientist had given way to put an end to the childish disagreement.

But Slane closed May's cabin door without discovering anything. The danger had passed for the moment.

"The Hawaiian Islands!" cried the airmen gathered on the bridge as they caught sight of the vague outline of the archipelago in the distance, which from here looked like no more than a little smoke floating on the surface of the Pacific.

The Hawaiian or Sandwich Islands, now annexed by the mighty United States, comprise eleven islands; one of the most important of them, Oahu, is home to the capital, Honolulu. All the islands were formed by a combination of volcanic eruption and coral growth. Jagged coasts with sheer cliffs alternate with sandy beaches. As you move away from the shore the land rises. Mountains reaching an elevation of ten thousand feet or more form ranges that are divided by high plateaus or lush valleys crossed by limpid streams tumbling over many waterfalls, where the accumulated flow of countless foaming brooks leaps down rocky cascades, each fall of which is two or three hundred feet high. Coffee, carob, agave, breadfruit, and so forth grow along the coast. Higher up can be found aromatic woods and trees for lumber. Higher still, you reach volcanoes, lava, and eternal snow.

Slane took over the steering controls from Bubany around ten o'clock in the morning. Once he was free, the captain carried his luggage up onto the roof deck. Then one by one the surviving crewmen were allowed back into the airship to pack up their personal effects. William stood by the hatchway with a revolver in his hand, to make sure only one man a time came inside. None of the men protested. Nothing surprised them anymore on an airship they considered haunted. And their eagerness to leave it, to get back on solid ground, to reach some town where they would no longer have to beware of evil spirits, put them in an accommodating mood.

Finally, the last man returned to the roof deck. William closed, locked, and bolted the hatch to seal it hermetically, and then returned to the control room, where he reported to his father that he'd faithfully accomplished the task he'd been given.

Slane nodded, then ordered, "Open the lowermost porthole. I believe we're nearing our destination, and I want to make sure I'm not mistaken."

William obediently turned a crank, and at the bottom of the wall a porthole was revealed, through which it was easy to see what lay beneath the airship.

"Land!" cried the young man after a quick look outside. Then he went on fearfully, "But if you want to keep our presence a secret from people here, of whom quite a few are Americans, you might want to change direction, because on the horizon I can see a breakwater and jetties that must be the port of Honolulu."

A minute passed. Then William said, "Bravo! We're speeding over a high plateau that blocks our view of the coast. What a bleak landscape: not a blade of grass, just rocks and more rocks. We could land here. I doubt anyone will come bother us here."

But Slane shook his head. "I've got a better hiding place. Not to leave you in suspense, I'll tell you that we're going to stop over the crater of the E'akiro volcano."

"Over it?" echoed William in surprise. "So we're going to stay airborne?"

"Why do you think that?"

"Because the crater of a volcano is usually at the summit of the mountain, which means that above it there's nothing but air."

That made his father laugh harshly. "E'akiro is the exception to the rule; its crater lies at the bottom of an abyss."

"Meaning?..."

"That around the crater, and overlooking it from a much greater height, there's a plateau that itself is divided into two levels, separated by an almost perpendicular cliff a hundred meters high."

"What a strange volcano."

"Strange, but secure. Once we've landed on the second plateau, no one in the world could possibly suspect the *Vulture* was there. And when I tell you this gigantic funnel consists of quaking, unstable ground made up of lava, cinders, and pumice, broken here and there by sulfurous springs and boiling sulfur geysers, and that the natives consider the whole area taboo, which is to say sacred and forbidden, then you'll understand we won't have to worry about being interrupted by nosy passersby."

William didn't say anything; he was focused on the landscape speeding by below them. The airship had left behind the wooded slopes, and now it was flying over heights left barren by volcanic eruptions. Lava flows glistened here and there under the sun like marble roadways, and the piles of boulders seemed to have been tossed there by the Titans. Everywhere he could see sulfur efflorescences that ranged from pale yellow to reddish brown, and boiling springs, and fumaroles. And among all those signs of the incessant action of subterranean fires stood snow fields and glaciers whose blocks of ice had formed strange shapes, with seracs rising like needles toward the sky. That frozen chaos broke apart the rays of sunlight, so that all the brilliant colors of the prism dressed the ice in a shimmering multicolored coat that provided the desolate mountain with an adornment of incomparable wealth.

Soon the turbulent plateau unfolding beneath the airship was broken by an immense, almost circular precipice. William couldn't help crying out in admiration. The *Vulture* had just flown over the upper rim of the caldera, at the bottom of which smoke and muffled booms and explosions of molten rock revealed the presence of the crater of E'akiro. Following a careful spiral, the airship dropped toward the second plateau, which—as Slane had explained—lay a hundred meters below the upper rim of the caldera.

There was a slight jolt, and the hum of the turbines ended. The airship came to a stop. It had landed with perfect ease, a credit to both the design of the machine and the skill of its pilot. Slane methodically set all the knobs and levers on the instrument panel to neutral, and closed off any portholes that were no longer useful now the *Vulture* had landed. Once he'd made sure the engines couldn't be engaged by accident, he got up from the pilot's narrow seat.

He rubbed his hands together in a way that was both mocking and threatening, while his hard eyes shone with wicked joy. "In ten minutes our rascals will be on their way, William. We'll be able to think about coaxing a confession out of your dear fiancée Liao, that sneaky little princess who scatters rubies along her trail."

His son snickered. He too was looking forward to the misery that was about to descend on the poor girl... who held the tender title of his fiancée.

"Good, good!" went on Slane. "You're as eager to learn what she's thinking as I am. I understand your impatience: what could be sweeter and more advantageous than hearing the confession of the girl who's going to beautify our lives?"

They both laughed. Princess Liao would have shivered if she'd heard them. She would have realized cold cruelty was not the exclusive domain of Asians, as the teasing of her American acquaintances implied.

For some time now the princess, having joined her friends gathered in the lounge, had kept her forehead pressed against the copper rim of a porthole and was absorbed in looking out at the landscape below the airship. The Chinese girl, whose thinking had been formed by the scholars of the Imperial City, was disturbed by the appearance of this unknown place; with the naive logic of an atavistic mind, she confused scientific reality and the chimeras of legend. For her a volcano was not the vent of a magma chamber—it was the lair of fire-breathing dragons, whose presence was revealed by the fumaroles, the loud explosions, and the eruptions of lava.

She was no longer listening to May and Lipson and the rest of her companions—and yet she was aware of their devotion, and she knew the risks they were running to help her. But her senses, her entire being, were now concentrated in the big black eyes that stared out at the view. That was the moment at which the *Vulture* had flown over the circle of cliffs, at the bottom of which lay the magma conduit of the E'akiro volcano, and begun the series of wide spirals that would bring it down onto the basalt slopes of the plateau.

And now the princess could see the molten igneous bottom of the great caldera: a sinister vision, evoking a visit to Hell. The blue flames of the sulfur springs and the boiling mud ejected from the geysers formed an unbroken ring of smoke and vapor around the central conduit, inside which rose and fell, like the movement of a giant piston, the column of molten matter that would be projected into the air when the pressure of the gases became great enough. Flames made pale by daylight danced among the mounds of cinders, pumice, and fragments of ejected rock that were piled into unstable hills, on the slopes of which the slightest tremor of the overheated ground would cause landslides. It was magnificent and terrifying. Like all natural spectacles, the volcano was a reminder of the insignificance of man, an insect who presumes to call himself the lord of creation.

The *Vulture* approached its landing spot. The hum of the engines ended, and the rapid spinning of the turbines no longer made the metal hull vibrate. The airship glided down across the plateau inside the caldera. With a slight bump it settled onto the rocky ground. That was all. The *Vulture* had come to rest a hundred meters below the circular crest, overlooking the depths of the crater itself by eleven or twelve hundred feet. It was now essentially impossible for anyone to know the American airship was on the island.

"The crew's going to disembark," said May quietly, as if from a distance, or as if she were talking in her sleep. This first great victory over their adversary had left her deep in thought.

No one replied, and she didn't seem to notice. All of her companions moved from the portholes that looked down at the ground to those that gave a view sideways.

May's prediction was already being fulfilled. A flexible metal ladder now ran from the roof deck of the airship down to the rocky surface of the volcanic plateau. One by one, Bubany, Black, and the crewmen climbed down, each of them carrying his luggage strapped to his back. Their movements showed how much in a hurry they were to leave the *Vulture*.

No sooner had they all gathered on solid ground than they started off into the distance on a narrow path that led up the cliff. For half an hour the passengers on the *Vulture* could still see them on that rough, difficult climb. The path followed a narrow ledge that clung to the rocky wall of the caldera, forcing them to walk in single file. And yet, as bad as the going was, the criminals following the trail seemed delighted. Their happiness at getting away from the haunted vessel could be seen in every gesture, and in their expressions of scorn every time they turned to look back at the sitting airship in farewell. Finally they reached the crest of the ridge, crossed it, and disappeared.

The passengers on the *Vulture* were now alone on board with the savage adversaries they'd vowed to unmask. And while they looked at each other, suddenly gripped by the anxiety that affects even the bravest when the hour has come for the pitiless battle to begin, the door of the lounge opened slowly, and Slane came in, followed by William.

They all shivered, not from fear but from revulsion. They felt the way a hunter does when he finds himself unexpectedly face to face with reptiles.

And yet the Slanes looked not at all menacing. They smiled, and affected an appearance of good nature intended to fool their passengers. Slane sounded almost gracious as he said, "Unexpected events have forced me to part company with my crew. That doesn't affect the continuation of our journey at all. A single person at the controls is all it takes to fly the *Vulture*. But we're going to spend twenty-four hours parked here in this volcano. No point in starving to death—wouldn't you agree?"

"Quite right," said May, recovering her presence of mind.

"I was sure of it. So I'd invite you to follow us to the dining room. The loss of my men will force us to make do with canned food, but we'll make up for the blandness of the solid menu with a liquid menu *di primo cartello*.[20] You'll sample my California rosé."

He offered his arm to his former typist, while William offered his to Princess Liao. Both accepted the unspoken invitation. May's friends followed, with Jane walking between Lipson and Sefra, and the little procession went to the dining room.

They all sat down cheerfully, each of them concealing his or her inner thoughts. Oddly, in that gathering, in which each person was plotting against some of the others, only the sweet little girl appeared lost in thought, troubled by serious reflection. Jane ate slowly, in an obviously distracted way, her eyelids lowered over her eyes like a veil. Occasionally she raised her eyes, and they gave off a fiery sparkle as she glanced quickly around the circle of diners. Then her eyelids dropped again, veiling her glance once more. Neither the Slanes nor any of the others noticed her strange behavior. A child of seven couldn't be considered a significant element in the battle, so what need was there to pay Jane any attention, especially since they all had to keep an eye on their serious adversaries? Even the wisest of us can sometimes be foolishly oblivious.

It would have been to Slane's and William's advantage to watch the little girl. If they had, they'd have noticed that, through the veil of her long lashes, she never took her eyes off the *Vulture*'s masters. They'd have observed that her glances around the table coincided with the uncorking of each new bottle of rosé. And they'd have been shocked to find out that Jane was pouring under the table the condensed milk she'd been given to drink.

Meanwhile the meal went on. Suddenly Jane rubbed her eyes, yawned several times, and fell limply against the back of her chair. For a moment she blinked, as if she were fighting desperately against sleep. Finally, her eyes stayed closed, and she breathed evenly through her open mouth, indicating she'd lost her struggle and had fallen asleep.

Princess Liao was the first to notice. "She's asleep," she said quietly. Prompted by the maternal instinct that precedes actual motherhood and leads young women to fuss over small children, she said gently, "I'll carry her to my cabin. I can't bear to see a child sleep so uncomfortably."

Slane and William exchanged a glance, as if they themselves had planned the circumstances. In a strange coincidence, Jane's eyelids fluttered at that very moment. But that too went unnoticed. Everyone's attention was on William as he said jokingly, "What a lucky girl! To have the daughter of an emperor for a nanny!"

---

[20] Italian for "of the first order" or "top quality"—literally a term for the headline act on a playbill.

The princess smiled as she got up, took the child in her arms, and left the table.

The rest of the company gathered there seemed barely to notice their departure. For a moment now, the tone of the conversation had dragged inexplicably, and the volley of remarks and replies could no longer be heard around the table. First one of them, then another, dropped some comment that apparently needed no response, because it seemed as if the speaker had no interest in being answered. Their eyes grew fixed, their voices thick. An incomprehensible weight seemed to make them slump. And then there was total silence. They were all asleep.

All? No: the two Slanes looked triumphantly at their companions. William went around the table on tiptoe, shaking each of the sleepers firmly. They seemed completely unaware of what he was doing. Derrick groaned like a sleeper being disturbed, but he didn't open his eyes, and his unconscious complaint end in a snore.

"Done," said William finally.

"Oh," snickered his father, "you do what you want, but there was no reason to shake them to make sure they're asleep. Poppy alkaloids are old friends of mine, and when I administer a dose of opiates, I can tell to within ten minutes how long the effects will last." His mirth increased. "Ha ha! Good old California rosé! Its tartness masks the sedative. Even a chemist couldn't detect the stuff by its taste."

He rose in turn and carefully brushed the crumbs off his clothes. William was looking at him questioningly, and he added, "It's eleven a.m. They'll sleep till eleven p.m."

"Twelve hours!"

"That's right, my boy. I set the dose for that interval."

And now Slane's voice rang like metal as he exulted in the success of his treachery. "For twelve hours we'll be alone with the charming Liao. We won't need all that time to get the explanations we want from her."

William looked surprised, and muttered, "Well, she must be asleep like the others, because I didn't see you give her a special glass to drink out of."

That made his father laugh, and when he'd recovered he said, "Of course she's asleep, my boy."

"So then?... We'll have to wait till she wakes up before we can make her confess."

"I'm worried about you, son. To have had an excellent education, to have lived for four years now at the very heart of scientific life in the United States, and yet still not to know that the effects of opium are counteracted instantly by the administration of a few drops of a mixture of caffeine, pyrogallic acid, and iodine!"

"And you've prepared a dose of that?"

Slane drew from his pocket a small crystal flask half full of brownish liquid. "Here it is, my boy. Thanks to this nectar, in less than ten minutes the lovely Liao will be ready to learn she has to choose between torture and absolute candor. Relax—she won't resist. Young women don't know how to bear suffering."

Then he pointed toward the sleepers around the table, and his voice grew cruel with sarcasm. "And if the darling princess has some ally among these people, nothing could be easier than to make that person glide from sleep into death. And to make all trace of the business disappear, right next to us we have the E'akiro volcano. No crematorium could possibly match the central conduit, right?"

The dining room rang with his laughter, and with William's echo of it. Still shaking with sinister laughter, the two Slanes went to the door that opened onto the corridor leading to the passengers' cabins.

CHAPTER V
Toward Freedom

Twenty-five steps brought those terrible men to the door of Princess Liao's cabin. There they stopped and listened. But even when they held their breath, not a sound reached their ears from the cabin. The lovely Chinese girl and her little companion must be sleeping in total silence under the influence of the juice of the poppy.

"In we go!" said Slane as he turned the doorknob and pushed gently. The door began to open. "The opium knocked her out so fast, she didn't even think to lock the door."

The door opened with a slight squeak. The cabin was lit by a sunbeam that came in through the portholes facing him. Princess Liao lay stretched out on a bunk with her legs hanging over the edge. It was clear from her position what must have happened: her head had felt heavy, she'd sat down, and gradually she'd tipped back. She was fast asleep. Facing her symmetrically, little Jane was stretched out on the second bunk. She too lay perfectly still, eyes closed, overcome by the irresistible power of the sedative—because Slane had also mixed some into the little girl's milk. But he didn't care about her: he just wanted her unconscious so she wouldn't hamper his plans, and now he paid her no attention.

While William watched in amusement, his father crossed the room to the sink, took a glass from the counter, ran a little water into it, and added a few drops of liquid from the flask he'd shown his son earlier. He handed William the glass, saying, "The antidote to the sedative, my boy." Then he added jokingly, "It's your fiancée who's asleep. She'll be happier being woken by her fiancé than by an old-timer like me. Persuade her lovely eyes to open again."

The young man didn't answer. Why would he? He'd certainly appreciated the sarcasm. He took hold of the glass. Then from his pocket he drew a short knife, and approached the sleeping princess. Why was he armed? Did he mean to stab the young woman with the sharp blade? No: he merely slid the steel blade between the princess's white teeth and applied a little pressure to force her mouth open. Then he slowly poured the contents of the glass between her lips. Then he straightened up, got rid of the glass, and waited. His father stood beside him, still and watchful. Two, four, five minutes passed. Then a shiver ran through the princess's body, and her slender fingers tensed.

"The remedy's working," whispered the two men happily.

A few seconds later, Princess Liao blinked slowly. She moved in the halting manner of an insect hesitant to take flight. But then consciousness returned, her circulation went back to normal, and the numbness caused by the opium wore off. Finally, she opened her eyes, then closed them as if she were dazzled by the bright light coming in through the portholes, then opened them again.

This time she was completely recovered from the effects of the sedative. She looked around, first in surprise, then with greater resolution. When her eyes fell on Slane and William standing by her bunk, a look of anxiety crossed her face. Obviously, she was wondering what they were doing in her cabin, and why they were observing her with such sarcastic, menacing pleasure.

They didn't leave her wondering for long. Slane, who'd stayed a little behind his son, now stepped forward next to him. He bowed. "Dear Princess, your fiancé wishes to speak with you. You seem to enjoy having your fellow passengers around you at all times. To arrange this one-on-one conversation, I wanted to separate you from them without using force."

"Without using force?" she echoed, like someone unable to catch the hidden meaning in what was said to her.

Paying no attention to her interruption, Slane went on, "So I quietly added a little opium to what my guests were drinking."

"Opium! Why?" The princess's voice shook with fear.

Her reaction presumably pleased Slane, because he smiled wider and his cheeks creased. "I'd like nothing better than to explain to my lovely and imperial passenger." After a short pause he went on mockingly, "Your friends are asleep around the dining room table. Thanks to a scientifically administered antidote, you alone are awake—along with us of course, who were never asleep, and for good reason!"

The way he said it intensified poor Princess Liao's fear. It was now clear to her she was in danger. She was both eager and afraid to find out what that danger was, what it would be. Her black eyes mirrored her painful emotional state—and her evident fear pleased Slane.

He laughed louder, and as he spoke, he gave his words a worrisome emphasis. "We're therefore sure to have privacy. No one will overhear the conversation we're about to have."

As he spoke, he sat down next to her on the bunk—causing her to leap up in fear. He seized her roughly by the wrist and forced her to sit again. He motioned to William to take a seat too, then went on, "Since our privacy is guaranteed, I see no reason to put off explaining."

The princess sat breathless under his gaze, like a baby bird hypnotized by a viper.

"Anyway," went on the terrible man, "if you feel for us the same affection we have for you, the conversation will be brief."

"What do you want me to say?"

"Not much. My demands are modest. You'll just have to answer one question."

"I'm listening," replied the princess dully. What Slane has said sounded innocent on the surface, and yet the young woman had the feeling—worse than that, the certainty—that they held some threat. Her whole being was braced for the unknown danger that was about to be revealed.

The poor child was unable to mask her feelings, and from her expression Slane could read her thoughts like an open book. His sly, cruel face brightened. He saw she was weak—helpless against him, who would stop at nothing. She would speak. She'd tell him what he needed to know. Slane said slowly, "Eight of my men are missing. The rest, terrified by inexplicable events—inexplicable to anyone not in on the secret of how they were performed—have obliged me to let them go and to put them down on land. I'm sure you can understand that I, having a scientific, logical mind, can't agree with those ignoramuses and settle for the explanation that the *Vulture* is haunted!"

Her throat was too choked to make a sound, and she merely bowed.

"I'm delighted to find you agree with me," went on Slane. "This conversation will be even easier and shorter…" But then suddenly he stood up. "But now that I think of it, I don't want to force you to listen to the babbling of an old man like me! White hair frightens young ladies. Lloyd, come forward and talk to your fiancée yourself. The future Mrs. Hibbett won't hide the truth from the man whose life she's going to share."

William's answer was to mutter mockingly, "Who knows?"

"I know," answered Slane harshly in annoyance at his son's clumsiness. "That kind of deceit would be treachery, and I'll have no mercy on traitors, no matter who they might be." He'd raised his voice. Now he calmed himself with an effort, and said again, "Question your sweetheart, Lloyd, go on."

The princess was now trembling hard enough to be visible. She was afraid, terribly afraid.

But events were hurrying along. The false Lloyd Hibbett sat next to the young woman. "Princess Liao," he said in a voice full of hypocrisy, "you heard what that worthy Mr. Slane said. He described the awful things that have been happening on board the airship. He told you the ridiculous explanation that satisfied the crew—and he made clear to you that neither he nor I can go along with such nonsense."

Though it cost her an effort that made her nerves jangle, the Chinese girl managed to say, "Yes."

As if her answer filled him with satisfaction, William went on, "Perfect! Perfect! So we're in agreement already! No surprise," he added gallantly, "for two people joined by mutual affection…" Then his tone changed. "But this is no time for love songs. Back to what I was saying. So, we don't believe the *Vulture* is haunted. But we haven't been able to figure out what caused the actions that afflicted the crew. You understand?"

She nodded.

"Great! So you can understand why we're quite concerned—and with good reason—right?"

She nodded again.

"In that case, this'll go smoothly. My fiancée's most important duty is to support me. So I won't have to beg you to tell us what person or persons are behind the stupid prank that just cost us our entire crew."

Princess Liao had gone deathly pale. For a moment she thought her heart had stopped. Oh, she understood now: they wanted her to betray those who'd risked their lives to protect hers. Energized by her revulsion at what she was being asked to do, she had the illusion that she was, simply and naturally, as heroic as the terrible circumstances required. Her eyes brightened and she replied firmly, "You're quite right. I'd be eager to tell you what I know… but I know nothing." After a deep breath she went on, "And it's no surprise an ignorant girl like me can't figure out scientific phenomena that have baffled scientists like you."

She broke off: her listeners were laughing rudely. "Does what I'm saying make you laugh?" she asked, instinctively using the strategy of the weak: to sidestep an accusation by means of a counter-accusation.

"Indeed it does," spluttered William through his spasms of laughter.

"What you're saying, exactly," agreed Slane, equally convulsed.

Taken aback by their replies, she said nothing.

William went on, "Before you incriminate yourself any further, Princess, listen to me." He took her hand, and she didn't try to withdraw it. "We never act blindly. You want proof? Here it is: we know you're colluding with whoever did all the damage."

"Me?! Me?!" she stammered wildly, her pretense of courage falling away in an instant.

"You yourself, and we know it from an indisputable fact our investigation revealed."

She stared at the Slanes with the terrified look victims give their executioners.

William didn't even notice. He went on, "You went into a cabin where you had no reason to be."

"What cabin?"

"Mr. Slane's control room."

At those words, the young woman looked absolutely shocked. The high arch of her black eyebrows, the sag of her open mouth, the wild look in her eyes, all showed that the meaning of what William had said completely escaped her. But in her expression the Slanes saw only another proof of her deception, and it just made them angrier and more bitter. Did this weak Chinese girl think she could fool them?

In an even harsher, more menacing tone, William said, "Don't bother to play dumb. There's no point in denying it. You left evidence in the control room that you'd been there."

"I left…" she stammered, completely lost.

"Come, come, Princess. You won't give up without a good reason, so here it is." William held out to her the ruby-studded bracelet he'd picked up from the dressing table when they came into her cabin. "You see this bracelet?"

"Of course."

"It's yours, isn't it?"

She tried to joke. "If you came here to tell me I own this piece of jewelry, you really needn't have bothered."

The young man shook his head scornfully, and raised the bracelet closer to her eyes. "Please observe, Princess, one stone is missing. It's been torn from the setting."

"So?"

"I found that ruby in the cabin I mentioned earlier. The stone being there, and the bracelet being here, obviously means that the person who owns this piece of jewelry went from there to here."

Princess Liao bowed her head. The truth had come to her in a flash. She'd given the bracelet to May overnight. And it must have been May who, without noticing, had lost the ruby in the control room.

Slane misunderstood her silence and assumed she was still resisting them. Meaning to strike the decisive blow that would break her will, he growled, "I'm no tenderhearted lover. I want to know who my enemies are, and I'll stop at nothing to find out."

He paused to let his words sink in. Then he went on even more harshly, "I've studied methods of torture where you come from, Princess. I'm sure I don't need to elaborate my point. You'll talk, or I'll put into practice what I've learned… on your noble person." He drew a knife from his pocket, and with a hideous cackle he went on, "What would you say if, for starters, I tore the delicate skin off one of your cheeks?"

She saw the blade glinting an inch from her face. Wild fear filled her entire being. She gave a hoarse, inhuman cry, and lost consciousness.

How long was she out? Princess Liao couldn't have answered that question when a fresh feeling of coolness restored her to awareness. It felt now like a cold rain was falling on her brow. She reached up quickly, and her hand came away wet from her damp forehead. And then another sensation drove away all thought of the previous: kisses covered her cheeks and her closed eyelids. She opened her eyes—and froze in surprise.

Little Jane was kissing her, while still holding a pitcher half full of water. Now the princess understood both her wet face and the shower of kisses. But how could the little girl be here with her? What had become of the Slanes? Still unable to speak, Princess Liao only asked herself those questions silently.

But the child must have had powers of divination, because her first words answered the Chinese girl's confused thoughts. "You were lying there, as if dead, with those wicked Slanes. I admit, I was afraid. But since you were still breathing I thought, she might just be asleep again. The opium those villains gave you…"

"You know about the opium?" stammered the princess in surprise.

The little girl nodded with mischievous self-satisfaction. "It wasn't hard. I overheard everything they said."

"So you weren't asleep?"

"No. At the table I poured my milk onto the floor."

"Why?"

"Because I was suspicious of those nasty Slanes. They seemed so pleased to be making you drink their California wine that I said to myself, 'The way to annoy them is not to drink.'"

Princess Liao clasped her hands; the child's precocious reasoning amazed her. But upon reflection she went on, "But didn't you fall asleep at the table?"

Jane's silvery laugh greeted the question. "Not at all. I was pretending."

"Pretending?"

"Of course. Oh, children often do that. The grownups don't suspect, and you can learn all kinds of things. I was watching through my eyelashes, and I could tell I was right. The two villains glanced at me out of the corner of their eyes, and exchanged a satisfied look. So I kept it up. And that's when I realized all our friends had been overcome by sleep."

She cuddled up to the princess. "You were very sweet. You volunteered to bring me here to your cabin so I could sleep more comfortably. I wanted to give you a kiss while you were carrying me. I didn't, because then you would've known I wasn't asleep—but I love you very much." She kissed the princess's face again.

The Chinese girl felt both gratitude for Jane's affection and the respect of an inferior before this child who was the only one of them to have protected herself from the Slanes' trap. That feeling only intensified after she asked, "And what about *them*?... Where are they?"

The little girl laughed openly. "Over there, on the floor. It's their turn to sleep."

Princess Liao sat up on her bunk to look in the direction Jane was pointing with her darling little index finger, and what she saw stunned her: Tom and William Slane were stretched out on the floor, fast asleep. Her eyes turned from them back to the child.

Vastly entertained, Jane went on, "You don't get it?"

"You can say that again, darling."

"But it's simple. They intended to hurt you. So I told them to sleep till I woke them up."

"You told them that?"

"That's what I'm explaining. You know I'm not lying."

It would be impossible to describe Princess Liao's astonishment. She stared at the little girl who claimed to have ordered her enemies to sleep. "Why would they obey you?"

"Because they couldn't help it." In a knowing way, Jane went on, "Unlike you, I have complete confidence in my dear May, who's so smart and so good. When she says we should do this or that, I don't need to understand before I obey. And look at the result: if you'd followed her instructions, you wouldn't have needed anyone's help to protect you."

Since the Chinese girl just stared at her in confusion, the child went on, "You don't seem to understand. If you'd worn the electric tunic, as May calls it..."

Princess Liao threw up her hands as if to ward off the idea. "Don't say that. That's the work of magic..."

She stopped, because Jane had burst out laughing. "You're funny!"she said through silvery peals of mirth. "It isn't magic, since May says it's science. I can't explain it, but I know my dear May wouldn't trick us, so I believe what she says." She pointed to her own body. "So when we were all given a tunic, and you refused it, I put mine on."

"You did?"

"Of course—and it's lucky for us I did. Just now, when those two men were standing over you, threatening you, I remembered what May said: if you're wearing the tunic you have nothing to fear. All you have to do is want something, and it'll happen. So I wanted those wicked men to fall asleep till I decide to wake them."

The princess was speechless—with admiration for the inventor of that marvelous device, and for the darling child who, by trusting what May said, had brought about the miracle of making their enemies powerless. But then she noticed Jane was bending over Slane's sleeping form and carefully searching through his pockets. "What are doing, dear?"

Jane glanced up. "I'm looking for the flask that lets you wake up someone who's been put to sleep by opium."

Liao couldn't help a cry of surprise. "You know how to counteract sedatives now, darling?"

Jane gave her a look of surprise at her surprise, and said in the most natural way, "I saw the way they woke you up, that's all. Our friends all drank wine at lunch, so they must be asleep just like you were. We'll have to wake them up the same way."

Jane certainly had a gift for logic. Princess Liao found nothing to say. And a moment later the little girl triumphantly held up Slane's flask.

Followed by the princess, still dazed by the whole adventure, she went back to the dining room. As she'd predicted, they found May and Lipson fast asleep next to Freda and Sefra. Derrick had slid out of his chair and was snoring under the table next to Stepan, whom he must have dragged along with him onto the floor. Princess Liao shivered with retrospective horror at the sight: the unconsciousness of her protectors made it clear how close they'd all come to disaster. And her affectionate admiration for Jane grew even greater with her understanding that, by her incredible presence of mind, the child had saved them all. She hugged the little girl and covered her blonde hair with kisses. Then the two of them—Jane lightheartedly, the princess in a kind of religious fervor—administered the antidote to their companions overcome by the sleep their enemies had provoked.

A few minutes later they were all awake, and had learned how their little companion, the weak child they'd have been afraid to rely on, had saved them. And saved was the word: saved from defeat, saved from death... It seemed clear that if the Slanes had managed to extract from the terrified princess a confession of the passengers' plot against them, they'd have struck back mercilessly while the opium-induced lethargy left their victims helpless.

The petting, cuddling, and congratulation they all gave Jane can be imagined—though she didn't act proud: in her own eyes what she'd done had been nothing special, nothing that would justify the fuss her friends were making.

She was more interested when, after the first effusions were over, Lipson asked. "Now, my friends, what should we do next?"

"Get off the *Vulture*," they all replied as one.

"I agree. We can longer stay in the presence of these villains. But leaving the airship isn't enough. We need to decide what to do after that. So let's talk it over while—thanks to our darling little Jane—our adversaries are incapacitated."

CHAPTER VI
The Unconscious March

"Come now, Captain Andrews, in the dumps again?"

"Always."

"Snap out of it! Hell, no one in the U.S. Navy would believe that—six months after we were posted to Honolulu—a brave officer like you, captain of Submarine B-23, can't get over some Chinese girl he left behind in San Francisco!"

"Well, Booker, Chinese or not, a lady's a lady, and a U.S. Navy officer is a man."

The speakers were two young men, smartly turned out in U.S. Navy uniform. Andrews, the tall, slim, elegant skipper of a submarine, had an air of authority and decisiveness. And that, no doubt, was the source of the surprise expressed by his fellow captain.

"It's already been six months since we left San Francisco," sighed Andrews.

"And tonight, old man, we'll get even further away, since we got orders this morning…"

"To sail for the Japanese and Chinese coast for a mapping survey… Bah! The distance from San Francisco doesn't matter. The misery is to be out of sight at all—the number of miles separating us adds nothing to the burden."

"Indeed, whether you're in Honolulu, in Yokohama, or in Shanghai, it's equally impossible to see the parks of Frisco[21] and make out the beloved figure of a certain amber-skinned little princess."

"Shut up, Booker."

Andrews had spoken vehemently, and a silence followed. But he soon calmed down, and held out his hand. "My dear friend, I beg your pardon. I'm foolish, and I know it. But I think I'd rather die than give up my folly."

"Don't give it up. To live is already to begin recovering."

"I think you're wrong. From the day I met her, I was helpless attracted to that young woman, whose race and social rank are so different from mine. No one was more critical of my folly than I was myself."

"And yet, once again, that criticism had no effect on your behavior."

"Not in the least. A humble naval skipper, the descendant of honest shop-keepers, is smitten with a young lady of imperial blood."

"Oh, the blood of a dethroned empire!" protested Booker lightly.

But Andrews shook his head sadly. "Throne or not, that doesn't change the distance between our races." All the reverence of democratic America for the privileges of birth were contained in those words.

While they spoke, the two men had been wandering up from the harbor through the meandering lanes of the old town of Honolulu. Absorbed in their discussion of romance, they hadn't noticed that they'd gone beyond the last houses and had reached farmland, divided into a checkerboard of cotton fields, coco palm groves, guava and banana orchards, and coffee plantations, displaying every possible shade of green.

A few months earlier, Captain Andrews had been living in San Francisco, his home port. By chance, while strolling in Golden Gate Park, he'd met Princess Liao. The mysterious phenomenon of attraction had struck again. The princess, exiled from the Chinese Empire, had big black eyes, in which the young man thought he could discern nostalgia for her lost homeland. And her exquisite pale amber complexion had disturbed the naval officer in unfamiliar ways.

He'd asked around, and had learned of the young Chinese woman's distinguished origins. All hope of marrying her had been dashed by that discovery. And yet he'd never stopped trying to find ways to run into her. Why? He couldn't have said. He had too much integrity to hope to win her in any way other than by taking her unawares, so he resolved that she would never suspect his feelings. Why wound her, since her birth placed an insurmountable barrier between them? Still, he wanted to see her, to fill his eyes with her image. That's often how the power of attraction disguises the illogical appearance of its own folly. And it's only appearance, after all, because mysterious fate takes pleasure in thwarting the most logical precautions.

---

[21] The nickname for San Francisco [*Note from the Author*].

That idyll—for which only Andrews was paying the price—had suddenly been broken off by Navy orders. Submarine B-23 had been posted to the Hawaiian Islands, and Andrews had three days to make ready to sail. What those days were like can be imagined. In a trembling fever, the young officer ran from his vessel to the places he'd be most likely to meet Princess Liao; and indeed he managed to reconcile the demands of his profession and his disappointed dreams. When they finally parted, he was aware that at each of their last meetings the young lady had betrayed a sudden flare of emotion—which she quickly veiled under the impassivity she'd learned at the imperial court.

Painful joy had whispered in his ear, "If she weren't of royal stock, she could've looked favorably on this humble skipper."

Then Submarine B-23 had carried Andrews across the blue-green emptiness of the Pacific Ocean. And now, in his new home, he spent all the time he had off from work immersed in his hopeless dream. And that was why Booker, his friend and Naval Academy classmate, was now trying, for at least the hundredth time, to show him the uselessness of his romantic illusions.

They ambled through the countryside in silence. Booker was gathering ammunition for another assault. Andrews gazed inward at the tender image etched on his heart. The road wound endlessly. Copses of trees of various sorts limited their view, and whenever they reached one of the countless bends in the road they caught sight of farmers, and of carts drawn by Asian buffalo, that were previously hidden from them.

Now, as they rounded another bend, Andrews exclaimed, "I'm going crazy, Booker! I can see her! There—there—up ahead!"

Coming toward them along the road was a small group consisting of four women, five men, and a little girl. Among the women Andrews had noticed only one: Princess Liao. There could be no mistake—it was she. Though he believed he might be seeing things, his eyes were in no doubt that they beheld the woman he thought he'd left behind in San Francisco.

The delicate Chinese girl was walking along, leaning on May's arm. On her other side, May held little Jane's hand. Behind them came Derrick and Freda, and Stepan and Sefra, all of them astonished by what they were witnessing, and also a little terrified by the proof of the almost infinite power of the electric tunics the engineer had invented. Down one side of the road, Lipson seemed to be escorting Slane and William. How had they all come to be a kilometer outside Honolulu, two days' march from the E'akiro volcano?

Once the princess was awake, a series of events had taken place on board the *Vulture* that the simple minds of Derrick and Freda and those teenagers Stepan and Sefra had yet to recover from: Their own awakening in the dining room. The princess and Jane taking turns explaining. Their shock at hearing how by her brave actions the little girl had effortlessly undone the Slanes. And then the long discussion. What should they do? After what had happened—and their lucky escape—it was no longer possible to stay aboard the airship.

Amid the general confusion, only May had stayed calm. It was she who'd persuaded her companions to go to Honolulu. And when they all protested, "Who'll guide us through this unknown land?" she'd laughed—which made Jane laugh in turn—and said, "Why, the Slanes! For once they'll be helpful to somebody."

Derrick and Freda had objected: to ask for assistance like that from their former jailers seemed insane. But little Jane, with comical gravity, stared down their objections scornfully. She went close to May, and the exchange that followed astonished everyone.

"I know they won't resist your will, big sister May," the girl began.

"Ah, you understand!" replied May affectionately, taking her in her arms. "Well, then, darling, explain to our friends the plan they don't seem to grasp."

The child was delighted to have a role to play, and didn't need to be talked into it. She assumed a serious expression. "The Slanes will sleep as long as I don't tell them to wake up, right?"

"We know that, but what's that got to with our needing a guide?"

"Our pretty May will order them to guide us. Without ever waking up, they'll lead us to Honolulu, if that's what it's called."

"Is that possible?" murmured May's adoptive parents.

May nodded. "Not only possible, but easy—though painstaking. One of us will always have to be with our enemies to steer them and keep them on the right track. That's the weakness of my apparatus: you have to be present to sustain the hallucination."

"So guiding us to Honolulu will be a hallucination?"

"At least the result of a hallucination. To persuade them, I'll make them believe it's to their significant advantage to guide us there."

"Bravo!" cried Jane, doing a little dance. "But if you like, instead of you always having to watch over the wicked Slanes, we can all take turns."

"Exactly, darling. And that'll make the job less tiring for each of us."

"Bravo! Bravo! So then, beautiful big sister May, we reach Honolulu."

In some embarrassment, May murmured, "But once we're there I don't know what we're going to do with those villains."

"We'll tell them to lie down in the shade under some trees and go to sleep, and not wake up till we've found a way to leave the island."

All had taken place exactly as planned. Under the influence of their adversaries' irresistible willpower, the Slanes had gotten to their feet, left the *Vulture*, hiked up the cliffs overlooking the volcano, and unhesitatingly crossed the plateau, following paths that led gradually down toward the port of Honolulu.

Ah, those two days of walking, led by a couple of people who proceeded with the stiff, mechanical motion of sleepwalkers—and with their eyes open and staring straight ahead, without glancing around like conscious beings! May, Lipson, Derrick, Freda, Stepan, and Sefra—those last two gradually getting used to the scientist's remarkable invention—had taken turns watching over their involuntary guides. That way, just as May had promised, none of them was unduly fatigued.

Andrews now felt his legs giving way under him. For a moment he thought he might fall to his knees, but then he straightened up and stood there, with his arms stretched out adoringly toward Princess Liao, overwhelmed by what he thought was a only trick of memory. Booker watched, stunned, wondering whether he too was the victim of some unheard-of mirage.

Now May's blue eyes fell on the two naval officers, and a smile flashed across her features as she thought to herself, "I knew he was in Honolulu, but I couldn't have hoped for a luckier encounter."

She leaned close to the princess's ear and spoke urgently to her in a low voice. Her words made the Chinese girl start and blush, but she nodded and—after gesturing to her companions to stay where they were—Princess Liao advanced to meet Captain Andrews.

He observed her, stunned that she was coming toward him, and that the dream that for the past six months had given him the will to live was coming true. His emotions made him sway like a reed in a north wind when she murmured, "Captain Andrews, you, here, in this remote land?"

"That's natural for a sailor. But as for you, miss, it's harder to explain."

She shook her head sadly. "Ah, I'd get even further away from San Francisco if I could, because I'm fleeing destiny."

"Could misfortune possibly pursue you, who so richly deserve to be happy?"

Princess Liao stammered, "Misfortune and death hang over me and over my father. Don't try to understand—I can't explain any better. All you need to know is that I'm doomed to die if within the next few hours I can't find a way to get off this island lost in the middle of the Pacific."

Andrews drew himself up. Knowing she was in danger had driven away his tender feelings. He was no longer the sighing lover: her words had promoted him to the rank of protector.

By all appearances, May had counted on exactly that transformation in him. Focusing the full force of her blue eyes on his pupils, and articulating slowly to emphasize every syllable, she said, "Am I right in thinking Captain Andrews is devoted to you, Princess Liao?"

"Devoted isn't putting it strongly enough," interrupted the young man impulsively.

"Yes, yes, it's enough," replied the engineer with a slight smile, "because you can provide us with the means we seek to get away from the Hawaiian archipelago."

The others started, because they didn't yet understand what she meant.

"What are you trying to say?" stammered the princess, making no effort to hide her surprise at the turn the conversation had taken.

But May thought it best not to answer her. Still addressing Captain Andrews, she went on, "I knew you were in Honolulu. We were on our way to town, meaning to ask for you, to find you, and to ask you for passage on board your Submarine B-23. Since here you are, I've seized the opportunity to get straight to the question."

Princess Liao stifled an exclamation. Up to now she'd thought they were going to Honolulu with only the faint hope of finding some steamer—maybe even a sailing ship—at anchor in the harbor and ready to sail. Any vessel, heading away from the islands in no matter what direction, had seemed to her the best chance the fugitives could expect. But now it occurred to her that—on this occasion just as on every other—May hadn't acted blindly. Their trek to Honolulu had been the result of a precise and logical plan. The Englishwoman had not come here in search of any ship that happened to be in port; she'd led the group toward a vessel she'd already chosen in advance.

But Andrews reacted to May's words with a gesture of regret. He mumbled with embarrassment, "Alas, miss! Though naval regulations forbid submarine captains from allowing anyone on board besides the crew, I wouldn't have hesitated to break the rules. But unfortunately, I have orders that require me to sail tomorrow for the coast of China..."

"The coast of China!" cried Princess Liao with evident joy. "But that's exactly where I'd like to be taken!"

"You would?" said Andrews, his face brightening.

"Didn't she tell you a moment ago," said May gently, "the danger that threatens her also hangs over her father?"

"That's true!"

"Her father is in China. He's unaware of the danger looming over him. The princess wants to go to him to warn him, to watch over him, and to share his fate."

With a gesture as sudden as the release of a spring, Andrews held out his hands to Princess Liao. But the young man remembered just in time that the Chinese girl was an "imperial young lady" whose royal fingertips he ought not clasp. He recovered by seizing May's fingers, which he squeezed hard enough to crush them, and all the while he stammered broken phrases in which his happiness and the respect of democratic America for beings of noble blood were mixed together. "To China!... The honor of crossing the Pacific with you!..."

May's laugh cut short his expressions of gratitude, which otherwise might have run on without end. "Understood: honor, pleasure, anything you like. But there's no need to notify the authorities of our departure..."

The officer's features clouded over once more. "But how can we manage that?"

"Don't worry," May replied. "What I'm asking is as simple as one plus one. You'll go back to Honolulu."

"I'll go back—easy enough."

"You'll take whatever measures are necessary on board to accommodate..."

"Ten people."

"No, only eight."

Once again Andrews looked surprised as he glanced around and counted off May, Princess Liao, little Jane, the foursome of Derrick, Freda, Stepan, and Sefra, and lastly Lipson with the two Slanes.

May hastened to explain. "Two people will not be coming with us on the voyage. So that makes eight."

He bowed respectfully and promised, "In that case, I'll be ready to receive eight passengers this evening."

"Perfect. When have you ordered your crew to return to be ready to sail tomorrow?"

"Everyone was aboard at noon today."

"Better and better. So, around nine tonight, send a boat to the cargo docks."

"Why the cargo docks?"

"Because after nightfall that part of the harbor is completely deserted. We'll be able to get aboard the boat and reach the submarine without drawing attention. Secrecy is of the utmost importance," May added with emphasis, "since we're trying to shake off the pursuit of ruthless enemies." She shook the captain's hand with typically American vigor. "Now go, Captain Andrews. Princess Liao is not permitted to express her gratitude. But I know I'm not mistaken in assuring you she thanks you with all her heart."

The young Chinese girl's cheeks glowed bright red; and, by a strange reflex effect, the young naval officer's face turned equally crimson. For a moment the two of them faced each other, speechless and without a thought, except for a confused sense that they'd just experienced one of those moments of shared aspiration between two persons that create unbreakable bonds.

After which the officer pulled himself together, bowed very low, and said in a trembling voice, "I'll carry out your instructions, miss. Tonight at nine the boat will be waiting at the cargo docks." He paused, as if he were short of breath. Then he managed to go on, "We sail at dawn."

Another bow, another glance at the emperor's daughter, and then the young man dragged his friend Booker back toward town—that officer being amazed at having witnessed the conversion of a torpedo submarine into a passenger vessel. Soon a bend in the road hid the two of them from view.

May looked around inquiringly, and her eyes fell on the flat land to the right of the road. A hundred meters away in that direction stood a small dense wood out of which rose the tall trunks of a few palm trees. Pointing to it, she said, "We'll wait for nightfall in that clump of trees. That's where we'll leave our unofficial guides."

No one offered the least objection, and five minutes later the whole group had disappeared into the thickets and were safe from prying eyes. Derrick and Stepan appointed themselves sentries and took up positions at the edge of the woods.

Meanwhile Lipson roughly ordered the Slanes, "Lie down!"

Strange to say, in perfect unison the two men stretched out on the heather and scattered ferns that covered the ground.

"Sleep," Lipson went on. "Sleep till we're out in the open ocean. After that we don't care what happens to you. We'll be out of reach of your satanic *Vulture*, and that's good enough."

Lipson glanced admiringly over at May, who, with the help of Freda and Sefra, was helping the princess get settled. "A submarine!" said Lipson under his breath. "The depth of the ocean itself will serve as a veil between us and the sharp eyes of the masters of the *Vulture*. Truly I couldn't even have dreamt of such a perfect solution."

Little Jane heard him, and she answered with the solemn tone that's so comical coming from a child. "My friend May planned all of this."

Strange: the little girl's affectionate words brought forth in the young man's features the same blush that earlier, out on the road, had reddened the faces of the princess and the submarine captain.

Dawn was approaching, tinting the gloom of night with an imperceptible touch of pink. In the woods in which May and her friends had found shelter the day before, no sign of them remained. But on the bed of heather and ferns that covered the ground two human forms lay unmoving, seemingly oblivious to the dew steadily dripping from the branches. Dew fall is abundant in the Hawaiian Islands; it sometimes dampens the ground as much as a real rain.

Suddenly the two bodies moved, sat up, and spoke in voices that rumbled under the dome of the trees.

"By the Devil! I'm soaked!"

"It's as if someone emptied a pitcher of water on me!"

"I'm not dreaming—I'll have to wring out my clothes."

"Mine are just as wet; it's not good for my skin."

"Some stupid practical joke that might lead to bronchitis."

"Even pleurisy, father, you might as well say it."

Snarling, growling, and roaring like that, Tom and William Slane emerged from the sleep imposed on them by Lipson's willpower, and returned to normal life. They were quite right about being wet. The sun, as we know, had barely risen; and from the branches of the trees the morning dew produced in abundance by the cool of the night condensed in drops as big as silver dollars and rained down on them like a veritable deluge. Those trees and that rain provoked a renew outcry from the Slanes.

"You see these woods, William?"

"Sure. I'm not blind."

"We slept outdoors, my boy!"

"I can see that as well as you can. But I have to admit I'm a little surprised."

"You're not the only one, son… But be so good as to tell me why you're surprised."

"Why? Ah, by Jove, I have no reason to hide it—I haven't lost my mind—and I'm certain I was overcome by a desire to sleep… in Liao's cabin."

"Overcome! The very word. I myself was seized by the exact same desire in the exact same spot."

"That's peculiar. To fall asleep like that, for no reason—or rather with every reason to stay awake… Because, if I remember correctly, our plan was to make that damned Chinese girl confess…"

The two men stared at each other, obviously astonished. Sitting up, with their legs stretched out on the trampled vegetation, they looked around them in amazement. To fall asleep in a cabin on an airship and wake up in the middle of some woods with their clothes soaked by cold dew—that certainly warranted the liveliest surprise.

"What are we doing here?" growled Slane finally.

"Oh, that's easy," joked his son. "What we're doing here is getting soaked! But what I'd like to know is, how did we wind up in these woods?"

That question brought Slane back to the main point of the mystery. William was right: what they had to find out most urgently was the reason for their presence in this shady, leafy, and above all damp spot. First of all, where were they? Where were these woods located? The foliage around them formed an opaque green screen. To orient themselves they had to breach the obstacle that limited their view. That thought occurred to both of them at the same time. They stood up, stamped their feet to recover the circulation in their benumbed legs, and pushed their way out through the thickets.

As will be remembered, the woods were small, and in ten paces the Slanes reached the edge. There they stopped, stupefied, their feet stuck to the ground by an astonishment that the reader will understand: before them a road wound through a varied landscape of assorted crops. Traveling along the road and raising a pale dust gilded by the first rays of sunshine, came a cart pulled by slow, majestic water buffalo, and several donkeys laden with baskets, on top of which Polynesian women—no doubt farm wives—basked in the sun on pyramids of piled-up vegetables.

"How about that?" stammered William. "We seem to have misplaced the E'akiro volcano!"

Though put in that jocular form, the idea frightened both men: the *Vulture* stood on the edge of the crater of the volcano, and its portholes looked out onto a charred, sterile, desolate landscape. The landscape that now greeted the Slanes' eyes, on the contrary, was pleasant, fertile, and well watered.

Slane's next words alarmed them both. "I can do without the volcano. What worries me is, I can't see the slightest trace of our *Vulture*."

They stared at each other, suddenly seized by the thought that the machine that guaranteed their incredible power over others had fallen into the hands of their enemies. And thinking about their enemies led them straight to their earlier perplexity: What enemies? Of what sort? Answering to what names? Taking what form? Driven by what motive, what hatred, what plan?

Their teeth began to chatter. Was it fear? Was it cold? They remembered the strange doings that robbed the *Vulture* of its entire crew. Those astonishing events had obviously not taken place without some cause. Common sense led inexorably to the certainty that what had happened had been intended, directed, carried out by some hostile will. But whose will? And whose hostility? What individual could feel bold and powerful enough to attack the Slanes—and could manage to terrify them by his unprecedented attack?

In their inmost thoughts the Slanes had to admit their enemy did have the power necessary: a peculiar and inexplicable power. They no longer doubted that their men had truly suffered all the torments they'd complained of. Hadn't similar things happened to them? Their sudden sleep, just as they were about to interrogate Princess Liao. Their transportation to this unknown land. All of that was only too real. All of that brutally swept away the sarcastic skepticism with which they'd dismissed their henchmen's claims out of hand. How bitterly they now regretted not having carried out their investigation more thoroughly. Instead of being sarcastic, of getting angry, of answering brusquely, they ought to have established the initial cause of the hullabaloo that had broken out aboard the *Vulture*. Scientific minds like theirs would certainly have solved the matter... if they'd approached it with the composure needed.

Now it was too late. The crewmen who'd fled had taken away with them the experiences and impressions that could have guided their masters' inquiry. Slane uttered a resounding curse and clenched his fists menacingly. "In any case, the first step is to find out where we are."

"Easy! Let's ask those people going along the road."

"Then let's hurry and do it, because I feel like madness is digging its claws into my brain."

The passersby had no trouble answering their questions, but what they said didn't make the two men any calmer: they were three kilometers from Honolulu, and therefore about two day's march away from the E'akiro volcano.

In front of their informants they could barely suppress the curses that rose to their lips. But why give away their secrets to these natives who could change nothing? The need to hide their rage only made it greater; and once they were alone the father and son gave way to echoing howls worthy of wild beasts. Two days away from the volcano! Two days from the *Vulture*! Their enemies must have made good use of that time. What now would remain of their airship, the brilliant invention that gave them mastery of the world till they were ready to donate it to the United States government?

The need to find out, mixed with a vague hope they didn't even dare put into words, drove them to return to the barren ground where they'd landed the airship. They turned their backs on Honolulu and walked all day, oblivious to the heat of the sun, to fatigue, to wind-blown dust, to everything.

That night they camped in the woods that cover the foothills of the plateau at the heart of which stands the enormous caldera that surrounds the E'akiro crater. In that blessed country they had no reason to worry about the nighttime dangers so much to be feared elsewhere: no ferocious animal haunts the Hawaiian night, and snakes—so common in certain parts of the world—are unknown in those islands.

At dawn, though their legs were somewhat stiff from the previous day's march, they set off again. They felt they couldn't afford to rest; their concern about the fate of the *Vulture* forced them to ignore their fatigue. Soon they passed the last bushes, and the grass itself thinned out and finally vanished. The Slanes kept going without a pause. They were unaware of any need to rest: all they could think about was their haste to get back to the *Vulture*.

They crossed the desolate lava fields, through pumice and slag, through the blueish clouds of sulfur that caught in their throats and stung their mucus membranes. They didn't slow down. Reaching the landing site of the *Vulture* had become a kind of obsession with them. They marched without feeling any effort, driven by an unconscious desire.

Finally, they recognized the plateau that bordered the ring of cliffs. A little further and they reached the rim, from which they could see down into the chasm, at the very bottom of which bubbled the crater of the volcano. They gave a cry of joy, but one whose strange tone was tinged with madness. "The *Vulture*! The *Vulture*!"

The airship sat on the rocky ledge, barely a hundred meters below them. From here it appeared to have suffered no damage. They could see the retractable ladder hanging down its side, and the hatchway leading to the interior was open. The vessel looked as if it had been abandoned, but there was no sign of looting. Could the reality match the appearance?

Like an avalanche, Slane and William ran down the steep path that connected the two plateaus. An unharmed *Vulture* would be their strength restored. Like gladiators knocked down for a moment, they would recover their sword and shield and rise up again ready for battle once more.

They reached the lower plateau, and their momentum carried them to the foot of the retractable ladder. William had already taken hold of the bottom rungs—but Slane grabbed his arm to stop him, and in a voice whose hoarseness betrayed the emotion filling him at that moment, he said, "Revolver in your hand, son. Who knows whether our quarters aren't occupied."

The idea was too plausible not to strike the young man as justified. So it was with his Browning at the ready that William climbed the ladder, followed closely by Slane, also armed, and with anxious eyes ceaselessly scanning their surroundings. No enemy, no obstacle could he see. They reached the roof deck. Still nothing! Still no one! The silence was encouraging. It crossed their minds that their mysterious enemies had abandoned the vessel because manipulating its controls had seemed too dangerous to them. Of course the two of them were still worried: they said "our enemies" without knowing to whom the words applied. But one fact stood paramount—they were about to regain possession of their *Vulture*.

They went down through the hatchway. They searched both levels: the cabins, the control room, the crew's quarters, the engine room, the holds— nothing escaped their inspection. Everywhere they found silence and emptiness. Nothing suggested that while they were gone anyone had even gotten inside the airship. Gradually they grew bolder. The conviction that they had nothing to fear made it possible for them to think again. And that led them to reach another conclusion.

"Liao has vanished!" said Slane, expressing the stark fact revealed by their meticulous search of the airship.

William completed the inventory of the passengers: "And along with her, that typist Miss May, Derrick the chauffeur, Miss Freda and that girl Sefra, that boy Stepan, James the valet, and that damned kid the princess was infatuated with, little Jane."

That darkened their mood. Their victim, the keystone of all their plans, thanks to whom they hoped to take possession of the wealth of vast stretches of Asia, was no longer in their hands. She was no longer subject to their will. The slave whose actions they could control at their whim had escaped from their tyrannical influence.

Slane slammed his fist down on the table next to him, and its varnish shattered under the blow. But almost immediately a cruel smile marked his face with menacing creases. "It doesn't matter!" he growled.

As was clear from his expression, William was interrupted in painful reflections. "What makes you say that?" he asked suspiciously. "You see a way to repair what looks to me to be irreparable?"

Slane chuckled. "Yes, my boy." And, his new cheerfulness seeming more dangerous than his earlier anger, he went on cynically and sententiously, "The daughter may have eluded us momentarily, son, but the father is still in our control."

"The father?"

"Of course! Don't we know where the deposed emperor of China is hiding?"

"Frankly, father, I don't see how knowing that will allow us to play our cards in such a way as to get our business back in hand."

Slane eyed his son scornfully; clearly the boy would never keep up with him! And there was sadness mixed with the scorn: the child of his own blood hadn't inherited his mental powers. He was certainly amoral, bloodthirsty, crooked... but the resemblance ended there. Intricate plots would forever remain beyond him. But, ignoring William's interruption, Slane went on explaining his idea. "The republican government of China trembles at the mere thought of the intrigues the ex-emperor could foment to regain his throne."

"That's obvious."

"It's also obvious that the government would deny no reward, no matter how costly, to the man who could put an end to that state of crisis by handing over the deposed ruler. Well, my boy, that man is me. Let's pull the emperor out of his hiding place, hold him prisoner on board the *Vulture*, and extract from the Chinese Republic every single mining concession and every single rail or river transport concession, in exchange for that fomenter of civil unrest."

William bowed. His father's schemes always took him by surprise. But this time, in the face of the vast plot conceived by that brain so fertile in evil, the young man felt his surprise growing into veneration. And yet one legitimate criticism arose by chance in William's mind. "Yes, but with Liao at liberty, and led by the unknown enemy whose attacks we've already suffered, she could reduce all our plans to nothing."

Slane nodded approvingly. "Well done, William. For once you're making good use of your gray matter. Rest assured, we'll work on getting on the trail of your... fiancée, and nullifying her potential accusations against us. Our *Vulture*'s speed guarantees that we'll reach China two weeks before the fastest ship, so we'll have time to make a careful investigation. Even the cleverest adversary always leaves behind some trace of his passing. It's up to us to find it."

CHAPTER VIII
In Which Slane is Astonished by
an Incomprehensible and Newly Acquired Power

"It's as cold as Siberia!"

"Ah, father, I think that expression doesn't even do it justice!"

That exchange reflected a reversal in the weather that had occurred in just a few hours on the high plateau surrounding the crater of the E'akiro volcano. Toward evening of the day on which the Slanes had finally returned to the *Vulture*, the sky had suddenly been filled with thick clouds that grew constantly blacker and heavier. A sharp wind had begun to blow from the north, causing the thermometer even inside the airship to drop to seven degrees below zero.[22]

Slane had quickly switched on the electric radiators that heated the vessel—but either they were malfunctioning or he was in a bad mood, because he couldn't get warm. And perhaps his ill humor was prompted by those clouds, which began to drop snow, whose white flakes fell past the portholes in endless flurries. He brusquely pulled himself together. "We paused to eat, William, but now let's go on with our investigation."

---

[22] About 19° Fahrenheit.

"For all the good the search has done so far..." grumbled his son.

"All the more reason to redouble our efforts. We've found nothing yet, I admit, but we have to find something: it's impossible for a whole group of people to vanish like that without a trace."

William shrugged, but, knowing from experience there was no resisting his father's will, he rose and waited for orders.

Slane went on, "We've checked all the rooms on board. We had to. The places most likely to hold a clue are those where the passengers spent most of their time: the lounge, the dining room, their cabins. That's where we have to go again."

"As you wish."

"All right! Come on, William. By Old Nick's clawed toes, we'll find some clue that'll help us."

And yet it was in vain that the two men searched the cabins, overturning the beds and the wash stands. What were they looking for? They would have had trouble putting it into words. In truth, their search was founded only on Slane's vague instinct that, "When an escape is planned, the fugitive leaves behind clues that are visible to someone who knows what he's looking for." But in fact the disappearance of the *Vulture*'s passengers had followed a series of unprecedented, incomprehensible events among whose singular qualities was that of not betraying themselves by any clue.

Slane growled furiously through clenched teeth. William followed him obediently, taking advantage of his position outside his father's view to shrug his shoulders, expressing eloquently how little success he expected from this search.

And the cold had now reached the very marrow of their bones, in spite of the bright glow of the electric radiators. Though at that time the temperature down on the coast must have been fifteen or sixteen degrees, in the crater outside the airship it had fallen to minus twenty.[23]

They'd searched the last of the private cabins. A rapid inspection of the dining room made clear to them that it held no clues to the disappearance of the fugitives. Only the lounge still remained.

William's discouragement must have spread to his father, because when they entered the lounge Slane let himself drop into one of the soft, thick-cushioned couches that lined the walls. Yes, the passengers had all gathered in this room. They'd stretched out on these couches that invited idleness. But what were the chances they'd left some impression of their thoughts on the furniture? If they hadn't done so in the privacy of their own cabins, they'd have been even more careful in the lounge, in some senses a public place accessible to anyone aboard the airship.

---

[23] About 60° Fahrenheit at the coast, 4° below zero in the crater.

His frown, the deep lines furrowing his brow, his clenched jaw—all suggested the tremendous anger filling a man who, for the first time in his life, had met an obstacle he felt powerless to overcome.

William philosophically sank into an armchair heaped with cushions, which had preserved an indentation showing someone else had sat there. Someone else… who? Perhaps that little Princess Liao, whom he'd flattered himself that he'd reduced to the slavery of marriage. How she must be laughing at him, now that she'd slipped between his fingers!

Those disagreeable reflections led William's features to grow as tense and menacing as his father's. Remembering his escaped fiancée made William angrier and angrier. He fired harsh curses in the direction of the vanished girl. At first, he cursed her under his breath. But rage, like a boiler, needs a safety valve, and the safety valve of an angry man is the noisy satisfaction of expressing out loud the insults he's been thinking up. William was true to form. His insults grew from the silent register to a murmur and finally to a roar. At last, he leapt to his feet so violently that he knocked onto the floor all the cushions piled onto his chair. He paid no attention…

But Slane, whose own train of thought had been interrupted by the racket his son was making, followed the boy's movements with a curious eye. The false Lloyd Hibbett's burst of temper didn't displease him, since it matched his own mood. He almost smiled at his son's behavior, which unconsciously cheered him up even in these grave circumstances.

The falling pile of cushions drew his attention. And then he gave a muffled exclamation. He stood up in turn, hurried to the armchair William had just left, and in the grip of intense emotion he stammered, "What's this?" He took hold of something that had been hidden under the cushions till now. William had turned to watch. Slane held up what he'd found and felt it carefully, saying again, "What in the world is this?"

William must have thought he was addressing him. He snickered scornfully and answered, "It looks like a knit undershirt. Put it on, if you're cold."

He stopped as Slane cut him off, saying, "No, this isn't made of wool."

"Oh, what does the fabric matter?" said his son. "It's some piece of clothing left behind by one of the passengers. May I roast in Hell if you find any better use for it than the one I already suggested."

Slane didn't answer. He moved to stand directly under the overhead electric light that spread its bright white beam around the lounge, and examined the garment carefully. The undershirt seemed to him, just as it had to his son, to be an ordinary piece of clothing. He had no idea he now held in his hands the terrible weapon conceived by May, thanks to which he'd been beaten, his henchmen had been killed or scattered, and his prisoners had escaped.

We remember that Princess Liao, who considered the navy-blue tunic that gave the power to impose illusions to be a form of witchcraft, had refused to put it on. She'd brought it back to the lounge, meaning to return it to May, but then

216

things had begun to happen quickly. She'd set the tunic down on an armchair, where it had been covered by a cushion and forgotten in the haste of their departure. And now it had fallen into the hands of their enemy... who, it was true, remained unaware of its unusual properties.

"No matter what you say," muttered Slane, "it's an odd kind of fabric. Like some sort of felt made from a mixture of cotton batting and metallic batting."

"It must be good and warm," joked William. "The metallic batting next to the skin would surely generate some heat."

"You're right. A little heat would be welcome, because I'm still freezing. And tonight, I mean to pursue our investigation in Honolulu."

"In Honolulu?" cried William.

"Of course. Let's take advantage of the storm. In this kind of weather everyone must be staying indoors, so there's no risk of meeting nosy people. The *Vulture* will get us close to town in just a few minutes. We'll land, you'll stay here to guard it, and I'll go see the harbor master."

"In the middle of the night? He won't receive you."

"A cash gift makes you welcome anywhere."

"Fine... but what's the point of your visit?"

"To find out what ships have sailed in the past two or three days: their names and destinations."

"Ah, now I understand. We'll find out where Liao is headed."

"I expect it'll corroborate my suspicions..."

"Which are...?"

"That her father, the worthy dethroned emperor, is the magnet drawing her..."

"So if we have one of them, we'll get the other one. Bravo, old man—you're going to get me back my fiancée."

Slane made a scornful face. "Do you insist on having her?"

"Oh, you know... The dowry and the expectation of those profitable concessions seem like the kind of solid qualifications you hope to find in your life partner."

"And you might be willing to have the solid qualifications without the burden of the partner."

"I'll admit it frankly. Is there a way to do that?"

"You'll find out in time. Right now, it's enough for you to know I have a way. And now I'm going to take your advice and put on this undershirt that turned up so fortuitously. Our former passengers will at least be useful enough to keep me in good health. Meanwhile go back to the control room and start the engines. You'll drop me off in the fields a few hundred meters from town. Go."

While William, under the influence of his father's greater intelligence, hurried off to the control room, Slane went into a cabin to put on the tunic—which he thought of simply as protection against the cold—and a heavy overcoat.

The gentle hum of the engines soon showed the *Vulture* was underway. The airship lifted off from its berth in the crater of the E'akiro volcano and flew away toward some still unknown destination.

Seated at the instrument panel, William concentrated on flying the vessel. In spite of the howling wind, in spite of the blizzard, the *Vulture* sped through the air like a bullet. The young man could see nothing through the portholes. An opaque darkness hid the ground from view, and the thick storm clouds above him let through no light from the sky. Only the compass showed what direction they were going. But a few minutes after they took off, it seemed to him there was now more empty space under the airship: they'd passed the high plateau of E'akiro and were now flying over the foothills that led down to the warm, fertile plains around Honolulu.

That led William to reduce speed and carefully bring the airship down a few hundred meters. He could no longer see snowflakes through the portholes, and an exterior light showed him that at their present altitude the snow had changed to rain. Certainly, it was still a downpour—but it proved that the layer of air they were now passing through was significantly warmer than where they'd come from.

"Proceed!" he said, giving himself orders. His hands operated the controls, and the *Vulture* resumed its forward course, but at a moderate speed: the forty kilometers separating the crater from Honolulu was no great distance for an airship capable of reaching two hundred kilometers an hour. A mere twenty-five minutes into the flight, the darkness was suddenly broken by points of light beneath the airship. By their pattern William recognized the web of streets and the layout of the port of Honolulu.

"Damn the night," he grumbled. "It won't be easy to land in the countryside without seeing what kind of surface I'm coming down on!"

"Well, well," said a mocking voice next to him, "yet again I observe you don't pay enough attention to the explanations you're given."

William jumped: Slane was standing right next to him. "Didn't I tell you," went on the latter, "about the Nightlooker, that device invented in our laboratories in San Francisco, which allows a pilot to land at any chosen point without the vessel being visible to the naked eye in the darkness?"

"So strangers, those gawkers scientists like us meet wherever we go, aren't alerted to our movements by even the faintest light—because light in the dark is the greatest foe, the one that gives away the traveler it's guiding."

"Good for you," said Slane approvingly. "Set the controls to a circle following the city limits. We'll choose an appropriate landing spot."

William pressed a lever on the instrument panel. When that was done, the young man—relieved that his father's scolding had been fairly mild—couldn't help observing, "You're in a better mood than you were earlier, when we parted."

Slane smiled. "I was freezing; now I'm warm."

"That undershirt, huh?"

"Exactly. The strange fabric seems to be ideal for concentrating calorific energy.[24] I'll have to get in touch with the manufacturer."

"To buy the patent?"

"Maybe. It's an invention that could be very profitable if capably exploited."

It should be obvious that Slane had no inkling of the real properties of the garment Princess Liao had left behind. And his response revealed his greedy nature: at this dramatic juncture, when he was at grips with an unknown enemy, he was reckoning the profit to be made from an innovative fabric. But this exceptionally gifted man—who would have deserved the full admiration of humanity if only he hadn't been attracted to evil—couldn't be distracted from present realities for long. He resumed his usual sarcastic expression. "We're about to land," he muttered, giving his son an odd look.

"Of course."

"Then don't forget to engage the Nightlooker."

It was a fair observation... but it provoked an unexpected reaction. Slane had barely finished speaking when William—as if impelled by some invisible force—leapt up, dashed to the panel that held the controls for the Nightlooker, manipulated them with feverish haste, and then jumped back into his seat.

Slane was on the point of expressing his astonishment at his son's behavior. But just then the Nightlooker began to operate. All the lights suddenly went out, and the ceiling of the control room began to glow as a new kind of overhead screen depicted a landscape in motion. A system of lenses, connected to prisms along carefully calculated angles, used radioactive materials—which, by means of a series of Roentgen rays, converted darkness into visible light—to capture the terrain beneath the airship and transform the indistinct night into a glowing image of the landscape projected onto the ceiling. The Slanes gave their full attention to the images unfolding above them. Trees, plowed fields, night watchmen's huts, houses at the edge of town—all were now visible to them.

Slane called out, "Stop!" The screen now displayed a broad meadow bounded at a considerable distance by a hedge of thorn bushes. "It'll be simple to land here." He consulted a dial mounted on the wall. "We're only eight hundred meters from the Honolulu city limits. I can easily rejoin you here after my visit to the harbor master."

As he spoke, his words were already being accompanied by the clicking of the controls: William was carrying out his instructions faster and more precisely than he ever had before. Unless Slane's authority and the effect of his willpower had suddenly grown, his son's obedience was hard to explain. He gave the boy a

---

[24] The calory is the unit of measure adopted to quantify the specific heat of a substance. It corresponds to the energy needed to raise the temperature of one kilogram of water by one degree Centigrade [*Note from the Author*].

curious look… but it wasn't a good time to ask questions. It was imperative that they learn in what direction Princess Liao had fled, so they could pursue her. As the old bandit put it to himself ironically, the *Vulture* would catch the songbird.

After a barely noticeable impact, the quiet hum of the engines ceased. The airship had landed in the middle of the meadow revealed on the Nightlooker screen.

"Leave the Nightlooker engaged, son. If some night patrol shows up, or some madman out for a walk—because you'd have to be mad to go for a walk in this weather unless you had webbed feet—just make a quick ascent. You can come back down when they're gone."

"Yes, sir. Consider it done."

Astonishing! William stood before his father with his heels together, his head thrown back, and his arms hanging at his sides, in the posture prescribed by American military academies for subordinates in the presence of a higher-ranking officer. He'd quite suddenly grown respectful. Well—the boy's new attitude certainly pleased Slane; no need to spoil things by making any remark.

"No doubt," thought Slane to himself, "in the current crisis he's realized I'm the brains of this team, and only I can lead us to victory."

Of course, he was wrong: the false Lloyd Hibbett's practically robotic obedience was caused simply by his inability to resist the will of a man whose powers of mind control were vastly magnified by the electric tunic Slane had put on. Unwittingly, unsuspectingly, as long as he was wearing that strange garment, Slane would draw from it not only the warmth he was aware of but a power of mind control whose effects, while inexplicable to him, would lead him from astonishment to astonishment.

But he had to hurry. Leaving William in the control room, Slane climbed to the roof deck of the *Vulture* and used the retractable ladder to reach the ground. The wind had dropped and the rain had stopped, in one of those sudden calms typical in the middle of the hurricanes that devastate those parts of the Pacific Ocean—as if the elements, worn out by their efforts, pause to rest before once more unleashing their fury.

"The ground is as saturated as a sponge," he said to himself as he set foot in the meadow. "No matter. The temperature has risen. The air feels almost warm—and I can't give all the credit to that undershirt my rascal passengers left behind."

As he advanced toward the hedge that enclosed the meadow, he went on, "Rascals? Are they really? Or did they just react like my crew, out of fear of the haunted airship?" He shrugged angrily. "Who can say?"

When he reached the hedge he followed it, and a moment later he came to an opening secured only by a rail mounted on two posts, forming a rustic gateway to the meadow. It took only a moment to move the rail aside and then put it back.

He now found himself on a path bordered by thick hedges, which in a few hundred feet led him to one of the large, excellent roads that crisscross the farmland surrounding Honolulu. When he reached the road he noticed, five hundred meters away, the first of the electric streetlights the American authorities had put up so many of in the Hawaiian capital. That sight pleased him: his journey would go that much faster, which—given his desire to avoid drawing attention to the airship—would enable him to get back on board as soon as possible and resume his progress in the sky, where he'd be safe from meeting anyone.

He walked quickly. Soon his heels rang on the basalt paving stones used for the urban sidewalks. The city slept. The tightly closed shutters on all the houses showed the population was abed. People in the islands retired early on stormy nights—a custom the occupiers had adopted. And there was wisdom in the practice: in the volcanic Hawaiian Islands, atmospheric storms often coincide with those terrible seismic storms, earthquakes. The natives had noticed the connection long before the arrival of Europeans and Asians. So when the wind rose they all went home, to watch over their precious belongings and to be there to take them away to safety in case an earthquake compromised the integrity of the house. The American administrators and colonists, guided by solid Anglo-Saxon sense, had easily adopted a custom whose usefulness seemed inarguable.

Though Slane was unaware of the cause for it, he was delighted to be able to walk the deserted streets, free of all other pedestrians. But he wanted to get to the harbor, and, while he enjoyed the security of the empty streets, he soon had to admit he'd be grateful to meet a native. He didn't know exactly where the harbor master's office was, and to find out he'd have to run into someone who could tell him.

Just as he came out onto the broad avenue known as Commerce Street, he ran straight into a police patrol charged with keeping the peace.

"Who goes there?"

That summons by the Hawaiian authorities made Slane jump, but he pulled himself together and answered in a voice that betrayed no emotion. "A stranger here, who's looking for the harbor master's office, to pass on urgent news."

"Harbor master..." echoed the men. "Too late now, him sleeping this time." The natives spoke a patois, a kind of Pacific pidgin made of English and Spanish and Japanese, enlivened by expressions in rudimentary syntax.

"He'll get up," said Slane, so as not to be left speechless by the men's awkward observation.

His words had a remarkable effect. The sergeant commanding the patrol cried, "If harbor master him get up, then you big admiral, all the way big!"

The master of the *Vulture* considered it beneath him to continue the conversation in that manner. He replied a little impatiently, "Kindly direct me to the harbor master's office."

He was stunned: all the policemen had frozen in respectful postures, and they were all speaking at once, crying, "Big admiral, you staying on Commerce Street. You pivoting right at Washington Pier. You seeing fine gold gate. Inside, you seeing little small sandy yard and house you looking for."

And then with very military coordination the men all sighed heavily, as if they were relieved they'd given their directions in perfect unison. Clearly, never in human memory had a police patrol answered a question at such length.

Slane had no idea it was the tunic he'd put on that magnified the persuasive power of his will and correspondingly increased his listeners' desire to obey. So it was in complete innocence that as he took his leave of the natives he said, "I thank you. Now go your way."

Before he'd finished speaking, the entire patrol was sprinting away, each of them trying to overtake the others. The whole street rang with the sound of that mad footrace, and in less than a minute Slane had lost sight of all the policemen.

CHAPTER IX
Slane is More and More Astonished

He stood there, stunned. "Am I dreaming?" he said to himself. "I feel like today everyone I meet is acting strange. Earlier it was William who seemed odd; now these honest Polynesian policemen…" But he cut short his reflections with a shrug. "After all, what does it matter? On to the harbor master's house."

Five minutes later he reached Washington Pier. The docks stretched away, their outlines marked by the electric streetlights along all the breakwaters, jetties, locks, and drawbridges. With a puff of arrogance, the crook was filled with American imperialism. He felt proud of the great port, designed and built in a few short years by American engineers.

But an attack of poetic sentiment doesn't last long in a criminal. Slane reminded himself of the purpose of his nocturnal journey. Twenty yards along the pier he came to the gate and the yard and the cozy little house he was looking for. But the blinds were down, and no light was visible, so he knew the occupants must be asleep, just as the policemen had warned him.

And there was something else: a tall mastiff was guarding the yard. Slane came to a sudden stop—which only made the dog nervous, and he flung himself against the gate, barking fiercely. His grimacing face and his menacing white fangs were so expressive that the visitor expected to suffer terribly if by chance the barrier separating him from the beast should give way. Anger drove Slane to answer threats with threats—a common reaction in people attacked by surprise—and he stepped up the gate and growled, "Stupid hound, will you shut up?"

O stupefaction! As if by magic, the mastiff grew calm. Slane attributed it to his own brave defiance, and he went on, "Back to your kennel!"

With trembling paws and tail between his legs, the beast scurried away to a wooden doghouse in a corner of the sandy yard. He didn't move when Slane opened the gate, which was unlocked and could simply be pushed open. Nor did the dog move when the intruder crossed the yard—though Slane was worried enough to watch him out of the corner of his eye.

"Damn!" he thought with inexpressible surprise. "I've missed my calling. Or rather, I'm just a man of universal talent. Now I discover I'm a tamer of wild beasts!"

Indeed the mastiff, furious just moments earlier, had completely lost his fighting spirit. He stayed in his doghouse, not the least interested in the movements of the stranger he'd greeted so unpleasantly at first.

"A lousy watchdog," thought Slane.

Then, no longer concerned about the four-footed sentry, he went up a few steps to a landing. From there a spiral staircase, making two turns before it was hidden by wisteria, led to the front door. Of course, the door was shut and locked. But a copper handle on the doorframe showed how to summon a servant to open up. This time Slane didn't hesitate as he pulled the handle twice. An electric chime echoed through the house.

"All right," he chuckled, "no one could sleep through that racket."

In spite of the apparent accuracy of that observation, the house remained silent. A second ring produced the same result. He rang a third time—and now there was a noise in response. A window on the second floor opened violently. Two figures dressed in white, one wearing a nightcap, the other a shawl, appeared at the window. Two angry voices, one of them distinctly that of a woman, cried, "Go away, or we'll throw things at you, like you deserve!"

The man's voice went on, "I have a hammerless choke bore!"[25]

And the woman added, "I'm holding a service revolver, a 1909 U.S. Army Colt!"

Indeed Slane could see one of them was brandishing a shotgun, the other the heavy automatic revolver that was standard issue for U.S. Army officers. Their hostile response exasperated him. Were these fools—and what were a harbor master and his wife compared to the Director of the Institute of Inventors?—going to persist in their stupid panic, and refuse him the information he needed? So he replied forcefully, "By Old Harry,"—one of the Devils's nicknames—"if you're blind, put your glasses on and see me for what I am: a perfectly honest gentleman, whom lots of people consider charming, almost saintly..."

---

[25] A breech-loading shotgun, first patented in the 1860s.

He broke off. Frantic cries could be heard from the window, at which Bill Tamm, harbor master, and his wife Lynn, still stood. Then, with a clicking sound, they both uncocked their weapons. Meanwhile they were both mumbling at the same time: "Accidents can happen so quickly..."—"We're taking out the bullets..."—"Because we'd rather die..."—"Than do any harm to your precious looks."

"My precious looks," muttered Slane, who suspected they were indulging in a kind of banter so popular in the United States, known as humbug. He was wrong—and what followed proved it.

Bill and Lynn Tamm went on with their explanations, in the singsong voice of worshipers chanting a litany. "Our only excuse is, we were woken from a deep sleep. That's why we were temporarily blinded. Without that, we'd have noticed your noble face haloed by divine light."

"Haloed?... Where are they getting this halo?"

But before Slane could ask that question, the Tamms, having unloaded their guns, left the window, saying, "Sainted man, we're coming down to open the door. We're honored to receive such a celestial visit."

Once again, the electric tunic Slane was wearing had done its job: the villainous gentleman had only to mention the idea of sainthood to trigger a hallucination in his listeners. The worthy couple had immediately seen him in Biblical form, with his head crowned by a bright halo. Of course, since he was unaware of the power he now possessed, Slane was unable to account for their behavior that way. So he was running through the entire official list of all the demons traditionally cursed at times of crisis... when the squeak of the opening door reminded him why he'd come here so late at night.

But the very next moment he was astonished all over again: Bill and Lynn Tamm were standing aside to welcome him in—but how strangely they were dressed! The harbor master was wearing blue-and-white-striped pajamas, but to do honor to his visitor he'd put on a top hat and was holding a gold-handled walking stick. As can be imagined, the whole outfit made him look like a chimpanzee about to perform acrobatics.

Lynn, a lively little woman of about thirty, as white and rosy as a baby—and as endearingly plump—had made sure to follow the example of her lord and master. The short skirts and modest camisole of her nightdress looked even skimpier, even more intimate, with the enormous black and white hat covered with feathers that the simple creature had added to her nightclothes, her curlers, and her hair papers.

"They're crazy," thought Slane as he came inside.

If so, they were crazy people who graciously made him welcome. He was led to a sitting room. Lynn hurried to find a teapot, to prepare the fragrant beverage so dear to all Anglo-Saxons. In vain the visitor tried to decline those attentions: Lynn announced firmly that nothing would make her let a saint explain the reason for his visit before he'd had a warming cup of tea.

"To come down from the Heavens, in the awful weather we're having to-night," she went on, "that takes courage. You might say a saint has more courage than an ordinary citizen, and I won't say no. But I—a creature of the earth, dust that will return to dust—I can only say what I think as a humble homemaker, isn't that so?"

Slane listened, utterly baffled. Apparently, he was a saint, descended straight from heaven. And Bill Tamm just nodded, fully in agreement with his plump little wife Lynn's mad babbling.

Slane remembered that psychiatrists all say you shouldn't contradict the mad, lest you trigger a serious reaction, even a violent crisis. While it was certainly surprising that the responsibility for overseeing the harbor had been entrusted to a household of lunatics, still, since here he was with them, he had to try to get out of it unscathed. So he went along with what seemed to be their obsession, and asked, half seriously and half mockingly, "How could people so devoted to the saints have begun by threatening me with firearms?"

"Oh, don't remind us of that awful blunder! We were woken by a terrible ringing, we got up, we were afraid... The truth is, we were walking in our sleep."

"Too bad you woke up at all," thought Slane to himself. "If you were asleep now I could happily slip away."

It was understandable that Slane felt genuinely concerned about being stuck at close quarters with these lunatics—which was what he considered them to be—and he'd have been delighted to head back to the *Vulture* even without the information he'd come here for.

But once again what happened next left him with his mouth hanging open. "Too bad you're not asleep now," he'd thought to himself... And immediately the Tamms stretched out in their armchairs, closed their eyes, and filled the sitting room with the gentle, regular sound of their breathing.

For one long a minute Slane sat there speechless—unable to say a word. He looked from Bill to Lynn and back again. Indeed, that peculiar couple had fallen asleep. Finally, as he pulled himself together, he put into words the thought that had been preoccupying him. "Now you're sleeping," he said out loud—but so quietly no one could have heard him.

And then he shivered, because the harbor master and his wife replied in touching unison, "Yes, since that was your will."

You can imagine the reaction of a man who suddenly, without preamble, discovers he's a mesmerist, a hypnotist—and one of such power that, without any effort on his part, randomly chosen subjects obey him even when his orders are delivered in a normal conversational tone. For a moment Slane was stunned—and who could blame him? He was an unwitting victim of the wonders of science.

He was like the hero in one of those classic mythic tales by du Châtelet,[26] who by a plot contrivance puts into his pocket—without knowing its power—some irresistible talisman: sheep's foot, Devil's pills, snake oil. We all know the story. The possessor of the talisman innocently wishes for something... and—bam!—his wish comes true in a sudden change of scene. It's a sure-fire success for actors who specialize in playing senile halfwits.

But when something like that crosses the footlights and infects real life, it provokes not just astonishment, but concern. Slane worried about his new mesmeric power, whose secret he still didn't know. Of course, no explanation came to him. The answer was too simple, too modest, to occur to someone who didn't already know it. A humble navy blue tunic gave its wearer the power of mind control. Incredible! Inconceivable! And therefore impossible to guess...

A clock chimed in the silence, and the shrill sound made him start. "Time's running out," he muttered impatiently. "I have to get back to the *Vulture* and hide it from prying eyes." With a grand gesture to underline his words, he went on to himself, "These numbskulls have been answering me in their sleep. Time to take advantage of their unconscious goodwill and learn what I came here to find out."

Now resolved, he turned to face the Tamms directly. Eying them with a commanding look, he waved his hands in the air the way mesmerists usually do, and asked, "What ships sailed from Honolulu in the past three days?"

"Only one sailed, forty-eight hours ago."

"Only one!" cried Slane, delighted. "So, there's no chance of following the wrong trail!" He went on interrogating the sleeping couple. "That vessel's destination?"

"The Chinese coast."

He rubbed his hands together. "Well, well... the very direction that little fool Liao would've taken." He raised his voice again. "The name of the ship?"

"Submarine torpedo boat B-23, of the U.S. Navy."

The answer struck Slane like a club. "A submarine! They don't take passengers—the rules are explicit."

Lynn Tamm replied softly, without opening her eyes, "Give me orders to follow the passengers you're talking about. I'll see them, and that way you'll know for sure."

It's well known that subjects under hypnosis can easily see a great distance, if they're told the starting point of the person or persons they're following in their thoughts.

"Follow them, ma'am, and tell me."

"I see them," she said suddenly, so positively that Slane looked around as if he too would be able to see the fugitives.

---

[26] Émilie du Châtelet (1706-49), a physicist, mathematician, and philosophical precursor of the French Enlightenment, who also wrote on questions of free will.

"Where are they?" he stammered.

"On Submarine B-23."

"Impossible, I tell you!..."

She paid no attention to his interruption and went on, "The skipper, Captain Andrews, couldn't say no to the Chinese girl."

"Andrews!" shrieked Slane. "Did you say Andrews?"

"That's his name..."

"Well, now everything's clear. Andrews, the naval officer who in San Francisco did his best to find ways to bump into that little Chinese doll! A man in love doesn't care about the rules... And, lovely, brilliant Mrs. Tamm, where's he headed now?"

"The Chinese coast, by Navy orders. Since the passengers also have business there, the arrangement was easily made."

"Thank you, ma'am!" cried Slane happily. "In China, I've got them! Well, well, their escape is only an interlude in the plot, whose resolution will certainly be comical. Farewell, good people, I've learned what I needed to know."

Leaving the Tamms asleep in their seats, Slane hurried out of the house and crossed the small yard... He was about to go out the gate when he noticed a police patrol a short distance away. "Hell," he thought to himself. "They'll stop me, ask for explanations. The Honolulu police is on the ball, and I certainly don't want anyone to suspect the *Vulture* is here..."

He stood very still. But a loud voice called out, "You there! What's your business at the harbor master's house?"

Slane had been spotted. He shook with anger. If he'd had that nosy policeman in his clutches, he'd certainly have hurt him. But—since even idle threats soothe the one who issues them—in his fury he groaned, "If only the horned Devil had blocked your eyes, and those of your men, till I'd gotten away!"

"By God, I can't see!"

"Nor can I!"

"Me neither!"

It was the policemen, who'd stopped a short way from the gate and were now sobbing and crying.

"What?" thought Slane, stunned.

"By God, I'm blind!" the representatives of public order wept in unison, and then they were all crying at once: "Blind! My wife will end up in the poorhouse!"—"My two boys will become gutter rats!"—"My daughter Dot won't be able to marry her fiancé Mallory!"—"Blind! Blind! Blind!" The pitiful noise rose over the pier and spread out across the water till it seemed to fill the furthest basins of the harbor.

Slane's hair stood on end, and for a moment he had to grab hold of the gate to keep his balance. He was terrified. What?!—he merely expressed a wish that they not see him, and the policemen went blind?! But further consideration calmed him. "No, no, it's just the power of suggestion. Clearly, I have stupendous mesmeric powers..." With a criminal's amorality he went on, "Ah, if only I'd know it earlier, life would've been simpler! I could've saved myself the trouble of so many complicated plots."

A harbor clock ringing the quarter hour brought him back to the present situation. "Anyway, let's take advantage of this to escape."

He went out the gate. The policemen continued to weep without noticing him. He headed back to Commerce Street. No sooner had he gone around the first corner that concealed him from the men still on the pier, then they began to cry out with joy.

"God bless the stars—I can see them again!"

"Me too, by God! It was just a dizzy spell!"

"A trick of the light!"

"Nothing to speak of, really!"

"And we'll forget all about it as we continue our rounds."

Slane, who'd heard them, had to admit reluctantly that the policemen had recovered their vision the moment he himself was out of sight... which was exactly what he'd expressed a wish for earlier.

But that thought didn't make him slow down. He was in a hurry to get out of town. Everything had gone the way he wanted—and yet a certain anxiety weighed on him. He had to admit that *everything had gone too well*. Like anyone who's gained some life experience, Slane believed that each person's existence was a web of compensatory balances: too much good luck seemed to him just as noxious as pure bad luck.

He got back to the *Vulture* without further incident. William hadn't had to deal with any crisis. Slane instructed him to start up the airship and fly west. He himself would take over the controls in the morning. He withdrew to his cabin. He wanted to sleep. When he woke his mind would be clearer, and he'd be able to make sense of the strange events that had marked his visit to Honolulu.

And then—perhaps as result of the stress of grappling with the inexplicable, or at least the insufficiently explained—he felt uncomfortably hot, as if his skin were on fire. He undressed and pulled off the undershirt he'd put on so eagerly earlier.

He got into his cot, saying to himself, "Sleep, devil take it—I have to sleep!" And then, with a violent gesture that almost threw him out of bed, he added, "The Devil! Ah, ever since we left San Francisco he seems to have been riding along beside the *Vulture*!"

The airship had already regained considerable altitude. Its turbines, rotating with dizzying velocity, drove the vessel at full speed toward the distant shores of the Republic of China.

PART FIVE: MODERN CHINA

CHAPTER I
The Chinese Customs Officials

You who overthrew the tyranny of the imperial court in its yellow-roofed palaces,[27] do not mistreat foreigners. Remember, it is those who come from overseas who will teach you about National Rights. Beneath that wise advice appeared signatures dear to the Chinese people, because of their very novelty: *the members of the Provisional Government of the Republic of China,* and *the President of the Republic of China.*

That notice hung on the pink brick wall, which was capped by a roof of light-blue glazed tiles that curved up toward the sky at the corners of the building. Ten meters away a wide muddy river carried its tons of ochre lazily by between low banks and a profusion of sandy islets.

---

[27] In China, yellow tiles were traditionally reserved for roofing imperial palaces [*Note from the Author*].

May, Lipson, and Captain Andrews looked around while Princess Liao translated the government proclamation for them. A launch moored to the riverbank held four oarsmen in U.S. Navy uniform; the passengers had just disembarked on the coast of China, near the city of Shanghai. The river was the Yangtze; the brick wall was that of the local customs office, located just outside the limits of the European Concessions in Shanghai.[28]

That very day, Princess Liao and her companions would have to part company with Captain Andrews, who had so opportunely helped them escape from Honolulu and had brought them across the Pacific in his vessel, Submarine B-23. During the long voyage from Hawaii to Shanghai the young man had done his best to make his passengers comfortable. Space is limited on a submarine, and amenities are few. But Andrews had worked so hard, and had made use of all the resources of his vessel with such a strong intention to be helpful, that they all felt truly grateful to him.

On the day that would mean their separation, May and Lipson had left their followers Derrick and Freda and Stepan and Sefra at the Royal Hotel inside the Concession to take care of little Jane, and had suggested that only the two of them go for a walk along the riverbank with Captain Andrews and Princess Liao—hoping thereby to give those two the comfort of relative privacy in which to make their farewells.

For all of her companions believed that the princess—that haughty descendant of the Manchu conquerors—had allowed a feeling sweeter than friendship to melt her heart. Anyone who observed her would think so: When the captain appeared, she blushed. If duty kept him away, she sat lost in deep thought, detached from the conversation of her friends. In the words of that philosopher of love, Kostigun,[29] "she withdrew from public life to concentrate on private life." If her companions spoke to her, she started, made them repeat what they'd said—in short, in the common expression, she acted like someone in a fog.

At this moment, Andrews stood right beside her, looking as pale as the princess herself. Soon they'd return to the Concession, where he would have to take leave of his passengers, since duty summoned him back to his submarine. During the short boat ride back together, he'd be able to gaze his fill on the emperor's daughter—and that would be the end. She would disembark, leaving him alone with his crew, who would bend to the oars, separating them irrevocably in

---

[28] Late imperial China granted foreign colonial powers—European, American, and Japanese—territorial enclaves in several port cities, where the occupying country's own laws were enforced by their own police, and Chinese subjects were usually forbidden to enter. The Shanghai International Concession belonged jointly to Great Britain and the United States. Many Concessions continued under the Republic of China, but all of them had expired by the end of the Second World War.

[29] The reference to "Kostigun" has not been identified.

a final farewell. Duty constrained them both: his was to cruise in Chinese waters till he was called back to his home port; hers was to journey into the interior, following the great winding river, to Tibet, the refuge of the overthrown emperor, Tipu Lia-Sou.[30] Any parting has its melancholy aspect; all the more reason why a painful sadness would hang over a separation that seemed likely to prove irreversible.

"Let's let them translate the proclamation on that sign," murmured Lipson into May's ear. "That'll give them a few moments longer to be together without thinking about us."

The scientist smiled gently, and her blue eyes suddenly grew moist. Unthinkingly, she squeezed the young man's hand. And then the two of them looked at each other, oblivious to their surroundings. In a flash, the veil concealing their feelings had been torn away. They realized that the four years that had passed since the sinking of the *Cyclopic*—years of shared fears, of dangers they'd faced together with a common goal—had joined their hearts together with unbreakable bonds.

They felt completely devoted to each other. Of course, he was still the heir robbed of the wealth of the Hibbetts, and she was still the foundling raised by the goodness of a couple of petty criminals—but those vastly different social backgrounds didn't feel at all mismatched to them. They remained on a footing of total equality. And now they admitted their attachment candidly, without hesitation, without second thoughts.

"I couldn't resign myself never to see his beloved face again."

"If I were an officer, like Andrews, I think I'd resign my commission to go with her."

"If I were a princess, like Liao, I'd give up my title to live by his side."

Well—it was certainly difficult to express such altruistic sentiments without feeling the effect of an emotion that made the blood rush to their hearts and left their cheeks pale.

Princess Liao finally came out of her sad reverie. Her delicate hand reached out to Andrews, while in a voice made hoarse by emotion she murmured, "I'll never, ever forget the friend thanks to whom I was able to reach China, thanks to whom I'll be able to see my father again!"

He seized her hand and brought her slender fingers, with their polished nails, to his lips. She could tell he was trembling, and that tremor spread to her own nerves. In a shaking voice she repeated, "Never! Never!" Her dream—born in a heart perhaps formed by the brutal winds of the Revolution—was coming to an end. To get back in the launch and return to the Concession would be to begin the final march to their farewells. A tear rolled down Princess Liao's pale amber cheek. What more was she going to say?

---

[30] This person corresponds to no actual historical figure, either by name or by description.

She didn't have a chance to put it into words. They all jumped as a stranger's voice rang out in a tone of command—though still politely—speaking slowly, in excellent English. "So these are the distinguished foreigners who came out of the fish-boat" (he meant the submarine) "anchored in Shanghai harbor!"

They all turned, their eyes wide with astonishment. Facing them were a dozen Chinese customs officials in uniforms modeled on Japanese dress; since the Revolution, Chinese officials had done their best to imitate European fashions, which in practice meant Japanese fashions. They'd eliminated the braided queue, which they'd once worn with pride. Clearly a simple change of clothing would seem much easier. In fact, wasn't their adoption of European fashions flattering to whites? It certainly proved that, in the Chinese mind, European dress represented freedom and civilization.

Some kind of captain, wearing a kepi loaded with gold braid, was in command of these "new style" customs officials—"new style" being the expression used all the time in modernizing China. He stepped forward graciously with a smile. "Ladies, gentlemen," he said in his passable English, "you have crossed outside the boundary of the Shanghai Concessions. In doing so, you have made yourselves liable—in the eyes of the Customs Department—for domestic taxes on travel."

While they all stared at him in surprise, seeming not to understand, he went into a lengthy explanation of the system of customs fees in the ports and cities that were open to foreign trade, and the domestic duties connected with the right of entry into the territories of the Concessions. Merchants couldn't be ignorant of those fees, because that complex system of taxation formed the great hurdle in all trade with the Republic of China. Some item for which the customs fee at the border of the Concessions was, say, one franc, might end up—once the domestic duties were included—taxed at ten times that rate.

But our travelers, not being in business, failed to see the beauty of the system the customs captain was explaining, and just wanted to put an end to the Chinese official's eloquence. Lipson said a little nervously, "We'll take your word for it, Captain. What should we do?"

"Excellent!" he answered, his eyes shining. "You pose the question perfectly. Well, not much at all. Be so kind as to enter the customs building, where you will pay the duties and in exchange get a receipt, which will give you the freedom to wander around outside the Concessions as much as you like."

Ten armed men backed up the customs captain's invitation—which was phrased in the most courteous possible terms. And, no doubt by chance, those ten men stood between the travelers and the riverbank, and therefore cut them off from the U.S. Navy launch—a pointless precaution, since none of the passengers from Submarine B-23 had the least intention of resisting. Princess Liao, and probably Captain Andrews, must secretly have blessed this complication for delaying their separation a few moments longer.

Surrounded by the customs soldiers, and led by the customs captain, the little group followed the pink brick wall to a gate of red and gold lacquered wood, on whose pillars symbolic dragons writhed in fanciful contortions. They went through the gate and crossed a small courtyard cluttered with crates, barrels, and sacks. Still led by their guards, they entered a small building, where a fat, wheezing customs major sat enthroned behind a pitch pine table of Western manufacture.

But that representative of the tax laws wasn't alone. Next to him stood a thin man wearing gold-framed glasses and an ample frock coat. The loose-fitting coat hung open to reveal a silk sash in the five colors of the flag of the young Republic of China.[31] That sash showed he was a government official. He examined the new arrivals with a sharp eye—and gave a grimace of delight on seeing Princess Liao. She was troubled by the insistent way he stared at her.

A little irritated by the man's rudeness, Lipson said, "Be so kind as to tell us what customs fees we owe."

The man with the sash put his long bony hand over the major's mouth. "Don't answer, worthy officer of the law. That duty is incumbent on me, as representative of the nation and inspector of foreigners."

They all looked at him in surprise. What could this official want with them? What was the meaning of his getting involved in a matter of customs duties? Had the post-revolutionary Chinese retained their love of the confusion of powers so typical of the former imperial China?

The man wasted no time before answering their unspoken questions. "Our country has just gone through an upheaval in which established norms were replaced by new ways. The Republic, so recently founded, can't be as liberal as governments that have had time to put down deeper roots."

"Damned chatterbox," muttered Andrews. "He's treating us to a political speech."

The official seemed not to hear, and went on imperturbably, "That will help you grasp, *with the mind's fingers*, why I regret the obligation I'm under to carry out the responsibility that goes with the position I hold. If I obeyed only my friendly feelings, I'd stop there. But the Republic commands me, and independence requires me, to root out not only the enemies of our poor young government but those who—by their race, their profession, their wealth or position—might possibly become its enemies at some future time."

"That doesn't apply to us," protested Andrews. "I'm an officer of the U.S. Navy, and the United States has unreservedly praised the constitution of the Republic of China."

---

[31] From 1912 to 1929 the Chinese flag consisted of five horizontal stripes: red, yellow, blue, white, and black.

"That's true, quite true, and we're grateful to and friendly with the United States. And yet allow me to point out that you weren't brought here as an American citizen."

Andrews's mouth hung open.

"We have nothing but friendly words for the American citizen," went on the bespectacled official, still smiling. "Unfortunately... oh, yes, very unfortunately... that isn't true for the sailor, considered purely as a sailor."

"What are you trying to say? A naval officer is by definition a sailor, and doesn't stop being an American on that account."

"Yes, your objection is very sensible."

"I'm sure it is."

"However, it's irrelevant in this case. The officer of the naval armed forces is not in question here, no more than the American citizen."

"So then?..."

"There remains, sadly, the commander of a passenger vessel, who tried to sneak into this country elements dangerous to the security of the Republic."

"What?!" That one word, conveying their astonishment, burst from all their lips. The Chinese official had genuinely surprised them. For maybe a minute the travelers were left unable to say a word. Then they recovered, and a chorus of recriminations rose and echoed in the customs hall.

Their accuser let them vent. When the first wave of their indignation had passed, he went on, as calmly as if they were having a friendly chat, "Ladies and gentlemen, you're tiring yourselves out for nothing. What you're saying proves only that you're regrettably uninformed about the situation you're in, and about our relative positions."

Those bold words reduced them to silence, and he continued, "I have a good enough opinion of your intelligence to feel confident that before long you'll agree with me. Americans are an intelligent people; we Chinese respect them for that."

He smiled, pleased by his own cordiality. Then, in a didactic tone, like a professor of Far Eastern languages at the lectern, he went on, "Let's consider: China is going through a period of turmoil. She has overthrown the Empire and proclaimed the Republic. She has made a clean sweep of all of her institutions, and replaced them with a new social concept: the nation."

"Damn," grumbled Lipson, "this Chinaman goes on like an orator at a European club."

"Everything is new here," continued the official. "Everything teeters in the balance, like a child's house of cards. Time alone can stabilize a society and give it a solid, unshakeable foundation. We must therefore watch carefully over our institutions."

"How are we a threat to them?" interrupted Andrews with typical American disdain.

"How? You're really asking that? Ah, truly, our philosophers are right when they say men from across the ocean have the smooth marble brows of inanimate statues!" The official underlined his words with a sour sarcastic laugh. "How? I explain the fragility of our improvised government, and you pretend not to see your crime—you, who are clandestinely bringing into the country the most dangerous moral explosive, the most disheartening of ideas, the most terrible political torpedo!"

"Where are you getting all this?" asked Lipson.

The man with the five-colored sash shrugged his narrow shoulders in scorn. "I don't know what you're aiming at with these pointless questions," he replied condescendingly, "but I'll remember traditional Chinese politeness, and assume you're asking in good faith, and answer accordingly." Looking Lipson in the eye, he went on, "What is the political concept most hostile to the newly installed regime—the one that can never be reconciled to it, that is incompatible by its very definition? It's monarchy, isn't it?"

"A perfect truism," snickered Andrews. "Everybody knows a monarchy and a republic can't mix."

To their surprise, the official accepted the wisecrack with delight. "Ah, excellent—so you're admitting it!"

"Admitting what?"

"That you're working against the sovereignty of the people, by bringing into China the beloved daughter of the emperor we overthrew!"

He pointed at Princess Liao. They all shivered. They suddenly understood the danger that was exploding over their heads. They'd been preoccupied with the personal drama around them for so long that they'd failed to think about the political drama convulsing Asia. Now, suddenly, that tragic story confronted them, wound itself around them, dragged them toward its terrifying resolution: annihilation. Should they speak? Defend themselves? What would be the point? Princess Liao knew nothing could rid Chinese minds of their preconceived notion of a conspiracy against the established government.

The official misunderstood their silence. He wanted to complete his victory by stunning his listeners with a display of the vast information possessed by the Chinese authorities. "Our global intelligence network knows its job. It was a serious mistake on your part to try to throw it off the track. See for yourselves: You were in Honolulu. Suddenly you vanished. Only one vessel had left port— the torpedo boat commanded by Captain Andrews, which is to say Submarine B-23. It wasn't hard to deduce he'd taken you aboard as passengers."

He eyed them with a look of authority. "Of course, American vessels travel fast. But not as fast as the *earth spirit*, as we Chinese call electricity. Electricity is the ally of the Chinese who've freed themselves from tyranny. A wire reached Canton, to be passed along the entire coast. You were expected. No matter where you landed, you'd have been caught. So don't blame yourselves for choosing Shanghai."

"But no one knew we were in Honolulu," murmured Princess Liao.

"Slane knew." At May's answer, all eyes turned to her. "Yes, Slane," she repeated. "Slane, who thought it through and deduced that the princess would be drawn inexorably toward her father. Anyway, the submarine's destination gave away our own. He's the one who sent the cable."

"But then," whimpered the princess, "we're doomed!"

May didn't reply. What could she have said? Prisoners recaptured after an escape always face harsher treatment. They're paying for the trouble they gave their jailers.

And now she thought of the electric tunics, which would have made them invincible: they were all tucked into their luggage, back inside the Concession. As of now she and her friends were in the power, no longer of one man, but of an entire hostile nation.

She jumped as Andrews spoke up. "Excuse me... I entered Chinese waters, with my vessel, by order of the United States government."

"And as a result," the official quickly replied, "we are impounding neither the submarine nor its crew. The American flag protects them. We are arresting only the man whose complicity in the plot is proved by his actions."

"Complicity?"

"Certainly. Did your government orders tell you to pick up passengers and to stop at Shanghai to put them ashore?"

Andrews bowed his head: his adversary was right. He would share his companions' fate. Nothing could save him from that. But that realization didn't sadden him, at least with respect to himself. He blamed himself for not having foreseen what would happen, and as result for having put Princess Liao in terrible danger. He held out his hands to the princess, and in a voice shaking with emotion he pleaded, "Forgive me, miss, for not having known how to protect you from danger."

But she gazed at him, and her big black eyes suddenly softened. "It's for you to forgive the unfortunate princess who drew you into the orbit of her fatal destiny."

"Oh, miss, don't be sorry for something that's a blessing to me."

Their eyes locked, as if through their pupils they were merging their souls, oblivious to all that wasn't them.

But the official broke into that ecstatic contemplation. "A junk is waiting on the river. You'll be put aboard. You can choose to go unbound, or to be bound in chains. Which would you prefer?"

The humorous side of the question made May and Lipson smile. To ask a prisoner to choose between relative freedom and chains seemed like the ultimate farce. But Princess Liao's next words made clear the real meaning of the choice. "Presumably to remain unbound we'd have to pledge not to try to escape."

They all listened, though there was little doubt as to the official's answer. So they were surprised when, writhing with irrepressible mirth, he chuckled, "No, no! No promises will be required of you!"

The princess gestured skeptically at the forbearance implied, and the official went on, "There'll be no need: you can't escape. In the Republic of China we're all Sons of Liberty, and we don't want to keep you from striving to earn your freedom. Try if you like. But I have to warn you, a failed attempt will force us to put you in irons."

He gestured to show the interview was over. Two customs soldiers flanked each of the prisoners.

"Odd work for the customs department," laughed Andrews.

"Clothes don't make the man," answered the official sententiously. "Under those customs uniforms they're all loyal *ti-paos*."

"Police officers?"

"That's right."

Before anyone could reply, the travelers were led across the customs courtyard and back to the edge of the Yangtze. The U.S. Navy launch had vanished. In its place floated one of those heavy junks that run up and down Chinese rivers and have a vague resemblance to a European river barge. Those large vessels use both sails and a towrope; the haulers therefore have to work even harder in a contrary wind.

A narrow plank ran from the riverbank to the gunwale of the junk. On the orders of the official, who'd escorted them conscientiously, the prisoners crossed the fragile gangway. They were now on their floating prison. Their jailers confined them to the stern, near the raised poop covered with grimacing carvings.

Almost immediately the vessel put off slowly. With its sails made of matting spread, and a line of haulers pulling on the towrope, it moved upriver against the lazy current, leaving Shanghai behind. Every cable length the boat advanced took the prisoners further from possible rescue. Their last faint hopes evaporated.

Of course, the crew of the Navy launch would report the arrest of their captain and his friends. But even if the United States Consul dismissed the claims of the Chinese government that the naval officer's actions had threatened its national security, even if the Consul insisted the prisoners be turned over to him to be brought before a European tribunal, his demands would amount to nothing: they couldn't be satisfied, since the captives had disappeared, led away into the interior toward some unknown destination, swallowed up in the vast human tide that was China.

That dismal train of thought gave Lipson a strong desire to know their destination. He stopped a passing sailor. "Hey, fellow, want to earn a few cash you can spend on rice or opium?"

240

The man laughed. "All the Benevolent Buddhas would turn their backs on a believer who answered such an offer with anything other than yes."

"In that case, enlighten me. Where will this journey end?"

"That's all you want to know, foreigner?"

"That's all. To prove it, I'll pay you in advance."

Lipson poured a few coins into the Chinaman's hand. The sailor's smile broadened, and without waiting for a second question he said, "Hankou[32] is where the Revolution began. It's become a holy city, and has been granted the honor of punishing the enemies of the Republic. It's been proclaimed the Sacred City of Torture. We're therefore going to Hankou. There you'll be sacrificed—no longer to the gods but to the people, whom you've insulted by your reactionary plots."

He spoke with a pomposity that in other circumstances would have seemed extremely comical. Political phraseology is the same at all latitudes. But Lipson wasn't amused. In the sailor's words he'd heard an irrevocable sentence, without appeal. He and his companions had been condemned, and nothing now could save them. His vision blurred with tears as he looked over at May, who was seated on a coil of rope and seemed lost in thought. Her pearly white eyelids veiled the blue of her eyes. A tear trickled down Lipson's cheek while he moaned, "Her? Her? Dead?" In a fit of impotent rage he brandished his fists toward some invisible enemy. "To have been stopped there in port, at the very moment I could've told her..."

He broke off, and studied the sky filled with light clouds. Then suddenly he seemed to come to some decision. He went to May, sat down next to her, and took her hand. His touch pulled her from her thoughts. She looked at him inquiringly.

"May," he murmured, "I thought we were close to the moment when, after defeating the Slanes, I would owe it to you to have given me back my name and the fortune of the Hibbetts."

"The heavens have determined otherwise, James. Let's accept that."

"Accept it—of course, we're forced to. But since our hopes won't be realized, since in all likelihood we're doomed, I want you at least to know what I'd promised myself to do after our victory."

May's eyelids trembled and her vision dimmed. In a dull voice she murmured, "I'm listening. Go ahead."

"I will. May, you've devoted your life and your engineering genius to avenging the crime my family and I suffered. When I regained my identity and my fortune, I would've said to you, 'May, I owe you everything. But I can only accept the privileges you've given me... if you agree to share them with me.'"

"Oh," she stammered, "thank you for the thought. Perhaps it's for the best we were defeated, since I couldn't have accepted... I'm just a foundling..."

---

[32] Hankou is now part of the city of Wuhan.

"Found to be divine, to be sisterly, to be devoted, and found by me. That's what kind of foundling you are. I'd rather sacrifice everything else than not have you for my beautiful wife."

The deep feelings prompted by his words made her stagger.

"Are you all right, May?"

"I... I... Oh, why not tell you everything? You're right—we're doomed. Already we're no longer part of life. Why be reticent? Why beat around the bush?" Her blue eyes looked right into Lloyd Hibbett's. "James," she said, her voice firm once again, "James or Lloyd, because you're both one and the other, I've been completely attached to you since long before you confessed your attachment to me. Let's turn a brave face to destiny. We've been denied happiness on earth; we'll find it hereafter."

And while the breeze from the shore carried the slow chant the haulers used to keep time, while the gentle lapping of the ripples as they ran down the side of the boat rose from the river, May and Lipson talked, forgetting that every passing minute brought them closer to the city with the sinister name: Hankou, the City of Torture.

CHAPTER II
A Seven-Year-Old Girl's Ideas

"They're doomed. Those stupid Chinese won't spare them."

"Our May convicted!"

"And that poor Mr. James!"

Freda, Derrick, Stepan, and Sefra were lamenting at the Royal Hotel in Shanghai, where the crew of the Navy launch, turned back by the Chinese customs militiamen, had brought them the news of the arrest of Princess Liao and her friends. The brave sailors also reported something that made matters look even worse: on their way back, they'd hidden their boat behind an islet overgrown with reeds. From there they'd watched as the prisoners were put on board a junk, which had sailed upriver under the dual power of wind and haulers. The European authorities in the International Concession could therefore no longer usefully intervene.

At first the thoughts of those loyal friends—so abruptly separated from those whom they served—had been filled with wild schemes. Then ran to the port and requested to go aboard Submarine B-23, which, having surfaced, now lay gently rocked by the waves that rolled across the water. Alas, the first mate, the quartermasters, and the sailors, being familiar with Chinese customs, all told them *nothing could be done*. The United States Consul would deliver a protest relating to the disappearance of Captain Andrews. Most likely the response would be some kind of monetary compensation, a fine the provincial government would agree to pay; but that would be all.

Freda—maddened at the thought of the danger now threatening her adopted daughter, that dear sweet May for whom the poor woman had killed and stolen and made herself into the manure out of which a lily grew—Freda cried out in a paroxysm of agony, "I'll go after her by myself! I'll save her or I'll die with her!"

And Derrick roared, "Bravo! Count me in!"

But, like an icy shower, the new commander of the American submarine replied, "You wouldn't get one day's march from Shanghai. The Chinese authorities would arrest you first thing. They'd wear you down with pointless arguments and flimsy objections to delay you. And even if they allowed you to proceed in some direction, you can be sure it wouldn't lead to those you wish to find."

Freda and Derrick stared at the officer, their eyes wide with vague fear.

"You have no idea," he went on, "of the sly cunning and the infinite diplomatic resources of the Celestial Kingdom, against which you struggle like a butterfly in a gauze net. You never meet open resistance that would justify firm action... always just a vague obstacle that gives way at the slightest pressure—but that reappears as soon as the pressure ceases. No one is against what you ask for. The most complicated politeness in the world prevails in all discussions. Everyone you address wants only to speed your journey—and yet some power beyond them opposes it. What power? They say they don't know. Is it the Benevolent Buddhas, the Tiger that creeps from South to North, the Dragon that slithers from East to West, the Ba Zi horoscopes that astrologers read in the stars, or perhaps feng shui—that inexpressible, paradoxical, shape-shifting art, whose name the whole country invokes in the most varied circumstances, and which not one Chinese is able to define? It's impossible to answer the question. You feel like you're in a prison made of steam, a tunnel of fog. The day that fog lifts and all obstacles are suddenly cleared from your path will be a day of mourning—because your freedom to proceed is proof that your friends are dead."

The navy officer was right. He'd given a marvelous account of the tortuous, convoluted diplomacy, adorned with every delicacy of refined politeness, that is the dominant quality of the Chinese race. It's irresistible, because nowhere does it present a surface firm enough to allow for a genuine struggle. It's the insurmountable barrier of the vacuum, the will-o'-the-wisp. The explorer Monnier[33] described it vividly as thrashing about endlessly in a cloud of opium smoke.

---

[33] Marcel Monnier (1853-1918) was a French journalist and travel writer. His best-known book was *Le Tour d'Asie*, especially Volume 2, *L'Empire du Milieu* [The Middle Kingdom] (1899).

Derrick and Freda, face to face with the man who'd just crushed their last hope, stood silent, their eyes wandering, fat tears rolling down their cheeks without their knowing.

Everything about them expressed so frightening a despair that the officer took pity on these poor people, to whom he'd felt it was his duty to tell the truth. He wished now to give them the comfort of some vague hope. Slowly, hunting for words, torn between wanting to soothe their distress and the fear of leading them to hope for too much, he went on, "You must've noticed that in my explanation *superstition* accounts for nine tenths of the artillery of obstacles raised against travelers into the interior of China. Superstition can only be defeated by itself. In other words, mythological beliefs block your way, but sometimes they can also ease your way. I hasten to say that the favorable effect is very rare; but it's been known to happen. If some official, the chief of some militia or the head of some administrative district, whether judicial or military or other, decides that *the spirits*—I'm purposely using that vague word to mean everything and nothing—that *the spirits* wish you to succeed, then instantly your way will be made smooth. Horses, boats, sedan chairs—all means of transportation will be available as needed. When you reach some district boundary, the passes allowing you to cross it will already be waiting for you. It'll seem like some kind of magical shield covers you... However, I'll say again, though sadly, because I wish I could be more encouraging: you can't count on that kind of luck."

May's friends came back to earth. At first, they'd been buoyed by the hope that the American Navy vessel and its crew, along with the U.S. Consul, would wield enough power to make the Chinese decide to hand over the prisoners. Now they bent under the weight of despair.

At the hotel, where Stepan and Sefra had been waiting with little Jane in her room for May's adoptive parents to return, Derrick and Freda recounted their fruitless, disappointing meeting. His voice hoarse, Derrick ended with angry mockery of the impossible chance the submarine officer had mentioned. "Those yellow-faced devils, take us under their protection? My poor children, can you imagine that? You'd have to be the ultimate idiot to expect a miracle like that to happen!"

"That's right," said Freda sadly; and Stepan and Sefra, their eyes reddened by tears, nodded in mournful agreement.

"You know, I'm small, so I may be the kind of idiot Derrick's talking about," chirped Jane suddenly. "But it seems to me the yellow devils would certainly protect us if we knew how to go about it the right way."

All eyes turned to the child, whose words were so much at odds with the prevailing feeling. Though not long before she'd been crying for her "big sister May," now her face was filled with joy and lit by a confident smile.

They all asked her questions at once, with the respectful formality they'd always maintained toward her. "What are you trying to say, Miss Jane?"

She placed her tiny index finger on the tip of her pink nose. "You remember our friend Liao never agreed to wear the electric tunic sister May gave her."

"Yes, of course, but what does that have to do with those devils?"

The little girl gave a silvery laugh. "It has everything to do with them! Wasn't it because of devils that Liao refused? Didn't she say the power of the tunic seemed diabolical to her?"

"Yes, that's true."

"Well then, I thought: Since it seemed diabolical to Liao, who's a great princess, it would surely have the same effect on ordinary Chinese people who aren't princes and princesses."

Phrased in her childish way, Jane's reasoning shone with the light of inarguable truth. The sweet little thing understood, by the look on their faces, that she'd persuaded them. "Well, then," she went on, "if you think I'm not babbling nonsense, we can leave Shanghai tonight... on a boat rented for a pleasure outing. Tomorrow we'll be among the Chinese, and we'll be able to say, like in the Mother Goose tales, 'I'm only a little fairy, but my powers are great, and I'll prove it to you, Mr. Mandarin.'"

Joy and decisiveness are infectious. All of them felt comforted by that brave resolve. Once again they admired the girl who, in the prevailing confusion, guided only by her childish logic, was pointing out a way that might lead to success. None of them thought about the danger of heading into the interior of the country. None of them thought of a single objection that could shake Jane's confidence. Instead Derrick and Freda—just like young Stepan and Sefra—without the slightest hint of resistance, gave in to the little girl's reckless audacity.

Jane rested her chin on her chubby arm and pondered before lifting her head. "The Tiger," she said. "I know what that is—a big cat with stripes... But the Dragon, is that some kind of soldier?"

They all laughed. "No, no," said Stepan and Sefra, "it's also an animal, but not a real animal."

Sefra ran to a side table to fetch one of those illustrated advertising fliers with which the Celestial Superfine Tea Company had flooded the country, and on which was emblazoned the logo of that powerful corporation: the symbol of China, the Dragon. "Here you go, Miss Jane. There's a picture of the nonexistent beast."

The child looked at it with amusement. "Oh, it looks like the animals in the book of fairy tales sister May gave me in San Francisco."

"And it's no more real than that," insisted Sefra.

Jane replied solemnly, "Oh, I know. It's a long time since I believed in fairy tales. May told me science has made real everything that imagination supplied in fairy tales. But with science there's no more magic, it's just learning."

They all fell silent, amazed by the dogmatic tone of the words coming of that childish mouth.

She went on, "In China, do the important people believe in the Dragon?"

"Yes, yes, they all do... Remember Princess Liao."

"I remember. She refused to put on the electric tunic." Then, more pensively, Jane continued, "So then, Liao, the officials, all of them—they're more childish than I am, since they still don't understand that Dragons, and magicians, and all those things don't exist." She expressed those ideas with such conviction that as the childish words left her lips they acquired masterful authority.

"How will we leave Shanghai?" asked Sefra timidly.

"The American sailors said the Chinese put our friends on a junk that sailed upriver."

"That's right."

"Well then, let's take a boat too."

"And what if they got off along the way?"

"We'll ask for information from time to time."

"Will the inhabitants want to tell us?"

With a confident smile Jane replied, "Those under the protection of the Dragon will learn everything they want to know."

Derrick and Stepan, having been promoted to the rank of oarsmen for the little group, quickly bought the boat of a fisherman who brought his catch to the hotel. They all went peacefully to sleep after little Jane rightly said, "Let's sleep, because we have to leave in the middle of the night, and we'll be too tired if we don't get some rest."

Clearly this child of seven had taken uncontested command of the devoted group who were about to plunge into the center of the most populous nation on earth to try to rescue May and her companions from captivity. Nothing troubled their sleep. The thought that a people four hundred million strong stood between them and those they meant to save didn't even cross their minds. Nightmares—which in Greek mythology issued through a gate of horn, no doubt to suggest their malevolence—didn't disturb them. Morpheus's poppies poured sweet peaceful tranquility over them.

It was about three o'clock in the morning when Derrick got up. Without a sound he woke his companions; silently, holding their breath, they left the hotel (they'd settled the bill the night before). Outside, all was quiet. Both the foreign Concessions and the Chinese city slept. The yelp of a dog, the clack of the beak of some night bird passing in the darkness overhead, the distant echo of the weapons of a ti-pao police patrol in blue and red, those were the only intermittent sounds they heard. Ahead of them the deserted streets stretched away, flanked by the double lines of European gas streetlights, between which swung the Chinese shop signs—multicolored paper lanterns that were just now beginning to go out.

Derrick and Freda led the way, followed by Jane, walking between Stepan and Sefra. No encounter interrupted their progress to the dock along the river: luck continued to favor them. They boarded the sampan—a Chinese rowboat—

Derrick had bought; he and young Stepan worked the long oars to push the boat out into the current, and then began to sail upstream.

The moon rose just in time to allow them to see in passing the brick walls of the customs house where their friends had been arrested only a few hours earlier. And then the last lights marking the location of Shanghai were hidden from view behind them. Now the sampan glided along between cultivated fields, where the riverbanks were lined with "gardens on rafts"—twelve million Chinese live on the produce from those floating gardens, created simply by transporting arable soil onto rafts moored to the shore—but the farmers were asleep at that hour. The boat passed the last farmers' huts on the outskirts of Shanghai. They were entering the unknown interior of China.

Dawn came. With sunrise, the countryside awoke. Peasants, teams of plodding water buffalo, and peculiar carts drawn by Mongol horses or even by men filled the landscape. From time to time the travelers spotted a farmhouse or a country pleasure house surrounded by a board fence whose planks were decorated with the name and titles and honors of the proprietor, and sometimes they passed a village.

Occasionally a servant, surprised to see people in European clothes heading upriver, hailed the sampan. Stepan had once lived in San Francisco's Chinatown, where he'd learned the strange lingua franca the Chinese use to make themselves understood all around the Pacific. When he answered the hail, the other man lifted his closed fists to his ears—a sign of kindly respect—and observed, "The Republic of China isn't barbaric, like the overthrown Empire. She likes the foreigners whose learning has allowed her to free herself. May the White Rooster perch on the tiller of your sampan, and may the river alligators swim clear of your oars."[34]

The travelers weren't surprised by their warm welcome. They didn't know China used to be the most closed-off country in the world—not only because of police or administrative regulations, but because of the intolerance of the people, who were conformist by nature, and whose customs, religion, and philosophical outlook all served to isolate them from the rest of humanity. In those days every foreigner was considered a barbarian, and every barbarian was thought to deserve being treated as an enemy.

However, Jane and her companions were soon to find that out for themselves. Near the coast, where contact with Europeans was almost commonplace, new ideas spread rapidly; but further inland the traditions of the Celestial Empire still persisted. Starting on their second day on the river, the natives exhibited hostility. They answered the travelers with nothing besides rudeness or threats, or sometimes with the endless circumlocutions of Oriental cunning. The Chinese are indeed past masters in the art of obfuscation; for anyone who has traveled in the Far East, the Turks—whose reputation in that art stands so high in Europe—seem by comparison no more than sincere, naive children.

Toward the end of the second day the hostility became clear. The sampan was passing a village by the name of Si-Fou, built at the foot of a hill on which stood a yamen (a Chinese palace) surrounded by gardens whose enclosed woods ran down to marshes lying to the west of the village, where stagnant ponds stretched to the horizon.

Suddenly Sefra, who was taking her turn at the tiller, cried out, "A junk is putting out from shore and heading toward us."

Freda stammered anxiously, "A war junk! Look, it's full of soldiers."

It was true. Behind the oarsmen, who sat in groups of four on the forward benches of the heavy boat, the benches aft were occupied by soldiers. The angled light of the setting sun showed they belonged to the new army of the Re-

---

[34] The White Rooster is a local superstition: white augurs good luck, black bad luck. As for the alligators, they abound in the Yangtze, and it's understandable that travelers would wish them to move aside [*Note from the Author*].

public: their hussar's jackets and trousers—copied from Japanese army uniforms—clashed a little with their visored conical caps; but their rifles of European manufacture, the belts holding their bayonets, and their soft leather bandoliers were a sufficient reminder of the drive to modernize that was characteristic of contemporary China. Nor were their intentions in doubt. Driven forward by the long oars that give river junks the appearance of the galleys of antiquity, the junk was making straight for the sampan, with the obvious aim of blocking its way.

"What should we do?" muttered Derrick, tightening his grip on the handle of his revolver.

"Fire away at them," answered Stepan.

But little Jane's chirping voice calmed their bellicose plans. "Let's be under the protection of the Dragon," she said.

Under the protection of the Dragon! The child's words reminded them all of the need to use deceit—a need they'd acknowledged before they set off. And certainly her advice was sound. To try to get through by force would have been folly. From the start they'd all understood that only finesse would give them any chance of succeeding in their risky mission. But there's a deep gulf between the time when, safe from all danger, you debate the best plans and strategies, and the time when—heart pounding and eyes blinking—you confront that danger face to face.

They all trembled... all except Jane. With childish carelessness, composed of her courage and her trust in May's scientific expertise, she remained calm, with a mischievous smile on her lips. Her darling face clearly expressed her thoughts: "This is going to be fun!" The Chinese intervention was nothing but a game to her. In fact, there was wisdom in what she said: the only way for them to continue their journey was to be granted permission to sail on—by controlling the imaginations of the Chinese through the power of the electric tunics all the travelers were now wearing.

The junk was now only a few meters away from the sampan. The rowers had lifted their oars to a vertical position, and the boat's headway allowed it to run alongside that of the foreigners.

"I'm the one under the protection of the Dragon," whispered Jane almost inaudibly. "Coming from a little girl like me, it'll amaze them even more. Plus they won't think I'm making fun of them. Grownups never imagine children are making fun of them. I don't know why," she added with a smile, "but that's how it is." Seeing the junk was right alongside, she added, "When I speak, use your willpower to reinforce my willpower. That way we'll be even more effective than sister May said... It's easier to push open a door if everyone pushes together."

Truly the child had taken command. The oddest thing was that none of them felt like opposing her. Jane's companions couldn't decide which was more frightening—the arrival of the Chinese soldiers or the calm of their dear little friend.

Luckily, they didn't have much time to think about it. The soldiers secured the prow of the sampan with a rope attached at its other end to the stern of the junk. Obviously they meant to tow the foreigners' boat.

Summoning his best Chinatown pidgin, Stepan asked, "What do you want with us?"

The officer in command answered merely by a two-part gesture whose eloquence cut off any further questions; he pointed to the riverbank, then to the army-issue revolver on his belt. They could all translate for themselves: they were being taken to shore, and they'd be shot if they tried to resist.

The oppressive silence that followed was broken only by the gentle slap of the waves along the hulls of both boats. The junk turned about, so its prow pointed toward the village of Si-Fou. Towing the sampan in its wake, it made for a wharf the travelers hadn't noticed earlier.

Jane was still smiling. She observed the oarsmen and the soldiers with shrewd curiosity—not at all intimidated by their forbidding expressions. After all, in the little comedy she anticipated, these men were only playthings!

And her air of careless calm made the Chinese consider her with anxious surprise. Who could this little European be, that she wasn't the least concerned by the sight of them?

The junk reached the riverbank. The sampan it was towing came to a stop alongside the wharf. The soldiers jumped out onto the wooden dock built on pilings and pushed back the crowd of curious chattering onlookers who'd gathered to see the prisoners. With an abrupt gesture, the officer motioned for the foreigners to disembark. Jane was the first to obey, and the other followed her out onto the wharf.

CHAPTER III
Under the Protection of the Dragon

Kuang, the mandarin Governor of Si-Fou, was a scholar of the second rank, and in the process of qualifying for the first rank, which would give him the right to replace the blue button on the point of his hat with a red button made of coral. In addition, Kuang was a philanthropist with a heart of gold.

Around Si-Fou the land along the Yangtze was low-lying, marshy, and clogged by mud banks that made access to the village difficult. The problem was made even more significant by the high proportion of the villagers who were fishermen. In his yamen, overlooking the crowded huts of the village from a great height, Kuang noticed the problem and decided to solve it by building a wharf that stretched twenty meters out into the river—twenty meters' worth of planks resting on solid pilings driven deep into the river bottom.

That public improvement was naturally carried out by means of requisitions. The laborers contributed work days. Men who owned carts brought materials to the site. Locksmiths and ironworkers furnished the rivets and bolts and metal framing that held the wooden structure together. Lastly, whatever had to be purchased elsewhere was paid for by a special tax on the merchants of Si-Fou. That was the only expense in cash, and even then it didn't exceed three hundred and fifteen or three hundred and twenty taels (about ten thousand francs).

After that Si-Fou could boast a spacious, solid, convenient wharf, which—as Kuang often remarked, with a smile that narrowed his almond-shape eyes—had cost the municipal treasury almost nothing. The only real cost—an enormous one—had been the expenditure of energy and thinking and devotion to the public welfare by the mandarin responsible for that magnificent structure.

Kuang was aware that during the course of the whole business he'd been outrageously cheated by his underlings, and he was in no mood to let an injustice like that pass. Every act of philanthropy deserved its reward—by the Tiger's claws and the Dragon's flames! But Kuang, a gentle soul by nature, didn't want to bully the people of Si-Fou. He found a way to be helpful to them while simultaneously reimbursing himself for his good works. Using plank walls that weren't watertight, he had the space under the wharf divided into compartments of different sizes. Before then the fishermen had kept whatever they hadn't sold of their catch in crates anchored out in the river to serve as fish tanks. Those crates naturally obstructed navigation and could have caused accidents. True, there'd never been an accident, but a catastrophe still remained within the realm of possibility. And to govern is to foresee.

Kuang's foresight led him to decree that from now on the compartments under the wharf would become the obligatory fish tanks. The use of them would be *free and without charge*. However, the mandarin with the blue button on his cap knew the villagers to be too honorable and too grateful to owe so much to their governor and to give him nothing in exchange. Therefore, out of respect for their dignity, and entirely from a desire not to offend them, he'd agreed to accept an annual rent, payable four times a year on the third day of the new moon—the most auspicious day of all.

As a result, Kuang collected about ten thousand francs in revenue each year—a pretty fine return, it must be admitted, on the equal sum spent by the well-to-do villagers to build that wharf. Those worthy citizens must have rejoiced at the knowledge that for a cost of less than three hundred and twenty taels each they'd guaranteed their beloved mandarin (a mandarin, as everyone knows, is always beloved) a perpetual annual income of the same amount.

So Kuang was a philanthropist... a Chinese philanthropist... But after all, can we be sure that in other places philanthropy isn't carried out in exactly the same way?

The prisoners now gathered on the wharf were unaware of the miracle of fiscal, economic, and administrative ingenuity represented by the planks beneath their feet. The soldiers surrounded them. Two heralds handed the captives boards on which painted letters displayed the Blue-Button mandarin's titles. Like the caps with their colored buttons, those honorific boards persisted in the Republic of China, though the travelers could see the writing had been simplified.

In the past, the lifetime of an educated man was barely sufficient for him to learn the forty-five thousand different ideograms that composed the Chinese writing system. Now the democratic rulers of the Celestial Kingdom had adopted an alphabet of thirty-three letters, whose various combinations made it possible to represent all the necessary sounds.[35] The writing on the boards they were holding had been done using the new system. What did the words on the boards mean? None of the travelers could tell. But, by the way the soldiers bowed low, they were led to assume that the holder of these titles must be very important indeed.

Once that ceremony was over, the soldiers set off, escorting their prisoners, with the board-bearers in the lead. Along the way, laborers, merchants standing at the doors of their shops, women gossiping in the middle of the street, even the children playing jacks or dice or hopscotch, all stopped what they were doing or saying to raise their closed fists to their cheeks to salute the boards that enumerated the titles and honors of Kuang, Blue-Button mandarin and Governor of Si-Fou.

Immediately behind the board-bearers came little Jane, walking with a firm step. She seemed to be highly amused. Her companions, more conscious of the trouble they were in, found themselves envying the little girl for her peace of mind.

But on they went. Leaving the narrow alleys of the village center—strewn with garbage like all Chinese streets—they passed through tiny fields, built one upon the next, and juxtaposing the most varied crops. Then they reached an open-work fence, lacquered in red and gold and twisted into fantastical arabesques. The board-bearers kowtowed. The officer made an announcement, which was simple enough for Stepan and Sefra to be able to translate it for their companions: "The Blue Button's estate!"—meaning simply that the procession was about to set foot on mandarin Kuang's property.

They entered that high official's grounds: admirable gardens, laid out in the Chinese manner, which is to say with exquisite skill, and in some ways reminiscent of the English style. It's worth noting, in fact, that while Japanese horticulture amounts to growing ridiculous contorted dwarf plants, Chinese gardeners by contrast have remained great decorative artists. The prisoners could have admired the flower-filled beds and the artificial springs and the manmade hills... if their capacity for admiration hadn't been diminished by the thought of the official who could put a stop to their journey.

Here and there, plaster statues lacquered in many colors flanked the dusty paths. One of them represented a dragon with scales highlighted in gold and

---

[35] The replacement of Chinese ideograms by some kind of alphabetic orthography was discussed after the 1911 Revolution, and "romanization" was adopted in principle by the Communist Party in the 1930s, but it has never happened in fact. Communist China merely simplified the number of strokes in some of the more complex ideograms in the 1950s. This detail is therefore an invention of d'Ivoi's.

with its menacing wide-open maw illuminated in vermillion. Jane stopped short in front of the statue. She prostrated herself, spoke in words no one understood, then stood up and went on walking calmly between the soldiers.

The commanding officer had observed that odd performance. Going close to the girl, and struggling to string together the few words of English he'd saved up during a short time spent in Shanghai, he asked, "Why does the foreigner worship *our* Sacred Dragon?"

Oddly, the question brought a smile to the little girl's face—as if she'd been expecting it! Without hesitation she replied, "Your Sacred Dragon is *my* revered master."

"Your master, and you a little white girl?"

"Exactly. And there's no doubt I'm under his protection."

"In what way?"

"I'll demonstrate it to the noble mandarin Kuang."

She spoke with such conviction that the officer couldn't help being impressed. He nodded thoughtfully and went back to the head of the procession. He couldn't have suspected that the darling little creature had just delivered the first speech of the scene that—in her childish audacity—she intended to perform before the mighty Governor of Si-Fou.

The trees here were spaced farther apart, and now between the slender trunks bordering the path they could see broad lawns, whose emerald carpet was punctuated here and there by luxurious planters full of flowers. By the eery light of the multicolored lanterns illuminating the gardens now that night had come, the flowers in those planters—following the whims of the gardeners—writhed like snakes or symbolic dragons, or spread out into cornucopias, or mimicked the outlines of the honored deities presiding over every intimate aspect of domestic life.

Those latter flower arrangements were said to be "reserved"—meaning that to have them in your garden you were required to (1) be a government mandarin, and (2) have donated to the Buddhist monasteries or nunneries in the district a gift as great as it was pious. As they passed those images in flowers, the soldiers presented arms, the commanding officer saluted with his sword, and Jane performed a complicated pantomime. She even turned briefly to her companions and said, "Do what I'm doing, since we're under the protection of the Dragon."

At the center of the lawns stood the buildings of the yamen. The main building had small square turrets and verandas opening onto terraces that led out to the gardens down broad stairs of a couple of steps flanked by bronze monsters. The roofs were upturned at the corners, and were stacked in layers according to the numbers considered lucky in Chinese religion: three, five, and seven. Everywhere the lacquer work, the gilding, the jade, the openwork wooden panels, had been meticulously sculpted by those patient Chinese craftsmen whose artistry was expressed in their care for detail and the perfection of their execution. Such was the sumptuous home of that Blue-Button mandarin, Kuang.

He himself, alerted by a messenger of the capture of suspicious foreigners, awaited them in the reception hall: a spacious room, whose walls were decorated in alternating white and red squares to symbolize death and justice, where the mandarin usually received his subjects, his petitioners, and dignitaries sent by the provincial governor. He had placed himself on the Dais of Government and was nobly sprawled across that dictatorial seat, which was green and silver—the Republic has yet to do away with those colors, symbolic of the imperial tyranny—and which was carved to represent a tiger crouching in one of those unrealistic postures that seem to be the proprietary secret of Chinese furniture makers.

At the sound of the footsteps of the soldiers and their prisoners, Kuang sat up straight and did his best to appear majestic. Perhaps he would have succeeded if he'd been dressed like a traditional imperial official, in a long silk robe embroidered with the wearer's titles and honors, and a high hat with a peacock feather, and leather boots decorated with gold trim. But republican simplicity, now imposed on all servants of the state, is ill suited for majestic display. Kuang—a small, slight, beardless, parchment-dry man—seemed further shrunk in his European jacket, his tight trousers, and his factory-made shoes. And his cap with its blue button, along with his glasses with bamboo frames, made him seem more comical than dignified.

But now footsteps rang on the flagstones of the veranda onto which opened the lacquered doors of the reception hall, and the procession of soldiers and captives entered, preceded by the household herald whose job it was to announce visitors. He called out in a ringing voice, "Yen, officer of the state, and his soldiers have brought prisoners to the worthy Kuang—foreigners who were traveling on the river without authorization."

Kuang nodded his approval. He studied the captives, and asked them various questions in Chinese. When no one answered—for the very good reason that they couldn't understand him—the governor thought of trying English... an English brightened up with a delightful Chinese accent, in which the sentences were decorated with unexpected syntax, but which at least conveyed a coherent meaning to his listeners. "Who are you? Why are you roaming through this district?"

A small, clear voice replied. "We're under the protection of the Dragon, and we're headed toward a destination unknown to us, but that he has promised to reveal to us." It was Jane who, bolder than any of her companions, put her head down and launched into the story she'd fabricated.

Derrick, Freda, and young Stepan and Sefra shivered, astonished by the little girl's self-assurance. The irreversible words had been spoken: what would come of this intrusion of the Dragon into their doings?

But their reaction was nothing compared to that of the Blue Button. The mandarin started, and greeted the name of the Dragon with a formal bow of the first rank, the one reserved for Buddhas and sovereigns. His wide-open eyes now examined the little girl menacingly, as if he resented her for having invoked the power of the mythical beast—a power so much greater than that of a mandarin. At the same time, he seemed afraid, as if he wanted to punish Jane for her presumptuous claim, but didn't dare... What if she were telling the truth! Here, like everywhere else, superstition was at work, and its influence ran counter to the governor's arrogance.

That inner tug of war was revealed by his tone of voice: he aimed to sound commanding but only managed to sound ridiculous. "Of course, we revere the lord Dragon. But it's not enough to claim to be under his protection; you still have to prove it..."

"That won't be hard," interrupted Jane.

He stared at her and echoed, "What? Not hard?"

"Of course not," she answered. "Think about it—if the revered lord Dragon is protecting us, he has to show it by lending us his power."

"Yes, yes," chuckled Kuang, who thought the little girl was just digging herself into a hole.

"So we're agreed, Mister Mandarin. Perfect. All right, look at me. I'm just a little girl."

"I see that."

"And you're an important grownup—because they only let people govern part of the country if they're important and educated."

He smiled at the compliment. "Quite right... However, child, let's get back to the Dragon."

But Jane didn't seem at all chastened. While her companions could barely breathe, so hard were their hearts beating with fear, she went on calmly, "We're getting there. You're strong, and I'm a little weakling. The Dragon will show that he's our friend, by making me stronger than you."

"Stronger! Ah, wonderful! Excellent!" Kuang gave way to loud laughter. Ah, this kid was too cute! She—stronger than him! Not even itinerant clowns had ever thought up anything more ludicrous.

But the grin froze on his face as Jane declared, "You're laughing, O Blue Button. The Dragon will make you repent that. He has whispered his orders to me. I, a girl of seven, forbid you to rise from your mandarin's throne."

As if in reaction to her words, Kuang tried to laugh once more. But in a confrontational, threatening voice, Jane added, "Try it and you'll see."

The child's tone was so firm, so commanding, that the governor automatically tried to stand up. A look of great amazement filled his parchment-dry face. He tensed his features, his hands pressed against the arms of his chair, and his entire body stiffened in his desperate effort... Incredible! He couldn't stand up. He felt as if his seat had fastened itself to him, that it had become a permanent part of his body.

Miss May's little protégée had simply used the ability of the electric tunic she was wearing to magnify the power of her will. And this time her companions had understood her thinking, and they too concentrated their wills to support their dear little friend—though Kuang's odd facial expressions made it hard for them to stay serious.

He was literally going mad: the "magicians" whose tricks took advantage of Chinese gullibility had never done anything like this. And then, a child of seven or eight didn't yet know how to lie! It must be true that the foreigners were friends of the Dragon. On the one hand he believed that; on the other, he still suspected some kind of fraud or trick—though the mysterious power that kept him in his chair seemed utterly inexplicable.

Above all, his dignity was wounded. He—Governor of Si-Fou, graduate of the College of Ritual and Literature, mandarin of the Blue Button, representative of the authority of the Nation—found himself immobilized, powerless in the hands of a child, and in the presence of a platoon of his soldiers.

Indeed the soldiers were still there, surrounding the foreigners like a squad of sentries. Seeing them gave Kuang an idea. If he gave the sign, his men would seize the prisoners—and then they'd all see if the Dragon would rescue them. Delighted with that plan, which he considered quite elegant, the governor gave the sign to arrest them... and then watched dumbfounded as the scene unfolded.

The soldiers took one step toward the prisoners—but only one. The foreigners turned toward them, and pointed. As if she had taken on the role of spokesperson for the group, Jane cried, "Halt! Present... arms!" She burst out laughing. "I know how to give orders—I watched parade ground maneuvers in Frisco!"

But all that was nothing. What shocked the mandarin was the behavior of his men. Their grimacing faces and contorted postures showed they were trying with all their might to resist obeying the order... but then they carried it out. They stood at attention, as still as statues, presenting arms—honoring the captives as if they were commanders of Banners. (A Banner is the name for a Chinese army corps.)

But that didn't last long. The diabolical little creature—who seemed to give orders to her grownup captives like some mischievous goblin leading a parade of sorcerers—spoke once again. "Good men, deploy out to the veranda, and keep anyone from disturbing us. Dismissed!"

With their captain leading the way, the soldiers left the reception hall. Through the open doors Kuang could see them space themselves out along the veranda, and fix their bayonets to the muzzles of their rifles. After that they stood perfectly still, vigilant guardians protecting those inside from the world.

Truly for the Blue Button that series of events had taken on the aspect of a nightmare. His anger began to rise, and his shock changed to annoyance. Mandarins are not accustomed to being made fun of by little children, nor to playing the role of someone's puppet. Kuang was eager to punish these bold foreigners who stood there before him, seemingly so respectful and deferential—though the look in their eyes and the occasional spasms crossing their faces betrayed a barely veiled mockery.

But, at least for the moment, these people had the upper hand. A Chinaman is no more in a hurry to be avenged than he is to conclude a negotiation. Patience and cunning are the watchwords of his strategy. So Kuang put on a cheerful expression, and made his voice gentle as he remarked slyly, "The Dragon's affection for you is clear to me, child. No doubt it was that powerful spirit who guided you to me."

Jane looked at her companions with laughter in her blue eyes. It occurred to her that, if it had been up to them, they would never have ended up in Kuang's presence. But she replied firmly, "Yes, it was he."

"Ah! No doubt he had some purpose for our meeting?"

"Exactly," said Jane calmly.

Derrick and Freda exchanged a worried glance. It seemed to them the child was headed down some mistaken path. What was she going to say? What good could the Dragon supposedly have foreseen in the events that had made them prisoners of the mandarin? Meanwhile Stepan and Sefra were observing the action as if they were watching a play at the theater, without the slightest concern. Jane simply fascinated them. The two of them, who'd grown up in the haphazard nomadic life on the road, admired the child for her intelligence—an inheritance of her highly cultured ancestry that seemed to them more sophisticated and more creative than anything they were familiar with.

"And can you tell me what the revered Dragon's purpose is for this meeting?" whispered the governor.

Jane bowed solemnly. "As you'll remember, Mister Mandarin, I said before that he's driving us toward some mysterious destination. He commands, and like good children we obey."

Kuang nodded his approval. "Well, then what?"

"Then the Dragon wishes our journey to be facilitated."

"Facilitated? How so?"

"By you, sir. He wants you to give us a safe-conduct as friends of the Republic of China, and a boat with oarsmen to take us upriver, and horses if we have to travel by land."

"What, me?" he grumbled. But soon he relented, because an idea he considered brilliant had just crossed his mind. He needed to dupe the prisoners, to appear to agree completely with them—and to lead them into troubles they couldn't get out of. With his voice all sugar and honey, he cooed, "Kuang is the worshipful servant of the sacred Dragon. He will obey the instructions transmitted to him via your infant mouth. But I'd like to pick out for you the best sampan, the fastest oarsmen, and the strongest and gentlest horses. Please accept the hospitality of my yamen at least till tomorrow. Don't deny me the honor of having the Dragon's favorites as my guests, and of organizing your journey to perfection."

He affected a tone of such goodwill and an expression of such sincerity that honest little Jane and her companions believed him without a second thought.

Only Sefra whispered into Stepan's ear, "This mandarin means to play a trick on us."

"Where do you get that idea?" he whispered back.

"I can feel it. We have to stick close to little Jane. Together three of us can exert a greater willpower; and if we're on the lookout for betrayal we won't be taken by surprise."

Meanwhile Jane announced, "Mister Mandarin, we accept your very kind invitation. If you'd like, you may now leave your seat and join us."

A flash of rage crossed the Chinaman's face but was immediately concealed. Smiling and obsequious, Kuang rose and joined his prisoners, who'd now become his guests. "With your kind permission, I'll have you shown to the rooms where you'll stay tonight. My servants will be your own. I invite you to join me in an hour for a dinner, and an impromptu celebration, that I would like to host in your honor."

He struck a loud gong. Servants in felt-soled shoes entered silently. The Blue Button pointed out the foreigners. "These are my guests. Show them to the apartments reserved for my dearest friends, and take care to satisfy their every need. If any of you displeases them, he will be caned to death."

That threat tickled Jane's sense of humor. So quietly that only Freda, who was standing next to her, could hear, she murmured, "You hear that? What a welcome! They'll even clean the servants' clothes by beating them like a rug!"

Still, she took her place at the head of the little group that processed out of the reception hall, led by the servants.

CHAPTER IV
A Tiger and Alligators

Kuang remained alone in the great hall. His expression changed. A thousand wrinkles etched his face; his clenched teeth and his burning eyes gave him a look of unspeakable cruelty. He paced the room from to end with violent gestures and loud exclamations, condemning those foreigners—who'd somehow tied him up with their mysterious powers—to the demons of Hell. It had to be some kind of sleight of hand. Why would the Dragon, that Chinese divinity, agree to protect foreigners, people whom it was against republican courtesy to harm, but that the Chinese mind—unchanged in spite of the Revolution—still damned with that insulting term, Foreign Devils?

He hurried out to the veranda, perhaps to give his men some sinister order. But the soldiers had disappeared, presumably in obedience to an unspoken order from the minds of those foreigners. The reminder that he was in fact alone pulled the mandarin back within the bounds of caution. "No, no," he muttered through his teeth, "no sudden moves. My first idea was my best: trickery."

For a moment he stood there, lost in thought. Then he gestured decisively, like a man who's just chosen his course of action. "I'll go see my musician, Tuoc, whose ivory flute can subdue the marsh spirits."

Five minutes later, after walking around the perimeter of the yamen buildings, Kuang stopped at a multicolored pavilion that stood at the far edge of the lawns directly surrounding the palace, on the very rim of the flat ground at the top of the hill. Beyond the pavilion the grounds fell away in a wooded slope, in the style of an English park. That descending slope faced west, toward the marshes that bordered the river on that side; lagoons of still water alternating with dark reed-covered islets stretched to the horizon.

Kuang knocked at the door, on whose green-painted background the signs of the Tiger and the Lizard stood out in yellow. Like the emperors formerly, practicing magicians had the right to use yellow paint—a privilege denied to ordinary mortals.

The door opened to reveal a man of athletic build, clearly from northern China. His great height, his broad shoulders, his complexion of the palest amber, all suggested the ethnic characteristics of a native of Zhili.[36] From his belt hung flutes made from the bones of water buffalo. He bowed ceremoniously. "Illustrious Blue-Button Kuang, Governor of Si-Fou and Tuoc's host and revered master... what do you wish of your servant?"

"To punish the sorcerers who paralyzed me and robbed me of my will."

Tuoc started. "What sorcery could overpower a scholar?"

"I don't know."

"Who are these sorcerers?"

"Foreigners."

"Enter, your lordship. Tuoc is your faithful servant. He will avenge you."

He stood aside to let his visitor come in. The green door closed behind them, concealing them from the yamen—where Jane and her companions rested trustingly in the rooms they'd been given. All of them were in good cheer. The little girl's plan had succeeded beyond hope. Here they were, guests of the mandarin governor, who'd also promised them a safe-conduct and means of transportation. Who would have believed a small child could so successfully ensure their travel through the Chinese countryside, filled as it was with obstacles of all kinds!

Stepan and Sefra performed comical dances for the little girl, whose superior intelligence they acknowledged. Derrick and Freda gazed at her affectionately: they were thinking of the past, and their simple minds were struck by the poetic justice of it all—how right May had been, aboard the *Cyclopic*, to save Jane from death, since now the little girl was about to return the favor. Indeed, May's adoptive parents were no longer in doubt: they'd find the captives and rescue them.

Bong! Bong! Bong! The solemn tones of a gong rang out, its humming echoes spreading through all parts of the yamen. Servants appeared and invited the Blue Button's noble guests to proceed to the hall where dinner had been prepared. They added that the grounds would be lit up in their honor, and that the scholar Kuang wished to give them the pleasure of an evening excursion by

---

[36] Zhili (also romanized as Chihli) was a region of northern China roughly corresponding to the modern province of Hebei.

sampan, so their souls would be bathed in the rays of the nocturnal orb, and all their undertakings would be blessed with good fortune.

How to respond to such pleasant overtures? Obey. The little group went to the dining hall, which was lit by an array of pink lanterns. On the table, set in the Chinese style, stood a multitude of tiny dishes and little bowls separated into groups by stacks of decorated paper napkins, which are the only kind used in China. At the far end of the hall there was a raised dais, whose purpose, though it eluded the foreigners at the moment, would soon be revealed.

Kuang awaited his guests, standing beneath an alcove that contained the altar where the household Buddha sat enthroned. Sticks of incense smoldering at the feet of the bronze deity filled the air with an exquisite fragrance. Bowing to each of them in turn, the mandarin pointed to their seats around the table. He himself didn't sit till all of them were settled.

And then the peculiar, copious meal began. The beverages they were served included aromatic tea, rice wine, grape wines—rosé, whites, reds, from Formosa and Tashuen and the Red River—and fermented palm juice... and all of that was poured, like flickering rubies and topazes and pale liquid sapphires, into cups the size of thimbles. Oh, Kuang was certainly treating his guests like people under the protection of the Dragon.

The household musicians appeared. Some of the women, seated in graceful postures, scratched a short bow across the three strings of the ao-lin, a kind of lute with a long neck;[37] others blew into the two stems of a three-note oboe known as the ha-tien.[38] There were also harpists.

Above all, the travelers noticed the excellent te-sme players. These women sat together in a close-knit group, each holding her own tambourine—but instead of the metal discs of the traditional Basque tambourine, their instruments had rattles of various sonorities.[39] A te-sme ensemble can perform complex pieces with remarkable accuracy, though each of the musicians contributes only one pitch. The vibration of the skin stretched taut across the circular frame of the tambourine provides the accompaniment. Nothing could sound more curious or more pleasant than the ringing of the rattles while the musicians rhythmically tap the vibrating skin of the tambourines.

Then came the dances. The slender Cantonese dancers, with flowers in their hair, performed their complex movements with an odd grace that seemed both pretentious and innocent.

Suddenly, as the meal was ending—and the guests were looking at each other, a little dizzied by so many new experiences—a series of explosions went

---

[37] Neither the name "ao-lin" nor the description corresponds to any real instrument, but the closest match might be the *erhu*.

[38] Again, "ha-tien" is not the name of any instrument. But in this case the description is close to the *shuangguan*.

[39] The Chinese rattle drum has several names, none close to "te-sme."

off outside. Kuang stood up, bowed to them all, and said gently, "The fireworks in honor of my distinguished guests will be lit as soon as they wish to leave the table."

No banquet in China would be complete without fireworks. The Arabs end their feasts with a fantasia featuring gunpowder. The Chinese prefer the colored powders of pyrotechnics.

"Fireworks!" they all cried with delight, pleased to leave the table and get some fresh air. Jane clapped her hands, rejoicing at the thought of the rockets whose flashing would light up the night.

None of them noticed the strange smile on Kuang's lips. He bustled forward to lead them out onto the veranda, scolding the servants who were bringing chairs. Once his guests were well settled, telling them he had to make sure the show went well—and accompanying his words by the most elaborate kowtows in Chinese protocol—he went away.

Jane and her companions laughed. Their treatment by the Blue Button mandarin put them in a good humor, and the seemingly infinite depths of Chinese superstition struck them as comical. All they had to do was to declare themselves acolytes of the Dragon, and to back up that claim with a scientific display, and China—a closed country in spite of its treaty agreements—was open to them. High officials placed themselves under their orders.

They spoke unconstrainedly, since they now found themselves alone on the veranda. The master of the yamen and all his servants had vanished. May's friends now faced only the lawns, beyond which the woods descended toward the marshes, which in this direction bordered the Yangtze River. In the trees, like unfamiliar stars, hung paper lanterns of many colors. From time to time a rocket—blue, green, red, or gold—traced its luminous path across the dark firmament, ending in a splash of gold, purple, lapis, or emerald rain.

Suddenly the five travelers started. A metallic squeaking had just rung out and was echoing across the landscape. Turning, they saw what had caused it: all the openings on the ground floor of the yamen were closing—not with ordinary shutters but with metal grills. In one coordinated movement, those grills had shut off every door and window that opened onto the veranda. What could it mean? That question had barely arisen in their minds before it was swept away by another.

Sefra—under the influence of her habitual anxiety, left over from her former life, in response to any unexplained occurrence—stood and pointed across the lawn. "There! There!" she cried in a strangled voice. "The earth has opened up!"

What could she mean by that? They all looked in the direction she was pointing, and stammered in distress, "It's true!"

A trapdoor had appeared where the lawn ended at the woods—a rectangular opening blacker than the grass that was dimly lit by the lanterns. Why those grills? Why that trapdoor? No one was there whom they could ask.

"Let's go have a look," suggested Stepan.

His companions began to move forward—but then stopped. A new figure had just entered the scene, rising up out of that trapdoor, whose purpose was now revealed to them: the opening led to an underground cage, in which the proprietor of the yamen could imprison his captives—either humans or wild animals, as needed. With one lithe and powerful leap, an enormous Bengal tiger had sprung out of the dark hole. He landed facing the travelers, and separated from them by only seven or eight meters.

"A tiger!"

"The mandarin tricked us!"

"We're done for!"

In their terror they all spoke at once. Unconsciously Derrick had picked up his wicker chair and was holding it out. Stepan bravely did the same, and Freda and Sefra instinctively took cover behind them.

But it was pointless. What could unarmed men do against a formidable predator? The beast considered the group with its glowing eyes. Its tail twitched gently against its legs, it stretched luxuriously, arched its powerful back with its alternating black and tawny stripes, and extended its enormous paws with their razor-sharp claws.

With the help of a little imagination, May's friends believed the animal was laughing savagely, that its muzzle was reaching out toward the prey it coveted, and that nothing could protect them from the monster's voracity.

The climax of the scene they all anticipated was approaching. The tiger had begun to move. It came slowly toward its victims. What need was there for haste, its behavior suggested, since its living dinner had nowhere to run? It advanced two meters, then three, then four, till it was close enough to eye their trembling forms with its blood-filled gaze. It hesitated for a moment: the beast was choosing its victim.

Terrified, their brows wet with the sweat of fear, they all wondered, "Who's going to die?"

At that moment Jane, filled with the panic that sometimes seizes children of her age, began to scream loudly and to cry out in broken fragments, "Shoo! Shoo!... I don't want to be eaten! I don't want to! Shoo! Shoo!"

Freda and Sefra reached out to the frightened child, but before they could complete the gesture they froze. Total astonishment filled them all. At Jane's cries the tiger had stopped. It wavered on its paws, as if embarrassed. It shook its head, as if to drive away a bothersome fly.

Jane kept on crying desperately, "Shoo, nasty tiger, shoo!"

The beast flattened itself on the ground, and crawling, with its head low, it backed up, and kept backing up. What could it mean?

The child's next words explained it: "The electric tunic."

In a flash they all understood. The tunic that vastly amplified the wearer's will had shown its power yet again. The little girl had cried "shoo!" and her desire to make the animal go away had broken the tiger's own momentum. Now they all joined her. Jane—reassured and trusting once more in her "big sister May," whose invention had saved her friends again—Jane led the way, advancing bravely on the tiger. Her companions followed her, focusing their wills on one goal: to make the predator go back into its underground cage.

It didn't take long. The pressure of all those wills converging on it caused the tiger to show signs of losing its mind. It spun around in all directions as if it were fighting off invisible enemies. Its enormous mouth opened, and it called plaintively. Finally, it turned and fled, vanishing into the black rectangle of the trapdoor.

When the travelers reached the opening they could see that, four meters below them, the tiger was huddled in the furthest corner of its cage, shaking convulsively. They fell into each others' arms and embraced. Then they thought of the one who'd saved them—dear May, who was absent, the captive of ruthless enemies. They had to go to her rescue as fast as possible. Either the mandarin Kuang would furnish them transportation—or he'd pay for the betrayal he'd just committed against his guests.

For they had no doubt: the closed grills, the open trapdoor, all were intended simply to force the travelers into meeting the tiger face to face. The Blue Button hadn't believed their claims, and didn't consider them worthy of being under the protection of the Dragon. Well, they'd show him a little something about the Dragon now!

It was Stepan who put their collective thoughts into words. Still astonished by the power they'd been granted thanks to May's ingenious invention, they all expressed their feelings amid joyful bursts of laughter that rang out at a great distance through the woods.

"Hey—music!" murmured little Jane, turning toward the slope that led down to the marshes.

"A Chinese flute," agreed Stepan and Sefra. "An ivory flute. We can tell, because in San Francisco we often heard them playing in Chinatown."

They were right: the melody carrying through the night came from a flute played by Tuoc, the mysterious musician who'd had that secret meeting with Kuang before dinner. And now the flutist was carrying out the orders he'd been given.

But the travelers didn't know that. They marveled at the strange melody flowing out of the darkness from the ivory tube. Sometimes the notes hurried, skipping gaily along, making them think of some dancing procession; then suddenly the pace slowed, and the music grew sorrowful. Laughter and tears leaped from Tuoc's instrument, and—a bizarre effect—the listeners imagined that at the foot of the hill, on the edge of the marshes, voices awoke and cried out, filling the valley with lamentations.

They'd all forgotten the tiger huddled in its underground cage. They were bewitched by the song of the ivory flute as it rose and fell, grew and diminished. The flowing sounds made their nerve endings tingle. All they could wonder was, who was that musician, and where was he hiding? He must be in the woods that blocked their view, and that the lantern light didn't penetrate.

But now the woods themselves seemed to come to life: leaves rustled, branches cracked as if moved by invisible beings. According to legend, Orpheus's lyre could bring stones to life and make them gather themselves into walls. Tuoc's flute seemed to induce motion in the trees and thickets. All around the mandarin's guests, life was stirring. They could feel it, they could sense it, but the mocking dark of night kept them from confirming it with their eyes. And yet there could be no doubt. The sounds from the woods grew louder.

"What's that?" murmured Freda and Derrick.

Sefra was leaning forward to hear better. "An army is climbing the slope, heading toward us."

"An army? Come on!"

Suddenly Stepan lay down on the grass and pressed his ear to the ground. He stayed still for a moment, listening, his hand held up to request silence. Finally, he got up, and inexpressible surprise filled his voice, his posture, his whole being. "There are things coming uphill..."

"Things? What do you mean, things?"

The boy shrugged. "I don't know. It's definitely not people. On the other hand, the footsteps don't sound like any animal I know. Horses, cattle, sheep, all sound different from that."

"So then what?" insisted Sefra.

The boy stretched out both arms, puffed out his cheeks, then let it all go. "Then... I don't know."

"Let's go back to the veranda," suggested Freda, instinctively lowering her voice.

"Why?"

"Because we'll be further from the edge of the woods."

"Is that any use?"

"Yes… If what's coming is dangerous, we'll be a little further away…"

"And we'll have enough time to use our wills, with the help of big sister May's tunics," added Jane. She went on, "Earlier, with the tiger, it happened automatically, without me thinking about it. Now we're on the alert."

She was right, and they all acknowledged it. They followed her back to the veranda—all of them suddenly aware that invisible eyes must be fastened on them, studying their movements and their faces. That was it! Those under the protection of the Dragon were being tested! Well then, they needed to keep their composure. They returned to the same seats they'd left earlier, and in silence they waited for *whatever was coming up the hill*.

Oh, the endless minutes, marked by mysterious noises! They could tell a moving circle was forming around them: small branches breaking, the ground ringing from the impact of heavy bodies, the rustling of leaves being shaken roughly, all were signs of their enemies' movements. The five travelers used the word "enemies": they had no doubt that whatever was approaching was hostile, and that it formed a multitude. All along the slope something was swarming in the night.

And still the flute played its tune—piercing, strident, painful to the ear— and in response to those annoying notes there came a painful bellow.

Suddenly Derrick slapped his forehead and muttered, "I'm an idiot! That bellowing… I should've recognized it. I've heard it enough times in the past."

"You know what that is?" They'd all turned to May's adoptive father.

He nodded. Then, slowly, his voice shaking, he said, "It's Yangtze alligators."

Their hearts froze. Those enormous crocodilians are not only fearsome foes, they inspire strong revulsion simply as members of the odious class of reptiles: lizards, snakes, crocodiles, and serpents all produce horror.

Now the thickets at the edge of the lawn parted or were crushed, and the woods groaned at the brutal stampede. Long brownish bodies emerged and trampled the lawn. Derrick was right: they were alligators. The mysterious flutist had summoned those sinister denizens of the marsh, and now they'd reached the yamen the diabolical music stopped.

The travelers were filled with rage: the mandarin hadn't dared to attack them face to face, but like a coward and a hypocrite he'd laid ambushes for them in which he hoped they'd die. But vengeance would have to wait: right now they had to ward off the danger—a terrible, repulsive danger!

Fifty alligators crawled across the lawn. They'd spotted Jane and her companions, and their eyes shone like red dots in their dark heads. Their jaws full of terrible teeth snapped with desire. They hurried toward the prey offered up to their hunger.

But this time Jane was no longer afraid. She had faith in May's genius. With a deliberate step she advanced toward the reptiles, calling out in her little child's voice, "Go back to the marsh, and make it snappy!"

Her actions and her words brought her companions back to the task. They all echoed her commands. And, just as they expected, the vile beasts stopped, seemed to struggle against some invisible opponent, snapped their jaws at nothing, and swept the air with their scaly tails. The sheer force of willpower, made irresistible by the electromagnetic tunics, constrained the alligators, as if great claws were squeezing them like a vise. Still struggling, they retreated and crawled back into the woods.

Two enormous alligators still remained—the terrifying rearguard of the routed army—and Jane had a brilliant idea. "Go eat the tiger. That'll teach him a lesson!"

No one laughed at her childish expression; what followed wasn't a spectacle to inspire humor. As if propelled by a spring, the alligators rushed to the trapdoor that led to the underground cage. Their enormous bodies vanished into the hole. And then a hellish symphony of frenzied roars and furious bellows filled the night. The underground battle was brief. Silence fell, suggesting the struggle was over.

Jane led the way as they all ran to the lip of the opening and examined the hole curiously. The tiger had vanished. The two alligators pushed their way pitifully up the sides of the cage—walls too high for them to climb. They'd devoured the great cat, but they remained prisoners.

And while the travelers all stared at each other, stunned by the almost unlimited power they seemed to possess, thanks to the tunics May had invented, suddenly their ears were filled with nonsense cries and giggles and words of praise right next to them. They turned to look.

It was Kuang, bowing down so low before them that he seemed to be kneeling. He spoke with the speed and volume of a stream that has burst its banks. "Distinguished guests... Yes, you are indeed under the protection of the Dragon... I didn't believe it—because it's wise not to believe in favor so rare, so priceless—and now I'm punished... A wonderful tiger, imported at great expense from British India to be given to the Coral Button, the governor of the province, has been devoured by alligators... I'm not complaining, that's the price I pay for not believing you. From now on you're my revered guests. Forget about my suspicions... they've evaporated! Tomorrow at daybreak I'll put everything—horses, carriages, a sampan, weapons, servants—at your disposal! Also the document, the safe-conduct, sealed in yellow lacquer with the delicate engraving of the Agate Seal, thanks to which no one will dare impede your journey. Glory to the Dragon! Glory to those he protects!"

The Blue-Button scholar, Kuang, Governor of Si-Fou, admitted his defeat. His guests didn't hold a grudge against him. They understood that this time the cunning Chinaman, finally beaten, was speaking sincerely.

Indeed, in the morning he kept all his promises. From now on the little party that had left Shanghai almost clandestinely could travel openly, guaranteed by the protection of the Agate Seal to receive the support and goodwill of all authorities.

CHAPTER V
Betrayals Loom

On a long narrow peninsula lying at the confluence of two rivers—each seven or eight hundred meters broad, each bearing its current of silty water, each crisscrossed constantly by heavily laden junks—stood a town filled with houses, yamens, temples, and gardens. On both banks stood other towns, with the same jumble of houses, the same peculiar buildings with multicolored upturned roofs, the same narrow filthy alleyways. And everywhere—in the streets, on the docks and wharves, in the shops, on the piers standing on pilings—a crowd of people swarmed and gossiped and discoursed and argued without end.

This was Hankou, lying five hundred kilometers from the sea, whose three districts contained more than eight hundred thousand souls: Hankou, cradle of the Chinese Revolution; Hankou, famous for its university that produced scholars and aspirants to the honorable rank of mandarin; Hankou, which carried out the spectacular feat of singlehandedly overthrowing the old aristocratic rule of the Celestial Empire.

The leaders needed for the Revolution were found within the city's schools. Their troops consisted of those who volunteered to put themselves under their orders: as always, there were plenty of malcontents ready to be recruited to form a revolutionary army—malcontents and looters. But the latter found themselves unpleasantly surprised: harsh discipline prevailed, so strict that foreigners weren't harassed.

The revolutionary leaders concentrated their forces against the regular army dispatched by the imperial court. And those regulars were either bought off or beaten, till their "Banner" regiments melted away and vanished. The triumph of the insurgents provoked both the emperor's flight and the proclamation of the Republic of China in all parts of that immense country, with its population of over four hundred million people. Hankou, consecrated "Mother of the Revolution," was decreed a Sacred City and granted the coveted privilege of being the City of Torture. From then on, anyone conspiring against the new status quo would be handed over to the executioners for torture within the walls of Hankou.

A denser crowd than anywhere else had now gathered for an execution of that kind in Red Square, the designated site for the punishment of the condemned. The square—irregularly shaped, and bordered by yamens whose balconies were ornamented with symbolic dragons and lotuses—had a sinister look under a sky streaked with gray clouds. The scaffold in the center rose about three meters above the flagstones. On the upper platform, red pillars decorated with the gilded symbols of justice were lined up pointing at the sky. To each pillar was bound a condemned convict. And the convicts now enduring the cruel mockery of the crowd—as bloodthirsty as all crowds—were none other than Princess Liao and her devoted friends.

The revolutionary tribunal had passed sentence: they were to be exposed to the public on the pillory, then to have their limbs broken with an iron bar, then to be left gasping and twitching till death delivered them from their appalling agonies.

Princess Liao, Miss May, James Lipson, and Captain Andrews stood bound, their faces tense with unspeakable horror. Every passing minute brought closer the moment when the torturers would appear, armed with the iron bars with which they'd break the flesh and bones of the condemned. And the thought that the young ladies were about to suffer that horrible ordeal dominated the minds of their companions.

In that terrible crisis, first one man, then the other, unconscious of the admission implied by their sorrowful words, moaned, "May, poor May, if only I could take on myself all of your suffering!" and "Liao, if only I'd died before I agreed to bring you here among these barbarians!"

Then once again silence fell on the scaffold, while all around it the stupid, pitiless crowd mocked on.

"Ah, the emperor's daughter must be delighted—she stands above the people the way she used to!"

"Bah," cackled a neighbor, "I'm not sure about that. There's no place like the Imperial City for putting you above the people!"

"That could be, but the Republic doesn't have the infinite resources of the emperors!"

"She's doing all she can, poor thing!"

Loud explosions of laughter greeted those brutal comments, their savagery born not out of love for liberty but out of the lowest emotion of all—envy.

But their sarcasm fell flat: neither Liao nor May moved. Their haunted eyes no longer saw, their ears took in nothing more than a vague humming, their pallid faces were rigid from a horror that was approaching its climax. Perhaps, by a supreme blessing of nature, they were no longer even conscious of where they stood.

Suddenly the captives shuddered, and the spectators howled and cheered: in the distance could be heard the solemn tones of the bronze gongs, the harbingers of justice. The crowd knew the musicians who customarily accompanied executions had left their quarters by the riverbank. In ten minutes or so, they would arrive in the square and assemble at the foot of the scaffold, and the bloody spectacle would begin.

For a moment the crowd froze—no more noise, no more motion—as if they'd all been metamorphosed into a collection of statues, like people turned to stone in some legend. The power of emotion—terror in the condemned, excitement in the onlookers—had overcome all of them to almost the same degree.

But soon a dull murmur arose, suggesting that the gawkers were resuming their insults and their vile jokes aimed at the captives. The approaching conclusion of the drama stimulated the wicked eloquence of the vulgar masses. The condemned instinctively bowed their heads under the hail of insults that was about to fall on them. The young women had closed their eyes against the menacing faces... Suddenly they opened them again, and trembling stupefaction filled their eyes.

The crowd was roaring—but the roar wasn't an insult to them. Their cheer rose to the sky, a cheer of acclaim. Yes, the crowd was acclaiming them. What? What? Irresistible curiosity drove the condemned to seek out the cause of that reversal of feeling. No doubt they were all thinking unconsciously, "Perhaps the cheers of the crowd offer us some hope." Doesn't hope endure to the last dying breath? Who knows what the next minute will bring?

All eyes had turned to the sky, everyone was looking up, with their heads tilted back. What was going on up there? Alas—the poor victims bound to the pillory found out all too soon, and the *mene, mene, tekel, upharsin*[40] of antiquity was no more menacing than what they saw. In the azure space between two clouds, some sort of airship hovered above the dramatic scene. And that airship was no friendly sight: with intensified anguish the condemned recognized the Slanes' flying machine, the *Vulture*.

---

[40] In the biblical Book of Daniel those words, meaning "numbered, numbered, weighed, and divided," appear miraculously on the wall of King Belshazzar's palace, foretelling Babylon's destruction.

Their enemies gathered around them on the ground had now been joined by their enemies flying overhead. Executioners below, executioners above, executioners everywhere!

"Them!"

"We thought we'd beaten them!"

"And now they're enjoying their triumph."

They spoke those words through lips that were bloodless and stretched in grimaces of horror.

"If only I could die instantly, without suffering!" sobbed Princess Liao.

Her cry shook Andrews. He tensed his muscles and tried to tear himself free of the ropes that bound him to the pillory. He would willingly have given his life to be able to go to the girl who was weeping for her youth and her lost life. His struggles were in vain. His efforts just made the wooden post creak, and drove the ropes deeper into his flesh, cutting a painful groove... but they didn't give way.

How had the *Vulture* come to be there, just in time for its sinister masters to witness the demise of those brave souls, who'd been undone by their selfless struggle against that despicable duo by the name of Slane?

As the reader will recall, when Tom Slane returned to his airship, on the outskirts of Honolulu, he briefly explained his reasoning to his son, the false Lloyd Hibbett. "Once Liao is free, she'll be drawn irresistibly toward her father, Lia-Sou, whom she plans to protect from my revenge. We must therefore get to China before her."

Before the *Vulture* carried the two arch-villains into the sky, they'd sent a detailed telegram to the government of the Republic of China, announcing that Princess Liao was heading to that country, with the aim of conspiring against the new regime. Thanks to that warning, the mandarin police officials, who were closely monitoring the arrival of all foreigners, had been able to arrest the princess and her devoted companions as soon as they disembarked.

Slane hadn't been there to witness their arrest, but his assurance that it would take place had restored his good humor. Wanting to share his confidence with William, he'd said, "Liao's going to be caught, my boy. We'll have done a tremendous service to the Republic, which will lead to rewards, commercial concessions, and so on. We know now that the typist May, and Derrick and Freda, and that boy Stepan and the girl Sefra, have all been bought by the Chinese girl. If we capture Lia-Sou, we'll have all the trumps in hand... All of them, my boy, and we'll break those simpletons who thought they could stand in our way."

The airship rose to a great height; the pilots didn't want to be seen from the ground or the ocean. Its speed was fixed at the maximum the motors could deliver. The Slanes, father and son, took turns at the controls. It was a tiring journey, during which they got almost no rest. So they sighed with satisfaction when they finally saw the Chinese coast ahead. But still they couldn't relax. Slane had no intention of landing in the coastal zone, too much frequented by Europeans. His destination was the provinces further inland, where no reporter would alert the international press. So over plains and rivers and hills and mountains the *Vulture* flew on, at the same dizzying altitude it had maintained over the long swell of the Pacific.

"Where are we going to land?" asked William, exhausted by three days of work without a break.

"At the Buddhist lamasery of Ayen-Talé, in upper Tibet."

"But that's where the ex-emperor, Lia-Sou, has taken refuge."

"Exactly. A refuge in all senses, because even if the emperor revealed his hiding place he'd have nothing to fear. No one in Asia would dare come seize him there: reverence for that sanctuary is too great. It'll take a couple of rascals like us to pull him out of there."

"You mean, your plan is to…"

"Yes, my boy, exactly that."

"You can't be serious. Our action would be called a sacrilege, and those stupid Asians would consider it a crime."

"That's true, if we abducted him by violence. You're quite right… But your mistake is to assume violence will be necessary."

William stared at his father in alarm, and murmured hesitantly, "You can't mean that Lia-Sou, whose life is threatened by an entire nation, is voluntarily going to leave a refuge where he's perfectly safe?"

"Yes, exactly, that's what I'm trying to tell you."

As the young man was about to question him further, Slane cut him off enigmatically. "There's no need to explain the future to you. You'll have the pleasure of seeing it unfold before your eyes… which are a little near-sighted," he concluded somewhat scornfully.

After a short silence he went on, his voice clouded by a mixture of the contempt and the tolerance that criminal felt for the beloved son who lacked his father's intelligence. "It's all right, son. I don't know if I could've thought up this plan at your age. But certainly, I would've understood it if someone explained it to me."

Slane's tone wasn't harsh. It expressed his secret grief: his son—as villainous as himself, as indifferent to wrongdoing, his equal in heartlessness and lack of scruples—was his inferior, by far, in terms of brains. No doubt William was excellent at carrying out orders; but his inability to put together a plan, in short to be a leader, was truly Slane's despair.

Their journey continued. There was no need now for the *Vulture* to fly at very high altitude: what did it matter if anyone spotted it? The mandarin officials who sighted the airship would notify the central government—and the master of the "great metal bird," as the Chinese referred to it, would gain importance in people's imaginations.

277

So, setting aside useless precautions, the *Vulture* flew at less than five hundred meters above the ground. The terrain had gradually risen, forming a complex mountain system, from the modest hills near the coast to increasingly prominent summits as they approached Tibet—that plateau that seems to be the central axis of the world, with its base at three to six thousand meters and its peaks above eight thousand meters: the highest points on the globe.

They'd left farmland behind. Now extraordinary piles of rocks and the chaos of a frozen desert presented to the eye a desolate, monotonous landscape, "every part just like every other part," as has rightly been observed by the rare travelers who have explored those bleak regions.

Sometimes there was a sudden change in the landscape: in a valley would appear one of the salt lakes that are so common between the Pamirs[41] and the border between Tibet and China. A lamasery with ornate construction, an impoverished village, a convoy of yaks or cattle serving as pack animals along a mountain trail, would be visible for a moment... Then a ridge would hide them all, and once again the chaos of granite and the confusion of boulders and snow fields and glaciers would flow by beneath the airship, seeming by optical illusion to be moving in the opposite direction from the travelers.

His eyes heavy with sleep, William watched everything without really seeing it. Physical fatigue had reduced him to a kind of stupor and robbed him of the ability to reason, to act, even to think. The goal they were pursuing seemed nebulous and unreal to him. He could almost have traded away his father's plans for the chance to sleep in peace. And it must be admitted that Slane's grandiose schemes didn't especially interest William. Not that they shocked his moral sense—he didn't have one—but that they were an obstacle to his desire for idle tranquility. Left to his own devices, the young man would have chosen above all other careers the one most agreeable to his own tastes: to live in the enjoyment of the fortune stolen from Lloyd Hibbett.

So he didn't hide his pleasure when his father called out loudly, "The lamasery of Ayen-Talé."

The false Lloyd Hibbett snapped out of his drowsiness; he rubbed his eyes vigorously, and when he could see clearly he ran to a porthole. In a steep valley that rose on all sides toward a sky full of sharp, jagged peaks, the bizarre buildings of the lamasery were stacked upon each other. Pavilions, courtyards, towers and turrets, all within a massive outer wall, were laid out beneath the *Vulture* with the clarity of a relief map.

As if talking to himself more than to his son, Slane said, "Courtyard number three, the one next to the pagoda, the holy of holies of the lamasery—do you see it?"

"Yes, of course. Our airship makes an excellent observatory."

---

[41] The Pamir Mountains form the western boundary of Tibet.

"It's the largest courtyard," went on his father. "So that's the one we'll land in. But first we have to be acknowledged as friends of Lia-Sou… indisputable friends." He gave a sinister cackle, like that of a hyena in the night. "Press the lever to the right of the door."

"I'm pressing it. What does it do? This is the first time I've seen it operated."

"It deploys at the rear of the airship the yellow imperial flag with the sacred dragon at its center."

"The imperial flag? What's the point of that ridiculous display?"

Slane gestured impatiently. He explained curtly, "That ridiculous display, as you call it, will show the lamasery that we're loyal servants of the overthrown emperor."

"So the lamas themselves are loyal to him?"

"Of course, my boy."

"Loyal to a dethroned emperor?"

"Who can regain his throne, you simpleton. My word, you talk as if you didn't know how republics evolve. First they overthrow the monarchy, then they overthrow religion…" He shook his head thoughtfully, then went on with a grimace and a laugh, "Unless they do like in our own United States, where religion has become an entirely commercial matter, and where anyone can start a new religion—which has allowed us to set the world record for competing sects, at a very respectable total of eight thousand three hundred and twenty!"

"Or unless the king, beaten temporarily, gets his revenge by stealing back the power that was taken from him," said William jokingly.

Slane didn't reply. He was focused on studying what was happening on the ground. In the courtyard he'd pointed out earlier, priests in long brown robes bordered with blue had appeared and were pointing emphatically up at the airship.

"They're summoning us," said Slane after a pause. "Let's descend."

They operated the instruments to lower the *Vulture* slowly along a gradual spiral toward the landing place. Lamas in robes of many colors were joined by soldiers with ancient helmets and scaly armor and copper shields of the kind once used by Manchu warriors, who now brandished lances bearing the triangular flags of the old divisions of the imperial army, known as the Eight Banners, and alongside those lances there were sabers in curiously decorated ivory sheaths—and everything assembled there in the courtyard showed that at the lamasery of Ayen-Talé the cult of the past was preserved intact.

The *Vulture* landed gently, without a bump. The air was filled with the soft humming of a chant, as the monks and the warriors sang, "Greetings, powerful spirits come down from the moon and the stars to honor our humble lamasery."

Indeed, these men who spent their lives in the high solitudes of Tibet couldn't understand—other than by magic—how a metal "chariot" could fly through the air like a bird. And now they kowtowed and fervently spun their prayer wheels.

Taking advantage of a moment of silence, Slane called out, "Lia-Sou, the emperor?"

He addressed his question to a monk who, he could tell from his insignia, held some important rank in the priestly hierarchy. That man bent his arms with his hands open, palms out, at shoulder height—in Tibet a sign of the highest respect—and said, "He is meditating in the cell where he defies the unjust anger of his rebellious people."

"Can you lead me to him?"

"I will proudly guide the divine messenger."

Slane bowed solemnly. It amused him to be called "divine," when all his ideas would more accurately have been described as "diabolical." He gestured briefly to tell William to stay there to protect the airship, then began to follow behind the lama.

They crossed the courtyard, entered the building by a low door, and climbed fantastical staircases that were sometimes set inside the walls and sometimes spiraled up the exterior of the buildings. When they reached a floor just below the stacked roofs of a corner tower, the lama pointed to a door decorated with curious copper arabesques.

"Man from the stars, that is Lai-Sou's room," he said. "Knock, and he will receive you."

After kowtowing once more, the Tibetan disappeared down the maze of corridors and stairs along which he had led the visitor. Slane remained alone. Smiling sarcastically, he muttered, "Idiots!" But then in a softer tone, and with his mockery barely noticeable, he went on slowly, "Let's not be critical of what's useful to me. An emperor will believe anyone who flatters his vanity. He won't doubt my devotion... so I've taken the trick."

He knocked twice, sharply, on the copper-ornamented door.

"Who comes to disturb the sorrows of a sovereign defeated by bad feng-shui?"[42] called a plaintive voice.

Slane shrugged scornfully. "The faithful messenger of Lotus Flower, born in the Imperial Palace, brings news to her father that his daughter is in danger."

Before he'd finished speaking the door was turning on its hinges. Facing him stood the ex-emperor, the Son of Heaven. Lia-Sou was a frail man of average height, with a look of dejection. His fine features, hollowed out by suffering, suggested the agonies he'd undergone and the torments he'd endured since the time, long ago, when the triumphant Revolution had driven him to flee. His black eyes, strangely like Princess Liao's, were veiled, as if clouded over by continual sorrow. His slender hands, the color of yellowed ivory, twitched unconsciously in his agitation.

---

[42] Evil spirits and omens [*Note from the Author*].

280

"Enter, messenger," he said. "Enter. The emperor's ears are open to your words."

Slane imperturbably repeated the gesture of greeting he'd seen the lamas use toward him earlier, then added solemnly, "O Lord of Jade, I do not bring you joy, but worry."

"Worry suggests the coming of misfortune. What greater misfortune could be added to those I have already suffered?"

To impress the man more deeply, Slane said nothing for a few seconds before replying, "O Son of Heaven, sovereign beloved of the Sun, of the pale Moon, of the sparkling Stars, has my feeble voice made no impression on your noble ears? No doubt the emperor has known the abyss of despair, and nothing more can touch him. But I weep—I, the messenger of Fate—at having to wound the heart of the father who consoled the emperor by saying, 'What does it matter! Liao, the light of China, the perfume of my love, has nothing to fear. She lives beyond the sea, among those Americans who, out of my ignorance of such things, I used to call barbarians. Those barbarians protect her now.'"

With an appearance of concern, the ex-emperor followed the bandit's tangled syntax. At this point in the villain's account he could accomplish nothing more. "Is she then no longer under the protection of the barbarians?" he asked, his voice shaking.

"She has left the sheltering soil of the United States."

"Oh, the ultimate shame! Have the men of that country driven her out?"

Slane assembled his features into an expression of feigned horror. "No, no, O Son of the Morning Dew, do not think that. The Americans were delighted to shelter the Flower of Mother of Pearl. They surrounded her beauty with praise."

"Then I don't understand."

The villain made his voice shake with emotion. "Refugees arrived from China. They told of your flight into the frozen, inaccessible heights of Tibet and your isolation at the lamasery of Ayen Talé. Other fugitives, demoralized by fear, spoke of rebel troops marching against your refuge, and described the horrible desire of those armies to seize you, to bind you to the pillory, to show the people what burden of torture an emperor can endure."

Lai-Sou gave a wan smile. "They were driven mad by fear, those prophets of torture. No one would dare violate the asylum of Ayen-Talé. Liao knew that."

"Alas! When rebellious subjects pursue their emperor, their father, a girl wouldn't believe them capable of drawing back from sacrilege."

"What did she do?"

"She left by night, on a submarine headed for Chinese waters. How did she persuade the commander to take her? No doubt she offered him gold and precious jewels; the barbarians like such things..."

But the emperor interrupted him. "You call them barbarians, and yet my eyes tell me you're of their race."

As if wounded by the remark, Slane stood up straight, and in a gentle voice he explained, "I call them barbarians to speak your language, sovereign beloved of the Buddhas. And anyway the word isn't offensive to me. While the civilized Chinese rushed to carry out massacres and start conflagrations, and drove out their rightful emperor, I feel honored and flattered to be counted among the barbarians who wanted to protect the fugitive princess."

Truly the man could play the part of a noble soul with rare perfection.

The emperor was taken in. He apologized, "You're right. In these upside-down times I myself would wish to take my place among the barbarians." His tone changed as he returned to the point of the interview. "On a vessel of the United States Navy, my sweet Liao has nothing to fear."

"She *had* nothing to fear..."

"Why do you say she *had*? Did that change?"

Bowing his head hypocritically, Slane quickly wiped away a nonexistent tear. "She left the submarine to make her way across Chinese territory to reach the lamasery of Ayen-Talé."

"She was trying to join me."

"And to share your destiny—yes, Lord Whose Brow is Crowned by the Dawn's Rays."

For a moment they considered each other in silence. Finally ex-emperor Lia-Sou went on haltingly, "Where is she?"

The question seemed to make Slane start sadly. Like a great actor, the villain simulated the embarrassment, the hesitation, the horror provoked by his coming words. He seemed to have to make a terrible effort to murmur, "Fallen into the hands of the rebels, along with the servants who accompanied her."

"Into the hands of the rebels!" cried the exiled ruler, his voice breaking. "But that means death!"

"A junk is sailing up the Yangtze, bringing Princess Liao to Hankou, where she will be bound to the pillory and tortured."

As if crushed by the news, the emperor stood frozen, his face distraught, his hands hanging helplessly by his sides. The shock was tremendous. In the gilded isolation of the Forbidden City, Lia-Sou had never known the kind of affection he could count on for support—nothing but flatterers, profiteers, lackeys, and courtiers whose fawning was just another form of falsehood. Only Liao had shown him filial love. Why had that child not adopted the worshipful artifice Chinese etiquette demanded in the presence of the Son of Heaven? Why had the emperor, unused to that kind of lapse in behavior, found pleasing in her what in anyone else he would have considered disrespectful enough to deserve the torture of gold leaf, yellow silk laces, or poison? A mystery of the imperial heart! What might have doomed the little girl had instead made her the sovereign's favorite.

And the shocking result was that in the Forbidden City, with its walls roofed in yellow tile, a tender relationship had grown up between father and daughter that was as bourgeois, as sincere, as open, as any that could be found in a typical European family. An evangelical missionary, Reverend Tosler, passed on his observation of that fact, but his report was so surprising that his words were given no credit. And yet the events to come would prove he'd been absolutely right.

So you can imagine how the exiled emperor's heart broke when he heard Slane's deceitful account, made up in equal parts of truth and lies. He was crushed, destroyed. His eyes filled with tears, and unconsciously stooping to the other man's level in admitting his impotence, he murmured, "What can I do? What can I do?"

A fleeting smile passed like a flash across the villain's face. Obviously he'd been waiting for those words. He'd steered the conversation so as to extract them from the despairing father. And while the question still rang in the room he answered unhesitatingly, "Save her!"

Those two syllables electrified Lia-Sou. He raised his hands toward his wicked visitor in supplication. "Is that possible?"

Slane pursed his lips doubtfully, then muttered bluntly, "We can always try."

Forgetting all etiquette, the emperor clasped his visitor's hands in his own as he stammered, "Speak! Speak! I'll do whatever you say. I'll stop at nothing to save my dear beloved Liao!"

So Slane revealed to him the existence of the *Vulture*, and his hope that it would enable them to rescue the captive princess from her jailers. He was careful not to point out that the new Chinese government was perfectly familiar with the airship, and that he'd negotiated a vile bargain with the nation's rulers: he would hand over Liao and Lia-sou to the Republic, in exchange for priceless commercial concessions. The contracts had been drawn up, and would be given to Slane upon delivery of the emperor in person. Those contracts were being held at the government offices in Hankou, awaiting the outcome of Slane's expedition to the lamasery of Ayen-Talé.

The emperor was already won over. An hour later, as the exile and the villain parted, the overthrown emperor said, "Tonight I'll slip into the south courtyard and get aboard your vessel. I'm entrusting my life, and my beloved daughter's life, to you."

"I'm prepared to sacrifice my own life in your service," replied Slane with perfectly feigned emotion.

"May the Ten Thousand Benevolent Buddhas braid your life with gold thread," sighed the unhappy father, pressing one last time the hands of the traitor who was leading him to his doom.

CHAPTER VI
The Pillory in Red Square

That was how it came to be that Princess Liao and her friends, bound tight to the posts of the pillory, saw the *Vulture* hovering over Red Square in Hankou.

Looking out from a porthole inside the airship, Liao-Sou in turn could make out the prisoners. He hadn't recognized them right away, but Slane stood by him, since William was at the controls. Keeping up his sinister act, the villain murmured, "They've made haste—we've come too late."

"Too late? What do you mean?" cried the emperor with sudden fierce anxiety.

Slane pretended to hesitate and collect his thoughts before he replied, "No use prevaricating. I can only tell you what you can see for yourself, and what you'll understand all too soon—alas!"

"All too soon? Is Liao?... Is my daughter?..."

The deceiver pointed through the lower porthole, through which they could see what was happening on the ground. "There she is!"

"At the pillory?"

"At the pillory," the villain echoed, hiding his face in his hands as if to catch his tears—which of course were nonexistent. In fact, behind his fingers he was laughing cruelly with delight at having reached the hour when his hellish schemes were finally triumphing.

For a while nothing could be heard but the dethroned emperor's sobs. And then he rallied and said to himself, "The death of one girl can matter little to the Revolution. Could she rally the partisans of the throne? Could she threaten the institutions of the new Republic? No, no, of course not!"

He was talking to himself, oblivious to the listener who was eagerly taking in his words. Yet Slane now answered, "Ah, that poor child couldn't possibly harm them!"

"So you agree with me. How much greater a victory it would be for the rebels if they held me in their power, if they could announce to the crowd, 'Behold your ex-ruler bound to the pillory and know that from now on the monarchy is defeated forever!'"

Slane nodded slowly in tacit agreement. Unwittingly led along by him, the emperor had arrived at a state of mind the American had intended, and to some degree created by his patient skill. Slane's approving nod, which seemed to submit to the logic of the emperor's thoughts, brought Lia-Sou's ideas into focus. "Well then," he cried exultingly, "why not give my rebellious subjects that satisfaction? Why not offer them an exchange?"

"An exchange?" stammered Slane, pretending not to understand. "What are you saying, Your Majesty?"

"Yes, an exchange! Freedom for that innocent child, who's incapable of harming the accursed Republic. And exposure on the pillory and torture for the sovereign hurled by the winds of fate to the foot of the throne his ancestors conquered!" And, at once pleading and commanding, without letting Slane get a word in, the emperor concluded, "Take us down to the ground. Open the doors of this place of refuge!"

Just then the doleful ringing of a gong reached their ears. Lia-sou shivered all over. "The gong of the Musicians of Death!" he stammered.

The traditional etiquette of executions was one of the few things the Revolution hadn't changed in China. The new government had kept the customary imperial protocol: just as in the past, special orchestras, whose members belonged to the department of executions, added musical accompaniment to the cries of agony of the victims dying under torture.

As a result, that advance toward the fatal conclusion in turn accelerated the emperor's gestures and words. Almost stammering, speaking in fragmentary, disconnected commands and prayers, he cried out, "You have control of the situation!... Hovering so high over the crowd, you can make them obey you!... There, look, just below us—the officials have cleared a large opening in the square... They're looking up at your marvelous vessel in fear and admiration. Take me down to them. Let them tear apart the father—but save the child!"

The poor man was right: soldiers in formation had pushed back the crowd to clear a large circular space that stretched from the government yamen to the platform on which stood the pillory at the center of Red Square. These soldiers looked nothing like the colorful warriors of the old imperial Banners in their strange helmets and robes; their uniforms were more like those of European and Japanese armies.

And inside that vast empty circle stood the members of the government of the Chinese Republic, wearing—over frock coats as ridiculously official as those of any European statesman—the five-colored sash that had been adopted as the national flag. With their noses in the air and their eyes fixed on the *Vulture*, they waited expectantly. A runner had been dispatched in the direction of that gong, and the gong had been silenced.

Lia-Sou was still pleading, and Slane pretended to resist. But now the distraught emperor seized a revolver that lay on a table—perhaps left there deliberately by the American—and pressed the barrel to his own forehead. "You won't stop me from dying, and you'll condemn her to death—my Liao, who can still be saved!"

That gesture seemed to make up Slane's mind. "Let it be as you wish, O Favorite Son of the Buddhas." He allowed himself the pleasure of sounding pitiful and looking desolate. The dramatic scene he'd prepared was being played out, and he found it amusing to act defeated. That vile actor, that despicable faker of noble sentiments, turned a few dials. There followed the clicking of some clockwork mechanism.

Lia-Sou looked at him questioningly.

"I'm sending down a telephone handset. I have twelve hundred meters of steel cable. From this distance we can talk to them and tell them what we want, without being in any danger."

The emperor nodded in satisfaction. He clasped the villain's hands in his own. "Thank you. Why didn't I know you before, when I was in power? With your help I could've held off the whole world!"

A sarcastic look flashed across the face of the Director of the Institute of Inventors in San Francisco. But he said nothing, and seemed to be absorbed in monitoring the device that was unspooling the telephone line. The clicking stopped, and was followed by a chime. "They've picked up the handset," reported Slane.

The emperor looked out the porthole. It was true: the President of the Republic of China—he knew the man by sight—held the receiver in his right hand. They could begin the conversation that would end in Lia-Sou's own death. With the feverish haste of the martyrs saluting Caesar before dying in the Roman arena, he commanded, "Offer him the exchange I described to you."

As if helpless against the tragic circumstances, Slane bowed. He leaned close to a vibrating membrane and spoke. The emperor listened in on an extra earpiece attached to the telephone apparatus. Slane had begun to try to keep him from picking up the earpiece, but no doubt quick thought had led him to change his mind, because he just shrugged, and with a chuckle he announced, "I'm going to pose as a friend of the Revolution to make them trust me."

"Good idea," agreed the unsuspecting emperor. "Thank you for your devotion." Devotion! How that word can sometimes be applied so strangely!

But the villain had already begun the conversation that would determine the final minutes of a sovereign's life. "Hello? Can the President of the Republic hear his humble servant?"

"Indeed, I can hear you."

"Good. But I would like to see that you have a clerk beside you with the paperwork needed for drawing up a contract that I'm about to offer you."

Lia-Sou put down his earpiece for a moment; no doubt he felt Slane's tone was less than ideal for a favorable negotiation. He didn't know that both speakers had already reached an agreement and settled on a horrific transaction. The paperwork Slane was asking to see was in fact the contract for the commercial concessions he and his billionaire partners coveted. And the price to get it was the delivery of the imperial victim... Perhaps if he'd known, Lia-Sou—that true Manchu—would even have been proud!

But he had no time to make a comment. To his great surprise, the answer to Slane's demand that came over the telephone line was, "No problem. The scribe Am-Hao will go get the papers."

Looking out the porthole again, the emperor could see a man hurry away across the cleared area maintained by the troops, inside which lay the government yamen.

"In exchange for those papers," went on Slane, slyly arranging his features in an inscrutable look of irony, "I can give you Lia-Sou, the last representative of the imperial dynasties."

Shaking with emotion, the voice at the other end of the line exclaimed, "Can you really?"

"Once I bring those contracts back aboard my airship, and once you promise to spare Princess Liao's life, I'll put the ex-emperor into your hands."

At any other time, the man whose fate was being discussed would have been surprised at the turn of the conversation. It seemed indeed as if the speakers were continuing a negotiation begun earlier, and not facing off for the first time. But the emperor, once all-powerful, now banished, was in no condition to sense that. And he was only partly paying attention to what he heard, since he also wanted to see: pressing himself against the porthole, he could make out Liao and her companions, and also the crowd, whose eyes were fixed on the airship in a kind of frenzy. Probably everyone standing in Red Square saw in the *Vulture* some sort of mythical beast, obedient not to scientific law but to the commands of a magician.

Similar ideas filled the emperor's head and made his mind spin. His vision and his hearing were troubled. Though his eyes and ears exercised their functions to the utmost, they contradicted each other, so that each sense performed no more than half of its duty.

Meanwhile the negotiation continued. The President of the Republic said banteringly, "Spare the life of former Princess Liao! Are you joking?"

"Not at all. You must promise that right now. Once I have those papers and your promise, I'll land the airship in the square. I'll hand over Lia-Sou, and you'll give me Princess Liao. An even trade. I'm aware I have to trust your word. Of course, once I've landed, you could keep both the emperor and his daughter. Still, my trust in you leads me to give you the opportunity to cheat me if you wish."

With hidden motives the emperor couldn't have suspected, the villain's words held a double meaning. Lia-Sou didn't pick up the almost imperceptible tone of irony in which Slane presented that idea. But the man at the other end of the telephone line must have understood the suggestion that he play false. With the cunning of any Chinaman, he deduced that circumstances must have forced Slane to put on an act. His reply showed he understood. "And you're right to put your trust in me. Everything will be done just as you request." He broke off. "The papers are here."

Indeed the scribe had returned, carrying a bundle of rolled-up scrolls, on which appeared columns of Chinese brushwork characters.

"Tie them to the handset, so I can pull them up to me!"

As the President did so, his last words transmitted in a murmur across the telephone line were, "Notice that I too am trusting you!"

The clicking of the machinery began again. The steel cable unwound earlier now wound back up around the spool controlled by the gears. Stop! The telephone handset that appeared in the niche designed to hold it was now accompanied by lots of documents covered in Chinese characters. In one quick, stealthy move—the leap of a predator falling onto his prey—Slane detached the papers, seized them, and carried them away.

But then he reconsidered: the emperor must still not be given any reason to guess at his double dealing. He went to a porthole and pretended to look over the papers with great care. Then he abruptly tossed into a nearby desk drawer the contracts that granted him all the riches of Asia. When he turned around, delight in his triumph made his voice shake uncharacteristically. "We can land now, if Your Greatness wishes!"

The emperor started. He'd noticed nothing wrong in the strange behavior of the villain who'd just negotiated his execution. Instead he was looking out the porthole at Liao. And since Liao herself was staring frantically up at the airship, the father felt as if she could see him in person, and he in turn could look straight into his daughter's black pupils, and their eyes had locked in a beam of affection like a caress that spanned the distance between them.

So he answered Slane's words with a mere nod. Soon the hum of the turbines filled the air, and the hull of the airship vibrated and creaked as it began to descend. Lia-Sou stood unmoving. Every spin of the turbines brought him closer to death. Was he thinking about that? No. He rejoiced in the descent, because in his eyes it brought closer the moment when Liao would be free. In his irrational fatherly egotism, he had no thought for his daughter's companions in torture. Perhaps he hadn't even noticed Miss May, and James Lipson, and Captain Andrews, all bound to posts and exposed on the pillory! He hadn't been moved by the look in their eyes—he wasn't even aware of it.

As the airship drew closer, everything in Red Square grew and became clearer: the soldiers, the crowd pressing behind them and even perched on the up-curving roofs and the balconies and filling the windows of the yamen... Now the noise of the crowd could be heard... Now they could make out the President and the members of the government giving orders. The soldiers pushed back the gawkers, forcing them to retreat into the narrow dirty alleyways that led away from the square, so as to give the *Vulture* more room to land.

There were a few more clicks of levers and buttons and dials adjusted by hand. William emerged from behind the screen that concealed the instrument panel and announced, "I've made contact. We've landed."

"Well done, my boy!" exclaimed Slane. "Stay at the controls. You never know, we may need to make a quick getaway. I'll disembark with His Imperial Majesty."

The words themselves were respectful. But Slane's tone was one of terrible sarcastic mockery of the man he referred to. And yet Lia-Sou still noticed nothing. Was this the time to quibble over someone's tone of voice? Was he even his own man anymore? Were his mind, his heart, his very soul not already up on the scaffold with his beloved Liao? With feverish haste he obeyed Slane's invitation to follow him. Together they stepped out onto the roof deck to show themselves to the mob greedy for bloodstained spectacle.

At their appearance a vast shout rose to the heavens, but it soon subsided. The President—who, with the sweet obliviousness of new-made Europeans, puffed himself up in a frock coat but still carried a brightly colored silk fan—raised that fan over his head. The crowd smothered its cries, fell silent, and waited.

The *Vulture*'s retractable ladder was extended till it reached from the roof deck to the ground. Slane pointed to it, and began to climb down. Without hesitating, Lia-Sou followed him down the slender, shaking gangway.

The square was now as silent as death. The government, the soldiers, the mandarins, the common people, all felt somehow that the critical scene of the Chinese Revolution was being played out at this moment. The emperor was putting himself into the hands of his subjects, he was accepting their judgment, whatever that might be. Autocracy was, once and for all, surrendering to democracy. Before, the throne had only been overturned; now the emperor's actions would reduce it to dust.

A minute later, the two men stood on the flagstone ground of Red Square. They walked toward the President, who awaited them—stunned by this easy victory, one so complete that even in his dreams of ambition and overthrow he'd never dared imagine it.

Stopping six feet from the man whom the acclaim of the people had raised to be foremost among the emancipated Chinese, Slane greeted him in the Manchu style, with his elbows at shoulder height and his hands open, palms out. "Great leader of the Republic," he announced, "here is the emperor I promised you."

The President said lightly, "We were both right to trust in our mutual agreements."

"Yes, we were both right."

They exchanged a look so cunning, with so suspicious a wink, that this time even Lia-Sou couldn't help noticing it. Suddenly he felt concern, and to drive it away he called for the carrying out of the agreement he'd offered. "Here I am, at the mercy of the people. Have Liao released!"

But before he'd finished speaking, brutal hands had seized his shoulders and his wrists. At an arranged signal, soldiers had rushed at him, surrounded him, immobilized him. He was about to protest, but the President spoke these sinister words: "When you kill the tiger, it's a good idea to kill its cubs too."

And Slane—now giving way to his natural barbarity—added, "Only an emperor could be dumb enough to believe a pardon was possible."

The words rang in the poor emperor's head. His eyes clouded over, and the beating of a gong seemed to fill his skull. He'd surrendered, and yet his beloved daughter was still going to die under torture by vile executioners. That sweet, innocent creature would suffer the fate of the most despicable convict. There was nothing he could do—nothing. Thousands of enemies surrounded him. In the numberless black eyes fastened on him he could see only hatred. The soldiers holding him kept him from moving at all. Tears now escaped from under his eyelids and rolled burning down his cheeks till they were lost in his thin, drooping mustache.

He could only just hear the words Slane and the President exchanged in a murmur. "Come with me to the Great Hall of Government," said the latter. "We'll exchange the signatures to ratify the concessions granted to you and your eventual successors in business."

"With pleasure," replied the villain cynically. "And allow me to express my gratitude for your lavish generosity."

"What is it compared to the service you've rendered to cause of the Republic today?" After a short pause the President went on, "Besides, you're a great American scientist. Your metal bird is proof of that. Who could be better than you at organizing our transportation, our mines, in short everything? I think putting you in charge of those matters will produce a fortune for the country."

They bowed to each other in the Chinese style, and shook hands like Europeans. Then side by side they processed toward the government yamen and disappeared inside it.

That seemed to be a signal: the shouts suppressed till now erupted again, and the common people gave way to their instincts, insulting the fallen emperor, and in their bestial cruelty they described in detail the tortures he would endure. They grew more excited, getting drunk on their own words.

But their captive's indifference irritated them—for Lia-Sou didn't seem to be listening… and in fact he couldn't hear them. All his attention, all his powers for thinking and suffering, were focused on Liao. Between the raised scaffold and the tiled ground of the square, the two victims exchanged a look of farewell: by the will of a delirious mob, they would be reunited in death.

As the emperor admired the princess's delicate features, he noticed that she occasionally turned her head toward her companions on the pillory. And now for the first time Lia-Sou observed them. Yes, yes, they were speaking to his daughter. They were probably comforting her, but he was too far away to make out their words. He noticed they were Occidentals; May's blonde hair and fine complexion showed she was English. The emperor was familiar with the English, with whom his ministry of foreign affairs, the Tsungli Yamen, had forever been in negotiation over trade duties and open cities and roads and diplomatic residences—in short over every little thing. He had despised the English, but now he felt affection for the pretty Englishwoman who was murmuring words of comfort to his daughter Liao.

He wept for them all now, joining them together in his affections. If only he could have heard their murmured farewells, to life, to love, to hope! On the execution scaffold, imminent death makes pointless the reserve that normally guards the secrets of the heart: Andrews told Liao of the vast love he felt for her. Lipson sighed as he revealed that he'd lost his heart to May. And the two girls received their homages with the boundless gratitude of those who, being condemned to die, linger over one last brief bliss.

The emperor watched. The crowd roared. And then suddenly their cries were extinguished. A terrified silence filled the square and spread out into the surrounding alleyways. You could have heard a fly buzz. What? What had happened? What had caused that terrified amazement in the mob?

Lia-Sou looked up, to his right, to his left, behind him. He wasn't mistaken: everyone was leaning forward, all eyes were locked on the scaffold. He looked in the same direction, and then he too was struck dumb.

The prisoners had vanished. Up on the pillory the torturers' assistants stood in ridiculous poses, holding the ropes that had bound their victims. They cried out, "The prisoners cut their bonds! They sawed through their ropes!"

What?! What could that mean? How could Princess Liao and her three companions vanish from right under the noses of that crowd, those guards, those soldiers? They couldn't have evaporated—human beings don't have that power.

So then what happened? How could their inexplicable disappearance be explained? Those questions prompted no plausible answers. As the emperor racked his brains to solve the inconceivable mystery, something new and just as surprising was happening. He'd been standing at the center of an open area, flanked by four Chinese soldiers with bayonets fixed to their rifles. Suddenly the men were mowed down—that was exactly the word: their legs gave way under them and they fell to the ground, with their rifles clattering on the flagstones.

Before Lia-Sou could recover from the shock, he had the terrifying feeling that an invisible hand had seized him by the wrist. A voice whispered in his ear, "Silence, father, and follow me. Devoted friends are rescuing us!"

He could have sworn he recognized his daughter's voice! But—by the Dragon and the Tiger—his Liao had never been invisible! But the series of recent shocks had broken down his resistance, and he let himself be led away. He was being taken toward the *Vulture*'s ladder.

"Climb, father!"

Again he heard Liao's beloved voice. It was beginning to resemble a magic show! Still he obeyed, though he said to himself, "Alas, the soldiers will easily catch up to us!"

While he climbed the rungs of the ladder, he turned to look at the soldiers who'd been guarding him earlier. Now that was strange! They weren't looking his way at all. It was as if no one in Red Square could see him—though he was perfectly visible as he rose up the side of the *Vulture*. He was so amazed that he stopped there, breaking off his ascent. Right away he heard Liao's voice below him, saying, "Go on! Once we're inside the airship, all will be explained."

Under the influence of his daughter's calm voice, he resumed climbing. When he reached the roof deck, the same invisible hand took him by the wrist again and drew him to the top of the spiral stairs that led down into the interior. The voice said, "Climb down!"

Two minutes later, guided steadily in the same way, he entered a cabin at the rear of the airship. He went to the porthole and looked out—and was disconcerted to see that no one seemed to be paying any attention to the *Vulture*. The crowd was raising a deafening cry, and even using blows from their rifle butts the soldiers could barely contain it.

At that very moment Slane and the President of the Republic emerged onto the front steps of the government yamen. They seemed surprised at the furious cries that greeted them. And then they understood. They turned toward the scaffold, now devoid of prisoners, on top of which the torturers' assistants flailed around desperately.

And now the general panic overcame them too. They ran to the emperor's guards and questioned them. It was easy to guess those unfortunate soldiers' explanations: they'd been tripped up and knocked down, and the prisoner had vanished, they had no idea how.

"Ha ha ha! Cheer up! This is all humbug! They've gone mad!"

Those words rang out in the cabin, right behind Lia-Sou. He turned, and gave a cry that was partly one of terror. Liao stood there, next to Miss May and James Lipson and Captain Andrews, along with newcomers the emperor didn't know: Derrick and Freda, little Jane, and Stepan and Sefra.

Liao flung her arms around him. Through her kisses and tears he heard the strange, incredible tale of Miss May's invention—the electromagnetic tunic—and its effects. A single person, wearing that newfangled armor, could impose on everyone nearby whatever hallucination he wanted, including that of making the wearer himself invisible, or of making the subject see some particular thing or person.

The prisoners' escape had been a simple application of that power, an application carried out by Jane and her friends Derrick and Freda and Stepan and Sefra—who, after their adventures in Si-Fou, furnished with the mandarin Governor Kuang's safe-conduct, had had no trouble reaching Hankou. From a house overlooking Red Square they'd watched as their companions had been exposed on the pillory. What anxiety they'd suffered before they figured out how to save them! And even if they could keep the crowd from seeing them, to rescue the captives they'd also have to free them from their ropes, and therefore they had to find a way to reach them on the scaffold. But how could they squeeze their way through the crowd? For though the tunic could render them invisible it couldn't make them intangible. Their progress would be noticed. Perhaps someone braver than the rest would seize hold of whoever was invisibly elbowing them aside. Hadn't May herself almost been caught that way aboard the *Vulture*?

But the appearance of the airship had given the engineer and her devoted companions a way to avoid that danger. When the troops pushed back the crowd to make a landing site, they'd slipped between the soldiers and reached the scaffold and freed their friends. And once the emperor himself was free, they'd all taken refuge aboard the *Vulture*, on May's orders.

"They'll look for us everywhere—except in our enemies' quarters," she said. "Besides, it'll be useful to have command of the *Vulture*, so we can return to America and make the two Slanes pay for their crimes."

"So you have a plan?" suggested Lipson.

"Yes. I'll tell you about it later. Derrick should stay on guard at the cabin door, so we can make sure to remain invisible when our enemies decide to come back on board."

With those words the emperor was led back to a porthole, as if by some power greater than his own will. His mind spinning, as though he were in a dream, not daring to credit the extraordinary adventure in which he was being tossed about, he stood there, with his forehead pressed to the glass, watching the chaotic panic of the Slanes, the leaders of the government, the army, and the crowd.

PART SIX: THE UNAVOIDABLE EAST

CHAPTER I
The Hunt for the Fugitives

"We've been combing the countryside for a week…"

"And nothing—always nothing! And yet they must be somewhere. Five people don't just disappear like the seed in a shell game!"

Their clenched fists brandished, Slane and William were arguing angrily. At first the unexpected escape of their victims at Hankou had stunned them. Then, constrained by circumstances to promise the prisoners would be recaptured, they'd suggested to the authorities that they make use of their flying machine to hunt for them.

No doubt that offer was welcomed. However—no trick being unknown in China—the Chinese had pointed out that since there were five fugitives (being of course unaware of the little group led by Jane), two men wouldn't be enough to catch them. As a result, twenty fanatics, members of two savage secret societies, the Green Fan and the Clenched Fist, were hauled aboard the *Vulture*. That ad hoc crew was officially there to guarantee the recapture of the escapees, and unofficially there to make it impossible for the Slanes to flee in their airship in case they failed. Slane understood completely, but, like a good sport, with a smile on his lips he accepted what he couldn't prevent.

So for the past week, flying thirty meters off the ground, the *Vulture* had been cruising over Hankou in ever-widening circles. They landed in villages and small towns, where they questioned mandarins and shopkeepers and farmers. Everywhere they got the same discouraging response: no one had seen anyone matching the description of the fugitives.

Discipline on board was satisfactory, though frequent quarrels broke out among the Chinese. No doubt those men—accustomed to making their living off riot and disorder—couldn't keep from stealing, because they were constantly accusing each other of petty theft. Oddly, it was mostly over food. The rations aboard the *Vulture* disappeared; pitchers of water and bottles of rice wine vanished. Even the serving platters on the table wandered away, and were found later in the control room or the engine room—of course minus any trace of their contents.

These strange ongoing incidents finally began to worry the members of the secret societies. As for Slane and his son, they grew more and more afraid. They remembered what had happened near Honolulu, events they'd never managed to explain, and they wondered whether the present phenomena were connected to the same unknown causes. Still, as long as the mystery remained limited to the theft of food, they gradually relaxed. After all, the members of the Green Fan and the Clenched Fist were known to be thieves. Perhaps their well-deserved reputation was enough to account for everything: since at the moment they couldn't rob either common people or shopkeepers, those rascals were staying in practice by robbing each other.

But one morning, a little less than a week since they'd begun their flights over Hankou, something more serious happened. The President himself wanted to watch the *Vulture* take off. Before the Slanes got on board he'd said solemnly to the older man, "Today may the Buddhas put those you seek in your path."

"Why particularly today?" replied the American, sensing a worrisome reticence in the man's voice.

The Chinaman made a sly expression, then went on with deliberate hesitation, "A decision by the Grand Council. I did my best to oppose it. Alas, I couldn't secure a majority."

"What decision?" asked Slane, annoyed by the man's circumlocutions.

"Here it is. Your image is locked in my heart,[43] and I'll prove it by applying the wise precept of our great Confucius: 'Friends have nothing to hide from each other. They share the good and the bad, and that alone is the friendship on which the Buddhas smile.'"

"Well, then, make the Buddhas smile," growled Slane in exasperation.

---

[43] "I'm your friend" [*Note from the Author*].

"I'll do it to please them and to obey you," went on the President, still keeping up the elaborate politeness of the Chinese. "So, the Grand Council met and decided that a powerful magician like you, who knows how to fly through the air in a metal machine, should've had no trouble finding the miserable fugitives, among whom there are delicate women unable to endure the rigors of a forced march."

"And damn it, I will find them! They've gone to ground in some hideaway, since no one's spotted them anywhere. They'll come back out, and then…"

"And then it'll be too late…" The President's answer cut him off abruptly.

Slane considered him, shocked by that straightforward statement, so little in keeping with the diplomatic customs of China. "How am I to interpret my friend's words?"

"That the warriors on board your vessel have been ordered to bring you back to Hankou tonight."

"I'd come back even without orders."

"No. If you had a choice, you wouldn't come back—not after I tell you what the Grand Council has decided." Raising his index finger—whose nail was extraordinarily long, in the supremely fashionable style of the Middle Kingdom—and waving it in rhythm to emphasize his singsong words, the President announced, "The great magician is certainly sparing the fugitives. Therefore he is betraying the cause of the People that rose up against its oppressors. If, this evening, he does not bring back the emperor and his daughter and their servants, he shall be condemned to take their place on the pillory and face torture. Thus will the nation know that its elected leaders strike without pity, and with equal justice, not only the recognized enemies of the regime but also their accomplices by commission or omission."

Slane and William, stunned by that sudden development—which made them prisoners aboard the *Vulture*, with twenty incorruptible jailors whose fanaticism placed them beyond any temptation—tried to plead extenuating circumstances.

But the President cut them off. "It's useless. I myself trust you. But as for the Grand Council, nothing can change their minds." He lowered his voice to add, in a whisper so quiet they could barely hear him, "That incomprehensible escape has frightened the people. They must be given victims to calm them down."

The airship had now landed outside a village named Kai Ping Yen, about a hundred kilometers from Hankou. William had gone into the village to pursue the methodical search they'd begun a week earlier. But the Chinese warriors had made clear their role as jailors by insisting that Slane stay on board. In their narrow-minded way, they assumed that one of a pair of people wouldn't escape if the other remained a captive.

William returned and reported that the fugitives hadn't been spotted in Kai Ping Yen. The Chinese warriors, who were stretched out on the sparse grass, didn't seem to be paying any attention to the Americans. But a closer look would have shown that they'd chosen their napping spots so as to surround the two persons whom the officials in Hankou had assigned them to guard. They were obviously prisoners.

Slane drew his son's attention to that with a glance.

"If they take us back to Hankou, we're doomed," murmured William.

"There's not the slightest doubt about that."

"So what then?"

"They can't take us back, that's all there is to it."

They fell silent as one of the warriors passed nearby. When he was far enough away, Slane went on cautiously, "Did you get the opium?"

"No. The pharmacist didn't have any, since the Republic has banned all forms of it. Or if he had any, he didn't feel like confiding in a stranger that he was breaking the law."

Slane gestured vehemently. "You say that so calmly..."

"Rightly so, my too easily angered father, believe me... True, I don't have opium—but I have crystalized chloroform, which is used in large quantities in Chinese medicine."

"Bravo, my boy!"

"We'll announce dinner. We'll put our friends in the crew's mess, after sprinkling a few grams of the crystals on the floor. We'll come back in an hour, when they'll be fast asleep..."

"An hour! What if some of them are dead by then?"

"Better yet," said William cynically. "Dead men are certainly less talkative than sleepers, with whom you can never be sure what they might report about their nightmares."

The father and son were a good match: the same moral makeup, the same indifference for the lives of others. Slane nodded his approval. "Let's get on with it, my boy. I don't know what's wrong with me today, but I'm worried. I feel like some catastrophe is getting ready to fall on my head."

"Nerves?" mocked William. "Could a Slane be getting cold feet?"

His father interrupted him brusquely. "Don't make fun of things you don't understand. What the ignorant call premonition, second sight, is simply an individual's electro-telluric connection with his surroundings. Science has proved it over and over. To joke about it merely shows your ignorance." Then in a more normal tone he went on, "Let's not lose precious minutes arguing—instead let's make haste to gain our freedom."

They slowly climbed the ladder leading to the roof deck of the *Vulture*, and entered the vessel by way of the hatch. Not one of the members of the secret societies stirred. Five of them, who were among the toughest, and were well armed, had remained on board. There was no chance these sentries were going to let the Americans fly away in their machine.

In any case, the Slanes didn't appear to consider doing so. They came back out on the roof deck to announce it was time for lunch. Now all the Chinese reacted. In obvious haste they climbed the ladder to the top of the vessel. With elaborate gestures of politeness they insisted that the Slanes go inside the vessel ahead of them. When they followed, the last man closed the hatch, made sure it was locked, and pocketed the key. None of them noticed the mocking smiles with which the Slanes observed that precaution.

The Chinese warriors went to the crew's mess. The Slanes locked themselves into the control room, where they usually took their meals. Just an hour of exposure to the vapor of chloroform could cause the death of some of the members of the Green Fan and the Clenched Fist. To make sure they all shared the same fate—equality being the guiding principle of the Republic, as William observed jokingly—the Slanes waited an hour and a half without returning to the mess.

When that time had elapsed, they looked at each other happily: any prisoner who gets rid of his jailors feels that unalloyed satisfaction. Their faces brightened with barely contained mirth as Slane, rising finally, joked, "Let's go see if those worthy Chinamen have dined well."

"I just hope they didn't overeat," responded William in the same vein. "There's nothing worse for your health!"

With that, they went along the corridor and down the narrow spiral staircase to the lower deck. They listened carefully, holding their breath. Not a sound. Nothing to suggest that twenty loud, hot-tempered fanatics were sharing a bountiful meal.

The Slanes' silent laughter grew, expanding into something monstrous and tragic. The "operation"—Slane used that euphemism to refer to the murder of twenty persons—seemed to have succeeded perfectly. Further precautions were therefore unnecessary. They both gave up walking on tiptoe; why bother, since footsteps wouldn't disturb the deceased in their eternal slumber?

They reached the door to the mess and pressed their ears against it. They heard nothing but total, utter, fatal silence. There could be no further doubt: they were free, and their jailors, now annihilated, would trouble them no more. With one triumphant shove they flung open the door, pressing forward in their hurry to witness their defeated adversaries—for they shared the opinion of the cruel Roman emperor who observed that an enemy's corpse is a pleasant sight, and a dead enemy *smells good*!

But the pleasure they'd promised themselves was suddenly denied them. And that unexpected rebuff left them frozen, their feet nailed to the floor, their mouths hanging open, their eyes starting.

The twenty members of the Chinese secret societies they'd left in the crew's mess had vanished without a trace. The Slanes said not a word. They both seemed to have been robbed of their voices by this strange incident, the latest in the series of which they'd been the victims. Indeed for a while now everyone they meant to make use of or get revenge on had disappeared. They'd put out chloroform, which produces unconsciousness and death; and chloroform, that joker, had produced a vanishing act.

"It's not possible! They're outside, on the roof deck!" William finally managed to theorize in the heavy silence.

His father, lost in thought, didn't answer, so William rushed out and climbed the spiral staircase at insane speed. He banged his head against the hatch, which was still locked. So he came back down, terrified, suddenly filled with a panic whose cause he didn't understand.

In the crew's mess he found his father sitting with his elbows on the table, which was still spread with the remains of the Chinese warriors' meal. "You could've spared yourself the trouble," murmured Slane in a blank voice. "Here's the key to the hatch. I found it over there, probably at the place where the one who had it was sitting."

"Well then, at least the key hasn't disappeared!"

"But that's not all."

"Now what?" stammered the young man, who found his terror magnified by his father's tragic tone.

Slane passed him a copy of the *Shanghai Daily*.

"What am I supposed to do with this newspaper?"

Through clenched teeth Slane said, "Read those excerpts from the American press—excerpts which must already have appeared in Europe and are now circling the globe."

"But how did this newspaper get here?"

Slane gave a furious shrug to say he didn't know. He set his hand on the table. "It was left here. No doubt one of those men had it in his pocket. And possibly the decision by the Grand Council in Hankou was prompted by that article."

"What article?"

"Read that! It's a terrible blow, and I'm at a loss. I can't see what hand is wielding the weapon that has struck us."

His son was no longer listening. His eyes had dropped to the printed page, and, shuddering from head to toe, he'd just read the sensational headline:

SHOCKING ACCUSATION—Research Institute and Billionaires' Syndicate Led by Murderers—Science and Wealth Suborned—Astonishing Crimes—Criminals of Former Times Like Children by Comparison.

Under that banner headline—which must have thrilled the paper's readers and guaranteed a vast circulation—William had trouble reading the body of the story. His temples were pounding and red circles floated before his eyes. What he finally managed to make out was the brief notice—menacing in its very brevity—Miss May had dispatched to the San Francisco dailies when Princess Liao was abducted at Buena Vista Park.

301

"What should we do?" The question betrayed William's dread, but it had burst from his lips without his even intending to express his dismay.

But Slane, on the other hand, was a bandit who never admitted he was beaten, and who seemed to grow stronger under the blows of adversity. As if his son's voice had given him back his usual composure, he lifted his head and looked the young man in the eye.

"People don't just evaporate like that," he began, recovering for a moment the tone of authority of the Director of the Institute of Inventors. "When they can't be found where they were, it must be inferred that they've left—or that accomplices have removed them."

William nodded in agreement; what his father said was obvious. Oh, it didn't solve anything—but the confidence with which Slane said it reassured his son.

"How did those accomplices manage it?" went on the general secretary of the syndicate of American billionaires. "How? I don't know. But the clear, undeniable fact is, they succeeded." He chuckled bitterly. "And in succeeding, they've given us a new opportunity, an excellent opportunity: they've left us alone on board."

William listened, but he certainly didn't understand what advantage he and his father could extract from their being alone on the *Vulture*. He spread his arms uncomprehendingly.

"To be alone is to be able to fly away in any direction we wish."

That helped the young man recover the power of speech. "So we can go to Frisco and tell off those stupid reporters..."

He broke off; his father was shaking his head.

"What! We won't dispute the story?"

"Not for the moment."

"Why the silence?"

"Because I believe we have an enemy more formidable than any malicious newspaperman. Formidable, because we've been the victims of his actions for a long time now, and not once, not for a moment, have we perceived the hand holding the weapon that strikes us." Slowing the speed of his delivery, as if to allow his son's limited intellect to absorb his words more easily, he went on, "We're free. Let's escape as fast as we can. Not toward San Francisco, but toward the Australian Outback! There, in the middle of the desert, we can remain hidden for a month, two months, longer if necessary."

"What do you hope to gain by that cowardly move?"

The insulting adjective made Slane laugh hysterically, and a minute passed before he could go on speaking. But then he rebuked his son in such a pitying tone, with such patronizing indulgence, that no nanny ever scolded a small child with comparable disdain. "Well, well, the world isn't about to run out of nitwits. It's painful for me to admit, but you try to raise a man and all you get is a pumpkin-head, and pumpkin isn't even much of a vegetable."

Under the lash of his father's sarcasm, William clenched his fists, and his lips grew white with fury.

But with a brusque gesture Slane kept him from speaking. "Calm down, son, calm down. Remember, one more stupid move won't wipe out all the rest!" Then in a different tone, resuming his quasi-professorial manner, he went on, "I'll explain what you don't get. To defeat an unknown enemy, the first step is to unmask him."

"Of course, but..."

"Shut up! Listen, that first step is all we need for now. Our enemy will only make himself known if we force him into it."

"Yes, absolutely."

"Now, the only way to force him to do that is to hide the target he's aiming at, which is to say you and me."

William's eyes widened. Like a man who still didn't get it, he stammered, "So, Australia?..."

"A hiding place, my boy. The target becomes invisible. The enemy hunts for it. He's forced to show himself,"—Slane exploded in laughter—"and that allows us to discover him, meaning that we reestablish parity in the struggle, which at the moment is tilted to our disadvantage."

He interrupted his son's exclamations of praise. "Enough chatter, my boy. Go to the controls. Take us up to three thousand meters, so our flight path can't be seen from the ground. Plus which, at first let's go east, as if we were headed for San Francisco. Then in an hour turn south, the real direction we want to go— to Australia."

By the time he'd finished speaking, William was at the instrument panel; from the pilot's seat, he operated the controls. The turbines began to spin, and their dizzying rotation made the whole vessel shake as the steel hull vibrated.

"We're off!"

Slane sighed with satisfaction.

Without taking his eyes off the instruments, William said, "At the risk of being called a pumpkin-head again... I have to say you seem almost excessively pleased."

His father came closer and lowered his voice. "You'll understand better once you hear what a part of me dreaded—what I hid from you so as not to frighten you."

"What the devil now?"

"My boy, I was afraid that whoever took away our Chinamen might at the same time have disabled the airship in some way, so as to keep us here."

William shuddered at the thought, and Slane went on, "Ah, that strikes home! You're thinking if we were in their place we wouldn't have neglected that wise move." He pursed his lips skeptically. "Who knows? They may've forgotten on purpose. They might've figured that, since we're on the outs with the Chinese authorities, we'd head back to California. Because it's possible our home town, Frisco, is the spot those people have chosen to carry on their battle against us." He laughed nervously. "And it's for that very reason we're headed elsewhere. Concealing our real intended route, by the trick I mentioned earlier, is a response to that possibility."

The *Vulture* was moving at twice the speed of an express train, and in a few hours they'd crossed the Chinese coast and were flying over the long gray swell of the Pacific. Slane waited another sixty minutes. He stood stiff and unmoving, with his face pressed to a porthole. A stranger seeing him then would have thought him devoid of any emotion.

But suddenly, presumably because he thought they were now far enough from the coast, he asked curtly, "Can you see land?"

"No, especially not in this fog," replied William. "Damn, we're speeding along!..."

Slane cut him off. "Are there any ships in sight? I can't see any from here, but the portholes around the instrument panel are better placed."

"None. The ocean is completely empty."

"So, no spies. In that case, my boy, set a course due south. They might be expecting us in Frisco, but we're going to vacation in Australia!"

Once it had made the turn, the *Vulture* raced on all day. But on his father's orders William had brought the airship down to a few hundred meters: why remain at such a high altitude now that they'd thrown off all pursuit? Still, when they'd dropped to an altitude typical for birds, Slane was surprised to see none of those great seabirds, the albatross and the gray gull. They've been known to venture two or even three thousand kilometers out over the ocean, and the *Vulture* was paralleling the Chinese coast much closer than that, so the absence of seabirds was puzzling. But it really didn't matter, and the two men on the airship considered the observation to be of merely zoological interest.

The sun set. The pearly blue gray of the midday sky darkened and was stained with indigo. A star came out, then a dozen, then a hundred, and finally the uncountable array of constellations, those eternal travelers through space.

"I'm hungry," said William.

Slane rose immediately and went to the pantry. Five minutes later he rejoined his son, who'd stayed at the controls. He brought a stoneware pitcher of foaming California rosé—limpid and certainly drinkable, but with their natural and incorrigible boastfulness Americans mistakenly claim it to be the equal of the finest European vintages. Even a superior plonk will never be a great wine.

The two men traded off at the controls. In turn, each one appeased his hunger and had a few glasses of rosé. Then Slane assumed the controls for good. William had piloted the airship all day, and his father would take over for the night. Feeling tired, William went back to his cabin, threw himself onto his cot without bothering to undress, and immediately fell into a deep sleep.

CHAPTER II
A Needle Gone Haywire,
Walking Dead, Absent Judges

Tom Slane remained alone at the controls. Through the portholes placed around the pilot's seat, above him he could see the celestial vault, and below him the surface of the sea, in which the stars that studded the infinite sky were reflected like golden sequins. "Clearly my *Vulture* is the dream of locomotion brought to life," he said to himself. "It can't run into anything—for now, anyway: eventually, when aviation has become normal, flight lanes will be as crowded as their terrestrial and maritime analogues!"

He broke off and raised a hand to his head with a terrible grimace. "I've got a headache," he muttered to himself. Then he shrugged with disdainful indifference at the fleeting images that were crossing his mind. "What can you expect after a day so full of unpleasant surprises? At least poor William can sleep! He knows nothing of the dangers I sense all around us. He's no genius, that boy. The eagle sired a goose." Again he pressed his fingers to his skull. "After all, it's just paternal self-esteem that makes me complain. A man always expects he's going to produce a masterpiece. Ridiculous! Pathetic! William is exactly what science would've predicted: my intelligence, hobbled by his mother's ineptitude!"

Those last words faded away in a blurry murmur. Slane's head tipped forward till his chin rested on his chest. His eyes closed slowly.

"That's it—he's asleep. Quick, James, take over the controls. Meanwhile I'll... enhance... the compass."

While those words were being spoken, May and Lipson had burst into the control room. Without being gentle, the young man grabbed hold of Slane and stretched him out on the floor, so he could take his place at the instrument panel.

"Oof!" he said. "It feels good to move around a little. What a long day! To have to stay hidden in the ballast compartments, forbidden to move—and then those twenty Chinese who don't smell very good!"

"They'll be useful to us," objected May. "They're one of the assets we'll need to break the Slanes down far enough to confess. Because, don't forget, Lloyd, we need their confession. They're still too powerful to defeat without it." But then May broke off, as if she regretted having spoken. "We'll worry about the Chinese later. It's the compass I have to take care of now."

She leaned over the instrument whose needle guides sailors lost on the empty surface of the sea. From a small bag she drew an assortment of tools. She removed a few screws, which allowed her, with a sharp pop, to break open the copper binnacle that enclosed the disc divided by lines to mark the cardinal directions. With a smile she examined the center of the disc, which was pierced by the point of the pivot that formed the axis on which the magnetized needle rotated to point north.

But what was she doing now? From her bag May drew a small half ring of iron alloy, and attached it beneath the dial of the compass. And then her intention became clear: the magnetized needle was attracted by that iron, and turned to follow it when May turned the half ring. Now the needle no longer pointed north, but west... and the *Vulture*'s course, when Lipson had slowly corrected it to match, no longer ran south to Australia but east to California.

All was now clear: May had driven the compass mad. From now on the Slanes would be flying toward the United States, though they thought they were headed for the island continent of Australia. The iron ring was firmly attached. The magnetized needle would forever point west instead of north. Once the copper binnacle was back in position and the screws had been replaced in their holes, no trace remained of the operation the scientist had carried out.

May went to the instrument panel. "James," she murmured, "we have to put the rascal back in his seat. Meanwhile I'll tickle the buttons!"

Without a word, Lipson picked up Slane, put him back in the pilot's seat, and made sure he was balanced. Then he drew a small flask from his pocket and passed it under the sleeper's nose. The effect was abrupt: though still asleep, Slane sneezed loudly. His eyelids trembled. His hands automatically reached out for the controls.

"Quick!" came a whispered hiss.

May and Lipson leapt to the door, which closed behind them just as Slane opened his eyes.

"Damn," he muttered to himself in a thick voice. "I think I was asleep. No time for that, old friend! Remember, losing concentration for even a minute could make us crash!" He gave a worried glance at the compass, but was instantly reassured. "No deviation from our bearing—I stayed on course. My word, I thought I'd been fast asleep. But this is a warning: it's a sign of physical fatigue." He pushed back the pilot's seat and stood up at the controls. "This way I'll be safe—even though some ignorant people claim you can sleep standing up."

That idea, or something like it, made him smile, and he went on to think about other things. The monotonous hours of the night flowed by to the cadence of the incessant hum of the turbines turning at high speed.

Through the portholes, dawn was approaching. The sky grew lighter, and shifted toward the golden colors of the sun. A single bright ray shone into the cabin and, through the beam of dancing dust motes, projected a blinding circle of light on the wall.

"My word," muttered Slane, "I hope William gets here soon to spell me. I won't be sorry to get some rest myself."

He adjusted a dial to correct their course, from which the airship seemed to have deviated slightly—but then he jumped: a muffled cry had echoed down the corridor onto which the door of the control room opened. What could that be? Slane was racked by the need to find out. And yet he couldn't leave the controls. To step away from the instrument panel for even a few seconds would trigger a catastrophe. Sweat beaded his forehead. Why? He couldn't have said. The truth was, the events of the past few days had shaken his nerves and robbed him of his usual composure. Fear had taken root in him, in a latent state, ready to manifest itself at the slightest provocation.

Now someone was running in the corridor. The footsteps stopped at his door. Then the door was thrown open so violently that it slammed back against the wall. William stood there, stunned, distraught.

"What's wrong?"

"It's... it's... it's the Devil again!"

Slane stamped his foot hard enough to shake the floor, and said harshly and scornfully, "Get out the habit of using idiotic expressions like that! You can explain what you mean without talking nonsense!"

His son didn't even take offense at his brutal welcome. "All right then," he went on, "we thought we were alone on board."

"Of course. Didn't we make a complete inspection to make sure?"

"I realize that, but our inspection must've been faulty..."

"Faulty!..."

"I mean, we didn't look carefully."

"Ah!" roared Slane, "this bumbling boy can't seem to say clearly what he means!"

"Yes I can. I said we didn't look carefully, and I can prove it. I just saw somebody at the intersection of corridors A and C."

"Somebody?" shouted Slane, whose teeth were clenched tight enough to crack.

"Maybe a corpse. I tripped over it."

"Take the controls!"

The order rang out so harshly that William hurried to obey. Now free to move, Slane ran to the still-open door and out into the corridor. He reached the intersection of corridors A and C. His son was right: a body blocked the way. Its immobility reassured him. He bent down to examine it. "Oh ho!" he murmured, "one of our warrior guards from Hankou!"

How had this body gotten here? For it was certainly a body—the chloroform had done its job. And how had neither William nor Slane himself noticed it here? His son was right: they must both have failed to search properly, to see properly. They'd followed corridor A on their inspection round. Later Slane had used it to get to the pantry, and William to get to his cabin. If they'd noticed nothing, it had to be either because they didn't pay enough attention to their surroundings or because the body of the Chinaman hadn't been here then.

The second option seemed absurd: if the dead Chinaman hadn't been here before, how could he have gotten here? In spite of all the old ghost stories, a dead man didn't wander, walking stick in hand, around a modern airship! And yet Slane shivered all over. One question sank into his brain like a steel fishhook: were inexplicable things going to start happening around him again? He was aware that his composure, which used to be imperturbable, had vanished, and that his reason was tottering. There was a crack in his courage, a hesitation in his boldness, an anxiety in his confidence.

But he had to act. He couldn't let his son guess at his distress. His son! That nincompoop would lose what little brains he possessed if he knew the thoughts now filling his father's mind. Slane therefore willed himself to be calm. He put on a carefree expression, and took his time as he returned to the control room.

"Well?" asked William immediately, without turning away from the instrument panel.

"Take us down. Land the *Vulture* on the ocean. It'll float like a boat. That way we can stop the engines and together we can haul good old Tai up to the roof deck so we can throw him overboard."

"Tai? So it was Tai! What was he doing there?"

"He was playing dead, silly boy—so I couldn't ask him." Slane did his best to joke, though he didn't at all feel like it.

His apparent high spirits reassured William; without pressing him further, the young man began to carry out the desired maneuver. Soon the airship—for now become a sea craft—was gently bobbing on the waves of the Pacific Ocean. The hum of the turbines had ceased. William had shut off the engines.

"Let's make it quick," said Slane. "No sense being spotted by some passing ship. So let's get on with it."

Together they returned to the intersection of corridors A and C. But there they stared at each other in astonishment: Tai's body had vanished. Unconsciously Slane pressed his hands against his head. Once again something mysterious, inexplicable, looking like magic... Magic! What could be more irritating to a scientist who knows perfectly well that the legends of the Middle Ages, driven by fairies and enchanters, are impossible? Yes, but what scientific explanation could there be for this nomadic corpse?

While Slane stood there thinking, bringing his wits to bear against the insoluble problem, William went off down the corridor to search. Suddenly he called out. His father's legs reacted like springs; forgetting his age and his weary joints, he ran toward his son's voice. When he reached William, he found him crouching by a body sprawled on the floor at the point where corridor B branched off from corridor A, a little beyond corridor C.

In a distant, almost absent-minded voice, William stammered, "It's Tai, sure enough... Before he was over there, now he's here. That's not possible, because he's dead, cold, stiff!... And yet it's true."

Slane certainly had no respect for his son's intelligence, but he couldn't have answered the questions implied in his words. Since there's nothing more humiliating than to remain silent when a lesser mind seeks guidance, the father reprimanded the son. "Everything has a straightforward explanation, my boy. You can't always find it right away, but you should never lose the conviction that it exists. We'll make a careful search later. For now let's toss Tai's corpse into the ocean—that's the urgent thing. We can hold forth on the question after that."

Once again, the habit of obedience settled William's distress. He willingly took hold of the Chinaman's shoulders, while his father grabbed the feet. Thus laden, they struggled up the spiral staircase leading to the hatchway. When they came out onto the roof deck they approached the steel railing, balanced their funereal burden on it for a moment, then heaved it overboard. An impact... A splash... The dead body sank slowly beneath the green water, its shape diminishing and growing indistinct, till it vanished.

"Let's go back inside," muttered Slane, "and get back up into the clouds. No sense hanging around here. Too many ships pass through these waters."

Dominated, taking refuge in submission as a shelter against his terror, William turned toward the hatchway leading to the stairs. But then he leapt back, his hair standing on end, and shouted wildly, "This time it's Miao! Miao's watching us!"

Shaken to his very depths, Slane turned to look at the hatchway. Miao, another of the fanatical guards they'd brought along from Hankou, seemed to be stretched out on his stomach on the stairs, with his head above the hatchway and his chin resting on the top step. His bleak unmoving eyes were fixed on the two stunned Americans.

Slane felt his own thoughts breaking down in confusion. This new corpse had to disappear. Hurriedly, with mechanical gestures, urging on his son—who was trembling so much he could barely help—he managed to hurl the Chinaman Miao into the depths that had already swallowed his compatriot.

But though the corpse was gone, the terrifying enigma of the ambulatory dead remained. How could those Chinese be reappearing? What macabre duel were they fighting—with dead men as the weapons—and against whom? Some power the Institute of Inventors in San Francisco hadn't harnessed, had never even suspected, was manifesting itself aboard the *Vulture*. What laws governed that power? Who was it who had uncovered those laws and turned them to his own use? And, above all, what were his intentions? Oh, his hostility was in no doubt: you don't play practical jokes as macabre as that on your friends! But his name, his hiding place, his means of action all remained unknown.

A kind of fog began to spread over the Slanes' minds. Their thoughts grew dim. An indescribable confusion prevailed in their intelligence, scrambled it, destroyed it. Fear came to dominate all other feelings, reducing them to the state of beaten soldiers at the dark moment when defeat turns into a rout. From now on the father and son no longer dared to be separated. Whenever it was meal time they brought the *Vulture* down to the ocean, so both men could go to the pantry together and then eat together in the control room.

Just as before, May and her friends were using the electromagnetic tunics. They'd decided at Hankou that neither the Slanes nor the Chinese guards should see them. To remain out of sight, they'd stayed in the ballast compartments, where no one ever went. When the Slanes—wanting to escape from the authorities in Hankou—had murdered the Chinese, the stowaways had carried the bodies down from the crew's mess to one of the ballast compartments they weren't using. And they were returning the bodies to their adversaries, one at a time.

"By the time we reach America," said May to her friends, "the Slanes have to be so broken down that they succumb to the first strong emotion they encounter. By succumb, I mean they won't be able to help confessing to their crimes. Because, as I've said a hundred times, men of their importance couldn't possibly be vulnerable to accusations from nobodies like us. The enormous scandal would be hushed up. Only their confession can put them within reach of the law."

"And you hope to obtain that confession?"

"I don't hope, I'm certain."

"How?"

"You'll see, my friends. For now let's focus on disturbing their minds."

And so began the macabre parade of the dead. After Miao came others. Stepan and Sefra and Derrick and Freda had taken charge of moving around the funereal loads. They kept on refining their methods.

More maddened by each new discovery, the Slanes took refuge in the control room. There they could pull themselves together and "apply the riding crop," to borrow a vivid sporting metaphor, before they resumed their lugubrious but unavoidable job as gravediggers.

That pair of teenagers, Stepan and Sefra, had the idea, which Derrick and Freda agreed to at once, of taking advantage of any delays by the Slanes. If the father and son recognized a corpse and, discouraged by the awful chore they faced, put off its disposal overboard till later—something that happened quite often—then May's companions quickly replaced that body with another one.

So when Slane—dragging his terrified, helpless, passive son along — returned, the sinister scenes that resulted delighted May's friends, because they understood that they advanced the Englishwoman's plans.

"That's odd," murmured Slane. "I thought I'd recognized Ming-No."

"Me too," said William with a shiver.

"Yet now this is Bien-Hoa."

The effect of that kind of experience can be imagined. Dead men seemed to be playing hide and seek, switching places, moving from one spot to another... For in one last burst of mental clarity Slane had declared, "Living people must be moving the dead around, that's obvious. Let's see!"

With indubitable logic, he'd hidden at the corner of one of the side corridors. He'd waited, pistol in hand, and he'd seen... Seen? When facing the inexplicable, can you ever be sure of what you see? He'd seen a dead body rise in the air, while still remaining horizontal, and float slowly toward him. He'd fled in terror. If he'd understood the properties of the electric tunics, all the manifestations would have made sense to him. But since he knew nothing about the tunics, he lived inside a nightmare.

And yet he retained enough presence of mind to keep a tally of the bodies they dumped in the ocean. "That's the last one," he said finally: they'd just submerged the twentieth Chinese warrior who'd been aboard the *Vulture*. "Now we can relax. The hail of corpses can't go on."

Indeed, they stopped running into bodies. But even so, the masters of the airship were no happier. Now they found themselves suffering from optical illusions. As they sat together in the control room, they suddenly couldn't see each other: they'd fallen victim to the hallucination of invisibility induced by May and her friends. Even if they'd known the cause, the experience would have been totally demoralizing; nothing is as disconcerting as the sensation that the faculty of vision is unstable or intermittent. But since the cause was unknown, it was truly enough to drive them insane. To combat that new torture, Slane had the idea of taking his son by the arm. When either one of them was at the controls, they stayed that way, holding each other. From then on they couldn't see each other; only contact proved they were still there.

In vain Slane kept asking, "What power are my eyes and my brain obeying? Where is the enemy who commands that power?" No answer came to mind. He considered every known means of transmission over distance, like wireless Hertz waves. But not for a moment did he think of the device—ingenious in its very simplicity—invented by that young engineer, May.

An invisible world seemed to have come to life around the two criminals. After one of their visits to the pantry together, they returned to find the dials on the instrument panel in motion: the *Vulture* had taken off and was flying without a pilot. But Slane—remembering that though some unknown power had made William invisible, he could still feel his son's arm against his—immediately reasoned that another invisible person was operating the controls. Quick as a flash, he fired his revolver at the instrument panel.

The result was astonishing: an extremely violent blow struck him in the stomach and knocked him to the floor, unconscious... But when he came to, he noticed a spot of blood on the instrument panel.

From then on he went everywhere revolver in hand. It was a temporary reassurance: his weapon was taken away from him, and blows rained down on his shoulders, his arms, and his shins all day long. He was scratched and kicked by invisibility.

Lipson and Derrick took turns punishing the wretch—because now they refused to let May come out of hiding. It was she, indeed, who'd been at the controls when Slane fired. The bullet had grazed her arm, not seriously. But Lipson had felt such strong emotion that he'd forced her to promise not to expose herself to further danger.

Tormented, struck, every moment expecting a blow that could come from anywhere, the Slanes had reached the point where they missed those dead Chinamen: after all, you threw one overboard and at least you got a little peace.

Sometimes, driven mad, at the end of their tether, with even sleep now impossible, the two villains, in the vague hope that their enemies could hear them, cried out in despair, "What do you want? Name it! We possess vast wealth. We'll pay a king's ransom!"

But they waited for an answer in vain. Their offer fell into a silent void. The enemy made no answer. And that very silence became a new source of fear. Because they knew he existed! That spot of blood on the instrument panel was material proof. So who could he be, that a king's ransom left him indifferent?

Then an even more terrifying, even more inexplicable discovery brought the Slanes' terror to its climax. One morning William pointed through the porthole at a coastline visible on the horizon.

"Australia!" roared his father in delight. "Courage, my boy! In a few hours we'll be able to land in some uninhabited area and get out of this damned *Vulture*, in which all the devils of legend have decided to gather!"

But their joy proved short-lived. As the airship rapidly drew near the coast they'd spotted, they were stunned to recognize the E'akiro volcano, where they'd landed near the beginning of their strange voyage. They hoped they were mistaken; they rubbed their eyes angrily. And yet the landscape remained the same: that familiar landscape where all their troubles had begun—that landscape, etched in their memories with lines of fire—that landscape unfolded beneath them now.

"The compass has gone haywire," muttered William dully.

But his father cursed. "Compasses don't go haywire like that. Where's the thunderstorm, where's the lightning that could throw it off track?"

William disagreed timidly. "Maybe it's those tricks with Hertz waves you thought were being used against us."

Yes, in truth, that was possible. Because the fact itself seemed undeniable: the magnetized needle had gone haywire. Following its guidance, they'd kept a steady course south, and yet they'd gone east. So, for some reason unknown but real, the needle no longer pointed north but west.

"What should we do?" whimpered William pathetically. The young man had been reduced to such a state that he was close to crying.

"Correct our course," said his father.

"Correct it?"

"Naturally. We'll offset the compass reading by ninety degrees. That'll show us true north. We'll set a course that's nominally northwest. Since by stupid chance we wound up in Hawaii, we'll head back southwest toward Australia."

William needed no further explanation; he'd reached the limit of his strength. From now on he let himself be pulled along, abandoning himself to his fate, indifferent to where it led him. He'd arrived at the desperate state of mind of those who have given up hope, which can be summarized as, "Go ahead and kill me, as long as I don't have to understand or suffer anymore!"

They immediately corrected their course. They didn't stop to eat, so they wouldn't have to bring the airship down to the water in an area so frequented by ships. But that night, when their stomachs were gnawing with hunger, they took the risk, and dashed to the pantry. They were gone just long enough for May and her friends to falsify the compass once again. Now the needle pointed straight south, so that the offset Slane had decided on led him to mistake west for north, as before. (May and her companions had a normal compass of their own. That was how they'd been able to detect the change of course adopted by the Slanes, and had immediately understood its cause.)

That night the two villains were left alone by their victims—who, thanks to May's scientific powers, had become their persecutors. Delighted by that truce,

314

and comforted by a meal eaten in peace and by the conviction that they were now headed the right way, they chatted almost lightheartedly.

They had no idea they were the subject of conversation in the bowels of the airship. Perhaps they'd have looked aghast if they'd heard the following exchange among their enemies:

"But when they recognize San Francisco," said James Lipson—or rather the genuine Lloyd Hibbett—"they'll change course again."

"No, because they won't recognize the city."

"Disguising an entire city seems beyond the power of our electromagnetic tunics!"

May smiled. "I know that."

"So then?..."

"Our enemies will be asleep when we approach Frisco. By the time they wake up the *Vulture* will have landed and they'll no longer be on board."

She laughed even more at the amazement on the faces of her friends, who couldn't grasp the whole of her plan. Only Captain Andrews and Princess Liao showed no surprise. The navy officer and the Chinese girl were no longer aware of what was going on around them. Since they'd left Hankou they'd been living entirely in a dream world lit by love, and nothing outside of it seemed worthy of their attention.

Five days later, when the Slanes, having brought the *Vulture* down to the surface of the sea, had left the control room on their way to the pantry, May and Lipson—on whose hand little Jane kept a stubborn grip—slipped toward the temporarily empty room. Through the partway open door May tossed a handful of small hard objects, which made a dry tapping noise as they fell to the floor.

"The crystalized chloroform is in place," she murmured softly. "It'll evaporate while the Slanes are eating. They'll be beaten by the same means they used against others. Now you see, James, why they won't recognize San Francisco?"

Lipson's only answer was to kiss May's hand, while little Jane murmured admiringly, "Oh, I was never in any doubt, because my sister May is never wrong."

"My sister!" Those two words made the young people blush. They exchanged a long look. Lloyd Hibbett had surely won his struggle. In spite of the colossal fortune he was about to recover, May would be his wife—and Jane her sister-in-law.

They hurried back to the *Vulture*'s hold before the Slanes returned to the control room and shut the door, not realizing they were thus leaving themselves defenseless against the vapor of chloroform. Half an hour later they were asleep.

Soon after that the door opened, and May entered, followed by all of her friends. Speaking slowly, she announced, "We're now within sight of the Golden Gate, the entrance to San Francisco Bay. It's time to rescue these men from the vapor of chloroform, because we want their confession, not their death."

315

Lipson, Derrick, Freda, Stepan, and even the ex-emperor Lia-Sou him-self—carrying out the instructions of the young woman whose scientific powers had saved his beloved Liao—picked up the villains' inert bodies and carried them away. Then May, along with Sefra and Jane, who never left her side, aired out the control room and sat down at the instrument panel.

"What time is it?" His voice thick with sleep, William stretched as he spoke.

"The time? I don't know. But it's clearly broad daylight." As he answered, Slane too was waking.

They both rubbed their eyes, stretched their arms, and yawned. Gradually returning to normal, they looked around curiously. Then they started; extreme surprise showed on their faces as together they exclaimed, "What?! Where are we?"

It must be admitted, the question was reasonable. They were seated on a bench in a vast oak-paneled hall whose beamed ceiling was divided into coffers painted red. Facing them, a long wooden counter was divided by a railing from the rest of the hall, which was slightly sunken, and in which stood other benches like the one they were sitting on.

"But... this is the courtroom of the Hall of Justice in San Francisco!" cried Slane.

William looked all around in astonishment. "The tribunal? My God, it's true!"

"What are we doing here?"

As if that question had been anticipated by those who could answer it, a door opened—the door to the chamber of witnesses. Through the doorway came a young blonde woman, whom the Slanes recognized immediately.

"Miss May!"

"The typist!"

They fell silent, because the person they were referring to shook her head. "No longer a typist, but in fact an engineer licensed in England. Known briefly as Mr. August, who once tested a revolutionary engine design on the *Cyclopic*."

"The *Cyclopic*!"

"Mr. August!"

Their exclamations rang gloomily through the vast hall, echoing off the deep-shadowed angles and cornices and beams.

Paying no attention to the interruption May went on slowly, "I was lucky enough to escape the death cloud you spread through the *Cyclopic*, before you set off the explosion that sent the enormous ocean liner to the bottom of the sea; lucky enough also to have rescued Lloyd Hibbett..."

"Lloyd Hibbett?"

"And his little sister Jane. Alas, I was unable to save their mother from death. She lies, along with the rest of your victims, at the bottom of the Java Sea."

The two men had bowed their heads. The memory of that monstrous hecatomb, now suddenly evoked after all the years they'd enjoyed in peace the fruits of their crime—the memory evoked by a survivor, coming at the end of the long series of unexplained incidents that for weeks had plagued their spirits—crushed them and robbed them of all powers of resistance.

May went on, "The five survivors of the *Cyclopic* are all here. I'll summon them, so that no doubt remains in your minds." Her voice filled with tragic force as she called, "Lloyd Hibbett, Jane, Derrick, Freda... and me: that makes the five I spoke of."

Those whose names she'd called entered in single file through the door to the chamber of witnesses. One by one they took their seats on a bench May directed them to. She called again, "Stepan, Sefra!" When the two teenage vagabonds had joined the others, she explained, "William Slane, these two witnessed the death of your mother."

A heavy silence fell. Then the young Englishwoman went on, "Tom Slane, your position as the Director of the Institute of Inventors, as well as that of your son, who under the stolen name of Lloyd Hibbett, took possession of the Hibbett fortune and now heads the syndicate of American billionaires, would make a public accusation damage the good reputation of this country. In any case, we've all reestablished ourselves. We're prepared to compromise. We've also persuaded Lia-Sou, the ex-emperor of China, and his daughter Liao, to accept whatever will be agreed to today."

"You're willing to compromise?" cried Slane, recovering his voice.

"I just said so."

"And the past will be buried forever?"

"Yes to that too."

"The *Cyclopic*, our doings in China, everything—everything?"

"Yes, everything."

The two villains exchanged an inquiring glance. From their satisfied expressions it was clear they considered the bargain to be to their advantage. Since they controlled incalculable wealth, they said to themselves, what difference would it make to buy, at whatever price, the silence of these dangerous adversaries? Besides—and of course the Slanes, those master craftsmen of deceit, had already thought of it—now that their enemies were unveiled, wouldn't it be possible to eliminate them later?

The result of all those rapid calculations quickly emerged. "Name your price, Miss May."

"Oh, I have to warn you, it'll be steep."

"It doesn't matter to us."

"We're talking about an heir robbed of hundreds of millions of dollars, about an exiled emperor whose daughter you handed over for execution…"

"I repeat, we'll agree to whatever figure you name, without haggling."

An ironic smile played across the young woman's mouth. "Whatever it is?"

"Whatever it is!"

"In that case we have a deal."

Suddenly straightening up sternly, the slim Englishwoman added a majestic grandeur to her role as lawgiver as she said:

"I demand that, since you cannot bring back to life those you've struck down, you at least make restitution of everything you stole."

The two Slanes, overwhelmed by the magnitude of the claim, remained silent. May extended both hands, with her slender fingers pointing at their skulls, and murmured, "Let the illusion of emptiness come to an end. See what is in fact the case."

Then suddenly the father and son saw the empty courtroom fill with people: on all the benches sat an attentive crowd, the lawyers stood at their rostrums, the judges sat on the dais of the tribunal, the bailiffs and the guards stood in their places. Stunned, dazed, the Slanes looked around in dismay, not understanding the cause of, or the chain of events leading to, the facts that now confronted them.

In the solemn silence, May's voice rose once again as she explained gently, "I, a humble engineer, invented an electric device to amplify willpower almost infinitely. Thanks to that device alone, I was able to fight against you—who seemed invulnerable in your vast power. Just now you thought you were alone with us, because I forbade you to see the audience. That way I could extract from you the confession of evil done by two men whom the country surrounded with admiration."

Her speech was greeted with thunderous applause. Cries of "Hip! Hip! Hurrah!" rang out, in spite of the judges' efforts to restore order and silence. The crowd wanted to apply the terrible lynch law to these criminals so suddenly unmasked. The Slanes had collapsed onto their bench. Terrified, they hid their faces in their hands, wishing to see no more and hear no more.

Three months later, Lloyd Hibbett—alias James Lipson—now restored to possession of his family's fortune, married Miss May. Little Jane was one of the maids of honor at the wedding. Derrick and Freda, now raised to the rank of personal assistants, wept behind a column in the nave. Beside them stood Stepan and Sefra in brand-new clothes, feeling very important.

A few days later, another wedding brought together all the figures in the drama once again. Captain Andrews—punished with a month's suspension for having taken passengers on board his submarine, and then promoted to commodore for his devotion to duty—slipped a wedding ring onto a radiantly happy Princess Liao's finger.

The ex-emperor Lia-Sou had decided to settle for good in San Francisco.

And—since Americans never lose sight of questions of *business*—it was being said in the crowd that the Republic of China, delighted by the voluntary exile of the dethroned emperor, had transferred to Lloyd Hibbett's name all the commercial concessions previously granted to Tom Slane.

The latter had hanged himself in prison. William had lost his mind, and, with no knowledge of who he was, now lived in an insane asylum.

Poetic justice had been done.

www.ingramcontent.com/pod-product-compliance
Lightning Source LLC
Chambersburg PA
CBHW060425030726
47495CB00003B/742